CHANGE OF FORTUNE

CHANGE OF FORTUNE

K. S. JONES

WHEELER PUBLISHING
A part of Gale, a Cengage Company

GALE
A Cengage Company

Copyright © 2022 by K. S. Jones.
Wheeler Publishing, a part of Gale, a Cengage Company.

LIBRARY OF CONGRESS CIP DATA ON FILE.
CATALOGUING IN PUBLICATION FOR THIS BOOK
IS AVAILABLE FROM THE LIBRARY OF CONGRESS.

ISBN-13: 978-1-4328-8833-6 (softcover alk. paper)

Published in 2022 by arrangement with K. S. Jones

Printed in the USA
1 2 3 4 5   26 25 24 23 22

To Sheri Groom
My sister of the heart.
Your strength, love, and loyalty
inspire me.

And

To Malinda Cobo Pettigrew Sackett
A true frontier woman born in the
wrong era.
Rest in peace, my storytelling friend.

ACKNOWLEDGEMENTS

From the first word to the last. Special thanks to Kathleen O'Neal Gear, W. Michael Gear, Amber Carter, Debby Beece, Pamela Nowak, Lanita Joramo, Ashley Sweeney, Michelle Ferrer, Alethea Williams, Irene Schubel, Jennifer Brown, and especially to Richard Lee Jones for making this a better book in so many meaningful ways.

CHAPTER ONE

Oregon 1849

The horizon over the Willamette Valley glowed fiery red, shooting daggers of sunlight through the fine glass windowpanes. Quinn squinted but dared not shield her eyes. She sat upright, proper, folding and refolding her hands in her lap. Strands of red hair, damp with nervous perspiration, clung to the nape of her neck. Though Henry's jittery knee bounced against the flow of her cotton day dress, she kept a tight focus on Hugh MacCann lest her inattentiveness unleash his rage.

"These are only my mother's things I'm asking for, Father." Quinn's tone was respectful, calm, although beads of sweat wetted her brow. "Her Dublin lace, the silver service, her blue Staffordshire . . ." Her eyes flashed to a simple wood framed painting of an autumn sunrise in Boston, her childhood home after leaving Dublin. "Her watercolors. All things she promised would be mine when I married."

"Then she should have lived to pass them on to you!" Hugh MacCann's bellow froze Henry's nervous knee. "And the two thousand dollars you've asked for was never your mother's money."

Though it was a warm summer evening, her father wore a thigh-length frock coat as he paced. In his hand, he held their crumpled marriage certificate. "The money she pledged wasn't hers to give."

Quinn sprang up. "You made a promise to Mother — on her deathbed! I heard it myself. She said her personal things and two thousand dollars would be mine as a dowry so that I could start a new life here in the West with a husband." She stepped toward him. "You promised!"

The back of his hand slammed Quinn to the floor. A shot of pain flared upward from her jaw and pulled one eye into a squinted blur, which she quickly cast toward Henry. Although their marriage was a sham, she had half-expected Henry with his sturdy build to defend her if the need arose, but there he sat, frozen, silent, his scared blue eyes fixed on Hugh MacCann.

A trickle of blood oozed from Quinn's bottom lip. She pulled herself to her feet.

Show no fear. Don't back down.

Expressionless, Hugh pointed to the man his daughter had married. "You there, what is it that you do?"

Henry's neck stiffened. "As in . . . work?"

"Well, I sure as Hades am not asking whether you pick your nose for pleasure, now am I? How do you make a living?" His Irish brogue was always thicker when he was angry.

Henry glanced at Quinn, who stood beside the davenport pressing a bare knuckle to her bloody lip to stop the bleeding.

"Don't tell me you need your new wife to talk for you?"

Steeling herself, Quinn said, "Father, no, but —"

"Then you needn't be answering for him." Her father gave her a hard glare before shifting his eyes back to Henry. "I'm waitin'."

After a throat clearing, Henry stood. His tan, coarse linen trousers bore the permanent wrinkles of a man more accustomed to sitting than standing, and his linen pullover shirt was drenched and smelled of sweat. "I'm going to paint houses and signs." When a raised brow met his reply, Henry started again. "It's my momma's idea. She likes painted houses. Like the ones in St. Louis. She says everythin' west of the Mississippi

11

might be uncivilized, but it don't have to look like it."

With a stern turn of his head, Hugh fixed his eyes on Quinn as he tossed their marriage certificate onto the floor. "You married this worthless know-nothing instead of the surveyor general's son?" When his arm rose again, she flinched, then stiffened. She didn't resist when he took a handful of her red hair. Used it to yank her to him. "California will be a state soon, but I'd wager a bet that the land I claimed there will be ignored by the surveyors, all because of you."

She grabbed hold of the hand that held tight to her hair. "Father, let go —"

"MacCann County!" he shouted, barely inches from her face. The reek of jerky and day-old coffee hung on his breath. "That's what he was going to call it. It was to be one of the first named counties in California." He twisted his grip tighter until her head tilted upward, facing his glare. Despite her best efforts, tears spilled. "And all you had to do was marry his no-good cripple of a son." He released her with a shove.

Quinn stumbled back. Had it not been for the steadiness of his high-backed reading chair, she would have ended up on the floor again. "I choose who I marry!"

With jaws clenched and both hands balled into fists, Hugh MacCann started toward her, only to halt at a knock on the door. As his housemaid scurried to open it, he uncurled his fingers. His hard glare softened at the sound of a feminine voice.

In the open doorway stood a woman dressed in a red brocade gown, thirtyish, tall, and thin with curly hair as black as overcooked coffee. Her rose-colored cheeks and red lips were akin to an undertaker's artistry on the newly departed.

The woman's eyes scanned the room, settling on Hugh. "You said seven o'clock, didn't ya?"

When Hugh turned, Quinn slipped back behind the davenport, putting her closer to Henry, which caught the woman's eye.

"Who is she?" The woman pointed to Quinn. "Ya never said they'd be more than one of us. I won't be splittin' my cost."

In a kindly tone rarely used, MacCann said, "My daughter has just come home from boarding school." He approached the woman and lightly touched her lips. "Lollie, why don't you wait outside 'til I finish here?"

"Wait outside!" Lollie snapped, but just as quickly, she gave a coquettish grin. With her head half-ducked, she said, "Why don't I wait upstairs for ya?"

Money aside, Hugh MacCann had a way with women. Charm tamed his mean spirit when companionship suited him.

"Father." Quinn spoke lightly. "I can pack Mother's belongings while . . . while your *business* is tended to, but I presume the two thousand is locked in your safe." The money was crucial to the start of her new life. She would never be dependent upon him again.

Hugh ignored her and gave Lollie a nod. "All right, upstairs you go." Once Lollie was out of sight, he turned to his daughter and settled his green eyes on hers. "I'll not be giving up your mother's things." His gaze shifted to the daguerreotype of Malinda MacCann, but her haunting, solemn eyes turned him back to Quinn. "None of the things you claim to be yours are yours. Everything in this house has always been mine and belongs to me still. It would take a ship six months to bring replacements, and I'll not be presenting myself as a pauper in an empty house. Her things stay." He crossed the room to the strongbox on the floor near his desk.

Quinn held her hand atop the cameo brooch pinned to her high-neck collar and quieted. Any word from her could stop him dead in his tracks, and she might never be free. Other than the clunk of a cast-iron skillet on the cookstove a room away, the house was nearly silent.

Her father took a drawstring sack out of the iron box and opened it. He withdrew several coins and held them out — his glare boring into Quinn.

With calculated steps, she drew closer, arms outstretched, hands cupped. Was it her heart or her ego that was sickened by her steady hands? The money was rightfully hers — it *was*!

"Two hundred cash," he said as he dropped ten gold coins into her palms. From his desk, he took out a blank paper. With a silver steel pen, he scribbled a note, folded it, and then handed it to her. "Take this to Richard at the bank in Portsmouth Square in San Francisco. He'll give you the rest."

He shut the desk drawer without taking his eyes off her. "What are you now? Nineteen? Twenty?"

"Twenty-two," Quinn answered.

"Twenty-two," her father repeated. "Twenty-two years you've lived a life of privilege. I've trained you to hold your place in society. You've had a home better than most." A sweep of his arm indicated the

15

houseful of well-to-do possessions. "You're the only Irish woman in a thousand miles who's never had to wash a dish, cook a meal, or clean your own garments. I've done my duty in trying to make you an obedient woman so that a man of worth might agree to take you."

When she said nothing, he continued. "You've always been ungrateful. A burden and a disgrace. Just a bad-luck charm. Your mother died from your negligence, and my son — my namesake — too. Both deserved this life more than you."

Old grief caught in her throat. Quinn was thirteen when typhus killed her mother, and just three when her younger brother toddled out the open door of their Dublin home, straight into the path of a passing carriage. Her eyes had only wandered from him for a moment.

He pointed to the door. "Go on, get out. See how different your days are without me."

"My mother's things . . ." Quinn started but was startled into silence when her newlywed husband jumped to his feet.

Henry moved swiftly to Hugh MacCann, took hold of his unoffered hand, and shook it. "Thank you, sir. I've wanted to see San Francisco for months. Men say there's monte and roulette, and the place is nearly doubling in size every day!" He reached for Quinn's folded paper, pulled it from her hand, and slipped it into his own pocket. "We'll be taking your note to the bank as soon as we arrive."

"But Henry, Mother's things . . ." Quinn's chest tightened.

Henry barely held back a grin as he took Quinn by the shoulders and fixed his eyes on hers. "We'll have two thousand dollars. We can buy whatever things you need."

"I don't want someone else's things. I want my mother's things." In a whisper, she said, "You agreed."

At Henry's hesitation, Hugh MacCann gave a scoffing laugh. "You'll need to be a meatier man than that if you plan to keep her as your wife." He headed for the stairs, but before starting up, he turned, his gaze shifting between the newlyweds. "Daughter of mine, I suspect you'll be fleeced of your money and dignity within a month, but it's time you learned the hardships of life, isn't it?" Then he made his way up the stairs.

Quinn grabbed her tan flannel shawl and whirled it around her shoulders. Through the haze of dusk outside the window, her eyes settled on the single-seat buckboard ranch wagon hitched to their gray mule. The beast stood stock-still in a mindless stance. What few belongings she had were stacked in the wagon's low-sided box.

Her two sage-green and apricot tapestry bags held her dresses and undergarments, two books, a pair of boots, and a few odds and ends. Also bundled up in the wagon were her three blankets and a feather pillow. All she owned. Her bed and furnishings belonged to the Oregon Institute. Even her paint box, watercolors, sable brushes, and vellum belonged to the school. Graduation meant when classes started again in a few weeks another student would be given her room, her books, and her supplies. She had stayed as long as was allowable.

Nothing remained, except to leave this house without a thing more.

She fought to focus on her long-awaited freedom — her father's heavy hand could never strike her again, and his berating words would no longer shame her. With the money, she could become an independent businesswoman, never again in need of a man for support.

Quinn started for the door only to be caught midstride by her mother's lonely eyes. Pulled by her heartstrings to the credenza, she picked up the daguerreotype. With gentle fingers, she wiped its dust. It

18

was agony to know she might never see her mother's face again. Unable to bear the thought, Quinn tucked the red leather case under her shawl and headed out of the house.

"You can't take that," Henry whispered with a glance over his shoulder.

"I'm not leaving it." Quinn opened the door and stepped out into the river-scented air of freedom. With a turn, she looked back. Silently, she bade good riddance to the painful memories within, but leaving behind the spirit of Malinda MacCann was a whole other matter.

Her thoughts came undone when Henry grabbed her arm, hurrying her to the wagon.

"Even though you didn't get your momma's things, we got the two thousand dollars. And you was headed for San Francisco from the get-go." With a look back at the house, he hoisted her up onto the seat. "Now, let's get before he figures us out."

CHAPTER TWO

The jangle of wagon chains and mule hooves plodding the bare ground overshadowed the sounds brought on by nightfall's approach.

"How much farther?" Quinn glanced at the man seated beside her. His self-barbered, sandy hair stood up defiantly at the crown of his head.

"We'll stop in a bit." He pulled a shelled almond from the muslin pouch tied to a button meant for galluses. One after another, he popped several into his mouth and chewed.

Quinn had met Henry three days earlier, and they'd married just this morning. Love played no part in it. Their marriage was one of convenience — he had needed her father's money to move south out of Oregon Country, and, at age twenty-two, she had suffered her father's brutal hand and cruel tongue too long. Marriage, and her promised dowry, was a way out for both of them.

She knew little of Henry, except that he was one of the few men her father didn't control. His insignificance boded well for her. He had come north a month earlier with men who sought work with Hudson's Bay Company, but when all except he were hired, he found himself penniless with no way home. She found him seated on the stoop of the Oregon Institute, from which Quinn was preparing to leave. He was head down, hungry, and angry after a wagon bound for California kicked him off. She'd offered to help him get home to Stockton if, in return, he would help her escape her father's rule.

Her green eyes studied the man who in an instant had become her husband. He wore tan trousers and a striped cotton shirt but had no hat to cover his head. Although she'd acquired their wagon just a day ago on her father's good credit in Salem, Henry handled it as if he'd owned it his whole life. He sat hunched forward with a good grip on the reins.

"How long will our trip take?" she asked.

"Thirty days or so, if the rain holds off." When their wheels bumped over a jumble of drought-dried ruts, Henry's blue eyes darted from the trail to Quinn. His gaze dropped to the unladylike bounce of her modest bosom.

In seeing his focus, she clutched her arms about her chest, then forced her eyes back to the trail ahead. "We'll need more supplies."

Quinn had counted on the dowry immediately. If successful, her pledge to Henry was three hundred dollars and the wagon to get himself back home to Stockton. From there, she would buy provisions for herself, hire a driver, and set out for San Francisco, an exciting new city filled with promise.

"Supposed to be a settlement ten miles south of here," Henry said. "We'll stop tomorrow and stock up." He took a swig from his flask. "Almost out of whiskey and almonds, anyway."

Thirty days with a man she barely knew. A drinking man. *Her husband.* But being free of her father was worth the hardship. With some luck, their first night's camp would be near a river so that Henry could wash away his stench.

When the evening's first star pierced the waning daylight, Quinn said, "Look there!" She pointed high above the horizon. "Is that the Dog Star? I'm all turned around."

Henry pushed up off the seat, balancing himself into a half-stand. He surveyed the ground around the wagon's southerly bound mule. "You say you saw a dog? Was it a wolf?"

"No." Quinn shook her head. When Henry reseated himself, she pointed again. "See that beautifully bright star? It must be the Dog Star, or the evening star. Do you know which?"

Henry twisted to look skyward. "Nah, I don't know. I never went to college like you."

She fixed her gaze on the bright point. "Do you have a compass? Are we headed west?"

"A little west. Mostly south." After a moment, he said, "We're on the trail to San Francisco, I know that for sure."

"It must be the evening star, which, of course, is not a star at all, but a planet."

"Did they teach you anything good at that college?" Henry's question didn't sound like a question at all. "Important things are here on the ground, not up in the sky."

Quinn's eyes never lowered. "I learned so many things, but the Ladies' Course focused on penmanship, poetry, the arts, and English literature." With a sigh, she said, "Astronomy was not an option for me, but I read the books." The feel of freedom beneath the stars was hers tonight.

Henry snorted. "None of it worth a damn."

Night darkened in the prairie land cradled between the Coastal Range and the Cascades, its only pardon being a meager light from the quarter moon. Near a huge cottonwood with broad, sweeping limbs, Henry stopped the wagon, unhitched, and then set about securing the mule for the night while Quinn set up camp by lantern light. She spread two woolen blankets a foot apart on the ground. She had never slept beneath the stars, and the clear night was full with a thousand points of light.

Wood smoke scented the air as Quinn made her way back to the wagon for their coffee and supplies. She pulled out their pot and a bag of roasted beans, but when she turned, she found Henry barely an arm's length away, his blue eyes ablaze like the campfire behind him.

"I heard a marriage needs to be consummated." He threw back his head, downed the contents of his flask, and then tossed it into the wagon. "Why don't you go on now and take off that pretty dress."

"I'll do no such thing! We are not married in *that* sense of the word." Quinn shifted, uneasy at the change in him.

"The preacher wrote us down in his

recordin' book. We're as married as anybody else." Henry inched toward her. He took hold of the empty coffee pot and tossed it back into the wagon box, then reached for Quinn.

Still clutching the bag of coffee beans, she stepped back. "Henry . . ." She steadied her voice to a reasoning tone. Miles from civilization, she had the choice to negotiate or fight, and she was far more adept at diplomacy. "What we have is a partnership. A business arrangement."

"Yeah, I know, but our *business arrangement* is called a marriage. I've been thinking long and hard about it, too, and the way I see it, that certificate gives me rights." His tongue curled over his bottom lip. He reached for her again, but she took another step back.

Smugly, he smiled. "You're just too damn proper. It's a daddy's job to teach you to be a lady, but it's a husband's job to teach you how to be a wife." With no more warning, he grabbed her wrist, knocking the bag of beans out of her hand. With a twist, he wrestled her arm up behind her back and held tight.

Quinn struggled to pull free. "We are not married as husband and wife!"

Henry gripped her delicate body. From

the backside of her ear, he whispered, "Ain't no other kind of marriage, and I haven't had a woman in a month or more, so I'm feelin' kind of edgy." He pushed himself hard against her. "You got wifely duties. Settle down, or I'll tether you down. Don't matter which to me."

Quinn stomped, but her heel barely grazed his boot. She bucked her head back, aiming for his nose. When neither blow connected, he wrenched her arm higher until she cried out in pain.

"I'd sure hate to tear this dress taking it off you, but I just gotta see what's under it. You gonna do it, or am I?"

"All right!" Quinn snapped. She had no gun. No weapon of any kind. Even if she had, this ruffian was her only hope of getting to San Francisco for a new life. She needed him, but trusting him had been a foolish thing. More quietly, she said again, "All right." She'd gotten herself this far with a purpose of independence in mind, and coupling would not change anything other than to bruise her self-respect. It's what men did, and women had to endure. The banker in San Francisco would soon release the remaining eighteen hundred dollars to her, and then she could settle up with Henry and send him on his way. Freedom and independence would be hers.

"Let go of me," she said with an arm jerk.

Henry released her, then stepped back. The low light of the campfire danced across the gray woolen blankets that lay spread atop tufts of yellowed grass.

Her back to him, Quinn disrobed down to her white linen chemise, knee-length drawers, and white kid-leather boots. After a deep breath, she gave a slow exhale and then turned, chin raised, and walked to the blankets. She lowered herself until she lay prone, arms straight at her sides. Her muscles tensed as she eyed the man she had willingly and legally wed.

Henry dropped to his knees. Pushed her legs apart, then undid the buttons on his coarse linen trousers.

When he reached inside the split of her white cotton drawers, she turned her face away and shut her eyes tight. His fingers probed her womanhood for only a moment before he entered her.

Though it seemed an eternity, it was over in minutes. There was no wedding night intimacy. Henry lay atop her, panting, heavy, and stinking.

With thumb and forefinger cradling her chin, he turned her face to his. "Bein' married suits me fine."

Bile rose in her throat. "Get off me!" She pushed until he rolled onto the blanket. Free of his weight, she rose, hurried to the tailboard of the wagon, and heaved, losing every ounce of her dignity.

"Might as well get used to it," Henry called out to her. "It's what men do to their wives."

As best she could, Quinn washed with water from their barrel, then unpinned her tangled red hair. With trembling hands, her splayed fingers combed through it. Then she twisted it into a bun and pinned it up again. She reached into the wagon, pulled out her only other blanket, and wrapped it around her quaking body. Silently, she stood and stared out into the darkness where the night seemed as endless as the wilderness itself.

She lifted her gaze to the quarter moon. *God, help me do this.*

CHAPTER THREE

The midday August sun baked the prairie soil, level to a fault, and dried the wheat, oats, and native grasses until nothing but thin, golden sticks of straw protruded from the cracked earth.

At a split-shake roofed cabin, Hugh MacCann sat poised atop his stallion, his broad-brimmed hat shading his face. "Anybody home?" he shouted.

The door swung open. Two men, both wearing dirt-encrusted boots, stepped out onto the hard ground.

"Mr. MacCann," the bearded one said. Galluses held up his moth-eaten, brown woolen pants. "Billy and me was just havin' coffee before headin' back out to the wheat field."

"You're both lazy. That field hasn't been tended in weeks." MacCann dismounted and handed the younger man his leather lead. "Water my horse. I've got business with your brother."

He pushed past the man into the cabin. The one with the beard followed him. Mac-Cann's eyes scanned the room. "The place is filthy."

"We been out workin' the fields. Ain't had much chance for upkeep."

"Remind me, Earle. Wasn't that part of the deal? I'd let you and your brother continue to live here, free of charge as part of your wages, as long as you kept up the place." MacCann's gaze dropped to his riding gloves. One finger at a time, he pulled until they were off.

"Yeah, but this cabin's looked the same for goin' on ten years now."

MacCann removed his hat, eyeing the man. "When I paid your brother's gambling debt, this cabin, and the land and crops growing on it, became mine." His tone was tempered, but his stare, cold. "I own it now. You both work for me."

Earle Conrad lowered his head. "That's right." Then he looked up again. "Billy'd be dead if'n you wasn't there that night."

MacCann gave a slow nod. "You're indebted to me. It's good you understand. Now, I have a job for you and your brother. It's extra money, if done right."

"What do we gotta do?"

"My daughter has married a no-account." Hugh MacCann gave scrutiny to the bearded man, scanning him head to toe. "Your type. Not fit to breathe the same air. His name is Henry Matheny. Well-fed boy. Know him?"

Earle shook his head. "Never knowed anyone by that name to live 'round here."

"Yes, well." MacCann slapped his sweaty riding gloves against his hand. "The two of them are headed to San Francisco. The bank in Portsmouth Square. They're traveling with a pittance on them, but they'll be getting more. It's my money. I want it returned."

"You want us to bring them back, too?"

"No. Just the money." Two strides and the midday glare fell through the open door onto his boot tips. He glanced back. "There'll be a two-hundred-dollar reward in it for you, but you'll not mention me or my name to anyone."

Then MacCann stepped outside. When sunlight struck his fiery red hair, he donned his hat and looked about for his stallion. "My horse!" he ordered.

When the younger brother ambled out from behind the cabin holding the leather lead, Earle asked, "So you don't want nothin' done to 'em for stealin' your money?"

MacCann mounted his thick-crested stallion, solid black except for a white patch shaped like a pine tree starring his forehead. "I never said they stole anything."

He lifted the flap on his saddlebag and pushed his riding gloves inside. "Hotter than Hades today, but I want you riding within the hour. They have two days' head start, but they're in a buckboard. You'll catch up soon enough."

"If'n we do the job right," Earle said, his head tilted upward, a hand shading his view, "might'n you let us buy back our land? Fair and square."

MacCann gave a half smile, then hesitated as his grin faded. "Fair and square," he repeated. "Return my money, with a full report on where my daughter settles. I'll consider it."

CHAPTER FOUR

California 1849

Dawn's light, coupled with the scent of coffee and roasted meat, roused Quinn from a fitful sleep. She threw back her blanket and rose, already anxious for the new day to end.

On the far side of the wagon, she slipped into her red and brown calico dress and then brushed and pinned up her coppery-red hair. Along the way, it had lost its silkiness to trail grime.

From the campfire came the hiss of grease dripping. Henry sat at the edge of the fire on a stump, his sandy-blond hair disheveled. In one hand, he held a cup of coffee. With his other, he balanced a crudely assembled spit upon which a grouse roasted. Its fat dripped onto the burning firewood, sending smoke spirals curling upwards into the bluing sky. Feathers littered the ground.

Quinn stepped around Henry and poured herself coffee.

"I went huntin' for us this mornin', but tomorrow you need to start cookin' the meals."

She lifted the metal cup to her mouth, wincing when its hot rim met her swollen lip — her father's parting gift. "I don't cook." Her gaze lowered. "I've never learned." Gently, she blew on the dark liquid to cool it, then gingerly sipped.

"Well, start learnin'."

The sun was up, shining bright against the swell of the distant mountains, when their wagon took to the road again. In fellowship with those who had gone before them, they followed the wagon ruts through a mosaic of grasslands and oak savannas.

A monotony of countless days came and went as they navigated the foothills of Northern California's Coastal Range, though its scenery — broad vistas and valleys with black bear, red fox, and elk — beckoned her artistry. She wanted brushes, paints, and vellum again. Instinctively, her right hand rose with imaginary strokes, her unseen paintbrush in a delicate dance replicating the breathtaking beauty of this wilderness.

Afternoons, the Pacific pushed graying clouds inland. Rain would slow them if it fell, but if a downpour came after sundown, they now had a tent — a beige canvas wedge with walls and a flap closure — purchased at their last supply stop.

With *Jane Eyre* open on her lap, Quinn read when the wagon's rough trail allowed. Pencil lines marked nearly memorized passages, declaring passion bliss, even bringing about a delirium of adoration between a man and woman. But Jane Eyre hadn't met Henry. She shifted on the seat — the soreness between her legs, chafed and itching, worsened each day.

Every mile of the long road to San Francisco wore on the loneliest part of her heart. As soon as her debt was settled with Henry, they would dissolve this marriage. Part ways, never to cross paths again. Until then, she needed soap and water, and liniment.

To lift her spirits, Quinn focused on the steps required to become a businesswoman of the elegant class. She calculated each one, readying herself for the city that grew nearer every day. San Francisco's population had grown from three hundred to almost twenty thousand in less than a year. Gold was the dream of every man, but surely, with so many striking it rich, people would welcome sophistication. Her thoughts fell on opening an art gallery, such as the Harding Gallery in Boston, or the Westminster Art Gallery in Rhode Island. After all, cultured people from every corner of the world were coming to San Francisco.

She'd studied art at the Institute, even finding joy in creating her own paintings, although hers were amateur compared to those exhibited at the Salon de Paris. They were the masters, but it was the landscape artists, like the painters living in the French village of Barbizon, who sent her daydreams spinning. Perhaps she would go to France, maybe Italy, to see for herself the artists' impressions of nature, and commission their works for her own gallery.

The elegant class.

Soon, this grime-ridden journey would be behind her. And Henry would be nothing but a memory.

CHAPTER FIVE

Ninety miles northwest of Sacramento City, while camped along the eastern foothills of the Coastal Range, two scruffy men on horseback appeared out of the darkness.

"Got enough rabbit to share?" The bearded man dismounted from a puny bay. His long, dark hair grazed the shoulders of his hide coat, worn unbuttoned. "Name's Earle. We ran into some bad luck a day back and lost our provisions." He motioned to the other man, still mounted. "My brother, Billy, and me is mighty hungry."

Henry braced his spit stick between two rocks and stood. With a shake of his head, he said, "Don't like to turn a man down, but it's a scrawny rabbit. We'd be glad to share our coffee, though."

Earle's brother dismounted. He was tatty-clothed and looked much younger. He pointed to Quinn, who stood several feet away braced against the wagon, and then to the campfire. "Your woman didn't make more than that rabbit for supper? What about beans? We'd be just as glad to get a cup of those."

Again, Henry shook his head. His eyes shifted to Quinn, then back to the two men. "She don't cook."

The brothers laughed as if Henry had joked them.

"Nah, I'm serious," Henry said with his own chuckle.

Earle shook his head. "Never heard of a woman who don't cook."

With her skirts raised boot high, Quinn marched forward. Her steady hand pointed to the blackened pot at the edge of the fire. "Henry offered coffee, which is generous, considering we have so little."

"Henry, is it?" After a moment of thought, Earle's dark eyes settled on Henry's face. "Well then, Henry. How 'bout we play ya for the rabbit?" From his ratty coat pocket, he pulled out a deck of cards and held them up. "Poker? Just me and you. Fair and square."

Henry's gaze steadied on the cards. The black and white Grandine deck was clearly old and heavily used. "Yeah, all right, but I got my own cards." He started for the wagon, but the sound of a cocking pistol stopped him dead in his tracks.

"Henry!" Quinn shouted.

With the flat of his hand, Henry signaled to her. "It's all right." He turned. "Seems they've got a special attachment to their own cards."

"Not tryin' to be rude, friend," Earle said. "But I've played one too many cardsharps who were dead set on usin' their own deck."

"I don't play much," Henry lied. "The deck was given to me a while back, and I just like the feel of 'em."

"I'll bet you do." Billy chuckled. With his pistol, he motioned to a spot of bare ground near the fire. His broad hat hid all but a few wispy, blond curls.

The three men knelt. While Earle shuffled and dealt, Billy rested his pistol atop his knee, trained on Henry.

Without lifting his eyes, Henry arranged five low-number cards in his hand. Not a chance of winning.

"Just take it!" Quinn shouted. "Take the rabbit and go!"

But Henry stood, his glare landing hard on her. "Go on to your tent now."

"My tent?" Her brazenness fell when the strangers snickered.

"See there, Earle. He does got enough spit in him to handle a little rich girl."

Quinn turned. *Rich girl?* Her curiosity probed their faces.

"Shut up, Billy." Earle eyed Quinn. "Go on." He nodded toward the tent. "Do what your man says."

Her throat tightened, sending a chill through her. "Henry, they'll kill you."

He leaned. Kissed her cheek. Near to her ear, he whispered, "Go on now. They don't call me 'Holdout Henry' for nothin'."

Bewildered, Quinn retreated to the tent. From inside, she listened to their muted voices and saw a play of flame and slow shadows crisscross the beige canvas walls. She strained to hear their subdued conversation but could only make out a few words — *flush, again,* and *double or nothing.* Soon, the dark-shadowed form of a flask passed hand to hand.

It was after midnight when Henry came through the tent flap stinking of wood smoke and whiskey. When Quinn sat up, he tossed her a strip of roasted meat.

"Saved you some." His words slurred.

"You mean you won?"

"Nope." He pulled off his boots, then kicked them to the side. "But the boys felt bad about you going to bed without supper."

She fanned away the stench of his stocking feet. "At least you only lost the rabbit and not your life."

Henry raised one brow and closed his other eye to better focus on her. "Lost more than that." He sat. Fell straight back onto the gray woolen blanket. With hips uplifted, he shed his tan trousers. In a mumble, he admitted, "Lost 'bout a hundred dollars of your daddy's money." Then in one fluid movement, he rolled on top of her. Face to face, he said, "Sorry."

Quinn gasped, then pushed her flattened palms against Henry's chest, but he grabbed her wrists. Pinned her arms to the ground above her head. Drunkenly, he kissed her. Intent on freeing herself, she bit down on his lip, drawing blood. When he cried out and released her, she shoved him off.

In a scramble, Quinn got to her feet. She burst through the tent flaps toward the wagon. Without a care about her night attire, she climbed into the wagon box and grabbed the smallest bag. Inside, she found the white linen handkerchief used to wrap the coins. It held just three gold pieces. *Sixty dollars!* Supplies at their last stop cost twenty, which meant Henry lost one hundred and twenty dollars gambling.

She wilted onto the apricot and sage-green tapestry bag and wept.

41

■ ■ ■ ■

First light confirmed that the Conrad brothers had gone on their way, leaving nothing behind.

Quinn climbed out of the wagon and made her way to the tent. She put on the same calico dress as yesterday while Henry snored.

After building a fire, Quinn brewed a pot of coffee. She knew nothing of catching grouse or rabbits. Even if she had, the plucking or skinning of it was not a thing she could stomach, especially this morning when she already felt nauseated over the night's monumental money loss. Stout-hearted wives, servants, and hunters possessed skills she never imagined she would need.

It was late morning before Henry crawled out of their shared tent in a drunken daze. He made his way to the cold, charred wood of the campfire and cautiously felt for heat on the sides of the coffee pot. When there was none, his eyes searched the area. "Hey, where are you?"

He spotted Quinn on her way back to camp. In the sunlight, her red hair shimmered.

"I see you've finally awoken," she said on approach.

"And I see you found the river."

"Yes." Sullen, she twisted the water from her long hair. "Please bathe, too. And quickly. We've already wasted enough of this day." Quinn went to her bag and retrieved her comb. With her back turned to him, she combed the length of her hair. Soon, she smelled the campfire and coffee but also heard Henry take down the tent. Within the hour, they were on their way. Henry was just as filthy as he was yesterday.

Gray pine, ponderosa pine, and cedar, each a different hue of green, timbered their path through the mountain pass until their wagon began its descent. Quinn held tight to her seatback, foot braced against the buckboard, to steady herself as the trail gradually dropped in elevation. Soon, conifers gave way to black oak and big-leaf maple, with leathery-leafed manzanita clinging to the rocky slopes.

Occasionally, the sure-footed mule veered too close to the trail's edge, causing Quinn to slide closer to Henry's mountainous side. Finally, bull pine, with their forked trunks, marked their transition into the lower blue-oak woodlands.

After barely a word all afternoon, Henry

glanced at Quinn, his swollen lip tinged blue, and said loudly enough to combat the wagon's rumble, "You still mad about the money?"

She turned to him, head cocked. "If you'd gambled away our supper, I would believe you did it to save our lives. But you didn't stop at losing supper. You continued to gamble until you'd lost one hundred and twenty dollars. More than half the money, which did not belong to you alone."

"I know. And I'm real sorry 'bout that."

In summers past, workmen had played cards when her father was absent. Poker, mostly. Although she'd never played, she listened. Its terminology still seemed foreign. "Why are you called 'Holdout Henry'?"

"Truth is, I like to gamble. Usually, I'm pretty good at it. I was just unlucky last night."

"Were you planning to use your own cards so you could cheat those men? Is that why they threatened us with a pistol?"

"You can't talk like that, Quinn. You'll get us both killed."

"There's no one here, except you and me."

Henry gave a cautionary glare. "You just don't talk about things like that — not ever. Do you hear me?"

44

Quinn turned away, focusing on the lush green, grassy valley ahead, until she mustered the courage to ask, "Is that why you were kicked off that wagon headed to California?"

Henry broke into a grin. "Those fellas didn't like my cards neither."

The thump of her heart made breathing hard. "Henry, where is the banknote from my father?"

"I got it safe, don't worry."

"I'd like to hold on to it if you don't mind." She held out her hand.

"I do mind." Henry eyed her. "Women have no business sense."

"But it's mine."

"No, it's *ours*. We made a deal, remember?"

Quinn turned to the horizon. The first faint sounds of crumbling dreams worked their way up from somewhere deep inside.

CHAPTER SIX

Nightfall's thunderous storm brought a torrent of rain, dousing their hastily staked tent, its top strung up like a teepee, tied overhead to an oak limb.

Quinn sat inside facing Henry, arms wrapped around her drawn-up knees. "Did you tarp the wagon?" Drenched, she shivered.

"Yeah, barely had time, though." The lantern between them lit both their faces as rain pelted the light-colored canvas. Henry's gaze skimmed her calico dress. "Should've grabbed your bag and a blanket, but the downpour hit fast."

Quinn looked up at the steep slant of the canvas, pulled high with rope. It sagged. Then billowed. "Will the tent hold?"

"Hope so. Got it staked pretty good, but I couldn't set the ridge pole in this wind." He scooted closer. Put his arm around her. "Try and think about somethin' else." When she nodded, he said, "If the storm blows over by sunup, we could be in San Francisco tomorrow afternoon." Then he cleared his throat. "Soon as we get there, I'm gonna meet up with the brothers at the Coffee Stand on the long wharf."

"The brothers? Those two ruffians who stole our supper and cheated you out of my money?"

"*Our* money." Henry fixed his eyes on the billowing tent top. "I got an idea as to how to win it back. Maybe a whole lot more. I'm gonna pay you back what I lost."

Quinn pulled away and stared at him. "And what money do you plan on using to achieve this great gambling feat? It certainly won't be my sixty dollars."

Henry shifted to face her. "I told you, I got a plan. Weren't you listenin'?" He grabbed her arm. "I need that money!"

Braced for a slap, her eyes scrunched shut. When none came, she opened them, then jerked free and pushed herself onto her feet. "Over my dead body!"

Henry tensed but then quickly cooled his temper. After a moment, he stood, slightly stooped below the pitch of the canvas top. "You're right. That sixty dollars is yours."

Taken aback by his lack of fight, Quinn firmed her shoulders. "Yes, it most certainly is mine."

He gave a slow nod. "I guess you'll need it 'til you can get on your feet."

"Yes." She lifted her chin. "As agreed, you'll get your money when we walk out of that bank with my inheritance, then we'll legally end the marriage and part ways. If you choose to gamble away your portion, so be it."

"All right. Fair's fair."

During the night, the tent collapsed in the storm, but the limp canvas covered them, a shield from the rain. At first light, they crawled from beneath it.

The horizon was a brilliant orange, gradually diminishing as the sun rose. Beneath their feet, the earth, parched by the summer drought, had already absorbed most of the deluge, leaving behind saturated brownish-black ground.

Henry raised his head to the bluing sky. "We best get moving."

"Without coffee? Or food? We had none at all last night."

"Do you see dry wood for a fire some-wheres?"

Quinn looked from spot to spot. Shook her head. "No, I suppose not."

"Then why don't you see if you can roll up that tent while I hitch up Berty."

"You named the mule?"

"Yep. She reminds me of my grandma, Bertha. That woman was a workhorse. Never tired. Always dependable. Folks called her Berty." Henry glanced at Quinn. "I've got fond memories of her."

The mule, still tethered to the white oak, lowered her head and gave a long, hoarse honk ending *aw, ah, aw.*

By the time Quinn folded and rolled the tent, both she and it were mud covered. Without a word, Henry picked up the canvas and carried it to the wagon, dumping it inside. He looked back at Quinn, who was mottled with mud. "You want to put on a clean dress?"

She stretched out her arms, palms up. "And ruin another?"

"All right, then. Get aboard." Henry hoisted Quinn up and then patted the mule's withers on his way around. He positioned himself on the seat, then slapped the reins. "San Francisco, here we come."

Two hundred or more square-rigged ships, masts bare, lay at anchor in the great bay. Quinn straightened on her seat, chin raised, stretching for a better view.

Between the rise and fall of bare hills, sparse with trees, was the new metropolis of the West. Adobe homes, canvas houses, wood shacks, blanket tents, and white canvas tents of all sizes rolled inland from the waterfront, over the sand dunes, and into a disorganized valley.

Berty pulled the buckboard through a throng of muddy hoofprints and wagon tracks — a path so bad, it was difficult to navigate safely until they reached named streets.

The air was rank with blasphemous oaths and gunfire. Pistols rode every hip.

Henry jerked up on the reins, halting the wagon, when two horses, with drunken riders clutching whiskey bottles, raced around a street corner, mud flying from their hooves.

The flat of Quinn's hand found its way to the high collar of her dress as a brawl burst out onto the street near lewd harlots with lifted skirts.

Men pushed and shoved their way into gambling rooms. Drunken sots lay where they fell.

Quinn covered her nose and mouth to dull the stench of animal dung and urine and then readjusted to ease the ache of her back and derriere. San Francisco was not the refined beauty she had imagined. It was not fancy. It showed no class or dignity, nor bore any resemblance to the Boston of her childhood memories, or the Paris of her dreams. How could she open a sophisticated art gallery in this crude, uncivilized place? A lawless city wild with drinking, gambling, and prostitutes.

"Hey, mister?" Henry called to an aproned merchant on the boardwalk, who stood amid great quantities of piled-high goods. "How do I get to the bank in Portsmouth Square?"

"You're headed there," the man yelled and pointed down the street before returning to his tasks.

Henry gave a wave and then slapped the reins.

Though Portsmouth Square — a plaza with sturdy buildings and wider streets — still had its share of monte, faro, and poker hells, it also bustled with businessmen in fine suits and hats. At the far end of the Parker House, she and Henry found the San Francisco Exchange and Deposit Office. Inside, they approached the only banker without customers, but when the dark-haired man ignored them, Quinn said, "Excuse me. We're here to see Richard."

Without so much as a glance up from his ledger, he said, "Not here. Can I help you?"

"Well, no," Quinn stammered. "At least, I

51

don't think so." She nudged Henry, urging him to hand over the note. "As you can see, this is specifically addressed to a man named Richard."

The banker took the note. Read it. Handed it back. "You'll need to see Mr. Naglee about this." He pointed to a closed door.

"But I was told to see Richard."

"Can't. He left the Exchange permanently two weeks ago."

Her heart thudded. *Had she been deceived?* "Yes, then please. Mr. Naglee will do."

When the clerk was out of earshot, Henry leaned close. "This wouldn't be a trick of yours to keep all the money, would it?"

"A trick of *mine*? I have betrayed no one. How dare you suggest it."

Henry cocked his head and eyed her. "Sorry, but money can turn an honest man, *or woman,* into a cheat awful fast. Seen it happen."

The closed door opened. Out stepped a curly-haired man with a mustache. His dark eyes surveyed the faces of the customers, stopping on Quinn, the only woman.

"This way," he called with a wave.

Inside the private office, Naglee read the note from Quinn's father, Hugh MacCann, and then he looked from her to Henry and back again. "Have a seat. It'll be a few minutes."

When he returned, he brought with him ninety coins. Exactly eighteen hundred dollars. He dropped them into a leather pouch and handed it to Quinn. "Tell your father I hope to see him soon. San Francisco has many new business opportunities worth his time."

Quinn nodded. No need to tell the dapper-dressed banker she would never see her father again.

By the time they reached the door of the Exchange and Deposit Office, Quinn's knuckles were white from the tight hold she had on the heavy pouch.

Outside the Portsmouth Square building, Henry took hold of her shoulders. "We got it!"

She'd done it. "I can't believe it. Not even a trick."

"C'mon," he said, urging her around the corner to a secluded area. "Ante up. I got places to be." Henry leaned against the building and pulled off a boot, removing his foul-smelling sock before slipping his boot on again. He held open the men's stocking and watched Quinn drop nine coins into it.

"Is that right?" He looked at her. "Nine?"

"Yes. Each coin is twenty. Nine of them

make one hundred and eighty dollars, which is exactly what you're due."

"We agreed to three hundred."

Quinn put a hand on her hip. "You gambled away one hundred and twenty dollars, remember? And I paid twenty for supplies, which included your whiskey and almonds!"

In a half-squint, he locked onto her green eyes. "I guess our business is finished."

"Yes." Her voice softened. "I suppose it is."

Henry gave a nod. His gaze shifted to the busy street. "This is a hell of a place for a woman alone. Sure you still want that divorce?"

Before her answer, a familiar voice said, "Well, hello, Henry."

Henry turned. At seeing the Conrad brothers, he grinned. "Hey, boys. I was just comin' to find you."

"That right?" Billy pushed his broad-brimmed hat higher up his forehead. His doubtful eyes fixed on Henry. "Thought you'd be here two days ago."

Quinn slipped the money pouch behind her back and then took a retreating step.

"Hold on, now." Earle had a lip full of chaw. "Where're you goin', little lady?" Tobacco-colored spittle flew through the opening where teeth used to be.

Henry extended his arm, separating Quinn from Earle. "She's just goin' across the street to the hotel to get us a room for the night while I make plans with you boys."

"I don't think so." Earle took hold of her arm.

"Your dealings have nothing to do with me." Quinn looked down at Earle's grip, then up again. "If you'll kindly release me, I'll leave you to your business with Henry."

The cock of a pistol came from Billy. He stepped close to Quinn and pressed the barrel of his gun hard against her side. He reached behind her, jerked the leather pouch from her grasp, and handed it to Earle. "Now you," he said with a nod indicating Henry's sock. "Hand it over."

"Please . . ." Weak-kneed, Quinn said, "It's all I have." She reached out. "I have no way to make more."

Billy chuckled. "You can double this in no time just by liftin' your skirts. Hell, I may come see you myself."

Henry shoved his coin sock at the thieving man. "Take mine. Leave hers be."

Earle grabbed the sock, but then with a *whack,* Billy hit Henry on the head with the butt of his pistol.

"Henry!" Quinn screamed as he collapsed onto the muddy ground, unconscious. She

55

yanked free of Earle and dropped to her knees.

"You didn't think you'd get off scot-free with the money, did you?" Earle laughed, then said to Billy, "Let's get!"

The thieving men ran, leaving Quinn with Henry. She cradled his head and then shouted, "Help!" When two men stumbled past the corner of the building, she called out again. "Please, help us!"

The passers-by barely offered a glance before moving on.

"Someone, help, please!"

In answer, a woman, dressed in a cherry-colored bodice and skirt, came and squatted by Quinn. "He get jumped?"

"Yes," Quinn said.

The woman turned Henry's head and stared at the rising bump, tinged barely blue, and then grimaced when a trickle of blood oozed from his left nostril. Her eyes caught Quinn's. "Never could stand the sight of blood. That's where I draw the line, you know? I'll do a man who's got some mud and filth on him, but blood's different altogether."

She stood. "Name's Pearl. Doc is a friend of mine. I'll send him back."

With Henry draped between them like a rag

doll, the physician and his assistant dragged him across the street, through mud and dung, to the medical office. Quinn held open the door while they hauled him inside and laid him on a cot. A whiff of strong salts roused Henry, but as soon as his eyes opened, he began to vomit. A bump the size of a chicken egg, lavender in color, had risen above his left eyebrow.

Queasy at his retching, Quinn stepped back. "Can't you do anything to help him?"

"Doin' what I can," the doctor told her. When Henry lay back, the physician said to him, "I'm Dr. Barton." He held up two fingers. "Can you tell me how many fingers you see?"

Henry squinted to focus. "Two," he said, breaking into a sweat.

"Good." Dr. Barton turned to Quinn. "He should be fine by tomorrow. Seen a lot worse today than this bump on the head."

"They get our money?" Henry asked Quinn.

"Yes." Without her willing them to, her hands went to her forehead. She rubbed at the ache starting there. "All of it."

Henry groaned. A moment later, he said, "You still got those coins in your bag?"

"Yes, but that's just sixty dollars, Henry. We had nearly two thousand!"

When Henry's eyes closed and he quieted, she turned to the doctor. "The ruffians who did this to Henry stole our money. I need to see the sheriff."

"Got a man comin' from Texas next month." Dr. Barton glanced at Quinn. "The one wearin' the badge now is a miserable thief himself. He won't do you any good."

Quinn bent forward, one hand on her stomach, the other on a chairback for steadiness.

"You sick?" the doctor asked.

She straightened, still gripping the chair. Her green eyes looked for decency in the doctor's face. "I have so little money left. What am I to do?"

Dr. Barton put his hand on her shoulder. "Why don't you go on and get yourself a room for the night. Sort it out tomorrow when you're fresh."

"What about Henry?"

"He'll be fine right here for the night." The doctor pointed to his assistant, a quiet young man who'd helped him drag Henry across the street to his office. "Jess here can take your outfit to the livery."

She forced a smile for the boy. "That's very kind. I'll need my bags from the wagon first."

In the beginning, owning just two bags

58

felt manageable, but now, as Quinn struggled to lug them across the plaza to the hotel, two seemed too many.

With the last remnant of sunlight fading into the bay, Quinn opened the hotel door. At the counter, she unlatched her smaller bag, then dug down until she found her folded handkerchief, which held her last three coins.

"How much for a room?"

The hotel clerk, a short, balding man, stared at her, silent.

"A room?" Quinn repeated.

"You alone?" he asked. "Don't see many women, 'specially ones unaccompanied."

"Yes." Quinn straightened her posture. "Just one night."

His brow lifted. Without a word, he lowered his head and rifled through an untidy stack of papers until he found his register book. "Five dollars. And you'll need to sign in." He handed her a pencil and pushed the green cloth-backed journal closer to her.

"Five dollars is a lot of money for just one night, isn't it?" She signed the book but then steadied her eyes on a doorway from which the aroma of beefsteak emanated. A blackboard advertised a breakfast special. *Ham and eggs served with redeye gravy and a biscuit. Three dollars.* "Quite a lot for a plate of food, too."

The man shrugged. "There's other hotels that can accommodate a woman, but they charge 'bout the same, and everybody knows Miss Tillie bakes the best biscuits."

Quinn handed him a coin, then briefly looked back at the restaurant. While he made change for her, she said, "I'll need a porter to carry my luggage."

He handed her fifteen dollars. "Everyone is their own porter here. Even ladies."

Her garret room was over the lobby of the one-story hotel. It smelled musky and dank. At the window was a single cot with gray blankets and a pillow so flat it barely had any fluff at all. A corner chair, lamp table, and a hanging mirror rounded out the meager furnishings. Overhead, the bare rafters gave little height to the slanted ceiling, and, after sliding her bags bedside, she stood, only to bump her head.

She sat at the edge of the cot and stared out a small, grime-ridden window. The salty sea air whistled around the eaves, imparting a gloomy loneliness. Beyond the rooftops was the shore, partially obscured by an evening fog.

How had this happened? Her fortune — stolen from her own hands. *"I suspect you'll be fleeced of your money and dignity within a month's time.*" Her father's words. She hated him for being right.

Education was to be her best defense against a life dependent upon him and his money. She'd expected her dowry to buy opportunity. Respect. A leniency to believe in oneself without regard to one's skill or experience. Yet she'd lost it.

If she'd chosen skill and ingenuity as a means to her independence instead of money, she might now be on a sailing ship to Paris.

Throughout the night, countless fleas and mosquitos awakened her — and at daylight, a cacophony of hammers banging across a hundred rooftops overtook a raucous uprising from the street below.

It was six o'clock when the hotel's breakfast bell clanged. Exhausted from her sleepless night, she lay listening to the commotion, unable to stop her short fingernails from scratching the incessant itch of flea bites. When the ringing stopped, she threw back the blankets and rose, only to bang her head a second time. "This godforsaken place!"

Hunched down beneath the low slant of the rafters, she made her way to the chamber pot and used it.

Her money was all but gone, her marriage

a sham. It was impossible to think of a future with any semblance of optimism. In this new city by the sea, she knew no one, except Henry. *Holdout Henry.* She needed to dress and go to him.

Quinn pulled out a clean blue dress from her bag and clothed herself. She brushed and pinned up her red hair and then tied her tan flannel shawl about her shoulders. Though both arms ached from the weight of her bags, she lugged them down the stairs.

The smell of ham and biscuits, wafting from the restaurant, assailed her senses, turning her growling stomach into a twist of hunger pangs, but a three-dollar breakfast was not within reason. Fifty-five dollars was all that was left of her fortune.

"Steward!" A man called out over the clink of restaurant dishes and silverware. "Where are my eggs?"

She hastened out the door to find Henry.

CHAPTER SEVEN

Quinn stepped onto the dew-covered planks of the hotel walkway. In each hand, she held a traveling bag.

Morning on Kearny Street was quieter, less active than the night before, but still, though daybreak barely peeked over the hills, Portsmouth Square was rife with tawdry women and bearded men with bottled spirits.

Outside, a man in tattered clothing lazed, his seated body held upright by the grace of a porch post. "How . . ." the man hiccupped, his slur disoriented, "much for a mornin'?"

"For a morning *what?*"

The man squinted up at her against the first strong rays of sunlight. "Well, you . . . ain't Pearl."

"No," Quinn said, softer than intended. "No, I'm not."

She crossed the street to the doctor's office and knocked lightly. When no one answered, she eased open the door. "Hello? Dr. Barton? Henry?"

In the silence, she set her bags down inside and then closed the door behind her. She went to the room where Henry had stayed last night. His unmade bed was empty.

It should not have come as a surprise. They'd agreed to part ways after the distribution of money. Nothing but a crumpled marriage certificate tied him to her now, and it had served its one and only purpose — her father had released the dowry. Henry was a free man.

Quinn closed her eyes. She rubbed the creases between her brows. What was she to do in this wretched city, alone, and without proper finances?

How quickly her hopes had become regrets. So many of her decisions proved wrong.

After gathering her thoughts, Quinn picked up her bags and headed for the livery. She knew nothing of driving a wagon. She would sell it. Surely, it was worth something.

She stayed on the plank walk as far as possible, but when she came to the building site of a new hotel, the boardwalk ended.

Before stepping off onto the road muddied with animal dung and urine, she set down her bags and shook the ache out of her arms.

Up ahead, children squatted on a dirt pile. With the head of a pin moistened in their mouths, they picked up glinting specks, which they deposited onto a folded white paper.

Quinn lifted her bags, carrying one in each hand, which left her unable to raise her skirts out of the muck. She trudged to the children. "Is that gold?"

A dirty-faced boy, no more than ten, glanced up. "Sure it is. See?" He opened his paper and showed her the tiny golden flakes. "I found nine dollars' worth yesterday."

"Nine dollars? Just by sifting through construction dirt?"

He nodded, refolded his paper, and returned to his hunt.

On the corner of Dupont and Union Streets stood the livery. The building was barn-like, built of wood, with a side corral. The odor of fresh hay and horses hung in the air.

"What can I do for you?" a bearded man asked as Quinn walked inside.

Quinn set her bags down. "A boy named Jess brought my mule and wagon here last night."

"The gray mule with a buckboard ranch wagon? Has belongings in the box?"

"Yes, that's the one."

The man turned with pointed finger. "There's a feller out back taking it right now."

"Taking it?" Quinn started for the back but thought better about going after the thief herself. "Stop him! That's my wagon."

Moving at a trot, the man shouted, "Whoa! Jacob, hold that rig!" He turned and looked back at Quinn. "C'mon!"

Past a line of a dozen new saddles, out through wide open double doors, she saw Henry seated on the wagon, reins in hand.

At the sight of Quinn, he pulled up on the leather. "Hold up, Berty." He jumped down. "Where you been?"

Quinn hurried to him. When she reached Henry, she said, "Were you stealing my wagon?"

Henry shook his head. His bump was bluer, meaner. "I was comin' to look for you."

"And you needed a wagon to do that? I was across the street from you, Henry."

"Well, how was I supposed to know that?"

"The doctor knew I was at the hotel."

"He wasn't there when I woke up this mornin'. Just that kid, Jess."

The liveryman, and the one called Jacob, stood swivel headed, listening to the back and forth. "Say, is it your wagon or not?"

"It's my wagon," Quinn told them.

"Well, he's the one who paid the livery bill."

Quinn turned to Henry. "You paid the bill? Where did you get money?"

Henry grinned. "Jess wanted to learn cards."

"You took money from that boy?"

"He lost a few coins, that's all."

"Well, I suppose I should look at the bright side. You paid a debt that would otherwise be mine."

He placed his hand lightly on her cheek. Leaning in, he whispered, "I got three dollars left, and I got a plan."

Quinn turned to the two liverymen. "Would one of you kindly bring my bags? I put them down when I thought my wagon was being stolen."

"Sure. Yeah, I'll get 'em." The bearded man hurried back into the building and emerged a minute later with her two bags. He set them inside the wagon. "Glad it all worked out."

"Yes, as am I," Quinn said. "Thank you."

Near Portsmouth Square, Henry stopped at a large canvas tent, twenty-five feet in length, which bore a sign that read El Dorado. Though it was just eight in the morning, shouts and laughter erupted within. "How much you got left?"

Quinn's eyes went wide. "I'll not give you a dime of my money."

Henry jumped down off the wagon. "Suit yourself." He fingered his coins. "I can turn three dollars into three hundred in no time at all, but if you can do what you need with what's left of yours, all right."

"Three hundred?"

"In no time."

"How much would you need?"

"Much as you can give me." He hopped into the back of the wagon. "Big bag or little one?"

"The small bag, but I've pushed the hankie all the way to the bottom."

When Henry withdrew his hand, he held Quinn's folded handkerchief. "So, how much you givin' me?"

"How much can you win with forty dollars?" she asked.

Henry grinned. "A bundle."

"All right. Forty dollars, then. That will leave me fifteen dollars, in case."

Henry refolded the white linen and lace, then pushed it back down inside. He jumped out of the wagon. Held open his hand. "Forty dollars, just like you said." He closed his fist around the coins and started for the entrance to the El Dorado.

"Henry?" Quinn called after him. When he turned, she stiffened. Her heart pounding. "Please don't lose. I don't know what I'll do if you lose." After his nod, she watched him disappear into the canvas hell.

The El Dorado had a constant stream of morning gamblers. Some stumbled toward it — fish reeled in by the sing-song voices of women — while others came with intent in their walk.

Mid-morning was fast approaching when Quinn recognized the woman who helped them after Henry was knocked unconscious. She climbed down out of the wagon and hurried to her. "Pearl?"

The blonde turned at the call of her name. Her eyes settled on Quinn. "What makes you look so downcast today?"

Was it so obvious? Quinn reached up and gave a pat to her hair in case any of it was out of place. "I wanted to thank you for yesterday." The two women stood facing each other, even though Pearl came only chin high to Quinn. "It was kind of you. I thought you might want to know that Henry is doing well."

Pearl peeked around Quinn's shoulder

and then scanned the area. "Where's he at?"

"Henry is inside. He's been in there an awfully long time."

"Whiskey, cards, and women — men can't seem to do without any of 'em." Pearl sucked in a quick breath. "Not that your man is looking for a woman. I didn't mean that at all."

"I understand." Quinn smiled.

"Want me to go look for him? You can come along. It's not really so bad in there."

Quinn shook her head just as a tall, stout man wearing a buff-colored vest came out of the El Dorado holding Henry by the scruff of his neck.

"He yours?" the man shouted to Quinn, then he tossed Henry — who scrambled to stay on his feet — at her. "Says you got money to pay off his debt."

Henry's feet knotted, and he fell face first onto the dirt. He jumped up and started for the man. "You son-of-a-bitch!"

"Henry, no!" Quinn ran and grabbed his left arm, pulling him back, but with his free arm, Henry swung at the man.

In a flash, the big man punched Henry in the jaw, knocking him back down to the ground. Riled and red faced, he turned his eyes to Quinn. "Twenty dollars is what he owes. You got it or not?"

Quinn looked at the burly man, and then down at Henry, crumpled at her feet. "I . . . I don't have all of it." A tear escaped. She wiped it away. "I have fifteen dollars."

He peered down at Henry, who lay staring up at him, dabbing his bloody lip with a bare knuckle. The man looked again at Quinn. "What's a lady like you doin' with this no-account anyway?"

Quinn lowered her head. Quietly, she said, "I'll get the money." She went to the wagon, retrieved the last of her coins, and returned.

He raked them out of her hand. Fingered them. "He owes twenty."

Faint, Quinn steadied her legs. "Fifteen is all I have. I don't have twenty." She recognized the defeated sound of her own voice. She had heard it too many times. When the man bent with gritted teeth and grabbed a handful of Henry's shirt, she cried out, "Wait!"

Hesitantly, her hand went to the high collar of her blue dress. She felt the finely carved lines on the sardonyx shell cameo. Tears flooded her eyes as she unpinned it and handed it to the man. "This belonged to my mother. I'm sure you'll find it worth far more than five dollars."

Pearl grabbed the cameo from her. "I'll give you five dollars for it, Frank." She opened her black silk handbag and pulled out a coin. "Here. Take it."

The man gave a slow nod. "All right." With twenty dollars in coins, he turned and went back inside the El Dorado.

"Take it, honey." Pearl handed the cameo back to Quinn. "I used to have Momma's pearl earrings, but some no-good who wanted more from me than he paid for took 'em. Gambled 'em away when I wouldn't give his money back. I shot him for it. Fact is, that's how I got the name Pearl. Mary Lizabeth is my real name." Her smile shrank. "Sounds too saintly for me anyway."

Quinn took the cameo but held Pearl's hand for just a moment, her green eyes misty. "Thank you, Mary Lizabeth."

CHAPTER EIGHT

A line of red had dried on Henry's chin, but blood still trickled from the corner of his mouth. His sandy-blond hair was dark with dirt and grime. He got to his feet.

"That's it for us then, isn't it?" Quinn's tone was solemn. "Not a dime left." She set her wandering gaze on the city. The buildings. The Square. The people.

"Honey," Pearl said to her. "I know it's probably not what you want to hear, but if you're needin' work, I got a place for you."

Quinn took a halting breath. It held. *A prostitute.*

"It ain't so bad, honey. Honest." Pearl gave her a gentle smile. She reached out and lightly squeezed Quinn's flea-bitten hand, which was frozen against her waistline. "I can get you some food and a new dress. A decent place to stay, too."

Henry grabbed Quinn's shoulders and turned her toward him. "They cheated me,

Quinn, but I'm gonna make it right. I'll pay you back. I swear I will."

Glassy eyed, Quinn looked at him. "How, Henry? How will you do that?"

Henry's chin jutted higher. He spotted Berty, right where he left her. "We still got a mule and wagon. Come to Stockton with me. I'll get the money from Momma." He glanced at Pearl, then back at Quinn. "Trust me, you ain't cut out to be a whore like her."

Snapped from her daze, Quinn's glare landed on Henry. "Trust *you*?" At his silence, her eyes drifted to Pearl and softened. "Thank you, but San Francisco is not for me. Henry owes me a great deal of money, and I intend to be repaid. Soon as I am, I'll book passage to the East. Back to Boston, where I belong."

Henry reached out and gently took hold of Quinn's hands. "I'm thinking I might want you to stay with me."

Slow, deliberate, Quinn nodded. After a moment, her steady gaze locked on Henry's blue eyes. She eased her hands away from him. "I will go with you to Stockton for my money, but I'll never stay."

Berty pulled the wagon east across miles of yellow grass and parched plains — a dismal journey, not because of scalding hot weather or dreary, dry scenery, but another, entirely personal, reason.

"I can't help it," Henry said for the hundredth time. "Quinn, I love you. We should stick together. And don't even say it isn't true love. It is. I swear it is."

But Quinn knew only one truth. There was no such thing as true love.

In Stockton, their wagon stopped at a gray, one-story, sawn-lumber house. Mature peach trees shaded the west lawn. On the eastern side was a dead, leafless almond tree. Wound around porch posts were delicate, pink wild bean vines.

The front door flew open, and a hefty woman in a lemon-plaid day dress shouted, "My Henry is home!"

Henry set the wagon's brake arm and wrapped the leather reins around it, then jumped to the ground. "What happened to my almond tree, Momma?"

"It died, Henry, but don't you worry. I found another place to get your almonds."

Quinn made her way off the wagon while the two bear hugged. She wove coppery-red straggles up under her hairpins and smoothed the skirt of her red dress.

Henry pulled away from his mother and swung his arm toward Quinn. "Momma, this is Quinn. My wife."

The wide-cheeked smile on his mother's face faded. "Your wife?"

"Quinn, meet Myra, my mother."

"Hello," Quinn said with a half nod.

Myra's eyes glided down the length of Quinn before she turned back to Henry. "Out with no bonnet? In a red dress? It's still daylight, Henry. Where in God's name did you find her?"

"C'mon, Momma," Henry groaned. "You'll like her, I promise."

Again, Myra turned to Quinn. Her gray-blue eyes traced Quinn's outline. "And already married?"

"Sure, Momma. I wouldn't have brought her home to you if we wasn't married."

Myra refocused on Henry and smiled. "Of course, you wouldn't have." She patted his arm. "You're a good, decent boy."

Henry kissed her cheek. "Sure is good to be home again."

Then Myra's eyes caught the fading bruise on Henry's forehead. She reached up, lightly touching it with her fingertips. "What's this?" Her head swiveled toward Quinn, shooting a glare at her, but her words were for Henry. "How did this happen?"

"Momma, I'm fine. Don't fuss about it. Can't we just go inside?"

Her glare lingered, then she wove her arm through his and guided him toward the house, leaving Quinn at the wagon. "You're home in time for supper."

Beckoned by the aroma of chicken and dumplings, Quinn followed.

Inside, the painted walls were straw colored, and a regal carpet in burgundy, green, and tan covered the living room floor. Yellow curtains hung at the windows, and at the far wall stood a gray stone fireplace stacked with pine-scented wood.

"Did you earn enough money up north to get a good start on your painting business?" Myra asked Henry while she ladled their bowls full.

"Yeah," Henry answered. "Yeah, did real good."

Quinn stopped at the lie — her linen napkin halfway to her lap — and looked at Henry, who did not look back.

"The thing is, Momma, I don't want to spend all my money on paint and supplies." Henry blew the steam off his bowl before taking a bite. He kept focused on the food. "I've got a wife to support now, and we need a house and a stocked pantry. I thought you could help out until the business gets going."

"Henry, I gave you five hundred dollars

two months ago to get you started — half the cost of what you said you needed." Myra filled her own bowl, then sat.

"I know, and three times that much come to me since, but I didn't count on coming home with a wife."

With a glance aimed at Quinn, Myra said, "It's a surprise to me, too."

Henry leaned back in his chair. Swiped a napkin across his lips. "I swear, Momma, there's just nobody who can cook like you." He straightened, then set his eyes on Quinn. From across the table, he took hold of her hand. "Momma, I need a favor. I want you to teach my wife to cook." His eyes shifted to Myra as his snicker tumbled out. "She can't boil water 'cept to make coffee, and, since you'll probably have a grandbaby before long, I know you'll want to help out as much as you can."

"A grandbaby?" Myra set her spoon down and stared at Quinn. "Are you . . ."

"Not yet, Momma, but maybe soon." Henry grinned at his mother. "So what do you say? Will you teach her how to cook and loan me another five hundred, or a thousand?" He stood and squared his thumb and forefinger, framing an imaginary signboard. "Myra and Son Painting — just think of it, Momma. Won't that be somethin' to write home to those biddies about in Saint Louie? They won't talk bad about you no more. Just you wait and see — I'll double your money. You'll be richer than all of them."

Eyes glazed, Myra spooned chicken and dumplings into her mouth. She chewed slowly. Swallowed. "I'll do it." She looked up. "For you, I'll do it." Myra stood and gave Henry a hug, then pulled away, leaving her cupped hands ahold of his shoulders. "Five hundred. Add it to all the money you've already saved."

Quinn spent her next several days taking orders from Myra, bearing insults, and keeping quiet about Henry's gambling.

"All haughty young wives like you are plain ignorant when it comes to household duties. Didn't your mother, or that college of yours, teach you anything?" Myra's girth bumped Quinn into a nook near the cookstove. "Don't just stand there! Put those eggs in the boiling water."

Quinn's scalded fingers were blistered red and so sensitive it was hard to shuck corn or peel the carrots laid out for her.

"Haven't you chopped those peaches yet?" With an arthritic finger, Myra pointed to the basket on the dry sink. "Remember, I need those pits. Don't throw 'em away."

Each time Henry passed their way, Myra's coddling arms captured him in a hug.

At week's end, Henry found and rented a furnished home near his mother — one owned by "Lucky Luke" Thornton, the man who had built the biggest gambling room within two days' ride. "So, what do you think?" Henry posed, arms out, behind Quinn, who stood in their own kitchen mixing flour and tallow for biscuits.

She turned and looked at him. With the back of her floured hand, she swept long, sweaty strands of red hair off her face. "How did you afford a new suit?"

"Momma bought it for me when I told her about my business meetings today."

"Is she going with you? She didn't mention it."

Henry shook his head. "Why would she come? A woman's got no notion how business works." He lifted a dark felt hat off the peg. "Momma filled a bean pot with brandied almonds for me as a wedding gift. I set it on the table."

"More almonds?" she asked. "Your mother was here all morning teaching me to make a peach pie with her new almond flour crust. Just for you, she said. It's cooling on the sill."

Henry grinned. "Momma knows I love 'em."

Quinn used her long white apron to clean the rendered tallow off her hands. "Henry, how soon do you expect to earn money? There's a ship sailing for Panama on the twenty-eighth of next month, and then on to Boston. I don't want to miss it."

"What's so all-fired important about Boston?" Henry crookedly tied a beige cravat around his neck, which Quinn reached to straighten. "Anybody can tell you, California's the place to be."

"Not for me."

Henry fitted the hat on his head. "We'll talk about it later." With a half grin, he said, "I might be late for supper." He was still smiling as he walked out the door.

Quinn wrapped her biscuits in a cotton cloth, then tightly lidded the stewed beef — its aroma scenting the house with a hominess — and then took the cooled pie off the windowsill. Just like Myra taught her to do, she made a tiny slit in the crust and tucked a sprig of sugared peach leaves into it for decoration. She stood back and smiled. Her first supper. Made entirely with her own hands.

With Henry off to his business meeting,

ship's passage was top of mind, so Quinn twirled her tan shawl around her and set off for Center Street to find some answers.

Near Reed's Landing, Quinn found the steamship office. She opened the door to a throng of ship hands and travelers crammed inside. Many crowded together to read the wall postings, but a few waited in line to talk to a thin, middle-aged clerk. The room reeked of river water, tobacco, and men fresh off their boats.

"Hello," Quinn said when it was her turn. She held onto the squared edge of the long, oak counter, which had nicks and gouges, and was without a sheen. "How much is ship's passage to Boston?"

The clerk's thick spectacles magnified his steely-gray eyes. "Just you?"

"Yes. I saw a posting for the twenty-eighth of next month."

He nodded. "Steamer costs thirty-five from here to San Francisco. You'll board a clipper there. Steerage to Boston is a hundred. Fifty more if you want a cabin." His oversized eyes stared at her. "You want a ticket?"

"How long is the trip?"

" 'Bout five months. Sometimes longer. The *Palmetto* came in at a hundred and sixty-two days. You want a ticket?"

"Five months," Quinn mumbled to herself.

"It's none of my business, but ain't you the lady who married Myra's boy?"

Absentmindedly, Quinn nodded.

"You shouldn't be goin' alone. Folks think passengers are noble pioneers, but they ain't. Most are gamblers, thieves, and drunkards. Scum of the earth, all of 'em. A lady alone will be bait, sure as beefsteak is to a pack of wolves." He laid his hand on top of the counter, palm up. "You want a ticket or not?"

"No," she said. "Not today."

"Good." He withdrew his outstretched hand. "Why don't you go on now and talk things over with that new husband of yours."

Quinn made her way home as the sun lowered, tinting the western sky yellow. The yard of their unpainted, unfenced house was flowerless and without shrubs, except for the two struggling white rose bushes that grew at the front corners of the wraparound porch.

Five months aboard ship with drunkards and thieves. Consumed in nightmarish thoughts, she stepped inside the house.

"Where you been?" Henry shouted at her, then tripped over his own foot. In one hand, he held the neck of a whiskey bottle. In the other, brandied almonds. "Supper s'pose to be on the table at five." He hiccupped. "Momma said so."

Overturned on the table, near a handful of spilled almonds, was Myra's redware bean pot. Beside it was the pie plate, empty.

Henry stumbled to a dining chair and sat. His blond head bobbed drowsily. "Need supper." He rubbed his forehead.

Quinn stared. Quietly, she said, "The biscuits need warming."

"Jus' give me wha'ya got." Red faced, he hiccupped again and then plunked down his near-empty whiskey bottle. It leaned drunkenly atop his scattered almonds.

Quinn went to the cookstove, filled a bowl with stewed beef and biscuits, then returned. She set it on the table in front of him. Hesitantly, she asked, "Henry, you still have Myra's five hundred dollars, don't you?"

Henry's head swung back and forth. "Nope." He took a bite from his bowl, then put down his fork. He rubbed his forehead again. His eyes were barely open. "Ever' last dollar is gone."

Then he collapsed.

CHAPTER NINE

Surrounded by Quinn, Myra, and an incompetent doctor who diagnosed food poisoning for every dying man without a bullet wound, Henry, faint of breath, said, "I love you, Quinn."

The truth was, he loved her no more than she loved him, but the words were expected at such a grievous time. "I love you, too, Henry."

"Hogwash!" Myra burst out through her sobs. "There's not a tear in your eye."

If a dying man could still hear words on his way out of this world, then those were the last ones Henry ever heard.

"You killed him!" Myra wailed. Her arthritic finger curled in an effort to point. "My boy is dead from your God-awful cooking!" She buckled under her grief.

Quinn stepped back, away from the deathbed of the man she'd married but barely known. Surely she hadn't done this, had she?

The gray-haired doctor picked up his black bag. "I'll send the undertaker."

Respectful of the mourning, Quinn let the breeze pull her to the open window where lace curtains rippled. Softly, she brushed a fallen strand of hair from her brow, then fixed her eyes on twilight's painted sky.

Through the window, she watched the doctor climb onto the seat of his wagon. He took hold of the leather reins but made no effort to leave as townsfolk gathered around him. His nod toward the house elicited gasps.

Word had spread — her beef and biscuits had snuffed out a life.

On the day of Henry's burial, Quinn had two bags packed. There was nothing left for her in this town now that he was dead, and, under Myra's threat of arrest, Quinn wanted out of Stockton before the sheriff and his deputies returned from a manhunt.

Food poisoning might have killed Henry, she'd decided, but it didn't make her a murderer.

"I'd like to sell this wagon and mule," she told the livery owner. With no notion of how to manage the rig, she knew money for it would serve her better, so when fifty dollars was offered, she gave a pat to Berty's rump and took the coins.

She crossed the street to the church and read the letter that hung tacked open on the bulletin board:

REPUTABLE WOMEN WANTED

The town of Fortune is rich in gold, but poor in women.

In need of saloon girls, cooks, wives for lonely men, and a schoolmarm for the children we expect soon enough.

Fifty dollars and an ounce of gold await any woman answering this advertisement within sixty days.

Signed,
Bill Beaudry
Fortune, California
August 15, 1849
P.S. Bring references, diplomas, or letters of moral character.

She tugged the posting off the wallboard and stepped out into the morning sunlight, only to have a gust of wind whisk the paper from her hands. She grabbed, snatching it midair, and then brought it down, smoothing its crumples against her skirt. The letter was already a month old, but surely, jobs were still available. She folded it into a square, then tucked it inside the long sleeve of her dress. Fortune, she decided, was as good a place as any for a fresh start.

Quinn stood outside the church with her bags, waiting for the Birch wagon as it made its way through to gold country, but by the time the high-sided ranch wagon reached Stockton, it was full to the brim with men. She shuddered at the sight of it. It had no shade bonnet and not a single seat cushion. When a boisterous boy, not much more than sixteen, jumped to the ground and grabbed the handles of her tapestry bags, she flinched. Without asking permission, he heaved them one at a time up and over the side, landing them in the bed before he climbed back aboard, taking back slaps and guffaws from the other men. When one slovenly fellow rewarded him with a chaw of tobacco, the boy tucked it under his lower lip and gave a brown-stained grin, then settled himself down on the splintery floorboards, leaving his seat vacant.

"Where you headed?" the wagoner asked as Quinn fumbled to pay the thirty-six dollar fare.

"Fortune," she said.

The man's quiet scrutiny settled on her plain, freckled face, but it didn't take long for him to drop his gaze to the tips of her white kid-leather boots and start working his way up. His eyes skimmed her cotton day dress, once a rosy-red but now resembling the color of a rusty nail, and didn't stop until they met hers. "Ever been there?" he asked. Then, without waiting, he said, "That ain't no place for a lady."

"Maybe not," Quinn said as she stepped up to climb inside the wagon. "But it's where I'm headed."

The only empty seat on the long bench wedged her between two sleeping men sprawled lengthwise on either side of her. She settled herself as best she could, showing only a brief jitter when Henry's mother came running.

"Stop her!" Myra shouted to the wagoner. "She's got all Henry's money!" She grabbed hold of the endgate and, huffing out what sounded like her last breath, said, "She killed my boy, then stole his fortune."

The wagoner turned to Quinn with raised eyebrows.

Quinn drew a fortifying breath and stared back at him. "Her accusations are unfounded, so, unless you plan to halt this wagon long enough to hear both sides, I suggest we get started. I'd like to make my destination by dark."

The wagoner gave an agreeable nod and climbed aboard, positioned himself on the driver's seat, and took hold of the reins.

With a hard rattle of the endgate, Myra shouted, "Where's this wagon headed?"

"Gold country," the driver answered, with a glance back. Then he slapped the reins, urging his team onward.

Myra ran a few steps and then stopped, her hefty frame exhausting her. "Where in gold country?" she shouted, but the wagon never slowed its pace.

It wasn't until the sights and sounds of her past faded into the rumblings of the well-worn wagon that Quinn breathed a sigh of relief. The farther north they traveled from Stockton, the more her burdens lifted. Talk of buying pans, pails, and picks in Sutter Creek came from the straggly men seated opposite her, which meant they had farther to go than she did.

"Are these two traveling with you?" She motioned to the men who lay in a drunken snooze on either side of her. It wasn't that she didn't appreciate the seat vacated for her by the boy, but almost thirty miles squeezed between two men who reeked of whiskey and hadn't visited a bathhouse recently was more than she'd bargained for on this trip.

"No, ma'am," came the answer from the scruffy auburn-haired man, who grinned as his two companions eyed her with brazen bad manners. "Them fellas said they was headed to Volcano, which anyone with half a mind knows has been all staked and claimed up."

"I see," she said, even though she did not. California purported to have enough land to satisfy the gold cravings of every man the world over. "What about you four? Are you going to the town of Fortune?"

The man snickered. "Fortune ain't even a town. 'Less'n that's what you call a tangle of tents and bush houses." That sent his companions into peals of laughter, which brought him a satisfied grin. He leaned forward. "Why don't you come on with us to the town of Muddy Horse? I'll be glad to let you bunk with me. These other fellas can get mighty mean if the spirit hits 'em."

"No." Quinn recoiled. When he continued to eye her, she turned her gaze to the distance. Not a real town? Was the posting a ploy? A swindle?

Though the route was wretched, the wagon rolled on at a good pace. Only occasionally did the driver find a trail, usually one beaten down by the hooves of cattle or horses or herds of one kind or another. Even from the back of a jostling wagon, the Sierra foothills inspired the artist in Quinn. Along its stream banks, complacent cattle drank while droves of wild horses and herds of deer and antelope, all fleet of foot, glided over the land in masterful rhythm. A time or two, animals dared to come close, showing more curiosity about the wagon and its passengers than the men did of them.

Being the only woman in this wagonload of prospectors, Quinn had nothing to say to the vulgar men who leered at her with lewd gestures. Loathsome, wealth-grubbing, women-ogling men had become commonplace. Perhaps her sufferings with Henry prepared her for the likes of these filthy gold miners, who seemed mostly bullies and braggarts, picking and prodding at each other when they weren't niggling her. If she'd learned anything at all from her father, Hugh MacCann, it was that paltry men like these tumbled when confronted, yet she hoped her parleying abilities would not be tested.

By midday, she found herself grateful to the sleeping drunkards beside her for taking up space the loutish Muddy Horse–bound men would have otherwise claimed for themselves. Before boarding the wagon this morning, Quinn had pinned her long braided hair atop her head and then tied on an ivory bonnet, but the jostling wagon was skilled at loosening hairpins. When a few unruly red stragglers worked themselves free, she delicately poked them up under her bonnet again, ignoring the men's elbow jabs and horselaughs that came whenever she displayed a womanly mannerism.

With Stockton far behind, the wagon descended into a valley covered in the amber of wild oats and luxuriant grasses, flowers in brilliant oranges, yellows, and reds, and timbered in groves of varying oak. Scattered about were dogwood, redbud, and buckeye trees whose silvery trunks stood encrusted with multi-colored lichen. Hundreds of horned cattle, fat and free, roamed undisturbed as herds of elk with immense antlers grazed atop sun-dappled hills.

The sun slowly wheeled through the sky, surrendering the last of its summer heat to the magnificent land, which by afternoon made it a struggle for Quinn to maintain a proper upright posture on the wagon's crude bench seat. Beneath her long sleeves, she sweated, and her back and derriere ached from the constant jouncing. She was almost glad when an especially hard bump dumped one of the inebriated men off the seat onto the rough floorboards of the wagon. With a groan, the man squinted one eye open for just a moment before his prone position sent him into new slumber. There he lay, face down, both arms splayed in flogging pose, which she presumed would likely be deserved. She lifted her feet and swung them over the man, then scooted closer to the endgate and repositioned herself, savoring an uninhibited breeze.

Soon, glimpses of the American River came into view, which captured the attention of the three Muddy Horse men. Without comment, Quinn leaned out, craning her neck from where she sat on the far side to see the river that had excited the world.

Although the rumbling of the wagon silenced the river's roar, its blue, white-capped water bared its beauty in the breaks between clusters of oak and dense strips of mottled sycamore. And when the river could no longer be seen through the thickness of the trees, she knew it continued to run alongside, because its dampness scented the air. Soon, tall stately pines overtook most of the other trees.

At close of day, amid the setting sun's golden light, the wagon rolled to a stop beside a narrow, steep-sided creek. Right away, the boy stood and grasped the handle of Quinn's biggest bag. He heaved it up and over the side, dropping it to the ground with a plop. Next went her smaller bag.

"This is the Fortune stop," the driver announced as he jumped down.

Quinn looked in both directions before turning back to the wagoner. "Where's the town?"

He pointed to a foot trail leading up an incline toward a clearing on the other side of the creek. "Hear them hammers? That's the town bein' built." He reached out his hand to steady her as she stepped down. "I got mail goin' to the supply store, so I can take one of your bags up yonder for you if you like."

"Ye-yes," she stammered. Reaching for her smaller bag, Quinn noted, "The posted letter said the town had businesses and a school. I thought I would see a church and houses."

"Oh, you probably will in another few weeks, now that folks are findin' the place. Most buildings didn't go up too long ago, and folks that followed went right to work pannin' gold, so the town has been slow comin'." In one hand, the driver held a stack of mail tied up with twine. With his other hand, he picked up her bigger bag. He turned and stepped onto the footbridge made of planks and walked across the creek as if he had done it a dozen times.

Quinn stood there alone, except for the wide-awake passengers who were cackling like a flock of crows and pointing at the dumbfounded look on her face. "Come on to Muddy Horse with us!"

She briefly felt tempted to climb back aboard that wagon and ride it to the end of the line, or civilization, whichever came first, but the simple fact was, her remaining fourteen dollars wouldn't last long. She needed the fifty offered in the posting, and she needed a job. The letter did not state how much an ounce of gold was worth, but she thought it must surely be at least five dollars. That would be fifty-five more than she had right now. With a look back and forth between the passenger wagon and the footbridge, Quinn made her choice. She hiked her dress hem above the tops of her ankle boots and started toward those planks.

The riverbank resembled land stampeded by bulls, or maybe just bullheaded men clamoring for their fortunes. Without recent rains, churned up dried mud formed hard, stiff peaks like a frosted cake, which made walking difficult in dainty-heeled boots. Further proof that no creek, big or small, was safe from gold miners anymore.

The stream flowed slow but steady in the

ravine beneath the barely built bridge. Once across, Quinn trudged up the incline carrying her bag. Near the clearing, she spotted the wagoner standing outside a store built of bare wood. He handed the bundled mail to a blond-haired man, then set her bag down on the ground near his feet. Both men turned to watch her approach until she was within a few feet of them. With a tip of his hat, the driver said, "Good luck to you, ma'am." He headed down the hill as if he were already late for his next stop.

Luck. She had a feeling that was exactly what she would need after seeing Fortune firsthand. The town had no streets, just one wide swath of tamped down dirt. Alongside the crude road, she counted five log and board buildings, with another partially built. Of those, three were canvas-topped cabins. Farther away, scattered amongst the trees, were dozens of primitive lean-tos and whitish-colored tents, most mud stained. All around, conifers and cottonwoods lay harvested with most already limbed and topped out, their long straight trunks strewed haphazardly across the hillside. A group of twenty or more men gathered at a field of felled timber with saws and axes. They looked more like lumberjacks than gold miners as they hacked and sawed.

"Hello," she said to the blond man holding the newly delivered mail. "I have a letter." She pulled the paper from inside her dress sleeve. With a nervous tremor, she handed it to the man. "It's signed by Bill Beaudry. Do you know where I might find him?"

"Yes, ma'am," the man said with a nod. "I'm Bill Beaudry. Pleased to have you here."

Her sigh of relief in finding the advertiser so quickly was louder than intended. "Good," she said, recovering from her unease. "Where do I collect my money?"

The man pointed to the letter. "Money is paid out after thirty days, ma'am. What was your name?"

"Thirty days?" Quinn dropped her bag and grabbed the letter out of his hand, then stabbed the words with her finger. "There's nowhere in this letter that says anything about thirty days."

"Well, that's how it works." The man motioned with an open hand toward the departing wagon as it headed off toward Sutter Creek. "Otherwise, women would be showing up, claiming their money, and then climbing right back on that wagon out of here. We got to have some kind of assurance you'll give Fortune a try before moving on to another town."

Slack-jawed, Quinn spent the next thirty seconds speechless with her eyes glued to his. Bill Beaudry wasn't the most handsome man she had ever seen, but if she could remember who was, he might surely have been second. His hair was the color of corn-husks, dried and darkened by too many days on the stalk. He wore it short, much like a university man, but with a longer, tousled top, and his eyes were as blue as a thunder sky over the Cascades in Oregon. His barely shaven face bore a few days of stubble, trimmed into just a hint of a beard and mustache.

"Mr. Beaudry," Quinn said as calmly as any lady could upon hearing this unexpected stipulation. "How am I to rent a room for myself without the money?"

"Ma'am . . ." He broke off. "Sorry, what was your name again?"

"Quinn is my name, Mr. Beaudry."

"Got a last name?"

A last name. If she used her married name, Myra might track her down and send the Stockton sheriff. Her innocence would not stop a vengeful mother. "MacCann. My name is Quinn MacCann."

"Ma'am, I'd appreciate it if you would just call me Bill. We're not much on formalities around here."

She gave a nod. "*Ma'am* won't do for me, either."

"Yes, ma'am . . . I mean, Quinn." Bill corrected himself with a quiet smile. Behind him stood a log and board building, big and sturdy, with a wood-planked porch where a young boy sat petting a sleeping, golden-haired dog. Above the door hung a sign with the words Beaudry's Supply painted in white, and displayed in its front window were cooking pots, kettles, tin plates, and stacks of gold-mining pans. He stepped past the boy and inside the store long enough to leave the mail, then stepped out again and closed the door. "Rooms to rent are upstairs at Medford's, but they might be full up by now." He pointed to the offering letter she held. "At least seven women have answered the ad in the last two weeks."

"How many letters did you send?"

"Well, let me think . . ." Bill turned his face skyward, mumbling numbers. "About twenty, I'd say. Where are you from, anyway?"

"Stockton." She saw no need to disclose the travel details of her journey to there from Salem via San Francisco.

He shook his head. "No, I didn't send a letter there, but I posted one in Sacramento

City. Maybe it got hand carried to Stockton."

Quinn nodded. Proper girls did not go looking for husbands or jobs, so it would not come as a surprise to find out that a respectable woman had forwarded the posting to Stockton in an attempt to save the good girls of her own hometown.

"Come on, I'll walk you to the boardinghouse. Medford's is offering a free bed in a shared room for seven days to anyone answering the advertisement."

Quinn's stomach knotted. "And what, pray tell, am I supposed to do during the twenty-three days that follow, Mr. Beaudry?"

"Call me Bill. And you got seven whole days to figure that out." He picked up her bags, then turned to the boy and said, "Blue, you stay here and watch the store, and if anyone comes for mail, just tell 'em I'll be back shortly, all right?" When the boy nodded, Bill headed for the two-story building at the end of the road. A sign on the building read Medford's Saloon and Boardinghouse. "Did you say you've come here looking for a husband or a job?"

His question came as if it were a perfectly acceptable inquiry. "I didn't say."

Bill glanced sideways at Quinn with that

same grin. "Well, if you're looking for a husband, seven days ought to be enough time. Fortune has more than a hundred men hoping for a wife and no more than a dozen women, so far. You're a handsome lady. You'll have some kind of roof over your head in no time."

A roof. An inconsequential thing she had taken for granted her whole life was suddenly of major importance. She could not afford a room on her own, not until she stayed thirty days to collect the money, anyway. How was she expected to pay for her boarding before wages could be earned? Her thoughts spun until they reached Medford's steps. Then Quinn stopped and turned to Bill Beaudry, looking him square in the eye. "I expect credit will be extended. After all, it's you who's holding my money."

Bill shook his head. "Room rates run four dollars a day, or twenty-five a week if it's all paid in advance. Your fifty-dollar stipend would be used up in about two weeks, which would leave me holding the bag on maybe a hundred or more if you was to skip out after a month." He extended his arm and made a sweeping motion across the hills. "If you're short on cash, you can always work the river. Women have done it before. Even bad prospectors get a few dollars a day."

Squatting in the mud alongside the riverbank was not at all what Quinn envisioned for herself. When her chin tilted upward all on its own, she said, "I did not come here to dig in the dirt." Then she winced at the rudeness of her tone. "What I mean to say is, I wouldn't know the first thing about being a prospector."

His blue eyes no longer smiled.

With a nod, Bill said, "You came in answer to an advertisement for matrimony or jobs, yet you're not laying claim to either interest, and you didn't come to prospect for gold. So, what are you doing here in Fortune, Miss MacCann?"

Quinn's eyes darted from Bill to the flyer and back again. Until that moment, it hadn't occurred to her that she would need to identify her intentions before receiving a payout, but her immediate need was desperate — she needed the fifty dollars to get on her feet again. She looked at the letter in her hands and silently reread it, considering all options. A saloon girl, she was not. Anyone would attest to the fact that she did not possess the friendly nature required, especially to men whom she had little use for anyway, and she had never been comfortable with serious drinking. She fingered the paper, her eyes shifting downward. Although she was well educated, having attended the Oregon Institute, she was certainly no schoolmarm. Children had never taken to her, nor her to them. The next offering was being a wife again, which was clearly out of the question. Just one option remained — a cook. An unintentional sigh escaped her. Though she had learned a little from Myra, what she knew about cooking wasn't worth a man's spoon, not to mention the worry of food poisoning. She took a breath. Steadied her eyes on Bill Beaudry. "I am a cook, but I am without references."

Bill took the letter out of her hand and pointed to its last line. "Says right here to bring references. Didn't you do that?"

Over the years, she had witnessed her father's ability to divert a challenge by being bullish. This was as good a time as any to try it for herself. "Sir, I am not accustomed to having my word doubted." She snatched the paper back from him. "I am a cook, but you'll not get references."

Bill set her bags down on the plank porch. With an admonitory stare, he said, "Your temperament grates a bit, so I suspect it might take you longer than seven days to find a husband, which by the sound of things might be your best qualification.

You're welcome to wait for the next wagon if you've a mind to leave. It should be back here next week." Then he turned and started back toward the supply store.

"Mister Beaudry!" Quinn shouted after him. When he failed to turn, she shouted again, "Mister Beaudry!" But he kept walking without a glance back.

From the open door of Medford's Saloon and Boardinghouse came a collective giggle of girls. Quinn turned to find three ladies of similar age to her own, all sputtering with laughter.

"Hello," Quinn said, doing her best to maintain an air of dignity. She held up the letter. "I've come to apply for the job of cook. Can you kindly tell me who I need to see?"

A giggler stepped out onto the wide wooden porch. Her black, slicked-back hair was bundled at the back except for a dozen shoulder-length ringlets, and one hand rested on her hip. With the other, she pointed to the retreating man. "That'd be Bill Beaudry. I hope you're a good cook, honey, 'cause I think you just cooked your own goose."

Chapter Ten

The giggler beckoned Quinn, who stood abashed on the steps. "I'm Monique. Come on inside. I'll introduce you to Marshall and Nettie."

"Who might they be?" Quinn asked, grappling for a dignified tone in the face of this disaster.

"Marshall owns the saloon. Nettie is his wife. She operates the boardinghouse upstairs." When Monique turned and headed inside, Quinn picked up her bags and followed.

Her father boasted about the grand saloon establishments in the East, and how they had polished bars with mirrored backdrops and ornate fixtures shipped from halfway around the world, but this saloon was not as he described. Medford's had twenty unadorned pine tables scattered about, each seating four, with individual spindle-backed chairs. Split-log benches lined the walls, and at the far end was a bare wooden platform, raised a foot high off the floor, resembling a one-man stage. The bar, built from fresh sawn lumber and carrying the heavy scent of pine resin and whiskey, had no stools or decoration other than plank shelving hammered into the back wall, which displayed an array of bottles and decanters. To the side were casks marked rum, gin, American and Irish whiskey, sherry, Madeira wine, and champagne cider.

Quinn's gaze settled on the man behind the bar drying glasses. Lanky and brown-haired, he wore an untrimmed mustache and a short beard.

"Marshall," Monique said, pointing to Quinn. "Another one came in answer to the advertisement. Should I take her up to Nettie?"

Marshall gave Quinn a pondering stare, then set the glass upside down on a towel. He leaned across the bar, inspecting Quinn as if sizing her for a dress. She shifted under his scrutiny.

"You a dancer?" he asked.

"No," she answered. "I do not dance."

"You a singer, then? Or piano player? We don't have a piano yet."

"No," she answered again, feeling utterly out of place. "I'm a cook."

Marshall's left eyebrow jutted upward. Skeptical, he sniggered. "Food isn't what we serve." He walked around the bar for closer inspection. "But if it's a cooking job you're after, Bill's hiring at the store. You met him?"

When Monique and her friends giggled again, Quinn ignored them. "Yes, but I fear Mr. Beaudry has taken a dislike to me. You have tables here." She motioned around the room. "Why can't I cook for you?"

"Men don't drink when they eat, and my money is made off drink." The man walked to the bottom of the stairs and called up, "Nettie, you got another one here!"

A short, sturdy woman with wispy dark hair leaned over the railing, looking down. "You answerin' the advertisement?"

"Yes." Quinn held up the letter.

"Then you'll be needin' a room. Come on up." Nettie beckoned.

At the top of the stairs, Quinn spotted the woman again, this time standing at one end of the long hall. She summoned Quinn once more with an impatient wave. A twist of the doorknob opened the farthest room. Nettie disappeared inside.

Quinn followed, stepping into the room where the middle-aged woman was fluffing a pillow, and set her bags down. "Mr.

Beaudry said you'd provide free rooming for seven days. Is that right?"

Nettie turned, looking Quinn up and down head to toe before answering. "That's right. You wantin' a husband, or a job?"

"A job." The room was crowded, with three single beds made up with a quilt and pillow, each having its own nightstand and oil lamp made of uncolored glass. Along the wall was one long pinewood clothes dresser decorated with only a Bible. A wood-framed oval mirror hung above it. "Who am I rooming with?"

"Nadine and Charlotte, but I expect Charlotte will be moving into Jake's tent 'fore long. Didn't take her but four days to find herself a husband." Nettie stared. "You Irish?"

"Yes." Quinn untied and pulled off her bonnet, revealing her redheaded ancestry. Feeling more at ease now that she had a room, more words than she'd intended tumbled out. "But I've been in America most of my life. We sailed from Dublin to Boston when I was just a four-year-old. My father made the trip a year before us when President Jackson, his distant cousin, retained him to strategize the Indian Removal Act. We came West when President Polk, may God rest his soul, commissioned Father to establish prominence. Father structured the Oregon Treaty, and then the Treaty of Guadalupe Hidalgo. We settled in the Willamette Valley."

Nettie stepped away from the bed, glaring at Quinn. "Your father made the Hidalgo Treaty?" Arch backed, she stood with both hands on her hips. "This land you're standin' on was granted to us by Governor Juan Bautista Alvarado nine years ago, and now we're hearin' that some Yankee lawyer says it don't belong to us, all because of that treaty." Her steely-eyed stare turned cold. "And *your father* is the reason for it? Folks say we got to go ask Congress if we can keep land that's already ours. Now, if that ain't the most fool thing." Nettie laid a room key on the nightstand. "Seven days. A daughter of that man will get no more, money or not." She strode past Quinn and left, thunking the door shut on her way out.

CHAPTER ELEVEN

When Bill stepped inside the store, his son Blue was waiting with two customers. He ruffled the boy's blond hair, then picked up the bundle of mail and headed to the counter where a man stood.

"Hello, Tate," Bill greeted him. Then he glanced at the other man, who was inspecting blades on a supply of shovels. "Hank, I told you, all those shovels are new. The blades are all the same. Just pick one so you can quit coming in here every few hours to look at them."

"I just want the best one, Bill," Hank said. "What's eatin' at you? You ain't never snapped at me before about inspectin' tools."

"Aw, it's nothing . . ." Bill said, guilty over his tone. He untied the twine around the bundle, then tossed the loose mail into a wooden box. "Tate, you lookin' for a letter from home?"

"Yessir, I sure am." The man pulled off his floppy hat and leaned across the counter to watch the mail sorting. "Want me to he'p you?"

"Naw, but thanks anyway." Bill came to an envelope plastered with stamps. "Look here, Tate, this one's got your name on it. It must be a two- or three-page letter by the look of it. Your wife must have something mighty important to tell you to be spending forty cents." He handed it to the man.

Without a word, Tate used his pocketknife to slice open the envelope. He pulled out two pages of black-inked scrawl and began mumbling the words as he read. Finally, he shouted, "It's a boy!" Both Bill and Hank shook his hand before Tate returned to his reading. "Mary says she birthed the boy on July twenty-fourth. What's today, Bill?"

Bill reached for his almanac and opened it to a dog-eared page. "It's the sixteenth of September. Your boy's near two months old." He held out the page, pointing to the date. "Maybe you should go on back home to New York. Be with your wife and new son."

Without looking up from the handwritten papers, Tate said, "No, I didn't spend over five months aboard a dad-blamed ship to get here so's I could turn around and go

112

back again still a poor man. I ain't goin' home a failure." Without taking his eyes off the letter, he mumbled his thanks and walked out the door.

Bill looked down at his son, who sidled up beside him. Their land journey to gold country had also taken almost six months, but they traveled by wagon, bringing with them the only people who mattered. Those left behind were dead and buried. Just memories now.

"I'll take this one, Bill." Hank held up a shovel as he walked to the counter with it.

"All right. Anything else?" When the man shook his head, Bill said, "That'll be ten dollars."

"Ten dollars! Hell, Bill, I could buy ten shovels for that amount in Sacramento City!"

"You're not in Sacramento, Hank. You're in Fortune. The shovel is ten dollars. You want it or not?"

The man swayed a little. "How 'bout seven? You know I ain't had much luck this past month, and I need that shovel to dig along the riverbank. I have this idea, Bill, that maybe if I can go deeper instead of relyin' on skim diggings, I might find them big nuggets where the river used to run but don't no more."

"You know I'd like to, Hank. But if I sell you a shovel for seven, then I'd have to sell everybody a shovel for seven." Bill's tone held some regret, but he straightened up tall and pulled his young son close to his hip. "I'm a businessman, and I shouldn't have to keep reminding folks of that. Now, do you want the shovel or not?"

"Yeah," Hank grumbled. He opened his buckskin purse and picked out coins. "What's aggravatin' you, anyway?"

"It's nothing," Bill said, softer. "It's just that even I'm getting tired of eating stew every night. I thought we'd have women flocking to us by now after sending out those postings last month. There's been a few good ones, but not one cook in the whole bunch."

"Not one, huh?" Hank asked as he paid for the shovel. "Most women can cook, cain't they?"

"Thought so, but either they don't know how or none of them wants to." Guilt reddened his cheeks. "Well, to be honest, there was one woman today, but I don't think she'd fit in too well with us. She sure is pretty, though."

Hank carried his shovel to the door, then turned around and said, "Got some cold nights headed this way. A woman layin' aside ya makes things look a speck better. You might want to mull over your priorities."

Bill nodded as the man left, but he knew what his priority was every time he looked at his blond-haired son. "I've got something for you, Blue." He patted the boy's back. "You've been such a good helper, I think you should have it."

The boy jumped up and down. "What is it, Daddy? What is it?"

From an open sack beneath the counter, Bill pulled out a polished toy top, oak with lime-green and brown lines swirled around its base. "This is what you call a finger top." With the pointy end against the floorboards, he twisted it between his fingers, making it spin.

"Whoa!" Blue blurted. "How did you do that, Daddy?"

With a laugh, he demonstrated again. "Now, you run out and practice it yourself. You'll get the hang of it." He smiled at his son's excitement as Blue darted out the door with his new toy.

An onslaught of miners hoping for a letter from home crowded into the store midway through the mail sorting. Bill handed out a dozen or more envelopes, then apologized to those who left empty handed.

"Could you check them letters one more time?" asked Horace Gardner, a skinny older man with no more than four teeth left in his mouth. "Rosie promised she'd write 'fore winter."

"Sorry, Horace. I looked twice already. Nothin' from Rosie. Maybe next time."

Horace nodded, hung his head, and started out. When he pulled open the door, a man with mink-brown hair wearing a wrap-around bow tie entered. His brown suede jacket, left unbuttoned, revealed a tailored white shirt.

The moment Bill caught sight of the man, his brow lifted. "Doss Parker," he said. "Didn't know you were back."

"Just got in. You should be glad of it, too."

"Why is that?" Bill asked, feigning disinterest.

"Because I'm gonna save Fortune, just like I promised." He pulled a plug of tobacco off the shelf and walked to the counter. "I told you and Marshall, gold alone will not sustain a town. And, just as I predicted, luring women and learned men with advertisements won't work, which means the miners will all leave, in time. This town will fade away along with our own fortunes." He smiled, but it was not friendly. "I've decided on a dance house, and I've brought a wagon-

116

load of men back with me ready to start work on it in the morning."

Bill stiffened but gave a nod. He had no right to dictate the kind of commerce in Fortune, but he knew Doss's penchant, and the town deserved better.

CHAPTER TWELVE

Quinn dug through her bag for her flat-heeled day boots in hopes of rescuing her aching feet, but her hands pushed only so far into the big, overstuffed bag. Frustrated, she pulled out her dresses, nightclothes, and unmentionables until, at the bottom of the nearly empty bag, she came to her shoes. She sat and pulled off her leather boots, then wriggled her toes and rubbed the soreness from her soles.

Before slipping her feet into the scruffy everyday brown boots, Quinn reached inside to the tip of one and pulled out the Irish linen handkerchief hidden inside. Within the soft folds of the hankie was her mother's pink sardonyx shell cameo. It brought back thoughts of Pearl, who rescued it for her from a debt collector's hands in San Francisco.

Then another good woman came to mind. Quinn fingered the delicate handkerchief made by her mother's own hands.

Abandoned, and nearly destitute with two young children, Malinda MacCann had taken a job in the Dublin linen factory after her husband accepted a position in America. Free passage, a promise of riches, and unimagined opportunity were his. He left his family behind but vowed to send for them. Neither his summons, nor his money, ever arrived.

While her mother worked, Quinn — just three years old — tried to care for her brother. The memory of the boy toddling out an open doorway only to be run down in the streets by a carriage still caused her nightmares. Not long after his death, her mother came home with ship's passage for two. If they made it to America, Hugh Mac-Cann was obligated to accept them into his home.

She rubbed her forehead for a moment, willing the memory to fade, then repacked it all. With the large satchel scooted aside, she reached for her smaller bag. In it were other belongings of worth: her hairpins and combs, a ten-year-old cotton apron upon which she had learned to embroider, two books worthy of a lifetime of reading: *Pride and Prejudice* and *Jane Eyre,* along with the red leather case that held the daguerreotype portrait of her mother.

Gently, she rewrapped the cameo and tucked it, along with her memories, safely away inside the tapestry bag.

Tortoiseshell comb in hand, Quinn's haggard reflection drew her to the mirror. In less than two months, her green eyes had sprouted crow's feet, and her complexion had darkened under too much sunlight and doubt. She pushed closer, peering hard at herself.

When she left Oregon, she'd counted on her strong spirit, intelligence, and ingenuity to get her through any difficulty, yet in a single hour, those very traits managed to offend the only man in town hiring a cook and the only woman with a boardinghouse.

Unpacking would have been the proper thing to do, especially since she had no money to leave this town, but she could not bring herself to put away a single thing.

With hair combed and pinned into a proper bun, Quinn summoned the courage to head downstairs. She needed to take stock of this new town while she still possessed the fortitude to assess its possibilities.

The earlier quietude of the downstairs was gone — replaced by laughter and loud banter. Men gathered at the platform stage where Monique, dressed in red, brandished a sheer, yellow scarf and danced. When her eyes caught Quinn's, she gave a high wave, which turned the men's attention, drawing them to Quinn like flies to honey. Miners, dirty and drunk, jumped to their feet, some knocking over their chairs, and shoved their way to Quinn. Excited prospectors surrounded her where she stood with her feet planted on the bottom step.

"Howdy, Miss Quinn!"

"Miss Quinn, my name is Jack, would you . . ." The voice of the soft-spoken man was drowned out by a dozen other men clamoring to meet her.

"Can I buy you a drink?" said another.

"Lord gawd, you're beautiful!"

A rough and calloused hand pulled hers into the gaggle of men, where the wet smack of a dozen lips slobbered her hand's topside. Quinn steadied herself at the railing and pulled back, but she could not free her hand until a swatting clangor sounded from the landing above.

"Here now!" Nettie yelled, repeatedly slapping two tin pans together. "Settle down, you heathens! Let her breathe!"

When Marshall shouted, "Half-priced drinks!" from the bar, at least fifty men launched into a shoving match, which pushed the tangle of men back across the barroom, deserting Quinn.

Only one remained. He was a black-haired man with soft brown eyes whose skin was the color of coal.

"You'll want to thank Marshall and Nettie for saving you just now like they did."

"Yes." Quinn caught her breath. "I suppose I will. Seems like the only two things worth attention here in Fortune are women and whiskey."

"And gold," the man said. He held his hand out toward her. "My name is Jack, but most folks call me Blackjack."

Quinn gave him hers, her fingertips resting on the unexpected softness of his palm. "No man should allow a nickname that degrades the color of his skin."

With downed head, he chuckled. "Oh, it's not that, ma'am." His smile was warm. "You see, there are three of us named Jack here in Fortune, and I am the best card player in town." He spoke of his nickname as if it were a distinction of honor.

"Cards. I see. Well then, Blackjack, my name is Quinn, and I have not eaten a single thing all day. I am half-starved. Surely, there must be someplace to get food in this town."

"Yes, ma'am. Come on with me. I'll walk with you to the stew pot."

The loud shouting and singing inside the bar made the evening outside seem quiet as a sleeping babe's nursery. The two walked toward several lit lanterns, which were set on stumps near Beaudry's Supply Store. A jabbering of male voices sounded far more civilized than the men they had left behind in the saloon.

Beneath a high-topped log shelter, low flames leapt out of a pit encircled by stones where a large black kettle hung from a tripod, astraddle the fire. There, with a ladle in hand near the pot, stood Bill Beaudry. Scattered about in conversation were at least three dozen men, with few taking notice of their approach, except one who stepped out from the gathering and tipped his hat as they neared.

"Evening." His eyes set on Quinn, he smiled. "I don't believe we've had the pleasure of meeting. My name is Doss Parker."

"No, we've not met." She struggled to tuck away her sudden shyness and drew instead on her assertive spirit. "I've just arrived. I'm Quinn MacCann. It's nice to meet you, Mr. Parker."

"We're on our way to get this fine lady some supper," Blackjack explained, his gaze urging Quinn onward.

But Doss stepped in front, stopping their advance. "I'm curious what brings a fine lady such as yourself to a ruckus of a town like Fortune?"

"I've come in answer to an advertisement for a cook," Quinn explained.

"Have you, now?" Doss leaned his head back and grinned as if he knew a secret he might be willing to share.

"Do you know of any such job?" Quinn asked.

"Bill is hiring," Blackjack announced. "Let's go talk to him about it."

"I'm hiring, too," Doss said, never taking his eyes off Quinn.

"You?" Blackjack asked. "Since when?"

"Since right now." Doss removed his hat, revealing thick, collar-length brown hair. His face was rugged, with deep-set wrinkles, or perhaps old scars too many to count. But it was his steely-green eyes — more like the eyes of a mountain lion than a man — that held Quinn's interest.

"Do you own an eatery, Mr. Parker?" she asked him.

"No," Doss scoffed. "But I'm building an establishment here in Fortune, and I plan to employ about two dozen people." He motioned to the stew pot. "I can't expect them to eat this slop day in and day out.

124

Part of the incentive for hiring on with me is knowing I'll provide free room and board along with wages. I'll be building a private kitchen, and I'll need a resident cook. Would you be interested, Miss MacCann? Your room and board would be included."

Quinn smiled. *Room and board.* "Yes, Mr. Parker. I would indeed."

"Now, hold on," Blackjack interrupted. "Miss Quinn just arrived. I think she ought to have some time to settle in before makin' a decision like that, don't you?"

Doss raised a halting hand. "I've got no issue with Negroes, free or not, but your opinion is of no value to me." He steadied his focus on Quinn. "Of course, I'll expect you to cook a meal for me first, so I can evaluate your abilities. Quality is important. Can you make biscuits?"

"Yes, certainly." Quinn repressed a wince, recalling Henry's last meal of beef and biscuits and his subsequent death. *Food poisoning.*

"Good," Doss said with a smile. "My Aunt Ella always says, 'If a woman can make biscuits, she can keep a man happy.' I'm guessing you're staying at the boarding-house?" When Quinn nodded, he said, "I'll call for you tomorrow evening to escort you to my cabin. We can discuss your employment over a home-cooked meal." Then he placed his hat atop his head and rejoined the circle of men who stood discussing the price of gold.

Blackjack turned to Quinn. "Not so sure that was a good idea, miss."

"I didn't say yes," Quinn said. "But he's offered a job, and I need a job."

Before Blackjack could answer, Bill called out with a wave. "Evening!"

"Evening," Blackjack greeted him, ushering Quinn toward the pot of stew, where a swirl of steam roiled upward out of the big kettle.

Bill's gaze fixed on Quinn. "Ma'am," he addressed her, adding a single nod.

"Hello again," Quinn said, their closeness igniting an unexpected fire inside her that had nothing to do with the nearby flames.

"Stew is a dollar a plate, but, Blackjack, you won't tell anybody about me giving this lady a serving at no charge, will you?"

"Not a soul, not a soul," Blackjack promised.

From a foot-high stack of wide, deep gold pans, Bill took two, filled them with stew, and then handed one to Quinn and the other to Blackjack. He spooned a ladleful onto another pan for himself, then motioned them toward an arrangement of log stumps.

The two men sat, leaving the middle stump open. After seating herself, she steadied her pan upon her lap. Using her fork, she cut a large potato chunk into bite-sized pieces.

Quinn had never known a man who could cook anything more than a rabbit or a grouse on a stick, so the fresh, flavorful stew came as a surprise. "This is a fine meal, Mr. Beaudry."

"Thank you," Bill said. "But you might not think so by week's end. Stew is all I know how to make." When their eyes met, both smiled.

As Blackjack pushed carrot chunks and potato pieces around his plate trying to cool them, he said, "Most men trap or shoot game, then cook it over a fire at their own camp, but sometimes a man is just too tired to make his own supper." He grinned. "I'm a pitiful cook myself, and I don't have time to hunt. I spend most of my time at the card tables, so I'm here for stew most every night."

"I see," Quinn said. "So you're a professional gambler, not a miner?"

"I can't say I won't pick up a pan now and again, especially when the excitement of a strike hits. But I'm a gambler by trade." He spooned a bite into his mouth and chewed. "Bill, you're lookin' to hire a cook, aren't you?"

"Yeah," he answered without looking up, as if fearing an awkward confrontation with Quinn. After a moment, his past annoyance apparently faded, Bill glanced at her. "We got off on the wrong foot, and I'd like a chance to start over." He cleared his throat. "I could sure use a cook who can make something other than stew."

"He sure could." Blackjack chuckled.

Quinn was quiet. Her eyes shifted from Bill to Blackjack, and back again. "If you're proposing a job, Mr. Beaudry, I'd like to thank you, but I've already been offered a position elsewhere, assuming my cooking warrants Mr. Parker's approval."

Bill straightened. "Doss Parker?" His eyes narrowed into a confused squint. "Doss doesn't own a restaurant."

"No," Quinn said. "His new establishment will need a private resident cook. For the employees, you know?"

The squint froze on Bill's face. He turned to Blackjack.

"It's a fact. I heard it myself just a few minutes ago."

Bill stood, holding his plate. "Well then," he said. "I should get back to work." He returned to the kettle without a goodbye.

The pot was near empty, but Bill stirred it anyway. He'd failed to hire the only woman answering his advertisement for a cook. She had slipped through his hands and was now cooking for Doss Parker, the only businessman in Fortune whose morals he questioned. Not only that, but she was a redheaded angel who stirred long-forgotten feelings in him.

He pushed aside tainted thoughts and fought to refocus his attention.

The money from his inheritance was nearly gone. Building a business in California was harder than expected — the outflow of money was more than what came in. Prospects for success looked worse than ever. Was he foolish to dream he could be a merchant like his father? Maybe he should cut his losses and move on while they still could. Sacramento and San Francisco were busting at the seams with prosperous businesses. Both towns had clerking jobs available for men with his experience, which came with a promise of five hundred dollars in steady wages every month. And the two towns had recently opened schools, too — he needed to think about Blue's future. The boy would be in need of proper education soon.

Bill glanced at Quinn. She was a bull-headed, blinkered woman, yet he found it hard to take his eyes off her. Beneath the lanterns, her coppery-red hair and faint freckles on alabaster skin hinted of fragility and innocence, but her sharp green eyes dared one to doubt her. This newcomer, Quinn MacCann — so out of place in this tent and tin-cup town — whipped his world into an unexpected flurry, and all he thought he knew and wanted was being reformed before his eyes.

CHAPTER THIRTEEN

Quinn sat on the edge of the bed, exhausted and damp from the light rain that began when supper ended. She pulled off her boots, then disrobed and put on her nightgown. The bureau had only one empty drawer, so she used it for her clothes, but before her unpacking was finished, the door creaked open.

"I saw you downstairs." The young lady stepped into the room, smoothing her disheveled brown hair with her hands. "But then, when Marshall offered half-price drinks, you disappeared."

Quinn stopped folding clothes. If words were sweet, this girl's would be candy. "My mind was on supper." Her eyes shifted from the girl's young face to her tapered yellow bodice, and then back again. "I ducked out to the stew pot."

"Well, it's nice to finally meet you." After closing the door, the girl started across the room. "My name's Nadine. Nettie said we'd be rooming together."

Nadine was younger. Quinn knew by the girlish sparkle in her eyes, and by her fresh complexion and the adolescent thinness of her body. "Do you mind my asking how old you are?"

The girl stood at the far bed re-pinning her mouse-brown hair, but her hazel eyes swung to Quinn. "I'm fifteen, but don't go tellin' nobody. Everyone thinks I'm nineteen."

"Why would you tell them such a thing? There's nothing wrong with being fifteen."

"Nettie won't let me work downstairs if she knows my true age. She won't allow anyone inside who is not at least eighteen. I added an extra year." Nadine grinned, proud of her ruse. "I mean, what's the difference between eighteen and nineteen anyway? Except to say nineteen sounds like a better marrying age."

"So, you're here in Fortune looking for a husband? Fifteen is young to be a bride."

Nadine slipped the last hairpin into her hair. "Young or not, I came looking for my one true love." She pressed her hands together in prayer-like fashion and looked upward at the ceiling as if she could see right through to heaven. "Lord, please make

Johnny fall in love with me. I'll be a good wife to him, I promise." Then she sat on her bed and said, "Quinn, you should see him! He is the finest man in this whole big world."

"How do you know my name?"

"Oh . . ." Nadine giggled as if telling schoolgirl secrets. "Every man in the saloon was talking about you tonight. Quinn this, and Quinn that, and, 'Oh, isn't Quinn beautiful!' "

"All men ever see in a woman is her beauty. Never what's in her heart or her mind. It's a shame, really."

"Well, thank heavens for that! Wouldn't no man look at me otherwise."

Quinn balked. "You're a very pretty girl. I'll bet you're smart as a whip, too."

"No, not me. Even my daddy told me to snag a rich man while I'm still young and pretty, and you know a daddy is always right when it comes to his daughter."

Quinn tensed at her own grimace. *You've always been ungrateful. A burden. A bad-luck charm.* The things a father said to his daughter were not worth discussing, so she sat on the bed, pulled her feet up, and tucked them under the quilt. "Do you mind if I turn out my lamp?"

Perplexed, Nadine said, "Bed so soon? I

133

thought we might get to talk awhile."

"I've had a long day. Maybe tomorrow?" Quinn wanted to be polite, but not so much she wouldn't be able to close her eyes and hurry through what was left of the day. She wheeled down the lamp's wick until it was snuffed out and pulled the quilt up to her chin. "Good night."

"Oh," Nadine said in a disappointed tone. "I suppose you have had a long day, what with your trip and all . . ."

Quinn was fast asleep by the time her roommate finished talking, but at the first light of day, Nadine was standing over Quinn's bed, gently shaking her.

"Wake up," she whispered. "Look at this note!"

Groggily, Quinn squinted her eyelids open. Nadine held a paper with fancy scrawl much too close to make out the letters. "What does it say?" Gently, she pushed Nadine's hands back, trying to find her focus.

"It's from Charlotte. You haven't met her yet, but she's our roommate nonetheless. She's eloped! Isn't that romantic?" Nadine pressed the letter to her heart.

"Yes," Quinn said and nodded as she propped herself up on her elbows. "That's lovely."

"Should we tell someone?"

"Who would we tell, and why?"

"No reason, I suppose. I just feel like spreading the happy news." Nadine turned and padded barefoot back across the room, re-reading the note the whole way. She sat down on her bed, and again, she pressed the paper to her as if it were her own private love note. "Just think, when we see Charlotte again, she'll be Mrs. Jake Fogarty!"

"Why did she elope? Didn't she want to be married here among her friends?"

"Fortune doesn't have a preacher. The town solicited for one, knowing plenty of women won't come without a man of God present, but none showed up. The town even volunteered to build a church for whichever preacher got here first."

"I should have held out for a better offering." Quinn intended humor, but her wit was lost on Nadine.

"No lady gets anything better than the one before her. Marshall says they don't need any brawls, and fair is fair. It is fifty dollars and an ounce of gold, and other than this room free for seven days, nobody gets nothin' extra."

"How much is an ounce of gold worth, anyway?"

"Johnny says an ounce runs fifteen dollars! Can you imagine how much a gold miner must make every day? A good one must be worth a bundle. Charlotte says not to let their dirty clothes and bedrolls in the scrub bushes fool us. She says they're only living that way until they can tote all that gold back to Sacramento City." Nadine's excitement sparked. "Johnny says he'll need to buy two extra mules to carry all his gold."

But Quinn's thoughts focused on her own promised nugget. "Fifteen dollars. That's more than I thought." The added boon would be helpful.

"Oh, but you won't need the money," Nadine said with confidence, looking back down at Charlotte's letter. "You're pretty as a peach. You'll have your pick of husbands." Then she turned with a worried glare. "Long as you don't turn Johnny's head. Johnny's mine, just as soon as I can get him to propose."

"Yes, of course," Quinn said. "Besides, I am not interested in finding a husband."

"You aren't? Why in the world not?"

"I intend to make my own way."

Nadine giggled and hugged herself as if holding tight to the man of her dreams. "That's just because you haven't met any-one like my Johnny yet."

CHAPTER FOURTEEN

At morning light, Doss Parker had twenty men and half as many oxen hauling logs along the mud road to a cleared area on the east side of town, which was the opposite direction from Beaudry's Supply Store.

Timber cracked under ax-falls, hatchets notched wood, and hammers pounded nails into sawn boards, waking just about everyone in town. Soon, miners and townsfolk gathered at the building site to watch the commotion, which seemed to suit Doss just fine. When the crowd grew big enough, he climbed atop a stack of resin-scented logs and shouted, "Fortune is about to become a real town!"

Quinn and Nadine joined the gathering, crowding through to the front.

"In a few days," Doss announced, "this new building will be the Dancehouse! Now, I don't mean to put Medford's out of business . . ." He stopped, his eyes scanning the crowd. "Are you here, Marshall?"

"Yeah, I'm here," came the call back amid a cluster of men. Marshall shouldered through, clutching his wife's hand, until they stood up front next to Quinn. "And I'm wanting to know what the hell is going on!"

Doss was dressed like a wealthy businessman in black jacket and trousers with a double-breasted vest over a white shirt and a stiff silk tie horizontally cinched into a flat half-bow. He looked like a man who had just come from New York City. He focused on Marshall with a grin. "You won't need that crowded little dance floor anymore, Marshall. Might as well use that space to set up more tables."

"You plannin' to serve drinks at this dance house?" Marshall shouted above the chattering crowd. "We made a deal that you wouldn't open a saloon."

"And I am a man of my word," Doss replied from atop the stacked logs. "Your saloon only sells liquor by the glass. The Dancehouse will only sell it by the full bottle."

"What about girls, Doss?" a man shouted from the crowd.

"Yeah!" other men echoed. "What about girls?"

138

Doss held out his hands to quiet the crowd. With a boisterous flare, he answered, "We got girls!"

Cheers and wild shouts erupted from the gathered miners, some stomping dance steps while others slapped backs and shook hands.

Nettie, who stood beside her husband, called up to Doss, "You plan on havin' sleeping rooms, too?"

Doss looked down. "Each of my dancers will have a private room as part of her wages," he said, "but rules at the Dancehouse won't be the same as your rules at the boardinghouse. No rooms will be rented to the public, but my girls can have men in their rooms for the night, though I doubt much sleeping will occur." The chatter turned loud, and laughter broke out amongst the men. "So, you can go on renting rooms to female newcomers and passers-through without any interference from me. Like I said, I gave Marshall and Bill my word. I've got no plans to cut in on your commerce. I will not sell liquor by the glass, and I will not rent rooms, but I do not intend to deny men their right to sleep and drink in my establishment."

More cheers erupted as Doss jumped flat-footed to the ground. He walked to Marshall and held his hand out for a gentlemanly shake. Although Marshall wore a frown, the two men gripped hands.

When they parted ways, Doss spotted Quinn and Nadine, so he stepped closer. His smile was all the encouragement the fifteen-year-old needed. "I've seen you around town," she said to Doss. "But we've not met yet. My name is Nadine."

Doss reached for her hand, which he kissed lightly, then said, "It's a pleasure."

"Are you lookin' to hire dancers? Because that's how I make most of my money at the saloon, and it sounds like I won't have a job there after you open."

The suave, boastful man looked into Nadine's eyes and smiled. "How old are you, darlin'?"

Nadine's expression turned shy, but her eyes beamed when she looked at Quinn. With an upward glance at Doss, she said, "Why, Mr. Parker, you know it's not polite to ask a lady's age." Then she smiled. "But I'm sure you're askin' purely for business purposes, so I'll tell you. I'm nineteen."

He tipped her chin upward with a light touch. "I always have room for a girl as pretty as a china doll. You come see me in a day or so."

The smile spread across Nadine's face as

Doss switched his focus. With a nod, he greeted Quinn. "Hello again."

"Hello," Quinn replied, adopting a businesswoman's stance. "I'm glad for the chance to see you this morning because it occurred to me that I'll need a few supplies, unless your cabin is well stocked."

"No, I'm afraid it's not stocked at all. I've been away for more than a week, just returning yesterday. But you can get whatever you need from Beaudry's store. Just tell Bill to put it on my account." He smiled and tipped his hat. "I have a few more people to see. 'Til this evening, Miss MacCann."

When Doss stepped away to address a passel of questioning men, Nadine turned to Quinn. "How is it that you already know Mr. Parker when I've been here a month and just met him?"

"We met shortly after my arrival yesterday," Quinn told her, hoping not to rehash the whole story. "I should be getting on to the store for supplies."

Nadine's face scrunched. "What kind of supplies? Surely, you're not buying prospecting tools."

"No," Quinn answered. "I'm hoping to be hired as Mr. Parker's cook." Not that it should have mattered, but admitting to being a work-for-hire cook didn't feel as prideful as saying she was an independent businesswoman. "If you'll excuse me." The lack of confidence in her newly created identity caused Quinn to dip her chin. With a quick turn, she angled across the road through tobacco-tinged air, leaving Nadine behind.

Miners scattered in hurried steps, most moving toward the river, hindering Quinn's pace. She found herself stepping this way, then that way, to maneuver between scurrying men as she walked. After reaching the store, she looked back. In the distance, she saw Doss still standing in the same place, except now four women stood beside him, nodding as he talked. Nadine was nowhere in sight.

Doss Parker had a rough, unrefined look about him, but still, he was a handsome man with his brown hair, sharp features, and stirring green eyes. His arrogance, however, reminded Quinn of her father. Normally, any resemblance would be repugnant, but it just so happened, her father's virtuous air had reaped her societal acceptance through the years, earned or not. Perhaps associating with Mr. Parker would produce similar respect, which would translate nicely into her becoming a full-fledged businesswoman.

As she stood staring at Doss and the gaggle of girls surrounding him, something tugged on her plain sepia-colored dress. She glanced down and saw the boy called Blue looking up at her.

"Hello, there," she said.

"Do you have kids?" the boy asked her.

"No," Quinn told him. "No children."

Blue sighed and sat down on the porch of Beaudry's Supply. He lowered his head until his face sank into the golden hair of a sleeping dog beside him.

"Aren't there any children here for you to play with?" Quinn asked, but when Blue answered with a shake of his head, she said, "Oh, I see. You must get very lonely."

"It's all right," he said without looking up. "My daddy promised they'd come. He said I just need to wait."

The store door opened, and Bill Beaudry stepped out, his presence capturing Quinn's attention. "Good morning," he said, friendly again. "What brings you here so early?"

The mere sight of him dressed in brown wool pants and a gray shirt that brought out the crystalline blue of his eyes caused a flutter inside Quinn. With her gaze caught on his beguiling smile, everything but her heart stilled. All the strength and independence she had walled within herself wobbled

143

when he neared, and she had no idea as to why. She fumbled for composure. "I was listening to all the excitement." She pointed to Doss and the dwindling number of girls. "A new establishment will be nice in town, won't it?"

With a dip of his head, Bill's eyes fixed on Quinn. "I'm surprised to hear you say that. In fact, I'm surprised all the women aren't up in arms over his brothel."

"But he said he's hiring dancers."

An eyebrow rose as he gave a single nod in Doss's direction. "Oh, it's a brothel, all right. Ask any man in town."

Quinn bristled at the accusation. "I'm here to buy provisions. Mr. Parker said to have you put them on his account." She brushed past him into the store, hoping he hadn't noticed her fluster.

"All right," Bill said, following her inside. "Tell me what you need."

She walked across the wood plank floor, searching the shelves and barrels. "I'll need flour," she said. "Saleratus, lard, salt . . ."

"No saleratus," Bill answered. "But I can bring some back with me next time I go to Sacramento City for supplies."

"No saleratus? How am I to make biscuits without a leavening?"

"I've got no idea how biscuits are made. I

make stew, remember?" Bill busied himself by scooping coffee beans into a sack and tying its top with a matching strip of cloth. He set it on the counter beside five other identical bags and started another.

"No leavening . . ." That put a new spin on Quinn's plan to make biscuits and gravy with salt pork for supper. Doss had specifically mentioned biscuits, and although she had only made them once, she felt certain she could recreate the recipe. However, she had no way of doing that without proper ingredients. She held a steady face and thought for a moment. "Then I shall need sorghum and . . ."

"No sorghum," he said. "But I have molasses."

Quinn shook her head. "I don't care for molasses. Do you have currants?"

Bill shook his head.

Shopping was more complicated than Quinn expected. She walked slowly, inspecting the available provisions in the store, hoping for a new supper idea. Of the things she saw, none met her cooking capabilities.

"I have fresh eggs in back, if that interests you," Bill told her. "They're straight out of the henhouse this morning."

"Eggs?" she repeated. "Yes, eggs would be lovely. Thank you."

145

"How many?"

"I think four will be plenty."

"Comin' right up." Bill retreated to the back room. When he returned, he had four eggs, which he set on the thick wood counter. "What else?"

"I'll take four potatoes, and do you have salt pork?"

"Sure do." Bill lifted the lid off a barrel, reached inside, and fished out a fist-sized chunk. He held it up. "Big enough?"

"Yes, that will be fine."

Bill wrapped the pork in muslin. "Anything else?"

"No, that should be all."

With his black ledger book open, Bill wrote down the items and totaled them. He turned the book around until it faced Quinn, then he handed her his short, over-used pencil. "Just sign right here to charge all this to Doss's account."

Quinn signed her name, wondering the entire time what she could possibly make when all she had was salt pork, potatoes, and eggs.

CHAPTER FIFTEEN

It was half past four o'clock when Doss called for Quinn at the boardinghouse. At Nettie's knock, Quinn answered, "I'll be right down." She smoothed the skirt of her best visiting gown, which was an earthy autumn yellow beautified with red wisps and thin striations of leafy green vines. Its long, slender sleeves fit her arms as though custom made, but the length of the dress was not as tailored. To keep the hem from dragging, she wore her white, too-tight, heeled kid-leather boots, which she had worn on the wagon journey.

With her eyes fixed on her mirrored reflection, she nodded with satisfaction. The next second, doubt crept in. This evening was strictly business. Surely, Doss Parker would respect that, wouldn't he? He had spoken to her like a businessman, but the way he looked at her was . . .

Nonsense. She shook her head to banish

147

the thought. *I need this job.* Before leaving the room, she tied on her bonnet and snagged her apron off the foot of her bed. It would serve as reminder enough of the upcoming dinner's purpose.

"Good evening." Quinn greeted Doss at the base of the stairs with the apron draped over her arm. When he tipped his hat, she said, "I left the provisions with Marshall." She headed for the bar, only to have Doss call out to the saloon owner before she reached him.

"Marshall, pour us two whiskeys, will you?"

Quinn turned, her eyes locked on Doss. "Two whiskeys?"

"To celebrate."

Her brow creased. "What would we be celebrating? You haven't so much as tasted my cooking yet."

A smile came as Doss joined her and shepherded her to the bar. "The vision of your loveliness has already enriched my tastes beyond expectation." The whiskeys were poured and waiting. He lifted his glass in a toast to her.

Quinn stared at the liquor in the second glass, then looked at Doss. "I'm sorry, but I do not drink."

"That's absurd. Some of the finest women

I know partake of this liquid gold. Try it." He scooted the clear beveled glass across the bar, closer to her.

With a shake of her head and a staunch posture, she said, "No, Mr. Parker."

"*Mister* Parker?" Doss lowered his head, grinning before his low laugh came. "It might help calm your nerves. Dust off a bit of that starch."

There it was again. Why was it that folks took offense at a woman's strength of mind? Myra said she was *haughty*. Bill Beaudry called her temperament *difficult*. And now, to Doss Parker, she was *starchy*. Quinn stiffened but forced a tension-easing smile. "Let's not let whiskey rule the outcome of our day."

Doss nodded. "Agreed." He swigged his whiskey, then took Quinn's drink and downed its contents, too. "We'll take our provisions now, Marshall." He gathered the items the saloonkeeper set on the bar top, and, without a word of direction, he turned to leave. She hurried after him. Outside, she climbed aboard the wagon unassisted and seated herself with pulled-back shoulders, intent on proving hardihood.

Atop a hill of golden grass not far from town, the Parker cabin stood tucked back, almost hidden among scattered conifers and other autumn-colored beauties. Its shingled roof jutted out in an overhang, which covered the porch and gently shielded them from a light, chilly rain that had started moments before they reached the cabin. Doss held their provisions in one arm, while opening the door for Quinn with the other. He followed her inside.

"I'll get a fire started," he said after setting the potatoes, eggs, and salt pork down on his rough-hewn pine table. The heady scent of charred wood, tobacco, and pine resin pervaded the place.

Quinn removed her bonnet, then turned and scanned the one-room cabin: a table with two chairs, a rocker, a bed stacked with calico quilts, one trunk at its foot, a bear-hide rug, several oil lamps, and a large blue cupboard with eight drawers and four doors that took up half of one wall. No curtains covered the windows, and nothing adorned the walls unless it was cooking, hunting, or gold related. Her eyes darted from one thing to another, all the while searching for a door to another room that was not there. "Where's your cookstove?"

Doss laughed. "In this little place?"

Angst rattled her previous verve. "But you have such a lovely cupboard . . . Surely it came from a well-stocked kitchen. Is there a separate cooking area?" Any man with the presence of mind to own such a fine piece of French-blue furniture should certainly have a cookstove, too.

Doss turned his attention to the cupboard, then looked back at Quinn. "You have an eye for the finer things, I see." His gaze skimmed the length of her. "We have that in common." With the fireplace ablaze, he stood. "A few wagons came through a while back in need of money and supplies. All they had in trade was that cupboard, which, if they had any sense, they needed to off-load anyway before the weight of it took its final toll on their exhausted oxen. Whatever possessed them to haul that cumbersome thing all the way from Missouri to California is a mystery to me, but when I agreed to buy it the wife bawled like I'd taken one of her children."

Many wagons, decrepit from months of navigating trackless plains and mountains, hauled similar cargo, too precious to abandon, to gold-bearing country. Along with the possessions rode the youngest children — their bewildered eyes peeking through split canvas flaps — as older ones walked, goading sticks in hand, mimicking their fathers. But the forlorn faces of the women were hardest to forget. Had they meant to be a prospector's wife, or had this thing called love persuaded them to chase a dream, which was never their own?

"Yes, well . . ." Quinn unfurled her apron and tied its strings around her waist. "Where might I find your water barrel?"

"Outside. South side of the porch." He pointed to a bucket on the floor by the fireplace.

Doss was on one knee at the base of the hearth when Quinn returned with the pail full of water. He was stoking the fire by blowing gently on its low line of flames. When she approached, he pulled back, giving her room to tip the pail so the water could pour out into the black pot he'd hung.

Quinn set the pail down. "May I look through your cooking pans?"

"All I've got hangs there on the wall." He motioned to several cast-iron pots, skillets, and long spoons hanging from nails near the hearth.

She inspected the array, then pulled down a long spoon and skillet and set to work on supper.

"Tell me about yourself," Doss prompted as he sat in a rocker near the fire. "And of all the places you could have gone looking for work, what made you pick Fortune?"

Since Doss had never asked for references,

Quinn steered clear of talking about Henry, their marriage, and his death, which was the very reason she'd lived in, and left, Stockton. After all, there was not a single good thing that came of it. "As I mentioned yesterday, I came in answer to the town's letter."

"But why?" he asked. "You're obviously an educated woman of higher class than most. I would expect to find a lady like you living in Boston, or Philadelphia, or Charleston."

Quinn was hesitant, but the pressure to answer caused the truth to spout out. "My mother and I sailed to America to join my father when I was just four. But you are not wrong — Boston was our home when we first arrived."

"Ah, that explains your charm and obvious education."

"No," Quinn said. She concentrated on gently dropping peeled potatoes into the pot of steaming water. "I only lived there for a short time. My father's family ties to America and its politics made him a respected man, but my mother and I surprised him with our arrival. Having a family he'd left behind in Ireland gave folks a different opinion of him, so he chose to accept an alternate position with the government that warranted a cross-country move. We settled in the Willamette Valley." She looked at Doss as she dried her hands on her apron. "But I did attend the Oregon Institute."

Quinn turned back to her supper chores.

Under Doss's scrutinizing eye, she sliced the salt pork into eight uneven slices, stacking them one atop the other in the palm of her hand, then moved to the fire, where the iron skillet heated. Carefully, she put each slice into the pan, nudging them with the long spoon as they crackled and sizzled. With a glance, she said, "I think it's only fair to tell you, I do not intend to be a work-for-hire cook forever. Someday, I plan to open my own business."

A guffaw slipped out, but a throat clearing steadied his tone. "You have experience?"

"No," Quinn said hesitantly, "but many people open businesses without experience."

He held his briar pipe, hiding a grin, and lit a match. Billows of strong-scented smoke roiled up until he pulled the stem from between his lips. "Men, yes, but women don't have the head for commerce."

With the long spoon angled like a pointer, she turned and snapped, "Women are just as capable of running a business, Mr. Parker . . ." Noticing her harsh edge, she softened her tone. "But it is no doubt harder for them." She turned back to the pot and quickly changed the subject as she lowered the four eggs into the water where the potatoes boiled. "Tell me about you."

"Me?" Doss rocked and puffed, his eyes steady on her. "I spent the better part of five years forging an east-west trade route for Hudson's Bay Company. Got tired of taking orders, though, and decided to start making my own rules. Stayed in Fort Vancouver for a while, then came south."

"To Fortune?"

"Monterey."

"What brought you here?"

"Boredom. Not mine — the gold seekers'. A man's got to have something to do when the sun goes down and his panning stops. Their boredom will be my fortune."

Grease popped in the skillet, flicking specks of hot oil onto her hand. She winced, wiping the splatter on her apron, then removed the meat from the pan.

"Supper is almost ready," she announced.

Quinn cracked the shell of a hardboiled egg and began to peel, but no matter how gentle she was, the eggshell did not easily slip off as it had when Henry's mother made them. When she finished, gashes and gouges pockmarked the eggs.

Doss seated himself at the two-person table while Quinn spooned potatoes, two boiled eggs, and six pieces of fried salt pork onto a plate and set it on the table in front of him. She filled another plate for herself. "Will you say grace, please?"

"No, but you go on ahead if it's important to you."

Quinn glanced at him without expression. Maybe the ruggedness of this land had a way of turning God-fearing gentlemen into hard-edged, disparaging men. She had no right to judge. With lowered head, she clasped her hands as if holding a tiny bird. "Oh, Heavenly Father, kind and good, we thank Thee for this ample food. Amen." Before raising her head, she heard the clink of a fork.

"Did you add flavoring to these potatoes?"

"Flavoring?"

Doss swallowed hard. "Yes, *flavoring.* Salt? Pork fat? Anything?"

"No," Quinn answered with a shake of her head. "Are they bland?"

"Bland might be one word for them." Then he took a bite of salt pork, which caused him to rise from his chair and spit it into the fire. He wiped his mouth on his shirtsleeve. "Did you soak this salt pork before cooking it?" When Quinn shook her head, he grumbled and reached for a hard-boiled egg. "And what happened to the eggs? These are the ugliest I've ever seen."

Feeling her defenses rise, Quinn said, "They'll taste the same as any other hard-boiled egg. Try one." She bit into a scarred egg from her own plate. With his full attention focused on her, Doss sat back in his chair and watched as she chewed and swallowed. "Delicious," she said.

"Did you use fresh eggs?"

"Of course they were fresh! They came from the henhouse today."

"Hell, woman, a cook of any worth knows a hardboiled egg needs to age a day or two before it'll peel right. Fresh eggs don't peel worth a damn." Doss leaned forward. "What exactly is your cooking experience, anyway?"

The needed words escaped Quinn entirely. She sat staring at Doss in hopes an answer would miraculously flow from her mouth, but none did.

"You've never cooked more than a dozen meals in your life, have you?"

If she said what she needed to say in order to keep her job, it would be an out-and-out lie. An unrecoverable falsehood should she be found out but, more importantly, a disappointment to God Himself to know that she could not tame her tongue.

"Mr. Parker . . ." She shifted in her seat. "You said yourself that I am an educated woman. I can learn to cook. It just takes time and practice."

Doss leaned back and howled with laughter, then slapped both hands on the tabletop as he tried to compose himself. He stood. "Well, well . . ." He walked around the table, stopping at her chair. "This is not all bad news." With a supportive hand, he prompted her to stand. When she did, he wrapped his arms around her and kissed her.

Quinn pushed back, leaning as far away as she could, though still trapped in his muscular arms. "What do you think you're doing?"

"Looking for another reason to hire you. Surely, you have talents more suitable to a man than cooking." He pulled her tight and kissed her again.

She struggled against him, grunting unladylike sounds. When one arm wriggled free, she slammed her fist against his ear, not once, but twice.

"Damn you, woman!" He shoved her backward, sending her flying. With a bounce, she landed on his bed. Like a lion on its prey, Doss was on top of her.

"Get off me!"

Quinn screamed when cold air whooshed beneath her skirt. She grabbed a handful of his hair and pulled, but his hand made its way inside her cotton drawers anyway — his male desire hard against her.

Doss forced his mouth onto hers. Quinn bit down, causing a roar of pain. Reared back like a stallion, he pushed up and off her, but with gritted teeth and fists balled tight in the fabric of his shirt, she held onto him. In a backwards stumble, they both fell to the floor. The clack of tooth on tooth and the coppery tang of blood told her she had bitten clean through his bottom lip.

With her disheveled red hair astray, she scrambled to her feet only to feel a hand grab hold of her ankle.

On the table was the knife she'd used for slicing the pork. She grabbed it, then turned its silver blade on Doss. "Take your hand off me, or I'll cut it off!"

Doss held on for a moment, then released her. He collapsed backwards onto the floor, breathing hard. His tongue lapped at his bloody lip. "Go on, get out of here."

Without wasting a moment, Quinn dropped the knife and ran.

Chapter Sixteen

The battering rain hammered the hillside, drenching Quinn in cold splats as she made her way through the trees to the place where the high hill became a grassy slope. She spotted the road below when a clap of thunder burst, sending a torrent of rain. She started down the hill only to have a cascade of mud *whoosh* her to the bottom.

At the level road, Quinn tumbled to a stop. She sat upright, sputtering, and then used her sleeve to wipe her mud-covered eyes. Anger raised her face to the heavens. "May God strike you dead, Doss Parker!"

With her boot heels dug in, she pushed herself up onto her feet. She looked right and then left, making her best guess as to the direction of town, and started off.

Why hadn't she seen Doss for the scoundrel of a man he was? How could she have gotten herself into such a predicament? Why had she gone to his cabin alone? She should have known better. She *had* known better, but she went anyway. Had she learned nothing from the brutal, untrustworthy men in her life?

The mudslide ruined the crisp newness of her autumn-colored dress, and by the feel of her white leather boots, she doubted they would ever dry out or clean up. She'd made a mess of everything.

On a muddy, hoof-pocked trail, she trudged into town. Drenched, filthy, and furious, she plodded toward the boarding-house, ignoring the light of an oil lamp that illuminated the inside of Beaudry's Supply, until a dip in the earth, camouflaged by puddles, caught her step. She fell with a *splat.*

"Blast it!" she cried out.

"Quinn?" Bill Beaudry called from his store's covered porch. "Is that you?"

She pushed herself up, only to slip and fall again. Flat on her derriere, she called out, "Yes, I'm afraid it is."

Bill hurried off the porch to her and grabbed hold. With his arms around her waist, he raised her up onto her feet and then helped her to the store. "What are you doing out here in the rain?"

Quinn swiped her drenched, straggly hair off her face. She looked down at herself, wet and muddy, and moaned. "This was all a very bad idea."

Bill opened the door and ushered her inside. He hurried to the cast-iron box stove, which warmed the room with its woody scent, and shoved another piece of firewood inside before setting down two stools. "Sit while I get us some towels." He disappeared into a back room.

Quinn sat and pulled off her boots, splattering the floor with dirty water. A puddle pooled under her stocking feet. The embarrassment, so unbecoming to a reserved woman, was almost too much to bear without tears.

When Bill returned, Quinn motioned to his wet floor. "I'm sorry for this mess."

"Naw, it's all right," he said as he handed over a stack of drying cloths. He sat beside her, but before grabbing a towel for himself, he reached down and stood her boots upright, setting them closer to the fire. "What was a very bad idea?"

"This . . ." She waved a limp hand. "All of it. Everything. Coming here. Thinking I could be a businesswoman." She glanced at him, unable to hide her tears. "Seems I don't belong anywhere." When Bill reached his arm around her, she shrugged it off, brusquer than intended, and he pulled back.

"I'm sorry, Bill, but please don't . . ." Whether caused by anger or shame, she wasn't sure, but tears came.

"Quinn, what happened?"

What hadn't happened? She stood. "Do you have a wash basin? I'd like to clean off some of this mud." Time alone to compose herself was what she needed.

"Yeah, sure." Bill led her to the workroom and lit a candle. Flickers of light barely brightened the room. Rain continued to pelt the building as he opened the back door, filled a bucket with water, and then came back inside. He set the bucket in the dry sink, handed her a mostly used bar of soap, and then left her alone to wash up.

Quinn scrubbed her face, refusing to acknowledge the trickle of tears, and then cleaned her hands and wrists, which was the farthest she could reach under her tight-fitting sleeves. She washed her red hair and then towel dried it, but with her hairpins and ivory bonnet lost between the cabin and the store, her baby-fine strands hung limp as if her duty to personal neatness had been all but forgotten. There was nothing to be done about her drenched and muddy gown except to wring its fabric, which she did, splattering the wood plank floor. Using her damp towel, she sopped up the mess as best she could, then returned to the cast-iron box stove where Bill waited with a steaming pot of coffee.

Wearing a forced smile, she said, "Much better now." She twisted her hair into a single shaft, pulling it over one shoulder. "Thank you."

Bill patted the stool. "Sit. Tell me how you ended up in tonight's rain covered in mud." He handed her a cup of coffee and waited.

The story was simply humiliating, but after his kindness, she owed him an explanation. She drew a breath and recounted the night's events.

Bill listened until she finished. "I'll have a talk with him in the morning."

"I'd rather you didn't. It would just seem as though I'm incapable of taking care of myself. As much as I appreciate it, this is something I need to handle." She looked at him and softly said, "Do you understand?"

"I suppose," he said with a nod. "Respect is hard to come by unless a woman is a worthy opponent. Is that it?"

Her hand moved to touch his, but she pulled it back. "Yes. How did you know?"

"My mother was a businesswoman. A darn good one."

Her shoulders eased. "I plan to become a businesswoman, too."

He shifted, then faced Quinn. "You've got just one problem . . ."

"What's that?"

"You don't have a business. In fact, it sounds like you don't even have a job."

Plainly stated, Bill Beaudry was right. Quiet, Quinn reached down, fiddling with the laces of her wet boots. "I had a silly notion that I was capable of owning a business — making do for myself. And perhaps that might be true somewhere else, but this beautiful, wild California country doesn't seem very welcoming to a woman." She looked up, her eyes meeting his. "I don't suppose you still have that cooking job available, do you?"

Bill shook his head. "I don't need a cook."

She straightened. "You've hired someone already?"

"No," Bill told her, sipping his coffee.

"But you said . . ."

"Quinn," he interrupted. "What I need is a business partner capable of running a real restaurant. My hands are full with the store, and it's getting busier every day. I need somebody who can take charge, do the cooking and serving, hire workers, order supplies, attract customers, and keep a tally journal." He set his eyes on hers. "Everybody can find their fortune where the river

165

runs, but digging gold isn't my way. When I first saw these foothills with their rich soil, rolling slopes, and big river, it set my heart a-beating. I couldn't imagine stopping anywhere else. After meeting Marshall and Nettie, I knew our fortune was here. They were the first to envision this place as a town. It was just too hard to do by themselves. When I told them about us moving West hoping to find enough gold to start a store, they sold everything except the boardinghouse and the saloon to me. They'd already built it all, even had a garden."

Bill shook his head. "I swear, it was like God told them we were coming." He smiled at Quinn. "And this fertile land can grow anything — vegetables, cattle, even kids. It was easy to see that our fortune was in commerce, not prospecting, so as businessmen, we three decided to put down roots and start a town."

"Business*men*?" Quinn questioned. "Don't you mean you, Marshall, and Nettie?"

Bill lowered his gaze. "No. I mean me, Marshall, and Doss."

Quinn's gasp was nearly silent. For a moment, she was too shocked to speak. "You're partners with Doss Parker?"

"It's not a partnership." Bill shook his

head. His blue eyes focused on her. "But the three of us did agree to work together — without competing — to build this town. Marshall and Nettie have their saloon and boardinghouse, and soon they'll have a hotel. I have the store, and a restaurant if you've a mind to give my stewpot a name, and rights to a butcher shop someday. Doss never officially declared his business interests until yesterday. There's no other agreement, except to say we'll make decisions together when it concerns the future of Fortune." He leaned forward without rising off the stool and opened the iron door of the stove. He stoked the wood, releasing a whirl of ash into the air before closing it.

"I see," she said quietly. Her gut wrenched.

"When we stumbled on this place in these Sierra Nevada mountains, I knew we'd found home." Bill raised his hand mid-chest and patted. "My soul breathes again. I'd almost lost that feeling before heading West. I don't ever want to leave here, but if I can't make a go of it, we'll have no choice." He paused. "A store needs customers, and, for now, gold is what's bringing them to Fortune. How long folks stay after they get here is another matter."

He picked up a pencil-thin kindling stick.

Lightly, he batted it against the floor where he focused his gaze. "Fact is, most men are gonna leave once they pan out unless we can give them a real town to settle down in, which means women, a school and church, a hotel and restaurant, law and order, and more commerce. If folks leave, our trade goes with them. We'll have to move on soon, too."

Although not a businesswoman, Quinn wanted to think like one. "Yes, of course, you're right."

Bill glanced at her with a pleased smile. "My plan was to open a supply store first, then a restaurant, and then a butcher shop. Miners need to eat, so food is always in demand. They need supplies, too, but it's all been a bigger undertaking than I expected."

"But there always seems to be a crowd at your store."

"Got no complaints about the store, but it's just one part of the plan." When the odor of burnt coffee stung the air, Bill moved the dry, empty pot to the back of the box stove. "I thought, since you're a cook, and your sights are set on becoming a businesswoman, maybe you'd consider a partnership." He shifted into a stiffer stance. "To be honest, I tried to do it alone, but the stew pot is a long ways away from being a real restaurant. It needs someone smart and strong. Like you." He glanced at her. "What do you say?"

Her own restaurant. Though her beating heart was jumping, she withheld any expression. The chance to be a full-fledged businesswoman, capable of earning her own way, was at hand, but she had to be sure of his intentions. Men could not be trusted. "I barely have a cent to my name, and I'll not take charity."

"I'm not offering charity. You'll carry half the load, especially once things get going. I'll be busy with my store, and this might free up some time for me to start a butcher shop, and sell hides and tallow, too."

It was a workable proposition, but she wanted no misunderstanding about her role. She stood and forged the courage to say, "Then I'll expect half the profits."

Bill took a slow sip of coffee. "I'll go thirty percent."

Quinn shook her head. This might be her only chance to become a true businesswoman, and she had to negotiate well. "Fifty percent — that, or you'll need to find someone else." Her heart pounded.

Bill tightened his lips until they were no more than a straight, thin line. After a long moment passed, he nodded. "All right, fifty."

"And half ownership."

His posture snapped. "Now hold on." Seriousness wrinkled his brow. "I've put a lot of work into my restaurant just to hand it away."

Hands on hips, Quinn fortified her gumption. "I'm not trying to be ungrateful, but your *restaurant* is nothing more than a big black stewpot that sits out in the open barely sheltered from the rain. It doesn't seem to me that you have much at risk."

To her surprise, Bill laughed.

He set down his cup. "Yeah. All right. Half the restaurant. Half the profits. But I get to keep the big, black stewpot. Are you willing?"

"Yes." Quinn extended her hand. "I'd like to give it a try." When Bill reached for her handshake, she gave a nervous laugh. "I fear we'll have nothing at all in common, though."

"We both want a restaurant. We've got that in common already." Bill grinned. "First thing tomorrow we'll work out the details, but tonight we should get you back to the boardinghouse so you can get out of these wet clothes and get a good night's sleep." He picked up her boots and handed them to her, though she did not put them on.

"Come on, partner. I'll walk you to Medford's."

At the door, Quinn stopped him. "Thank you," she said.

"For what?"

"For being a friend to me tonight. I can't say I've had many, so accepting kindness doesn't come easily."

A smile crossed his face as he opened the door.

The rain had all but ended by the time they stepped off the porch, but the day's torrent had flooded the road. Water still stood almost ankle high, mercilessly soaking Quinn's stocking feet as the two trudged to the boardinghouse. Before going in, Quinn placed her hand on Bill's forearm. With a thought that her quivering nerves might make themselves known, she pressed her other hand to her stomach. "I won't get a wink of sleep tonight unless I confess something to you."

He focused on her hand as it lay atop his arm. "What is it?"

"It's silly to say, but the fact of the matter is, I'm not a very good cook."

His eyes swung up to hers. "You just agreed to open a restaurant with me."

"Yes, well, unfortunately, cooking doesn't quite suit me." When Bill's eyes veered to

171

the ground, she had misgivings about mentioning it at all. "That's not to say I know *nothing* about cooking — I do, but perhaps it's less than you were expecting."

Bill held a steady expression as he contemplated her confession. With a nod, he said, "Looks like we have more in common than you thought."

CHAPTER SEVENTEEN

Although it was just eight o'clock in the morning, the store had been open for hours. Prospectors were hurried men trying to get to their lucky spot along the riverbank before someone else beat them to it. Beaudry's Supply was usually their first stop. Since most gold miners did not have much more than a lean-to roof over their heads, they had little space to store food supplies. Many came early and bought enough jerky or pemmican and plug tobacco to last the day.

When the steady stream of customers died down to a trickle, Bill went out back where Buck Garvin was cleaning and butchering a bull calf, which he had brought in as payment on his overdue account. "Be sure to clean up out here when you finish, Buck. Bury those innards and carcass good and deep out there in the woods, so no hungry bears or wolves come looking for leftovers."

Buck, a gray-bearded man in his sixties, straightened up tall and raised his arms in a long stretch. "I'm gettin' too old for this kind of work."

Bill grinned and gave him a wave before he returned inside to clean up his own mess of potato peelings and carrot tops from his preparation of tonight's stew. For weeks, he had only served two variations, vegetable or venison, so word had gotten around quickly about the beef. Almost every man who came into the store had asked whether the rumor of beef stew was true. He expected a big crowd.

As he cleaned his workspace, Bill thought about the future. He could use a man like Buck, who had butchering skills and needed a job. It would be a plus if the man was a hunter, too. Not only could he add butcherings to the store, but he would have a supply of meat and fowl for the new restaurant.

As the last two customers left carrying rations, picks, pans, and a shovel, Quinn entered.

"Good morning." She motioned to the men leaving the store with their supplies. "I'd think most miners would already own their own tools, but you seem to sell a good many. Why is that?"

Bill's blue eyes settled on Quinn. Strands

of her bundled red hair hung softly against the high neck of her floral dress, which held the faint color of a blue California lilac.

"Newcomers don't usually walk out of here without a pan in their hands." Bill smiled. "Those two were newcomers, Peter and Percy Weatherlow. Identical twins, they said, and they must be because I couldn't hardly tell them apart. They got here yesterday leading a group of twelve wagons from the East. Their story is that they came to scout out the town for the others, but I think they wanted to be the first to prospect." He was unable to keep his eyes from scanning the length of her before lowering his gaze. "They said another caravan is on its way, led by a man named Joe Keegan. Percy said they're a day or two behind, but they're only planning to stop for supplies and a few days' rest at the river. He said they're going on to Jamestown, but they want to pan a little first. No doubt they'll be buying tools, too."

"Why wouldn't they already have tools if they've come all this way hoping to prospect?"

"Because," Bill said, prideful, "I bought up every kind of gold-mining tool for miles around. New folks have to buy from me or get themselves used ones in need of repair from the men already here. It's a good business."

"Is that fair? You buying up all the supplies and making yourself the only one with rights to resell them?"

"It's business. Why wouldn't it be fair? I paid the asking price for everything, then hauled it all up here. I use my own space to store it until needed, too. And I got a right to sell for a profit, don't I? Wouldn't be much of a businessman if I didn't."

"Yes, I suppose you're right." Quinn studied his face until her scrutiny sparked improper thoughts. She turned and straightened sardine cans on a shelf. "Running a profitable business is not a charity affair. Or that's what my father would say."

"Your father sounds like a man I would like to meet."

"No," Quinn said. Her voice hardened. "I doubt that, Mr. Beaudry."

"Bill — you've got to call me Bill."

"Yes, of course. I'm sorry, Bill. My thoughts got away from me." Quinn's gaze fell on a barrel full of apples. She picked up a red-skinned beauty streaked with various shades of yellow. "I've always loved apples. My mother baked pies with them."

"Mine baked blackberry cobblers, mostly, but I was raised in Georgia where the brambles grew enough berries to feed half the town."

"That many?" Quinn asked, wanting nothing more than to keep listening to the smooth, sweet sound of his voice.

Bill began filling one-pound bags with Indian meal, tying them shut with twine as he talked. "We had a pear tree, too, but Mother said we couldn't do much with them other than eat them, fresh or preserved, which we did." He grinned at Quinn, already feeling as though they were friends. "Any chance you could make a cobbler out of these apples?"

"Pies are all I know how to make. I never learned to make a cobbler. If you can tell me how, I will be happy to try."

"Pie is just as good." Bill finished tying off the remaining filled sacks and walked to the barrel. "These are the last of the fresh apples. How many would you need?"

Quinn put back the apple, then held out her empty hands. "I have very little money, and certainly not enough to purchase supplies every day."

Bill smiled as he picked up an apple. "You'd be making pie for tonight's customers. It will be the first sweet thing these men have had in a long time." His tone was patient. "The way this works is that the store will furnish the supplies and then, as partners, you and me will split the profits. Just tell me what you need."

Her gaze dropped. She knew cost versus income was a big factor in the success of any trade, but without experience, an intellectual discussion on the subject evaded her. Stalling, she picked up another apple, and, as if inspecting its freshness, she raised it to her nose and sniffed, giving her an added moment to think. Was Bill offering to buy supplies for her? If so, it didn't bode well for her independence. Opening a charge was her only other option, which would put her in debt before her doors ever opened for business. That couldn't be a smart business move, either. She lowered the apple. With her thumb, she rubbed its smooth skin. How was she to make pie without the needed ingredients? Her throat tightened at the realization she had not thoroughly thought this through. She put down the apple and glanced at Bill. "Are you extending credit?"

Bill shrugged. "In a roundabout way, I guess I am. But only for a few hours. At the end of the night, the supply costs will be paid back out of the nightly profits." He pulled out eight apples and set them down on the counter by his cash drawer. "Other than apples, what would you need to make a pie?"

Credit for just a few hours? Then she would repay the debt to him leaving herself on level ground, financially speaking. Her businesswoman's spirit sparked. "Let me think . . ." she said with steady voice. Her eyes scanned the shelving. If she used apples instead of peaches, perhaps she could use Myra's recipe. "I'll need flour, salt, fat, sugar, and mace, as I recall." She turned to him with a satisfied nod.

"I don't have mace, but I have nutmeg."

Were they the same? "Yes, nutmeg."

"What else?"

"Other than a bowl and knife, I'll need an iron skillet. Do you have a cookstove?"

"No, but I'll sure share the fire pit."

Quinn nodded. She would do the best she could, because she had no other choice.

Bill pulled out a tally journal, then turned it for Quinn to see. "So, eighty cents for apples, seventy cents for flour, sugar at a dollar, twenty cents for salt . . ." Bill continued to write prices on paper. "Nutmeg is a dime. All that comes to . . ."

"What about the fat?" Quinn asked. "I can't make piecrust without fat."

"That's right." Bill slid a big hide bag from beneath the counter. "Got tallow right

179

here. Ten cents' worth ought to be enough."
He mumbled numbers while adding the
figures, and then he looked up at Quinn.
"Comes to two dollars and ninety cents."

Quinn gasped. "I can't charge three dollars for a pie!"

Bill laughed. "I should say not . . . three
dollars for a whole pie is ridiculous." He
raked the apples off the counter and into a
bucket. "You'll be charging a dollar a *serving.*" He smiled at her teasingly. "Sell three
servings, and your whole supply cost is paid
in full. The rest of the pie is all profit."

"Can the miners afford a dollar a serving?
Bill, if it doesn't sell, I'll be in debt before
midnight."

"Prospectors make good money off the
river, and they don't mind spending it.
They'll be hungry for something sweet after
filling their bellies with my stew. They'll
happily pay a dollar. In fact, the pie earnings are yours tonight. That way, if it doesn't
sell, you're not out anything but a day's
work."

Quinn rubbed her forehead, her thoughts
riddled with doubt. She'd only made pie
once — peach. What if the recipe didn't
work with apples? To herself, she mumbled
aloud, "Tonight is my only chance . . ."

"Actually, you'll be able to make three or

four pies with these supplies. Other than apples, the next few pies won't cost you a cent." He glanced at the remaining apples in the barrel. "But when these run out, you'll have to use dried, because the season is about over. Your cost will change some."

"Yes, of course." A headache set in, but that wasn't what worried her.

Quinn unfolded her long apron, then pulled its strings around her waist and tied them into a bow behind her back. "Where shall I begin?"

Bill walked her to the back room where she had washed up last night. In the daylight, she saw the room was larger than she thought. It had a table and two chairs and fastened along one wall, as if were a bar top in a saloon, were two long planks of pine squeezed tightly together, which made a wide counter for working. Wooden crates filled with potatoes, carrots, and onions from the garden lined the wall underneath. Each crate had straw strewn across the top with some mixed between the vegetables to keep them fresh. A bucket of water sat at the end of the counter and nearby were more neatly folded drying cloths.

Quinn glanced around the room as if taking inventory. "Do you have a rolling pin? I'll need to roll out my pie dough."

"No . . ." Bill's hand went to his chin. His brows creased. "I'm not a baker, so I've never needed one." He looked at Quinn. "What now?"

"Do you have whiskey?"

His eyebrows arched. "Yeah, I got a bottle that I keep handy for personal use."

"Thank goodness. Empty it out. I'll use the bottle as a rolling pin."

"Empty it out? You mean you want me to pour out perfectly good whiskey?"

"Unless you know of a place I can get a rolling pin for my pie dough."

Bill did not intend to waste his private stash of liquor, so he pulled a bottle from its hiding place and held it up to the window light. One-third remained, too much to drink himself, especially before noon. "Maybe the weight of this whiskey inside the bottle will make the rolling easier."

"No," Quinn said, shaking her head. "I'll not risk spilling a drop of that vile liquid on my pie crust. You'll need to drink it, serve it, or pour it out."

"Can't serve liquor without stepping on Marshall's toes. It's part of the agreement. He runs the saloon, not me."

Quinn looked at Bill, and, in seeing his unhappy face, she realized her request might be an unreasonable one. A man without an occasional sip of whiskey often finds himself led to a saloon in search of a nip, especially on cold nights. And the temptations in a saloon were far greater than keeping a bottle hidden away for personal use, whether it was for warming one's insides, sterilizing wounds, or for other medicinal purposes.

"You're right, of course." With eyes cast upward, Quinn slowly walked the length of the room searching the high shelves, which looked like long sticks from a woodpile nailed up without the least bit of alteration. "There." She pointed up at a dozen quart jars. Leaning into the work counter for support, she reached, and, using her fingertips, she scratched at the too-high jar, hoping to tip it just enough to get her fingers inside and pull it safely down.

Instead of retrieving the jar for her, Bill froze as his gaze locked on Quinn. The radiant morning sun shone through the room's only window, casting its light on her slim figure as if it had purposely searched her out with the intent of illuminating every curve — her bosom, her waist, her hips . . .

"Are you listening?" Quinn asked, unaware of the attention she had drawn.

Bill shook his head to refocus, but the fog did not easily clear. "I'm sorry, what did you say?"

"The jars, Bill." Quinn recoiled from her reach. "They are too high. Can you get one down so that I can pour your whiskey into it, saving the empty bottle for me?"

Before he could take action, the back door flew open, and Bill's barefoot boy burst through, bumping Quinn into a spin as he sped past into the store.

CHAPTER EIGHTEEN

"Blue!" Bill shouted as he hurried after his son. "You almost knocked over Miss Quinn. How many times have I told you not to run in the store?"

"But there's puppies out front, Daddy!"

"No puppies," Bill told the boy, although both stood peering outside through the front window.

"Aw, Daddy . . ."

Bill put his hand atop the boy's blond head. "Well, I guess it won't hurt if you just pet a few. Go on." When the boy made a smiling dash out the door, Bill called after him, "But don't bring one back with you."

"So, he's your son?" Quinn had never considered the boy might be his. In fact, it hadn't occurred to her to ask whether Bill had any family at all. But then again, why wouldn't a handsome, successful business-man be married with a family of his own?

"Yeah," Bill said with a satisfied grin as he

watched Blue slide into position on the ground, giggling as golden-haired pups pounced on him.

"He's beautiful. So pure and innocent."

"He's the best thing I've ever done, and he's the reason for everything I do." Bill had a dreamy gaze as he watched the boy.

"I've never gotten on well with children," Quinn admitted as she looked away from the window and smoothed her apron. "I should get busy peeling apples." She started back through the store, leaving feelings of family warmth behind her.

Within the hour, Quinn had two pies in the black cast-iron pots ready for the fire. She topped them with lids, then left the pies on the work counter before going into the store to find Bill. "Hello?" she called out, perplexed when she didn't see him.

"Over here," he answered from a squat position near a table beneath the store's front window. As Quinn moved closer, her eyes followed Bill's gaze to where his child hid. "Blue, come on out and say a proper hello to Miss Quinn."

With a pouty face, Blue scooted out from his crouched position under the table and then leaned against his kneeling father. The boy pointed to her long white apron. "Do you have a real puppy like that one?"

Quinn raised her apron and fingered a patch of colored threads — an embroidered pup amid a patch of daisies. She smiled at Blue. "No, I never had a dog. I suppose that's why I put this one on my apron so long ago. I always wanted a puppy of my own."

"Yeah," Blue said, and nodded. "Me, too, but Daddy says I can't have one."

"But you have that shaggy dog out there." She pointed to the porch, where an aging retriever slept. "What's his name?"

"That's Rufus, but all he wants to do is sleep."

Bill turned Blue around until they faced each other. "That's because Rufus is four-teen years old. He's not a young sprout like you anymore." He poked his finger in Blue's belly and twisted, causing the boy to grab his tummy and giggle.

"He's delightful," Quinn said, pushing away the happy feeling that came with hear-ing a child's laughter. "How old is he?"

Bill looked at his son and said, "Tell Miss Quinn how old you are, buddy." Blue held up three fingers, which caused Bill to laugh. "That's right, but how many is that?"

"Three," Blue said and grinned.

"That's right." He gave the boy a pat on his behind. "Now run on out back and help

Mrs. Crawford gather the eggs from the henhouse so we can get them in here and sell them."

As Blue hurried through the back door, Quinn said, "Blue is an unusual name for a child, isn't it?"

"My wife, Katy, died shortly after his birthing. She only got a glimpse of him before passing, and she thought he was the girl she'd dreamed of having. She'd picked the name Bluet, after her favorite flower, if the baby was a girl, but she never decided on a boy's name. Her last words were 'my precious Bluet,' and I just didn't have the heart to change his name after she died. I started calling him Blue right off, and it just sort of stuck."

"I'm so sorry," Quinn said.

Bill nodded but then began stacking bagged coffee beans into one of the many wooden crates nailed to the wall. "The boy doesn't know any difference between life with a mother and life without one. Mrs. Crawford has made sure of that."

"Mrs. Crawford?"

"Yeah," Bill said as he turned to Quinn. "She's a sweet old dear. I don't know what we'd do without her." Then he smiled and corrected himself. "I shouldn't call her *old*. She'll turn sixty this coming May, and I'd venture a guess that she has plenty of good years left in her." He moved to the front window as he talked and began to stack one gold pan on top of another for a window display. "She's my father's cousin. Blind since birth. My parents brought her to live with us about twenty years ago after a bandit shot her husband. She helped raise me. I was five when she moved in." Memories made him grin. "She taught me to play the piano. She's still nagging me to have one hauled in here from San Francisco." His smile faded. "A month before Blue was born, my folks died in a fire. Our house and store burned to the ground. Afterward, Mrs. Crawford came to live with me."

Quinn placed a hand over her heart, steadying the emotional tug.

"That was a hard year, what with losing my parents and my wife. Mrs. Crawford has been a godsend." Bill walked toward her with a modest smile. "That was quite a ramble all about me, wasn't it?" His laugh held uneasiness. "I'll bet you need help getting those pies on the fire."

Quinn was captivated. Bill was so unlike any man she had known. He seemed so genuine and sincere about everything that had ever touched his life. If he had flaws, he was hiding them well. As he moved closer, a fire lit deep inside her, stirring unfamiliar desires. Even while wed to Henry, this wifely sensation, an arousal new to her loins, had never been lit. She fanned herself, inhaling a great gulp of air.

"You all right?" Bill asked.

She spun herself around to face her pies. "Yes, of course." *Shake this feeling!* "I've made two pies. We'll want to get them on the fire right away. They'll need time to cool before supper." It took a moment to find her composure, but then with a glance at Bill, she said, "I'm anxious to see if even a single serving sells." It would be an embarrassment if the pies went to waste after she had used his supplies to bake them.

"If a crumb is left when the night is done, I'll buy it myself."

Bill gave a reassuring pat to her flour-covered hand, which sent a spark fluttering through her veins, jump-starting her heart as if bringing it back from the dead.

CHAPTER NINETEEN

Rain began again by mid-afternoon, turning the town's only street into a river of muddy water.

The cook fire, although still burning strong beneath the wide lean-to roof that jutted off the side of the store building, was now puffing out enough smoke to look like a house on fire. Wet wood was Bill's reasoning when Quinn asked.

Her apple pies had baked, mounding high with syrupy goodness that bubbled up through the half-moon slit she'd cut for venting. They sat on trivets in the workroom, and, every so often, Quinn glanced at them, admiring her handiwork. She had followed Myra's recipe exactly, with the exception of using apples instead of peaches, and nutmeg instead of mace.

With a bucket of water hefted up onto the dry sink, Quinn was preparing to wash the stew vegetables for tomorrow when an older woman came in with an apron full of carrots. She wore a plain tan-colored bonnet, but it was as soaked as she was by the rain.

"Hello, dear," the woman said and emptied the carrots onto the counter. Turning her head in Quinn's direction, she went on, "I'm Mrs. Crawford. Bill asked me to bring these carrots to you. They're filthy dirty. The mud pulled right up out of the ground with them. He says he'll be back to help as soon as he can, but he's behind schedule carving out his stew meat." She wiped her hands on the underside of her apron, then reached out for a handshake. "Nice to know another woman is around."

Sprigs of blondish-silver hair poked out from beneath Mrs. Crawford's bonnet. Her lips were thin, as was her nose, but it was her crystalline-blue eyes that captured Quinn's gaze. The eyes had no focus whatsoever.

"Hello," Quinn greeted her as she shook the woman's hand. "Bill has told me about you."

"He did, did he? What tales did he tell?"

Quinn smiled at the woman's easy manner. "Well, he said you taught him to play the piano."

Mrs. Crawford nodded. "That's true, I did. And if he'll have another shipped in,

I'll teach Blue how to play, too. It's easier to learn the art when you're young, don't you think so?"

Art! If only she could talk about her painting, but how foolish to converse with a sightless woman about brush strokes, colors, and imagery. "I'm ashamed to say that I don't have a musical bone in my body."

"Is that so?" Mrs. Crawford asked, her eyes directed at Quinn even though they could not see her. "There are all kinds of instruments one can play, dear. Although, piano is my favorite. Once, in Saint Louis, I heard an accordion played, but to my ears, it was just caterwauling. It sounded like a perfectly good pipe organ completely out of tune. Nowadays, the only music I hear is from a fiddle or harmonica. I like them fine, but I sure miss the sound of a piano. If Bill hauls one in, I can teach you to play. It sure seems to warm a man's heart. Blue's mama played, and those ivory keys sang as if they had a heartbeat all their own when she touched them. Bill swears no man should be with a woman who has no musical talent."

Quinn silently admonished herself for not squelching the attraction she had felt for Bill. How could she think any man had no flaws? "Yes, well, men seem to have a way of dismissing their own faults while talking about the flaws of women, don't they?"

"Do you need help with these vegetables?" Mrs. Crawford asked. "I don't peel, chop, or dice, but I can help wash off the mud."

"No, no," Quinn told her. "I'm sure you have other things to do. I'll be fine here."

"Well, then," Mrs. Crawford said as she walked to the back door, felt for the latch, and opened it. She stepped out into the rain, closing the door behind her.

Quinn watched through the window as the older woman walked along a puddled path that led to a cabin about a hundred feet behind the store. She stopped just long enough to pick up a few sticks of firewood before she opened the door and went inside. Surely, not all three lived together in that tiny place, did they? Her gaze searched the area for another cabin, and, although she found none, she did spot a smokehouse, a large fenced garden, an outhouse, and a chicken coop, fenced and then secured with a curious honeycomb-shaped wire. She was still peering through the rain-splattered window when Bill entered the workroom.

"What's out there?"

Quinn jumped. "You startled me!"

"Didn't mean to. Wish I could sneak up on a turkey as easy." He laughed. "Did you see something out there? Ol' Buck was supposed to haul off a calf carcass so it wouldn't attract any bears. You didn't see a bear, did you?"

"No," Quinn told him with a shake of her head. "I was watching Mrs. Crawford. She makes her way quite well without sight, doesn't she?"

"She does fine." Bill peered out the window, inspecting the area.

"Do all three of you live together in the cabin?"

"That little one-room place?" Bill shook his head. "That's Mrs. Crawford's house. She says a lady needs her privacy and swears it's plenty big. Blue and me sleep upstairs over the store. She doesn't like climbing stairs, so it works out."

"I didn't realize there was an upstairs."

"It's not much of one. Stairs are out back."

"There are so few homes and so many men, what happens to the miners when it's cold or rainy like today?" Quinn asked.

"Most have lean-tos under the trees. They're hard to notice, but if it's still raining tonight, you'll spot a lot of them by the shirts thrown over the pine boughs for shelter. Folks are working hard to get cabins built before winter sets in."

Quinn motioned to the walls of the store.

"You're set well in comparison."

"That's true, but we arrived August first." He picked up a broom and began sweeping up the dark garden dirt.

Before her thoughts could settle, the store's front door banged open, and a man yelled, "Eureka, Bill! Eureka!"

Every man within a thousand miles knew the word *Eureka!* It meant gold had been found. A lot of gold.

Bill grabbed Quinn by the shoulders, eyes wide with excitement. "Watch Blue for me, will you?" Without waiting for an answer, he dashed through the connecting doorway into the store, grabbed a sack, a pan, and a shovel, and then, on his way out, he yelled, "Blue, stay with Miss Quinn. I'll be back!"

She and Blue watched Bill and every man who wasn't already at the river, running full speed toward it through a deluge of rain. Their boots slapped the muddy water, sloshing shin-high as they ran.

Quinn looked down at Blue. "You would think they could wait until the rain stopped, wouldn't you?"

"The rain washed it up, and the rain will wash it away."

"Oh, I see." Quinn nodded with a better understanding.

She hadn't cared for a child since her

year-old brother died a lifetime ago, so her feelings of inadequacy roared to the surface when Blue looked up at her. Determined not to let weakness overtake her, she forced a poised tone. "You're terribly smart. Tell me, what is one supposed to do with a little boy on a rainy day?"

"Well, I was waiting for Daddy to come outside because he said it was time to stir the stew."

"Is that your job?"

"Only when Daddy helps. He says I'm too little to do it by myself."

"I can help. Will you show me how?"

Blue nodded, then took hold of Quinn's hand. He led her around the side of the building, walking beneath the overhanging porch roof until they came to the fire pit shelter and stew pot. Blue pointed to the waning fire. "It needs more wood. It's not hot enough."

"Oh, dear. There's more to cooking this big pot of stew than I thought." Quinn spotted the scantily built woodshed at least twenty feet from the shelter. "I suppose we can't let the fire go out, or none of us will eat tonight." She raised a hand to her pinned hair. No bonnet. "Is it kindling we need, or bigger wood?"

"It's the big wood."

"Yes, of course, it is."

Quinn dashed toward the woodpile, sloshing through puddles. By the time she reached the woodshed, she was rain soaked. She picked up one, two, three sticks of firewood, then hastened back with it cradled in her arms. Halfway to the shelter, she slipped, landing on her derriere with a *splash!*

Blue started toward her, but Quinn yelled, "No! You stay put! I'm all right." She stood, gathered the wood off the wet ground, and then hurried to the shelter.

Blue moved back, away from her sopping wet dress. "Want me to run and get Mrs. Crawford?"

"You don't need to be running anywhere in this deluge." Quinn shoved the firewood into the low flames beneath the stew pot. "I suppose we'll need more before too long. Stay here, Blue. I'm going for more wood now, while I'm already soaked." She hurried to the woodpile, picked up another four sticks, and then rushed back. She stacked the firewood on dry ground. "Now," she said as if everything were perfectly normal. "Where's the stirring spoon?"

Blue pointed to a black long-handled ladle hanging from a nail on one of the shelter's support posts.

Quinn swept strands of wet hair off her face, then said, "I see it now." She pulled it down and handed it to the boy. "Stir away, but be careful of the fire."

Blue dipped the ladle into the slow bubble of stew. Holding tight to it with both hands, he stirred.

Quinn watched a swirl of sliced carrots, corn, chunked potatoes, and onion wedges with an occasional piece of meat. Only when Blue pushed the ladle farther down into the pot did more meat rise to the top and then drop down again, out of sight.

"That looks good, Blue."

Back inside the store, Quinn searched for a coat or blanket to wrap around herself, and clean water so she could wash, but found neither. She extended her hand. "Come on, maybe we'll go see Mrs. Crawford after all."

Instead of taking her hand, Blue sat down on the floor with his toy top. "I'm gonna stay here and play." He spun the top.

"Oh, no, you don't." She reached down and took hold. "I allowed a little boy to play by himself a long time ago, and I won't make that mistake again."

"What other little boy?" Blue asked as Quinn helped him to his feet.

"Some other time," she said.

They hurried to the little cabin out back and knocked. It wasn't more than half a minute before the door opened a crack.

"Yes? Who is it?" Mrs. Crawford asked.

"It's Quinn MacCann. With Blue. May we come inside?"

The door opened wider. "Yes, come in. What are you doing out in this rain? You must be drenched, by the sound of the storm."

"Yes, I'm afraid I am." Quinn closed the door behind her. "Bill left with the other men when word of a strike came, so Blue has been showing me how to keep the stew stirred and hot. I was gathering wood when I slipped and fell in the mud. And, well, I'm soaked to the gills." She looked down at the boy. "And so is Blue now that I've dragged him out here with me."

"Land sakes!" Mrs. Crawford grabbed a wool throw, held it out for Blue, and then took a green quilt, unfolded it, and handed it to Quinn. "Wrap up, dear. Now, tell me, are we about the same size? Can I loan you a dress?"

Quinn took a look at the woman, then shook her head. "No, I'm afraid that won't work." Mrs. Crawford was a short, plump woman, whereas Quinn was tall, five feet eight inches to be exact, and she weighed at least a hundred pounds less than the older woman. "I think if I could wash my face and hands and dry myself, I'd feel a bit better, but the workroom water is like mud itself after washing the potatoes and carrots. Of course, I could go stand in this rain shower."

"No need for that. Bill has whiskey barrels out back filled with rainwater, so we don't have to lug buckets back and forth from the river. I'll show you where." Mrs. Crawford tied on her bonnet and then whirled a black cape around her shoulders.

The rain had lessened, but it was still steady. Quinn took the blind woman by the elbow and guided her down the muddy path to the workroom entrance.

At the door, Mrs. Crawford stopped and motioned to the casks set along the outside back wall. "Those are rainwater barrels."

Inside, Blue sat down on the floor and began spinning his toy top.

"Thank you for your help, Mrs. Crawford," Quinn said.

"You're welcome, dear."

"If you don't mind my asking, why do Bill and Blue call you Mrs. Crawford, especially being family?"

With a chuckle, the woman said, "Because my given name is Faddie, and, considering the extra weight I carry on these old bones of mine, it sounds quite ill mannered."

Quinn stifled a giggle. "Yes, I understand. Thank you for explaining, Mrs. Crawford."

CHAPTER TWENTY

Quinn wandered the empty store after Mrs. Crawford took Blue back to her cabin to "give the boy a good bathing." Alone in the quiet, the world inside the unpainted wood walls felt deserted with the only sounds being the tapping rain and crackles from the burning wood inside the knee-high box stove. As she stood looking out the grime-blurred windowpanes, she spotted a lone man, head down, shielded by a dark wide-brimmed hat, hurrying through the rain to the store. She had no idea what to do with a customer. Bill hadn't left storekeeping instructions, and the man was approaching too fast for her to summon Mrs. Crawford. Quickly, she grabbed a crumpled cloth and began dusting, hoping to appear as if she belonged all alone inside Bill Beaudry's store.

When the door opened, the sound of boots stomping off mud rattled the floorboards. With her eyes focused on the shoulder-high shelf of dusty forks, spoons, and knives, Quinn stiffened. Who was this uncouth man who cared so little about the cleanup that would be required after his mud stomping ended? Annoyed, she turned, intent on chastising him for his shameful disregard, but froze when she saw the rain-drenched man was Doss Parker.

Head down, Doss removed his felt hat and shook it dry before replacing it. Only then did he look up, his green eyes settling on hers before skimming her muddied dress.

"Well, well . . . you working for Bill now?" His bottom lip bulged — its swell extending all the way to his jawbone. The punctures from her bite had reddened to a bruised crimson-blue.

"Yes," Quinn answered, then quickly said, "I mean no . . ." With gathered courage, she straightened her posture but otherwise did not move. "I'm starting a restaurant here." She gave a slanted nod indicating the west side of the building. With scarcely a movement, she loosened her fingers from the cloth and let them glide across the utensils until they found the sharp edge of a knife.

Doss chuckled. "Restaurant? You mean that burnt up old stew pot Bill uses every day? So, you're cooking his stew now?"

"No, I mean a *real* restaurant."

With no hint of surprise, Doss walked to a shelf holding tobacco. He picked up a pouch and sniffed, then lowered it, studying its brown color. "What sort of deal did Bill make with you?"

"The details of our arrangement are none of your business."

"Tough talk for a woman," he said. "But just so you know, I've never met a woman I couldn't break. I doubt you'll be the first."

Quinn steadied her eyes on him. "I was born broken, Mr. Parker, which takes me out of your equation."

His amusement faded. "Heard your days at the boardinghouse are numbered. Seven days, no more, is what I heard. At least with me, you had room and board coming. My bed might look mighty inviting after a night or two outdoors under the trees." He snickered. "When it gets too cold out there, you'll come looking for me. You've got the stench of an amorous woman all over you, so just remember, I'd be glad to forgive your bite for a good bend-over." Then he held up a plug of tobacco. "Tell Bill to put this on my account."

The sun had almost set before Bill returned to the store, wet and muddy head to toe, where Quinn, Mrs. Crawford, and Blue waited. He carried his dirty, half-full canvas sack slung over his shoulder.

When he opened the door, Quinn hurried to him with the same green quilt Mrs. Crawford had lent to her. "You're soaking wet."

He set down his sack and took the blanket.

Blue, clean and dry, got up off the floor with his toy top. "Did you find gold, Daddy?"

"Yeah, got some," Bill told the boy as Quinn took his muddy shovel and pick and set them outside the back door.

When Quinn returned, Mrs. Crawford was pulling off Bill's waterlogged boots and socks. She set them near the woodstove.

"How much, Bill?" Mrs. Crawford asked.

"The whole lode is probably worth twenty thousand."

"Dollars?" Quinn gulped.

"The rain uprooted an old tree along the riverbank, which started men scrambling to get their hands on any rock or pebble with a shade of gold before it got washed away. Hopkins got swept downstream when the bank gave way under the rain and weight of men. Blackjack and me went after him so he wouldn't drown, but it took us a half mile to catch him. He lost both shoes and his hat in the raging waters. He was coughing and sputtering when we pulled him up, but that boy hung on to his bag of gold."

"How much did you get, Bill?" Mrs. Crawford asked again.

"I don't know for sure. As soon as the rain dries up, I'll take it to the assay office in Sacramento City on my next supply trip."

"I know very little about gold," Quinn said, "but wouldn't this fortune rightfully belong to the landowner?"

Bill turned to her. "It's on common land, and Fortune doesn't have set rules about staking a claim. There's just been a few of us here up until lately, so we haven't needed any."

Quinn eyed the canvas sack with its lumpy bulges. "I thought gold was just dust and pebbles."

"I got a few nuggets, but then up come those tree roots, and out popped fist-sized chunks of quartz with veins of gold running right through it." His eyes shone. "They came up out of the mud, just like digging potatoes. I got my hands on two, but I don't have any notion as to how to get gold out of a rock. But I sure wasn't going to just leave it there."

"Are you sure it ain't pyrite?" Mrs. Crawford asked him.

"No, it's real gold, no doubt about it."

"Sure wish I could see it," she said.

Quinn could have listened to Bill tell his story for the rest of the evening, but frankly, she was nervous about her pies. "Will the other men be back soon? I think the stew is ready, but you should check it before they arrive for supper," she suggested. "And how are they going to keep this rain out of their stew bowls? Not to mention, my pie. The crust will be soggy before their first bite."

Bill used a corner of the blanket to dry his hair while he talked. "They'll huddle under the trees and beneath the cooking shelter." When he looked up again, he realized Quinn was wet and mud-splashed for a second day in a row. His eyes scanned her up and down. "What happened to you?"

"Oh . . ." She brushed the front of her blue floral dress as if smoothing wrinkles. "I slipped and fell in the downpour. It hasn't stopped raining long enough for me to get back to the boardinghouse to change into a clean, dry dress."

"Miss Quinn carried firewood, Daddy. She did real good," Blue said, as if his opinion was all that was needed.

Bill patted the boy on the back. "She did?"

Quinn nodded, showing more embarrassment about falling than pride in carrying wood.

The door swung open as a drenched and dirty miner came into the store. "Bill, I need supplies real quick. I'm leaving for San Francisco."

"Tonight, Isaac? It's still raining."

"I gotta go, Bill. I promised Mary I'd send for her and the kids six months ago, and I ain't had the heart to tell her I was bust. Now that I'm a rich man, I'm gonna put my money in that there Miner's Bank, and then I'm sending for her and the kids. After that, we're coming back here to settle."

Quinn's heart jumped when she realized a free roof might be in sight. "What will you do with your lean-to while you're gone?"

Isaac turned and tipped his hat to her. "I ain't got a lean-to, ma'am. I got me a ten-man tent. I was expecting my family to join me someday, but I didn't expect to be a rich man when I sent for them. Now come spring, I'll be building the family a proper house."

"A tent?" Quinn asked. "How much do you want? For your tent, I mean."

"You want to buy it?" Isaac asked as Bill turned to Quinn with a confused squint.

"Yes, how much?"

"Well," Isaac said, rubbing his chin. "I'll

gladly take five dollars for it, I guess. I got more money than I know what to do with now, and shedding it would sure lighten my load. But I don't want to take advantage of no lady."

She turned to Bill. "I know we haven't sold a single serving of pie yet, but could you give this man five dollars, then take the money out of my pie earnings? I'd like to buy his tent."

"Why do you need a ten-man tent?"

Quinn's stance stiffened. "I don't recall questioning you when you ran out of here today asking me to care for your son. I trusted you were making a reasonable decision."

Bill winced. "All right." He walked to the cash box, pulled out a gold half-eagle coin, and handed it to Isaac. "The lady just bought your tent."

"It's on the pack mule. Soon as I get my supplies, I'll toss it on the porch."

Mrs. Crawford took Blue into the back room while Isaac settled his account with a few gold nuggets. He headed for the door, not noticing Quinn on his heels.

With eager eyes, she watched as he untied the rolled-up canvas tent and threw it onto the porch, all the while talking about his wife and four kids. When Isaac finished cinching up his supplies, he patted the mule's backside, then mounted his own horse. "See ya in the spring!"

Quinn turned to Bill. "Thank you for fronting the money." She bent to check the weight of the tent. "Will you help me carry it inside so that I can store it safely until tomorrow?"

"Sure." Bill picked up the other end of the rolled canvas. "But I'm stumped about why you bought this big ol' tent."

She smiled at him. "Don't you know a restaurant when you see one?"

CHAPTER TWENTY-ONE

Twenty-seven prospectors came for stew. Thirty-one, for pie. Quinn sold sixteen servings before it was gone, leaving more than a dozen disappointed men. With pea-sized gold nuggets weighing down their pockets, most wandered off toward the saloon with a grumble.

At the end of the night, Bill took pencil to paper and calculated their pie earnings.

"Less the five you spent buying Isaac's tent, you come out with nine dollars." He grinned. "You want your earnings now?"

Quinn stood staring in disbelief. "Hold it for me, will you, Bill? I don't have a safe place to keep that money yet."

So emboldened, she decided on four pies for the next night, plus bread to accompany the stew, raising the cost of supper to two and a half dollars, and another dollar for a serving of pie.

"Still don't have a leaven," Bill reminded

her. "Can bread be made without it?"

"I'll try my hand at Poor Man's Bread," she told him. "Or that's what my mother used to call it when I was a child, God rest her soul. Father never allowed me to do anything that had the connotation of being poor, so it's been a long time since I've made it, but it needs no leavening."

With her apron untied, Quinn gently shook out its dusting of flour. Her first day was a success. She had earned money with her own hands!

Rain ended before Bill walked Quinn back to the boardinghouse, but the dark, drifting clouds, illuminated by the moonlight, suggested the storm was not over.

He escorted her through the raucous saloon, stopping when they reached the bottom of the stairs leading up to the private rooms. Laughter and shouting drowned out the faint sound of a fiddle, which played while dozens of men hollered and stomped in convoluted steps on a small space cleared for dancing. With only a few women in attendance at the day's celebration, the men danced together as partners. Of the two dancers, one man wore a red bandana tied around his upper arm indicating the other had drawn the right to lead the dance.

"Good night," Bill said to Quinn, but before either could continue, a miner, still wearing the dirt of the day, reached in front of Bill and grabbed Quinn's hand. He pulled her to him.

"I got me a girl!" the miner shouted.

Bill seized the man's wrist. "Let go, Jim. The lady isn't wantin' to dance tonight." He slid the man's hand off hers and nudged Quinn up the stairs, staying a step behind all the way to the top.

"Thank you," she said when they reached the upper landing where a sign hung: *No men allowed upstairs!* "I can make it safely to my room now." Her tired smile was genuine. "In spite of the mud and rain, I've enjoyed today."

"It was a good first day for us." When his eyes met hers, his voice softened. "See you again early tomorrow?"

She struggled to shift her green eyes from the striking blue of his, finally managing a nod. "Yes, early tomorrow." Her gaze focused on the floor until she had taken a few steps down the hall. When she glanced back, Bill was still there, eyes watchful.

"Good night," she softly said.

She reached her rented room, turned the doorknob, and pushed, letting herself inside. For a moment after closing the door, she leaned back against it with her eyes shut, reveling in her independence after a well-worked day. With her face turned upward, she said a silent prayer, thanking God for giving her the courage to make her own way. She had a future, and, although succeeding would not be easy, she had confidence for the first time in months.

When her eyes opened, she saw a neatly folded drying cloth, big enough to wrap herself in, and a palm-sized brick of lye soap on her bed. Quinn walked to the mirror hanging above the clothes dresser and looked at her reflection. Her face and hair were as dirty as they felt. Although it was late, she could not go to bed without washing. Nettie had not talked about a bathing room, but she knew it must be on the rooming floor. She stepped out into the hall holding her towel, soap, and sleeping gown just as another woman came hurrying down the hall, stopping at the door of the next room. Her shoulder-length dark hair was wet, and her nightwear was saturated collar to hemline. All but her back was drenched.

"Hello," Quinn greeted her. "Can you tell me where I can wash?"

"Last door. It's marked." Her glare scrutinized Quinn as she turned her room's doorknob. "Better hurry. That little brat won't have a job anymore when I find Nettie." The woman hurried inside and closed the door.

Without any understanding of the woman's remark, Quinn hastened her steps to the room marked *Bath* and knocked before opening the door. Inside was a brown-haired girl, down on her hands and knees, using a cloth to mop up water. Her dark dress was as wet as the floor.

"Hello, miss," the girl said as she glanced up at Quinn. "I didn't know anyone else was waitin'. I'll have your bath ready in a bit." Although her Scottish brogue was noticeable, the language of Westerners had softened it. "Just have a seat on me bench."

The room was small with just one window. Beneath it was a long and thin tin tub. Three buckets — two full and one empty — sat beside a wooden bench. Quinn made her way across the room. "Would you like to use my towel to dry yourself?" When the girl looked up, Quinn noticed old burns scarred her young face.

When their eyes met, the girl lowered her head. "It's all right, miss."

Quinn laid her towel on the bench, then returned to where the girl was drying the floor and knelt. "Let me help you." She unfolded another cloth and began cleaning.

When the floor was as dry as a wet wood floor could be, both stood. The girl took Quinn's wet cloth along with her own and went to the empty bucket. She twisted the cloths, wringing them dry over the pail, then set them aside.

"If you'll get in the tub, miss, I'll wet yer hair and wash it."

Quinn glanced at the tub, half full with gray water that had probably bathed half a dozen women already. She hesitated, then said, "I suppose carrying a dozen buckets of water upstairs for every bath would not be reasonable, would it?"

"No, miss." The girl shook her head, then motioned for Quinn to get into the tub.

"My name is Quinn, by the way," she said as she undressed and stepped into the soiled water.

After Quinn lowered herself into the tub, the girl set to work removing Quinn's hair combs and pins. "Now lay back so's I can wet yer hair afore soaping," the girl instructed. Her voice was soft, gentle. "Yours is red, like me maw's hair was. I wish mine was the color of your'n."

"Your brown hair is lovely," Quinn remarked, but the girl did not respond. "I'm sorry if it seemed I was staring earlier. Do you mind my asking how you were burned?"

"No miss, I don't mind. It happened when I was four. Me brathair and me were playing a game of pretend. He was an Indian tracker, and I was the Indian. Donnan had just smeared cooking fat on me face as war paint when I turned and ran from him. I tripped and fell into the fire Maw had lit to cook supper."

Quinn gave a quiet gasp. "You could have lost your life. You're a lucky girl, but I can't imagine how difficult your recovery must have been."

"That was ten years ago, miss. I don't think much about it no more," she said as she took a bucket and tipped it until water poured out, gently rinsing Quinn's long red hair. "Not unless some no good like the woman afore ye comes in here throwin' insults at me."

"Is that what happened? I was wondering . . ."

The girl stepped back from the tub and propped her hands on her hips. "You know what she says, miss? She says, 'Turn your head away — don't look at me — yer face makes me sick.' Then she says, 'Yer cheek looks like a smashed apple, all pushed up here and there.' So I throws half me bucket of water on her."

Quinn repressed a grin. "I might have

218

thrown the whole bucket."

The girl burst into a crooked smile and began vigorously drying Quinn's hair. "Me name is Catherine, miss. I'm glad ye came in tonight."

After she dried off, Quinn dressed in her sleeping gown, covering her hair with the damp towel. "Do I owe you anything?"

"Aye, miss. A bath is fifty cents."

"I'll be right back with your coin."

Quinn had just opened the bathing room door when Nettie pushed through with a glare for Catherine. "Ivy says you threw a bucket of water on her for no good reason!"

Eyes wide, Catherine stepped back. When she hesitated in answering, Quinn intervened. "I imagine it's difficult to rinse one's hair when you're ordered to look away while doing it, wouldn't you agree?"

Nettie's eyes shifted from Quinn to Catherine. "Is that what happened? It was an accident?"

With lowered eyes, the girl mumbled, "Aye, an accident, that's what it was, ma'am . . ."

"Well," Nettie said. "Don't let it happen again or you'll be needin' a new job. This is the third complaint this week!" She turned and left, closing the door behind her.

Catherine breathed a relieved sigh.

"Thank ye, miss. Nobody has ever stood up for me afore, and I never thought a lass so fine and bonnie as ye would give a care at all about the likes o' me."

Quinn smiled. She placed her hand softly on the girl's unblemished cheek. "You and me, Catherine, we're not so different."

Bill locked the store, then walked the worn path back to Mrs. Crawford's cabin. He found Blue sleeping in her arms as she gently rocked him.

In a whisper, Bill said, "He's too big to be rocked to sleep."

"It's just love, and no one is too big to be loved." Mrs. Crawford released her grip on the boy as Bill cradled him in his own arms. "I swear, this boy is the sweetest thing alive."

When she stood up from her chair, Bill kissed her cheek.

Blue slept soundly as Bill carried him back to their room above the store.

Moonlight illuminated the place as he laid his son on the bed, covering him with quilts. Quietly, Bill lit an oil lamp, which sat at the far side of a scarred wood table abutting the wall, and then sat to sort through papers he had left there near his pencil. Before he finished his list of needed supplies, he added mace and saleratus.

At the foot of his bed was an iron safe. It had been a prized possession belonging to his father, made especially for him by his old friend Thayer. It held a few important papers, money, keepsakes belonging to Bill's dead wife, and several pieces of his mother's jewelry. Most important of all were the memories. Bill used his key to open the safe, then put today's earnings inside with his journaling book. On top, he put Quinn's nine dollars. Before closing its door, he picked up the wedding ring once worn by the woman he loved. He slipped it onto the tip of his pinky finger, then rubbed his thumb over the back of its band, his eyes catching a glint of light from its tiny diamond. Would Katy be proud of the father he'd become, and the life he was building for Blue? He'd brought his family a long way from Georgia trying to find peace.

Bill slipped the ring off and returned it to its confines inside the safe, then glanced at his sack that held today's modest collection of gold and gold-bearing quartz. There was no need to stuff it inside the safe — it would be fine on the floor near the woodstove. Most prospectors had their own sacks tonight, and many were worth far more than his own.

Wearing nothing but his long johns, Bill

slipped into bed beside Blue. Thoughts of Katy invaded his slumber. Through closed eyes, he saw her face and flaxen hair, and the soft gentleness of her smile. Though the words never left her lips, he heard, "Wish, and it will be so."

Then his thoughts drifted to Quinn.

CHAPTER TWENTY-TWO

By mid-afternoon rain was falling again, but not before the ten-man tent had been set and staked. Although it wasn't ideal, the cleared land on the other side of the store — near the workroom, not the fire pit — was the only place for it. Using the tent as a makeshift restaurant had stirred almost as much excitement among the townsfolk as the Dancehouse.

When word got out, several men put down their gold pans and picked up hammers, nails, and saws to build tables and benches for the restaurant. To direct customers to the tent instead of the fire pit, one man carved the words *the stewpot* onto a broken board and then etched an arrow pointing the way. Quinn had taken one look at it and envisioned a real sign someday: THE STEWPOT RESTAURANT, Quinn Mac-Cann, Proprietress.

Tonight, the miners would eat supper in a

dry shelter, rather than huddling beneath tree limbs and lean-tos.

Quinn worked to keep her focus on her pies and bread, instead of letting her eyes wander to the activities of Bill Beaudry, so instead of depending on him to muscle the lidded iron skillets to the fire, she carried one around back to the fire pit herself. She set the pan on a riser to cook and then returned for the other pie. With both set, she scooped up red-hot embers with a shovel and laid them atop the iron lids, hoping for a crisp brown top crust.

From the fire pit, she looked at the ten-man tent, thirty yards away. Her restaurant. The jitters of being a businesswoman had her heart racing. There were so many things to do! *Focus on the food,* she reminded herself. *Tasty meals bring in paying customers, not just a dry place to eat.*

Fretting over her cooking skills, Quinn hurried back to the workroom. She started mixing flour, a little at a time, in a bowl with melted fat, and then added salted water. When the dough had a suitable consistency, she divided it into fist-size pieces and then rolled each into inch-high rounds the size of a flapjack and set them aside. When the pies came off the fire, her rounds of Poor Man's Bread would take their place.

Footfalls turned Quinn around to find her new partner entering the workroom. "We could certainly use an oven, Bill. Any chance of getting one?"

"Matter of fact, two Mexicans came by a few weeks ago and offered to build a clay oven called a *hornos* in exchange for provisions. I was low on supplies at the time and didn't need an oven that bad, so I told them no." He hesitated then said, "But I've given it more thought in the last day or so, and I think I can build one myself."

Though she had admitted her dearth of cooking abilities, she feared the whole truth about her limitations might halt her farce entirely. A cookstove was her best hope.

"I know nothing about cooking on such a thing. I'd rather have a nice cooking stove like the one my father had brought to Oregon. Surely, there must be ships with such supplies." She gave Bill a steady look. "Perhaps you can ask about a stove when you go again. How far is it to Sacramento City?"

"Two days, there and back. I close the store while I'm gone, so I lose two days' income each trip." Bill pointed to the rounds of bread she had laid out on the work counter. "Quinn, a *hornos* won't take much to build. I've already got most every-thing here, and that bread will cook up nice in one of those." His eyes came to rest on her lips, where a dusting of flour had settled. He stepped closer and gently wiped it clean.

When a tingle surged under his touch, she turned away. "Yes, well . . . I would prefer a stove."

Supper that night saw more than forty men chowing down on bread, stew, and pie in the comfort of a warm, dry tent.

Quinn collected supper payment from the diners, seated in shifts, then found herself proudly wandering amongst the miners as they ate, pouring coffee as needed. She paid little attention to the discussion between Bill and Blackjack about building a clay oven.

Solid ground, Quinn thought. *That's what I feel beneath my feet.*

"Pardon me, ma'am," a prospector said as Quinn refilled his coffee cup. "Do you think you could fry me a chicken sometime? I ain't had fried chicken since my mama died, and that's been near on four years."

Quinn smiled at the man's politeness. "I'll ask Bill," she promised him. "He's the one who owns the chickens."

The end of the evening brought the counting of money again. "Your half comes to thirty-nine dollars and fifty cents," Bill announced with a proud grin. "You've been here just a few days, and you're already making near forty dollars a night!"

It was far more than she had imagined, and the prideful feeling of being an honest-to-goodness businesswoman was growing.

Quinn returned to the boardinghouse, expecting to pull off her shoes and fall into bed, but as she neared her room, she heard the unmistakable sound of a woman crying. She opened the door, but without lighted lamps the room was too dark to make out anything more than a silhouette near the window.

"Nadine, why the tears?" she asked as she went to her bedside table, struck a match, and lit the oil lamp. Quinn turned the wick higher, its light brightening the room, only to find a plump, brunette, twentyish-girl gazing back through tear-flooded eyes. "Charlotte?"

"Libby," the girl answered.

"I'm sorry, I assumed . . ." Quinn stopped short of further explanation.

"I got the room this afternoon." The girl began to sob, wiping her tears with both hands.

"Why the tears?"

After a deep stuttered breath, Libby said, "Just feelin' sorry for myself." She wiped her eyes dry again, then placed a hand on her midsection. "Pa tossed me out when he learned I was with child. I was already burden enough, I guess, and he wasn't wantin' me with him no more."

"Where's your husband?"

"Ain't got one." Libby swiped her face one last time, then lit her own bedside lamp before reaching down and grasping the tie of a stuffed-full burlap sack. She heaved it up onto her bed, emptying out a bundle of crumpled clothes. Piece by piece, she shook out the wrinkles, then folded the garments. "That's why Pa don't want me no more. Ever since Ma died last spring, he says I been nothin' but trouble." She turned and faced Quinn as another sob broke free. "I didn't mean to be! One minute Ma was teaching me to cook and sew, and the next we was buryin' her. It was Clive who helped me get through the days after she died. Then one morning, out of the clear blue, Pa woke up with a sparkle in his eyes, shouting, 'Pack your clothes, girl, we're goin' to Californie!' I asked what in the world for? He said we was gonna get us some of that gold he kept hearin' about." She sat down on the edge of her bed, forlorn. "I tried to

228

talk him out of it, but he wouldn't listen to nobody. I didn't know I had Clive's baby in my belly when we left Saint Louis. I didn't know myself until we was halfway across Nebraska, and then I was too afraid to tell Pa. He figured it out on his own this morning."

"And he just threw you out?"

The girl nodded. "Pa used almost half the money we had left and rented me this room for ten days. He was spittin' mad about havin' to spend it, too."

"How old are you?" When another sob escaped the girl, Quinn rethought her tone. Softer, she explained. "Around here you'll either need to work or find a husband. In your . . . *condition,* finding a man to marry might prove difficult."

Libby snuffled up a sob and turned toward their shared chest of drawers without meeting Quinn's eyes. "I turned eighteen last month." She took her folded clothes to the dresser and filled the middle drawer with them.

Remembering Nettie's age rule, Quinn said, "Well, thank goodness for that. It gives you a few more employment options, at least."

Quinn undressed while Libby talked, cried, and talked some more. Listening, she

229

crawled into bed, exhausted by the day. When Nadine arrived, Libby told the whole story over again with Nadine hanging on her every word. By the time their conversation turned to love and Clive and Johnny, Quinn's eyelids were closing. She didn't fight it, for she did not want to be the one to tell them — if true love did exist, it was highly overrated. She dozed off wondering if she'd voiced her thoughts aloud to the two lovesick girls, or whether she had just silently recommitted her own heart to the steadfast belief that love was just a fairytale, made up entirely to entice women into satisfying the urges of men and bearing them children.

CHAPTER TWENTY-THREE

Hammers, saws, and the sound of men yelling *Gee!* and *Haw!* to their mules woke Quinn. Her roommates awoke soon after and padded their way to the window beside her to see what the commotion was.

"My heavens," Nadine stammered. "Where did all those folks and their wagons come from?" She pulled the curtains further back, and all three leaned closer to the glass windowpanes.

Quinn focused on the scene below. "Bill said a man named Keegan was on his way here with a caravan of wagons, but I had no idea he would be leading so many settlers."

Without more words, each woman dressed. Quinn wore her sepia-colored day dress, which was one of two still clean and mud free.

By the time she reached Beaudry's Supply Store, customers had overrun the place. She squeezed through the crowd of men to where Bill stood, then asked him, "What can I do to help?"

Flustered, he said, "I've got crates stacked under the front table. They're full of panning supplies. Can you pull 'em out and restock? There's so many people waitin' to pay, I can't get up there to do it, and everybody is asking for them."

"Of course." Quinn took his hammer off the counter, then hurried to the front of the store, where she pulled two crates from under the table. Soon she was stacking columns of pans atop the table and piling small knives and hatchets in any available space. When she heard men asking for more dried peaches and apples, pemmican, and almonds, she moved to restock the food supplies. It was almost noon before she realized supper had not been started, and, gauging by the last few days, stew usually took hours to prepare and cook.

"Bill," Quinn began, sidling up close to him as he stood at the counter taking payments. In a whisper, she said, "I need to start on my pies and bread. What about the stew?" When he stopped and dropped his hands to his sides with a distressed look, she knew he had forgotten all about it.

"It's too late in the day to start it now. I haven't even carved the meat," he said to her. "What am I going to do?"

The feeling of ineptness grabbed hold. With her sleeved forearm, Quinn dabbed beads of perspiration off her brow. If she were a *real* cook, she would have a ready remedy, but every idea she had fell flat until her own self-disappointment barked, *Stop thinking like a cook and think like a business- woman!* "I'll find something."

It didn't take her long to hurry back to the boardinghouse in search of Libby. She found her dressed in black, sitting on the front porch steps, her brown hair loosely bundled and her big blue eyes red from cry- ing. Quinn sat down on the steps beside the girl and asked, "Libby, are you feeling poorly today?"

With a turn of her head, Libby said, "Just brokenhearted, which I 'spect I'll be the rest of my days."

"Libby, dear, I know it's hard, and I don't mean to sound callous, but things are going to be different for you now, so you might as well get on with it."

"Get on with what?"

"Life," Quinn answered. "You have a babe depending on you."

Libby pressed a hand to her midsection.

"Getting your mind off your troubles may relieve a few of your worries, earn you some money, and help me at the same time." She touched her hand to the girl's forearm. "Would you like a job?"

"A job? For me?"

"Yes." Quinn nodded. "I need someone who knows about cooking, and last night you mentioned your mother taught you sewing and cookery. Do you cook?"

A glimmer of hope twinkled in Libby's eyes. "Yes, I can cook. Well, a little. I'll never be as good as my mama."

"No cook is ever as good as their mama." Quinn stood and reached for Libby's hand. "Come with me."

The distance between Medford's Saloon and Boardinghouse and Beaudry's Supply was only a half mile, but in that stretch, at least fifty newcomers crowded together to survey the town. Another fifty scoured the hillsides pitching canvas tents and felling trees for fast homes.

A gaggle of human chatter, mostly men, filled the air, but women and children mingled, too. The hullabaloo dwarfed the sounds of yesterday. Inquisitive folks stopped Quinn and Libby with their questions, but being newcomers themselves, they had few answers. The bustle was extraordinary for a previously undiscovered town.

Quinn and Libby skirted the street but

stayed their course toward the store, missing completely the confrontational approach of a male suitor until a hand clamped around Quinn's upper arm, yanking her back in mid-stride.

"You're a purty one!" A brown-haired miner, bathed and shaved but still wearing dirt-encrusted clothes, held tight to her as he pulled himself closer. "I got me a pocket full of gold and a hankerin' for a woman." His slurred words smelled of whiskey.

"Let go of me!" Quinn jerked, trying to free her arm.

The man's grip tightened. With a wayward slant of his head, he said, "I got me a place up yonder in the trees where you and me can go get friendly." His free hand dug into the pocket of his brown coat, and he pulled out a half-dozen gold nuggets, each the size of a robin's egg. He held them for her to see. "I can make you rich."

Quinn jerked again, freeing her arm from his grasp. She nudged Libby hard aside, urging her onward, but the miner cackled and blocked their way. "Didn't ya see them nuggets?"

A flare of Irish ire lit Quinn. She stepped toward the miner, not away. Faces close, she said, "I will not be bullied by you, nor any man." She grabbed hold of Libby's hand. Pulled her around the fellow, and marched forward.

"Hey!" the drunken miner shouted after her. "I'm not finished with you!"

Without turning, Quinn roared back, "Well, I'm quite finished with *you*!"

Hastily, Quinn and Libby made their way to the supply store. Instead of going inside through the front entrance, which was still over crowded, Quinn took Libby around back to the workroom entrance. Once inside, they closed the door, and both leaned back against it as if they might keep out the world.

After a brief respite, Quinn dismissed the drunkard's harassment as crass male behavior, then re-gathered her confidence. She explained to Libby her quandary of what to do now that noon had come and gone without even the beginnings of meal preparation. "Do you have any notion as to what we can make that will take less than three hours to prepare, cook, and serve?"

"Depends on the supplies," Libby said as her gaze inventoried the room. "And how many folks you're plannin' to feed."

"About thirty, I'd say. Although with this swarm of people in town, I can't be sure. But that's about how many we served last night."

When Libby's eyes spotted the topless, straw-filled crates under the work counter, she moved toward them, bending down for closer inspection. "Are these vegetables?" She turned to Quinn. "You have *fresh* vegetables?"

"Yes," Quinn said, missing the importance of the question.

Libby raked the straw aside, exposing the crate's contents. "Carrots, onions, turnips, parsnips, potatoes," she reported before straightening up into a stand. "We've been crossing the territory for so long now that I thought I'd never see another fresh vegetable. I am so sick of dried everything! What a sight to see."

"But can you do anything with them?" Quinn asked. "In time to serve supper, I mean?"

"Sure I can. Do you have meat?"

Quinn took her to the workroom window and pointed to the smokehouse. "Bill takes meat from it every day." Remembering her debacle of a meal with Doss, she added, "And a barrel of salt pork is in the store." Then she pointed to an old shed, which stood on the other side of the garden near Mrs. Crawford's cabin. "If our potatoes run low, the shanty is full of them."

"Land sakes!" Libby pressed her nose to

237

the windowpane. "You got chickens, and a garden, *and* a smokehouse?" When Quinn nodded, she said, "And you own the store, too?"

"Oh, no!" Quinn stepped back, shaking her head. "None of this is mine. Everything except the tent belongs to Bill Beaudry."

"He must surely be a rich man."

"Well, I don't know about that, but he seems to do well."

"You work for him?"

"Yes," Quinn said with a nod then, "Actually, what I meant to say is, we're partners in the restaurant." Maintaining her business-woman status was important.

Libby gave a nod. "I'm grateful to you for the job."

Before long, Libby had the back work-room of Beaudry's full of supper fixings and had meat cooking over the open fire outside. She peeled and diced potatoes, carrots, and onions, then tossed them together in a large wooden bowl. Quinn had no idea as to what she was making, but it looked and smelled heavenly, and Libby seemed well versed on how to handle herself in a kitchen.

Quinn had used the last of the fresh apples yesterday, so today she was using dried apples, but their soaking was taking longer than expected. While waiting for the apples

238

to soften, she said, "I'm going to check on Bill, to be sure everything is going well in the store. I'll be back in a bit." She untied her apron and laid it over a chair back.

Upon entering the store, she saw Bill seated on an empty keg at the counter with his journal open, writing in it. He had one leg of his tan and brown plaid wool pants hiked above his boot top to accommodate his propped foot. He paid no attention to the few remaining miners who stood talking at the box stove where a pot of coffee brewed. His store shelves and wooden bins were nearly empty.

Quinn went to the grimy front window and glanced out. Crowds of newcomers and old-timers dispersed over the hills in every direction, laden with their purchased provisions.

"Bill, there's virtually nothing left in the store."

Bewildered, he looked at her. "I know. I didn't expect this at all. *One* wagon train has nearly cleaned me out, and another is on the way." He stood. "I can tell you this — I was unprepared."

"What are you going to do?"

"I've got to go to Sacramento City for supplies." He adjusted his stance, then focused on the floor. "Do you think you might be able to operate the store *and* cook supper tomorrow night while I'm gone?" He looked up at her. "Mrs. Crawford will take care of Blue, and they can gather eggs and pull any vegetables you need from the garden, but the rest would be up to you."

"I don't know, Bill . . ." Quinn hesitated. "I wouldn't know how much anything in the store costs."

Bill picked up his journal. "It's all right here." He showed her the open pages. "I wrote it down for you, in case you were willing. I'd pay twenty dollars a day, and you'd get full profits off the supper."

A good businesswoman would not turn down such an opportunity. "I suppose I could try."

Bill gave a relieved sigh. "It'll be a big undertaking, so, if you have to, you can always close the store at sundown."

"Oh! I completely forgot to tell you . . . I've hired someone."

"Hired someone? Who?"

"Her name is Libby. From the smell of her cooking, I think she'll be a nice addition to the restaurant."

"Is that what I smell? I figured the new-comers were cooking up a big community meal. I was afraid they'd put our restaurant out of business."

"No," Quinn said with a smile. "That heavenly aroma is coming from us."

The ten-man tent was full to the brim with supper patrons, and more waited their turn. Many congratulated Bill on the restaurant's official opening, but most of all, the men were glad to see something served other than stew.

Quinn collected supper payment from the miners the minute they sat at an open table and then poured coffee into the tin cup left by the previous patron.

One after another, Libby dished up plates of beef hash topped with an egg, sunny-side up, and corn cakes, which she said were too thin without saleratus. "Those hungry men won't even notice."

The pies made with dried apples instead of fresh didn't get the same rave reviews, but they still sold out. Pies being the thing she did well, she asked Bill, "Do you think you can bring more fresh apples while they're still in season?" With a nod, he marked down her request.

As he did, the realization hit her: she was a real businesswoman, with one employee.

At sunup, Quinn readied herself for a full workday as Bill and his hired men drove off in two empty, high-sided ranch wagons. If the weather held and they didn't meet with any unfortunate circumstances, he would return late Saturday.

Wearing her green and tan plaid dress — the last clean dress she owned — she watched as Libby donned the same black dress she had worn for two days.

"Do you have other dresses?"

Libby looked down at herself, smoothing her skirting. "I have more, but most of 'em are fittin' tight now." She looked up at Quinn again. "Don't you like this dress? It's loose, and it hides my growin' belly. Besides, the color suits just how I'm feelin'."

Quinn could not think of a single good reason to suggest brighter wear. If one was feeling gloomy, the color of their dress was not going to change it.

Wholly unsure as to whether she could manage Beaudry's without Bill, Quinn felt good knowing Libby was with her.

As they headed down the boardinghouse stairs, Nettie called to Quinn. "It's the seventh day. I'll be needin' your room by evening."

"Am I not allowed a seventh night?"

Nettie's hands went to her hips. "The agreement said seven days. You have 'til sundown to move out." Then she turned

242

away, knocking on the door of a nearby room.

Libby turned to Quinn. "Can't you pay for more days?"

"It wouldn't matter. Nettie was quite clear about saying seven days for me, money or not. That's all I am allowed to stay."

"Why? She's in business to make money. Wouldn't she *want* you to stay?"

"Sometimes it's not about the money." Quinn started back toward her room. "Go on to the store and get a fire started. I'll be there in a little while."

After packing, Quinn gripped the handles of her two tapestry bags and left the board-inghouse, head held high, choosing to walk right down the middle of the only road in Fortune.

Beaudry's Supply Store was just steps away when she caught sight of Blackjack talking to a miner. Quinn veered toward them. "Excuse my interruption," she said to the men, then with her attention directed to Blackjack, she said, "Would you be able to stop by the store and help me with something today?"

"I'll he'p ya!" the scruffy miner blurted, stepping closer to Quinn.

Blackjack's arm jutted out, blocking the man. "I'd be happy to, Miss Quinn. What can I do for you?"

"I plan to buy a tent, but I'm not sure I can stake it alone. Would you have a few minutes to spare?"

"Another tent? What in the world do you need another tent for when you already got that big ol' ten-man tent?"

"This tent is not for the restaurant." She hesitated, then said, "I'm in need of housing."

He shook his head. "A lady like you shouldn't be livin' in a tent. Not even a new one. Why don't you just stay on at the boardinghouse?"

Blackjack had been the first friendly man to show her genuine kindness, and she didn't want to dismiss his suggestion without explanation, but she had no time to waste. She had not yet opened the store, which put her behind schedule, and with a glance, she saw impatience in the crowd gathered at its door.

"I don't mean to sound impolite," Quinn said, "but can you help me or not?"

"I said I'd he'p ya!" the sunbaked, unwashed old miner offered again. " 'Cept you don't need no housin'. You can just bed down in my tent free. I won't need much from a purty thing like you. Just a little now and ag'in."

"Oh, for heaven's sake!" Quinn turned on her heels and started for the store.

"Miss Quinn, wait . . ." Blackjack sprinted after her. By the time Quinn reached the back door and opened it, Blackjack was apologizing. "I'm glad to help — it's just that I'm not sure you're makin' the best decision."

Quinn set her two bags down, then walked through into the store with Blackjack in tow. "There," she said, pointing to the canvas tents for sale, each rolled and stuffed beneath a table stacked with candles, lamps, and oil. As she hurried to the front of the store, Blackjack heaved her new tent atop his shoulder and left through the back. After sliding off the locking bar across the front door, Quinn opened it. "Good morning," she said to the gathered men.

The store stayed busy throughout the day but not in the same overrun manner as the previous day. The store was nearly bare, and it seemed most newcomers had already purchased their needed provisions and returned to their wagons or home sites.

For the first time since arriving in Fortune, Quinn witnessed several fisticuffs, most of which were claim-jumping accusations, but one was over a girl, and another escalated into a fracas between a man and his heavy-fisted wife, who bloodied her husband's nose. Afterwards, the woman plucked coins from the man's pocket and huffed away.

Quinn stayed busy helping customers find needed provisions in the store and made notes about requested items, but she was especially careful about taking in the right amount of money. Many men left without their purchases when she refused their gold exchange.

"Bill's got a scale right back there!" a man shouted at her. "I always pay with gold!"

But Quinn had no idea how to calculate gold — did its worth change daily? She turned away every customer who tried to pay with nuggets or gold dust.

"I'm sorry, but Bill isn't here today. I am."

When the workroom door opened, Quinn turned to see Mrs. Crawford, dressed in a boot-length blue dress and garden bonnet, making her way toward her.

"Hello, Mrs. Crawford," Quinn greeted. "Is everything all right?"

"Fine," the woman answered. "I just came to see if *you're* all right." She held onto the counter with one hand as she talked. "Say, I like that Libby girl you hired. She reminds me of a friend I had back in the olden days. She's good with Blue, too. He doesn't distract her a bit."

"Yes, she's a lovely girl," Quinn agreed, "and a wonderful cook."

"She sure is, and she's indebted to you. Wants to do right by you. She said so."

Quinn couldn't remember a single person who ever gave a care about her, except perhaps her own mother. She smiled. "Is everything going well for supper? Did she say?"

Mrs. Crawford gave the counter a happy slap, then said, "Do you know what she's cooking up for tonight?"

"No," Quinn said honestly.

"She's mashing carrots and turnips together. Says it's one of her favorites. Never heard of such a thing!" Mrs. Crawford chuckled, then said, "But I'm game to try it. Oh, speaking of game, Buck Garvin came by this morning with two wild turkeys for Bill. Libby's got 'em both cleaned and seasoned, and she's almost ready to put them on the fire. Will you tell Bill, so he can credit Buck's account? I told him I'd do it, but I get more forgetful every day."

"Of course," Quinn promised.

Mrs. Crawford made her way back through the workroom as Blackjack sauntered in wearing a friendly grin. "I just come by to tell you that your tent is set and staked beside the cabin out back. Do you need anything else with Bill gone?" Before Quinn could answer, he picked up a half-pound bag of coffee and carried it with him to the counter. "And I was just wonderin' if you wanted me to show you how to weigh gold?"

Quinn's hands went to her hips as if glued there. "The men are complaining, aren't they?"

"Well," Blackjack said with a shy smile. "Yes, ma'am, they're a-grumblin' some. I thought I might be able to help."

"That's very nice of you." Quinn softened her tone, mostly from embarrassment for not knowing something evidently so simple. "I'm just not comfortable taking gold instead of coin."

"But gold is the same as coin, Miss Quinn. Fact is, most folks think it's better." He set down his bagged coffee on the counter, then said, "Look here, let me show you something real easy, then you decide." He pulled a hide pouch from his pocket, picked out a gold nugget, and laid it on Bill's scale, balancing it. "Now, this nugget is almost an ounce, so it's worth about fifteen dollars." He pushed his bag of coffee nearer to Quinn. "And this here coffee costs fifteen dollars, so taking this ounce of gold would be the same as takin' three half-eagles for it. You're still gettin' fifteen dollars, no matter how you look at it." He smiled again. "So, it's up to you now . . . you want to take this nugget for the price of this coffee or should I pay with coin? I'm happy to do whichever you decide."

Quinn nodded. With a pursed smile, she held out her open hand. "The nugget will be fine."

CHAPTER TWENTY-FOUR

Libby refused a summons into the dining tent for compliments, claiming the fire needed tending, but the intermittent redness of her eyes suggested a different reason.

"I've never heard such food flattery!" Quinn told her. "The roasted turkey and mashed turnips and carrots are all but gone. Although I regret serving the rice pudding cold — the men became demanding, which gave me no time to warm it."

Libby grinned. "It's meant to be served cold. It's better that way."

"Oh, then no wonder the men liked it so much." With a smile, Quinn took Libby by the shoulders. "You are the perfect cook! Won't Bill be surprised when he returns tomorrow to find us a success?"

"I counted servings — we filled forty-seven plates tonight." Libby's tone lacked energy.

"Forty-seven!" Quinn leaned against the

counter. "No wonder we're tired." Then she thought about all the disappointed men who walked away when the food ran out. "But we need to do more. No man should be turned away hungry."

"I've been thinkin' about that. Stew is what feeds the most people, so I thought maybe I should make a kettle of it for supper tomorrow."

"No!" Quinn stiffened. "We might be the first women lynched in Fortune if we serve stew to these men. It's all they've eaten for months."

Together, they rummaged through the near empty vegetable crates, then lifted the last flour sack, finding it only one-quarter full, and then peeked into the open bag of corn kernels, which sat ready for grinding into meal, only to find it crawling with grain beetles and maize weevils. With a gasp, Quinn dropped the top of the bag and backed away.

Curious, Libby reopened it and peeked inside. She raised her head with a grin. "It's all right. My mama always said a little extra protein never hurt anyone."

In spontaneous reflex, Quinn gave a shivering shake. With a hand to her heart, she said, "I'll leave that to you." She made a staunch turn toward the door. "None for me tonight."

Once inside the store, the two women split up inspecting the shelves.

When Libby came upon four twenty-five-pound bags of dried beans — two white and two red — she asked, "What about beans and bacon with more corn cake? And rice pudding again? I can rinse the beans and set them to soaking before I leave tonight."

"Soak the beans?"

"In salted water," Libby explained. At Quinn's blank stare, she added, "So they'll soften."

Quinn had no notion as to how to cook beans. Servants simply served them. She'd assumed it was the cooking itself that made them soft and edible. "Oh, yes, I see." Though she didn't. "Beans and bacon. Fine," she said. "When Bill returns with the supply wagons, we'll have more choices, and hopefully fresher product, but until then we'll just have to make do."

Early Saturday afternoon, two heavily laden wagons with Bill and his supplies aboard rolled into town. He drove the lead wagon, which he steered around back past the tent's opening. Nailed to the outside wall of his store was his black slate announcing *Beans and Bacon* as the nightly meal.

Libby briefly greeted Bill as he climbed down off the wagon, but her hurriedness to get to the cooking fire gave little time for pause. Just as quickly as she scurried away, Bill's son, Blue, darted out from Mrs. Crawford's cabin and leapt into his father's waiting arms.

"Did you bring me anything, Daddy?"

"You know I wouldn't forget about you." Bill hugged his son and then handed him a peppermint stick. "Put it away 'til after supper." He patted the boy's behind. "How did everything go around here? Did you earn your keep?"

"Uh-huh." Blue nodded, clutching his candy. "I earned my keep good. I pulled weeds and gathered eggs. Miss Quinn and Miss Libby cooked." Quizzical, he said, "But they didn't make stew, Daddy."

Bill was laughing when the back door opened and Quinn came out wearing an apron, now soiled from the work of several days. "I'm glad to see you back. Did things go well?"

"Better than planned." He stood with a proud grin. "Come take a look." Bill held his son's hand while they walked to the second wagon. They waited as the workmen pulled the canvas off the load, then Bill stepped up onto a wheel spoke, hoisted himself into a far-reaching stance, and grabbed hold of a rolling pin, holding it high. "I found one for you!"

Quinn attempted a grateful smile. "It's not the oven I wanted, but one thing at a time, I suppose."

While the men unloaded the wagon, Quinn showed Bill the tent Blackjack had staked for her on the far side of the little cabin. "Mrs. Crawford said it would be fine if I used a square of your land for my tent. Is it?"

"Yeah, sure, but why are you in a tent?"

When Quinn explained the need, Bill went into his store and came back with two woolen blankets and a lantern for her, then carried extra canvas to Mrs. Crawford's cabin. After a nod to Bill, the older woman threaded a sturdy needle and set to work sewing together canvas sections.

On his return, Bill explained, "She's been saving cornhusks for mattress stuffing. You'll be sleeping on one in no time."

Quinn had never slept on a cornhusk cushion, but the idea of sleeping on the hard ground another night without one sent an ache through her.

It took an hour for the hired men to unload

both wagons, and then another two hours to restock the store, only retaining the help of one man, Harve, who had handled the second wagon on the trip. The men replenished shelves, tables, floor space, the counter, and back room until the store was chock-full with supplies, mining tools, some dry goods, and a few specialty items. Of the new things, smoking pipes, umbrellas, castile soap, linseed oil, and playing cards would be sold, and, instead of purchasing cumbersome barrels filled with flour, salt, and sugar, they were now in cloth sacks, which made stacking easy. By the time the men finished, a line of fidgety miners had formed outside the tent restaurant.

At five o'clock, just as supper service began, the sign went up on the front of the Dancehouse. At six o'clock, Doss Parker opened for business.

Bill stood on the front porch of his store with a cup of hot coffee, his gaze scanning the growing town. With sundown came the lighting of oil lamps, whose glow seemed brightest at the far end of town where dancing and drinking ruled.

He stared at Doss's hastily built building, which stood where the only road in town ended. It was bare and dull with no design or embellishment, not even a porch or balcony. Its main floor was without windows, but its second floor had four, all facing frontward so that its occupants looked down the length of the main road, as if the street existed for the sole purpose of luring newcomers to the Dancehouse.

With his cup empty, Bill gathered Harve, and together they went to the food tent. Libby was cleaning up, but Quinn headed for them with two full plates. After their supper, she served dessert, explaining, "The rice pudding is supposed to be cold."

With a quiet, "Good night," Libby slipped out for her return to the boardinghouse, passing Blackjack on his way inside.

"Evenin'," he greeted the remaining three.

"Good to see you, friend," Bill said as he stood to shake hands. "No card game tonight?"

"No," Blackjack said, seating himself across from Bill and Harve. "No use competing with Doss. My usual players are over to his place tonight."

"Big turnout for the Dancehouse, is it?" Harve asked.

Blackjack shook his head. "Forty or fifty men were there, but Doss was grumblin'. He said liquor was the reason for the low turnout. His delivery wagon is late, and he's got just two girls, so far. Clarice and Rose, both from San Francisco, and then there's that sweet little Nadine who has no business bein' there. They're the only entertainment. Doss said his other dancers are comin' soon." Blackjack took the steaming cup of coffee Quinn handed him. "He's got a big to-do planned in a few weeks after everything's in place. Even got a stage performer comin' from San Francisco for the night. It'll be quite a goings-on for Fortune."

The four sat with a single lamp light in the tent restaurant. "Sacramento City is booming, too." Bill split his attention between Quinn and Blackjack. "The livery owner said there's more than five hundred buildings in the town now, and the place is growing every day. He said they even have a steamer running between Sacramento and San Francisco."

Quinn quieted, remembering her plan to sail from Stockton to San Francisco after Henry repaid his gambling losses. Nothing had gone as she'd meant. It seemed she had been destined to find Fortune.

"A steamer? Runnin' just between towns?" Blackjack asked.

"Yessir," Harve agreed. "Last spring, hardly nobody was here, and now people are thick as in New York. Ever'body is clamorin' for gold," he said before he fell silent. After a last sip of coffee, his voice softened. "Folks say the Feather has got more gold than the American. Maybe I'll pack up and head north tomorrow."

Bill set down his cup. "Fortune is just as good as any place up north. I think you should stay."

Harve shook his head. "Not for me, it ain't. Lately, I can't find a nugget any bigger than a nose hair, and living on one meal a day in a leaky tent without a woman for company . . ." His gaze jerked up, landing on Quinn. "Sorry, ma'am. No disrespect. It's just that a man gets awful lonely, and it ain't like I'm pluckin' a fortune out of the river to keep me here."

Quinn nodded her understanding as Bill said, "I thought you had a spot upriver that was paying off?"

"Did!" Harve straightened up so his lungs could release the bellow. "But I ain't got it no more. Got throwed off it by a bunch of boys bigger and younger than me. That's why I signed on with you for this supply run. A man needs coins in his pocket one way or another."

"Sorry, Harve," Bill said. "I didn't know."

With scrunched brow, Quinn asked, "How can they do that? Throw you off, I mean.

Don't you have a legal claim on your site?"

Harve shook his head. "The only rule anybody is followin' was laid down by a bunch of bullyin' buggers and thieves." He looked at Bill and said, "With you, Marshall, and Doss bein' the landowners and town founders, you three has got the rights to enforce a man's claim. Ain't no one gonna stay here workin' a plot of land if he's just gonna get throwed off soon as he hits pay dirt."

Quinn's focus settled on Bill. "That's the same as stealing!" But her bluster lay silent on the three men who seemed intent on studying the bottoms of their empty cups.

After a few moments, Harve, his voice deep with resolve, said, "Yessir, up north sounds purty good."

Bill rubbed his forehead. Folks were already packing up and moving on.

CHAPTER TWENTY-FIVE

In the darkness of night, with nothing but the sound of crickets, night birds, and drunken sots wandering the woods, Quinn settled down on her mattress in her new tent. She covered herself in woolen blankets and then tucked a butcher knife between her and the canvas sidewall. She had decided to bed down with the knife for the duration.

What felt like ages ago and hundreds of miles away, affluence had softened her beyond reason. Luxuries were routine, and — as long as no one put too much stock in love and family — the whole MacCann lifestyle had spurred envy. Her two-story Willamette Valley home, built by workers, was still one of the largest in Oregon Country. She'd had sufficient schooling, ample food, books, warm clothing and good shoes, and fine Boston-built furnishings.

She brushed her hand across the top of

her cornhusk and canvas mattress. Gratitude for the simpler things settled inside her.

A weary slumber pulled her eyelids closed, but when the moon was full, bright, and high in the night sky, the voice of a frightened girl woke her.

"Don't, please don't . . ." a bemoaning voice, young and familiar, pleaded, ending with a whimpering, "No."

Clad in a white-cotton sleeping gown, Quinn rose from the mattress and slipped her bare feet into boots, then draped a folded wool blanket across her shoulders. She struck a match and lit her lantern, but before she stepped out into the night, she grabbed the knife.

The cool air raised the scent of pine needles and damp earth, which cushioned her already light steps. In the distance, a band of coyotes yipped. Although the voices stopped, she ventured cautiously up the incline anyway. "Who's there?" she called, but no answer came. It wasn't until moonlight broke through the trees that she saw a man strong-arming a woman against a tree. His flattened hand covered the woman's mouth.

"Who's there, I ask?" When a muffled cry of *help* escaped, Quinn started for the tree. With so few women in town, the sweetness of the meek voice was undeniable. "Nadine? Is that you? Are you all right?"

A gruff male voice answered. "Mind your own damn business!"

Quinn raised the lantern, moving closer. "Who's there with you?"

"Go on now," the big man ordered as he muscled the woman face first into the thick-ridged tree bark. Her skirt back was bundled at her waist. When another whimper came, he said, "We're just havin' a little fun. Go on. Get outta here! My business needs doin', and it don't need no spectators."

Quinn's muscles tightened, sending a quiver through her legs. "It doesn't sound fun for the lady. I heard her say 'no' to you."

Less than ten feet from the two, she stopped, a tight grip on the knife. With it raised high for the fellow to see, she took another step, but a charging man whose face she never saw snatched the weapon from her.

The knife-wielding rescuer barreled into the big man, knocking him to the ground.

Quinn ran to the girl. Seeing Nadine's tear-streaked face, she wrapped her arms around her and hurried her away from the brawling men.

Rolling, grunting, growling — glints of silver flashed from both combatants.

Quinn shouted, "Help!" then, "Bill, *some-one!*" but when the door to Bill's upstairs room slammed open, all else fell silent except for Nadine's night-piercing scream.

The girl pushed free from Quinn and ran to her savior, who lay bloodied and deathly still. "Johnny!" she screamed. Sobbing, Nadine fell to her knees. "Oh God, not my Johnny."

Within moments, Quinn and Bill were at his side, but his heart had taken the fatal stab of a stag-handled knife. His tan-checkered shirt was blood soaked.

Nadine's gasping sobs became guttural screams.

Mrs. Crawford frantically called from her cabin, "Bill, are you all right?"

But Quinn's attention was riveted on Nadine, collapsed at the body of her beloved beau.

In the lantern light, Quinn eyed the young man's face for the first time. It was fresh and innocent, not dirt-ingrained or weathered like other prospectors.

Kneeling, Bill did a cursory check for signs of life, then stood and took Quinn's lantern with him to the other man. He held the light above the sprawled form for an identifying glimpse. "It's Bob Riddle." Bill leaned down and pulled a knife out of the man's throat, which had nearly decapitated him. He held it up by its dark-wood handle, inspecting it. "This is one of my knives. It's branded 'BB,' and, far as I know, I have the only set made." He stood up with the knife and walked to Quinn. "How did one of my knives get out here?"

Quinn stood and stared Bill Beaudry squarely in the eye. "Two men dead, a traumatized and violated girl, and you find it important to know the whereabouts of your knife?" She took a breath, then answered, "I had your knife. For my own protection. I never anticipated using it to defend another, but I heard the cries and came outside with it."

Bill bent and wiped the bloody blade on the grass. "Well, it's a murder weapon now."

"It was always a murder weapon, even before it was used as one."

Bill lowered his gaze, nodded, and then looked up at Quinn again. "Bob Riddle already killed two other men in fights since he got here in August. This is the third one."

"Then why was he free? Where's the law, Bill? Surely, there's a sheriff somewhere willing to come here!" Incensed at the lack of forethought, Quinn said, "This town is responsible for these deaths, and there is no excuse for allowing this kind of lawlessness."

Saloon patrons, bunched together like birds in a nest and reeking of whiskey, approached.

"What's goin' on, Bill?" one asked before their group chattering began. "Look, it's Bob." And, "Sure did it this time." Then, "Got hisself kilt."

"Boys," Bill called out. "There's no kin here for either of these men, so we might as well get a grave dug so they'll have a place to lie tonight." He walked to an enclosed lean-to, tall but thin, attached to Mrs. Crawford's cabin near the garden and opened it. Inside were his personal tools — shovels, pickaxes, and more. "Help yourself. I'll get some canvas to wrap the bodies."

Mrs. Crawford made her way toward Bill's voice. When she reached him, she laid her hands on his face, his head, his chest. "Are you all right, Bill?"

"I'm all right," he answered, "but we got bodies to bury."

Quinn comforted Nadine as the men set off for the town cemetery, each carrying a shovel or pick.

Sunrise on the plateaued hilltop left the hungover gravediggers sweating. Though a few townsfolk stood beside Quinn and Nadine at the fresh mounds of dirt, there was no preacher to call on God.

"If any of you has got words to say, go on and do it. It's been a long night," Bill said with bowed head, his eyes on his son, Blue.

"I'm no man of God," Marshall said. "But I'll do it." Holding his broad-brimmed soft felt hat waist high in his hands, he focused on the two graves, which were mounded a foot high with no more than three feet of dark, fertile ground between them. "Dear Lord," he began. "These men, Bob Riddle and Johnny Gant, met with fatal adversity in this life. This is hard country, and a man's good sense is easily lost. Don't hold it against them." After a moment, he said, "Dust to dust. Amen."

Nadine, eyes swollen red, said, "I got words for Johnny." Then the sweetness in her voice turned dark. "But I'll not talk over Bob Riddle, who I hope is already burnin' in Hell."

Bill nodded. "Understood. Go on and say your words."

Nadine knelt at the simple wooden cross marking Johnny's grave, brushing her fingertips over the knife-engraved letters of his name. "I-I never . . ." Her voice faltered. "Sorry," she whispered and started again. "I never gave much thought to the will of God 'til last night. I guess I thought He never paid any attention to me at all."

She broke into a sob, stilling the breath of those gathered until she regained composure. "I surely broke my mama and daddy's heart when I left home without a word to them. It was the first time I ever disobeyed them, but the calling that brought me to this gold country was as strong as any calling God gives to men. When I got here, I knew why — it was because my Johnny was here. My one and always true love." Tears came again, but she wiped them away. "My Johnny was honest and decent and good. I don't know what he saw in me." She glanced up at Marshall, her old boss. "I know I disappointed you, too, when I quit and went to work at the Dancehouse, but I didn't know what I was doing. I thought it would be the same as working for you at the saloon. I didn't know men were expectin' anything different. Nobody told me . . ."

Nadine looked at the others. "Except Johnny. He tried to tell me it wasn't the same." Her strength broke. "Johnny's dead because of me and my wrongs."

Quinn placed her hand on the girl's back. "Nadine, none of this is your fault."

"Yes, it is. I'm the reason God gave up on us."

In quietude, people dispersed, slowly

267

disappearing down the hillside. When Quinn was alone with Nadine, she turned her gaze to the surrounding land, giving the fifteen-year-old time to say her final goodbye to the boy she loved.

The season had turned most of the tall grasses from pale green to autumn gold, while the trees still held tight to the deep green of their leaves. The earthy scent of freshly dug soil infused the still air with life and hope, not death, as was its purpose today. Only a cloud or two marred the bluing sky.

After a time, Nadine rose off the ground and dusted her paisley skirt.

Quinn, without taking her eyes off the land, said, "Johnny has a lovely eternal view from up here. No place can possibly be as beautiful as California."

As if she hadn't heard Quinn's words, Nadine said, "See that spot?" She pointed to the narrow space between the two graves.

"Yes."

"That's mine. I'm thin enough to fit between the two of them. It's a fitting punishment to bury me beside Bob Riddle, so one foot rests in Hell with him for what I done to the only ones who loved me, but I can't bear not lyin' near my Johnny."

Dismayed by the young girl's thoughts of

death and dying, Quinn said, "You have a lot of years left. There's plenty of time before deciding on an eternal resting place."

Looking straight at Quinn with dour eyes, Nadine said, "You'll remember, won't you?"

"Yes, of course," she said in hopes of pacifying the girl. "I'll remember."

With her arm around Nadine's shoulder, the two started down the hill through amber oats and tufts of grass with long, needle-like awns. Below was the town of Fortune, tucked in amongst the trees at the lower-most flatland between two sloping hillsides. At the west end of the town's only road stood the Dancehouse — a dull, planed-board monstrosity.

"Have you considered going home?" Reflecting on her own difficulty in leaving Stockton, Quinn said, "The ranch wagon will be back soon. I could help you pay the fare."

When waterfowl in flight darkened the sky, Quinn turned her face skyward, missing the sullen glance Nadine cast back at the graves. "I won't ever leave Johnny."

Though Nadine had a room at the Dance-house as part of her wages, Quinn did not take her there. The boardinghouse was a better, safer place. When they arrived at Medford's, Monique hurried to Nadine, then whisked her up the stairs.

Although the burden of committing to another was not in her plans, kinship overtook Quinn. "I'll pay her room rent for seven days," she promised Nettie. Whether in sympathy for Nadine or blind trust of future payment, she couldn't be sure, but Nettie nodded before making her way up the stairs.

By the time Quinn returned to the store, Bill was busy with customers, so she went straight to the back room and tied on her apron. When she turned to retrieve her flour, Bill was standing silent in the doorway.

"I didn't hear you come in," she said, but his silence was heavy, and his blue eyes carried a burden. "Are you all right?"

"I've been giving thought to what you said earlier. I'm feeling responsible for that boy's death and for the attack on Nadine. Even though there isn't a town with a lawman within a hundred miles, I should have pursued finding one. If I had, Bob Riddle would be hung by now, and none of this would have happened."

"Having a lawman is overdue, but you are not the only man in Fortune who has decision-making abilities. There are others who should share the blame."

Bill studied her. "You could have gotten killed last night."

"I had no choice but to go out," she told him. "I could hear the girl. She was in trouble."

"Well, I'll take the notion of finding a sheriff more serious now."

"As you should. Fortune needs a jail, too. Perhaps if you build one, it will show the town you are serious about law and order." Quinn picked up the butchering knife that had killed Bob Riddle and washed it. "A man who has no fear of the devil often becomes him."

CHAPTER TWENTY-SIX

The rising sun painted the dawn pink, tinting its layered breaks in lavender and blue.

Quinn arose, shivering, thinking only of wool socks and hot coffee. She dressed and then made her way to Bill's firepit, where she set three split logs atop kindling before lighting it.

Of the four rough-cut tree stump stools, she walked to the one closest to the fire and then sat, warming her hands. The damp, sweet-scented pine popped and crackled, sending up smoke whorls. The coffeepot was inside the locked store, so she tried to take her mind off it, but her senses imagined the aroma of roasted and charred beans brewing.

Her thoughts were alone and far away, when Bill approached from behind.

"Mornin'," he said. "Brought you some coffee."

"Coffee?" Quinn raised up off the seat and

took the offered cup, sipping before sitting down again. "Thank you. I didn't know anyone else was awake at this hour."

"I'm an early riser. And it's really the only time of day I can have a peaceful minute." He sat on a stump beside her and sipped his coffee. "I smelled the fire and knew somebody was up."

Quinn smiled.

"I was wondering," Bill said with a sip of coffee. "Since Libby does most of the cooking now, do you think you and me might slip off for a picnic lunch? There's a little valley not more than twenty minutes east where a trout stream runs."

Picnics were not something she was accustomed to having. In fact, she had *never* been on a picnic. Those seemed to be reserved for close families and good friends.

At first, she stared blankly at Bill. "An outing?"

"Yeah," he answered.

"Together? Such as a *family* picnic with Mrs. Crawford and Blue?"

Bill chuckled. He lowered his head, but his eyes swung to hers in a soft glance. "No, I mean a private picnic — just you and me."

"To discuss business?"

"No. All we've done since you got here is work, and I feel like I barely know you."

It was true that except for the one unfortunate night with Doss Parker, there hadn't been much time to strengthen their business relationship. "I see," she said. Partners should have a good understanding of one another. "Yes, that would be fine."

"All right then. Good." Bill stood, empty cup in hand. "You talk to Libby about us being gone for a while today, and I'll tell Mrs. Crawford and Blue." With the matter settled, he walked back inside the store.

At noon, Bill put on a clean shirt, washed his face, combed his hair, and then hung a Be Back Soon sign on the front door of the store. A wooden crate held picnic supplies, which included smoked ham, cheese from Sacramento City, and two clusters of purple grapes picked from a wild, headstrong vine, twenty feet tall, that grew behind Mrs. Crawford's cabin. He set the packed box in the bed of his wagon, then tossed in a gray wool blanket, two willow poles, and a can of earthworms and grasshoppers that Blue had caught. When Bill went looking for Quinn, he found her out back shucking corn with Libby.

"Ready?" he asked her.

Quinn untied her apron, then asked Libby, "Are you sure you'll be all right with both of us gone?"

"I got enough to stay busy," Libby said, motioning Quinn along. Then looking at Bill, she said, "If you're plannin' to catch trout with those worms and grasshoppers Blue brought in, I'll need at least a half dozen to make it a worthwhile offering on the supper menu."

With a nod, Bill opened the door for Quinn, waiting while she whirled her shawl around her shoulders.

"You didn't mention anything about fishing." From the buckboard seat, she spotted two poles strung with strong thread and a hook in the wagon bed. "Bill, I've never fished, and I know nothing about catching trout."

"I'll teach you," he said with a grin.

The thought of sitting on a riverbank fishing for water-bound food sounded as ridiculous as digging in the dirt for gold, but being disagreeable was not her intent today.

Just as Bill described, twenty minutes east of Fortune the wagon crested a grassy hill, below which a line of trees traversed the valley, their roots clinging to the banks of a winding, rapidly moving stream. After spreading the gray blanket atop tufts of native grass, he walked Quinn to the river's edge. Beneath the surface, riffles whipped the current into whitecaps, then sent it downstream over partially buried rocks, splitting its flow at the boulders before sending it onward toward swirling eddies. Where seams converged, black-dotted trout bearing shades of golden green rested.

It wasn't long before a willow pole, from which an earthworm dangled, was in Quinn's hands. She held it straight out, the tip far from her, with a mild-mannered shake of her head. "I don't think this is a good idea. Wouldn't it be easier to buy fish in Sacramento?"

Bill chuckled as he hooked a worm onto his own willow. "Somebody's got to fish 'em out for folks to eat. Might as well be us. Besides, I like fishing. I carried these poles all the way from Georgia so Blue could learn angling the way my father taught me." He stepped nearer the water's edge. "Now," he instructed. "You're going to toss your hook into the stream like this." He cast his hook and line into a deep pool where the current slowed, then dropped. He gently yanked. "Go on, you try it now."

But when Quinn hurled her threaded hook out over the water, pole and all flew.

"That's all right," Bill said. He handed her his pole to hold, then waded in, retrieving hers from the water. He untangled its line, then handed the pole back to her. "Try again."

Giving it a high flick, her pole went sailing again, careening into the water where a faster current flowed.

Quickly, Bill sloshed out, grabbed the willow pole from the river's pull, and then returned to shore with it. This time he stepped behind Quinn, and, with his arms encircling her, he placed the pole in her hands, positioning her fingers around the willow. Gently, he moved the pole back and forth while she held it. "Feel the balance?"

But all she felt was his breath against her neck, warm, sultry, and dizzying. She forced a nod.

"All right," he said. Releasing the pole, he stepped off to the side. "Give it another try."

Quinn took a deep, calming breath. Then, with the hook in her sights, she swung the rod and released, sending the pole flying again. With a huff, she said, "What am I doing so wrong?"

"You've got to hold tighter to it." He waded out, grabbed it up, and started back. "Angle it so your line glides out over the water, but don't let go of the pole." When her next cast ended up with the hook and line wrapped around the lowest branch of a nearby tree, Bill conceded. "Maybe you're right." He took hold of her pole with a smile. "Fishing might not be for you."

Bill took both willows, and they walked back from the river. When they reached the wagon, he laid the poles inside, then grabbed the crate holding their food. He carried it to the blanket spread upon the grass.

Quinn pushed the shawl back over her shoulders, allowing it to hang behind her while she ate ham, an occasional grape, cheese, and crackers.

As they picnicked, Bill asked, "So, you don't like to cook, and you don't like to fish. What do you like to do?"

Will he laugh like so many others? She hesitated but then said, "I enjoy painting."

"Painting?"

"Yes. Art. Watercolors on vellum, or oil on canvas."

"Never known an artist before. Do you have anything I could look at?"

"No." She shook her head. "My supplies are gone. Left behind."

"Well, you should get more. Maybe you can ride into Sacramento City with me next time and order new supplies."

He didn't laugh.

"Perhaps so." More at ease, she said, "My mother painted, too. Lovely sunsets."

"How old were you when she passed?"

"Thirteen," Quinn said. "She caught typhus after our arrival in Oregon Country."

"I'm sorry." Bill put down his half-eaten roll of ham, then wiped his hands clean on his pant leg. He reached for her slender fingers, cradling them in his hand. "So your father was left to raise you when you needed a mother most of all."

Quinn bristled at the common assumption that girls only needed their mothers when they themselves were entering womanhood. "I suppose so, yes. Although I wouldn't call what Father did *raising* me. He actually had little to do with my upbringing."

Bill cocked his head. "Sometimes it's hard for fathers to show their feelings."

She rubbed her hands together, which sent cracker crumbs flying. "Father's feelings were clear. He resented Mother and me for following him to America. Frankly, he resented everything about us, or me, anyway."

She brushed more crumbs off her skirt. "As soon as he could, he sent me off to boarding school, which was the only kindness shown to me. I was never more than a burden to him." She put the remnants of their lunch back inside the carrying crate.

"I left home as soon as my schooling was complete."

"So, you came all the way from Oregon Country to California on your own?"

Why couldn't the past stay in the past, untold? She was finally making her own way, and she hated to be hobbled by memories and mistakes. "It must be two o'clock by now," she said as her eyes gauged the distance of the sun to the horizon. That's when she caught sight of a rider alongside a wagon.

The man stood in his stirrups and waved an arm back and forth in a wide swath, shouting, "Hello!"

When Bill raised an arm in acknowledgment, the man lowered himself into his saddle and galloped toward them. He rode a sorrel gelding without a mark or blemish, other than a small white star on its forehead. He dismounted, maintaining his hold on the lead. "Glad to come across you folks." His dark-blue pants, tan shirt, and hat had seen the dust of a lengthy trail, but he still appeared neatly kept. He reached for a handshake with Bill as Quinn's gaze shifted to the decrepit wagon that followed. Its bonnet, torn through the middle and barely mended according to the wind that lifted it, was a putrid brownish-yellow, and the left back wheel was cockeyed. When it came to a stop, its swarthy driver stayed seated, sipping from a canteen as the young rider talked. "We're lookin' for a town called Fortune, but I think we got bad directions."

"Well, what do you know," Bill said, cheerful. "We're from Fortune, and we'll be headed back in just a bit. Why don't you give your animals a good watering, then you can follow us?"

"Much appreciated." The young rider gave a wide grin and then a nod before he led his horse off to the stream. While his horse drank, the man filled his canteen, and then his hat, with water. At the wagon, he let the mules drink from his hat before returning for more.

"Funny how it all works out," Bill said as they stood repacking their picnicking items.

When out of eyeshot of the strangers, Quinn looked at Bill, noticing his blue eyes settled on her differently. She turned away, busying herself by putting the folded blanket into the wagon bed, but her beating heart was pounding out a warning — her defenses against the charms of this blond-haired man were about to fail.

With a gentle hand, Bill brushed the length of her arm.

A tingle coursed through her, settling in

the hollow of her belly. Quinn closed her eyes, hoping to refute the heated desire building inside her. She glanced up, searching his eyes. Had this same wondrous energy overtaken him as well? When he smiled, she said, "Bill, I . . ."

But without a word, his hand slid behind her neck, pulling her closer until his lips touched hers, lighting a flame deep inside. In delicate surrender, Quinn melted into his embrace, her lips pressing against his with an unfamiliar yearning.

After a moment, Bill pulled back, his gaze studying her green eyes, her rosy lips, and her red hair as it graced her face. Softly, he said, "I know I should apologize for the kiss, but a fire I never expected to feel again overtook me."

"Yes," Quinn said, her hand touching his cheek, restrained in its caress. "Well . . ." She pulled back, reining in her desire. A romantic relationship would compromise their partnership. "I suppose we should head back to Fortune." But they both lingered, searching for the unknown in each other's eyes until the young rider cleared his throat.

Bill stepped back, away from Quinn, to regain his lost composure. To the rider, he said, "I didn't catch your name."

"Clive," he announced as he patted his horse. "Clive Bennett. Me and Sketch come all the way from Saint Louis."

Quinn gasped. "Clive? Libby's Clive?"

The stocky, brown-haired rider faced Quinn as if the power of the Lord Almighty had her tongue. "Yes, ma'am," he uttered. "I been searchin' for Miss Lowell for months now. I almost give up finding her 'til a man we met yesterday told us about a fusty old coot in Jackson who was moanin' about dumpin' off his daughter named Libby in the town of Fortune. His description sounded a lot like Libby's pa. Do you know her?"

"Yes," Quinn said with a pleased smile. "Libby is our cook."

The trip to Fortune had Clive riding alongside them, chattering the whole way. Pointing back to the old driver on the rickety wagon, he said, "Riley Boles and me met a month ago on the trail, and we been travelin' together since. When I come upon him, he was in a bad way with a broken wheel. He's half crippled, and I couldn't just leave him out there all by hisself, so I did what I could to fix it, but it's unreliable." He chatted on. "He says he was a blacksmith back in Connecticut, but he got both legs broke and ain't been able to work 'em right since, so he give up blacksmithin' for gunsmithin'. He moved on to Saint Louis last year to learn riflesmithin' from some fellas named Hawken, but when gold was struck he got all-fired up about movin' west."

"Well," Bill announced, "Fortune is without a gunsmith, so he could do well if he's of a mind to stay."

"He'll stay. He's got no kin and don't wanna miss out on being part of the expansion. His last adventure, he calls it."

Quinn struggled to focus on Clive as he rode alongside their wagon, but more often than intended, her glances glided to Bill. Had they been alone today, would she have succumbed to her desires?

Clive rattled on with his chatter until the town of Fortune came into sight.

The afternoon clouds, so frequent of late, rolled in, turning the sky into one big savage bruise, warning it was ready for another good cry. As proof, by the time the foursome arrived around back of the store, flea-sized raindrops were falling. Without waiting for Riley Boles and his wagon to pull to a stop, Clive dismounted and then hurried to Quinn, helping her down from her wagon seat. With a nod toward the store, he asked, "Is that where Libby's at?"

"Yes, she's probably working in the back room." Quinn motioned toward the door, and Clive was off in a near run. When Quinn arrived inside a moment later, the two were already in an embrace, and Libby was crying, tears of joy by the sound of it.

"Thought I'd never find you," Clive told her. Holding her out at arm's length, he said, "I rode all this way to ask you to marry me, Libby Lowell."

She wiped her tears. "It's a good thing, 'cause I'm havin' your baby."

Clive's eyes dropped to her rounding belly. "You're havin' a baby?"

"We're havin' a baby. I wrote you a long letter tellin' you about it, and how I was crying every day just missin' you, but the mail just left with it."

Libby's eyes met Quinn's when Clive dropped to his knees. Bowing his head, he tenderly pressed his forehead against her expanded middle. "Thank you, God, for keepin' 'em safe for me 'til I could get here."

CHAPTER TWENTY-SEVEN

On the second Sunday in October, the passenger wagon returned, carrying a doctor, two lawyers, an aging preacher, and no women.

As the newcomers gathered outside Beaudry's Supply with Bill and Marshall, Quinn stared past them. She watched a man, thin and feeble, trudge uphill with the lead rope of an overburdened pack mule pulled tight over one shoulder. A heavy-bellied woman swayed atop the white-muzzled mule as the bearded stranger plodded to a stop.

With concern for the exhausted-looking woman, Quinn approached. "Hello."

The man nodded in response, then reached to help the woman down. Beneath her yellow bonnet, wisps of blonde hair strayed. Her face was pale, and her diminutive lips were dry and chapped. As her feet touched ground, the man patted the mule's withers, then slipped his arm around the woman. They approached the gathering of men.

"Sorry for the interruption, but I'm looking for Bill Beaudry."

"That's me," Bill answered with outstretched hand. As they shook, he asked, "What can I do for you?"

"Name's Greely Brown." He nodded to the woman beside him, whose bowed head never raised while she held one hand to her belly. "This is Martha, my wife. Three months 'fore, I accepted a call to the Methodist Church in Stockton, but our trip took too long. By the time we arrived, another pastor had taken up my parish duties. The good people of Stockton told me you were in need of a minister here in Fortune, so we have come in answer."

"Friend, you are too late," one of the newcomers interjected. "The town's proposition of building a church was extended to the minister who arrived first." The man reached out for a handshake. "I'm Reverend Albright."

The gaunt man's pleading eyes settled on the reverend. "We're not able to travel farther. We've come so far already." His voice had the ache of a beaten man. "It'll be winter soon . . ."

"Then you'd best be on your way," the

reverend told the late-arriving pastor. "They said one church."

Head down, Greely Brown nodded. Pulled his wife tighter to him.

Still several feet away in his approach, Doss called, "What's this gathering about?"

Bill's eyes settled on Doss's lower lip, which still bore a deep, half-circle scar. "Seems Fortune is suddenly popular."

With a nod, Marshall said, "Looks like our offer of a free building for professional folks worked after all." He pointed from one to the other, identifying the newcomers. "This is Dr. Weber. These two are Kent Hawley and Conny Steele, both attorneys at law, and that man over there is Reverend Albright. Pastor Brown and his wife, Martha, just got here." Marshall glanced at Bill before his eyes shifted back to Doss. "With the blacksmith, livery, and Bill's new butcher shop opened last week, all we're missing is a schoolmarm and a sheriff before we can call ourselves a real town!"

Although the Meat Market bore the Beaudry name, it was Clive who built and opened it in less than a week. When he realized Libby couldn't travel until after their babe was born — and after learning Bill planned to open a butcher shop as soon as the right man came along — Clive worked night and day for him until the shop was built and stocked.

Doss turned his attention to the new arrivals without any word of acknowledgment to Bill, Marshall, or Quinn. "I'm Doss Parker, owner and proprietor of the largest establishment in Fortune, and one of the town founders. The biggest infirmity of a new town is its inability to draw learned people, so imagine my surprise to find a whole passel of you here today." He pointed to the two lawyers. "I, myself, am in need of a competent attorney, so I can guarantee enough work for one of you, but not two. Here in Fortune, head-to-head merchant competition is discouraged." He glanced at Bill, and then Marshall. "Although I can't say I am in agreement with that rule, it is the rule nonetheless. Seems one of everything suits us fine."

Conny Steele, a balding, skeletal man with round eyes and an oddly thin nose, wore an oversized chocolate-brown suit coat and pants. He announced, "I have a multitude of experiences in drawing up mining claims and settling the disputes that invariably follow. And, being a gold hunter myself, I am drawn to this fine new community of Fortune to find, well, my own fortune. I intend to stay one way or another."

Doss faced the other attorney, a young, baby-faced man. "Kent, is it?" The sound of workers wielding hammers nearly overshadowed his words.

"Yes, sir, it is." The younger man took off his stone-gray hat and held it in his hands as he leaned in to make himself heard. "Kent Hawley is my name." He wore round spectacles and a suit with an almost indistinguishable plaid design in gold and brown.

Doss spoke up. "You look fresh out of law school. If I were you, I wouldn't bother to unpack. A wagon should be back in a week or so, unless you've a mind to buy yourself a ride out of here. The town of Muddy Horse will suit you better. A lot of young bucks, still wet behind the ears, have gone there to lay claim to their futures. You'd be better off to do the same."

The young man leaned closer. "You've not thought this through, Mr. Parker. Securing a man's rights through legal documentation should not be left in the hands of just one man. Fortune can use more than one lawyer, especially one like myself who is newly educated in a variety of legal documents. And, since it is commonplace for folks to oppose each other, two attorneys are necessary for any town."

Conny Steele grumbled. "Drafting and

enforcing mining claims does not require more than one legal mind," he said in defense of his newly granted position.

But Kent stayed his course. "What if I were to say that I am also a surveyor?" He reached down and opened his traveling trunk, which carried folded clothes on each side cushioning a wooden box squarely in its center. When he opened the box, it revealed a new brass compass, telescope, tripod, and level. "In case you have not heard, it is the right of our manifest destiny to mark this land as our own." Kent reclosed the trunk carrying his belongings. "Unless you have one already, this town will need a provisional plat to refute unjust claims. I am willing to share the office with Mr. Steele, if necessary."

Doss grinned, pleased with the negotiation. Then he turned to Bill and Marshall. "Looks like we got a need for two lawyers, after all." To Conny Steele and Kent Hawley, he clarified the town's position. "But only one building."

In spite of Steele's protest at sharing an office, Bill nodded, which prompted Doss to turn a deaf ear to the older attorney, focusing instead on the physician. "Finding a doctor so soon for a newborn town like

Fortune is a boon. You'll be next to the law office."

The men shook hands as a chain-rattling team of oxen approached, lumbering down the main road dragging logs toward the new hotel site. Their racket overtook the other sounds that came with building a town.

When Doss spoke to the remaining newcomers, he had to shout to be heard. "But we sure as hell don't need preachers, so you two can quit worrying about who gets the new church, 'cause there won't be one."

"Now, hold on, Doss," Bill interrupted. "Folks here want a church, and that offering was made months ago."

"Not by me, it wasn't. You and Marshall cooked that up." Though the oxen and their noise moved off down the road, Doss continued to shout. "All a preacher does is shame folks into not drinking or dancing, and I'll not have that kind of condemnation hanging over Fortune."

With the sound of a seasoned attorney, Kent Hawley asked, "Was the church offering in writing?"

Bill shifted, one foot to the other. "Yeah. I mean, I suppose so. Same as you. We put a notice in *The Placer Times* over in Sacramento City and sent out a few postings."

Kent looked to Reverend Albright and

Pastor Brown first but then directed his attention back to the three founding men. "I believe California is on the precipice of statehood, but as of now, the law of the territory seems to be whatever circumstances require it to be. Given this — as people of reason — I'm sure you'll agree that these men might have a legal claim against this town if the offering is not upheld."

Not disappointed by the news, Bill said, "So, that settles it. A church it is . . ." His words were cut short when Martha Brown collapsed, nearly taking her frail husband down with her.

Quinn hurried to the woman as Pastor Brown steadied his feet — his arms grappling to hold onto his wife — but his legs were too wobbly to lift her off the ground.

Bill and the doctor lifted the woman for Greely. "We need to get her to a bed," Dr. Weber said.

"Bill, what about using Mrs. Crawford's cabin?" Quinn asked.

"Sure, run ahead and tell her what has happened. We'll bring Mrs. Brown."

When Quinn started for the cabin behind the store, she saw Doss, seemingly unaffected by the woman's fainting. He was headed off in the direction of the Dancehouse.

With Mrs. Crawford holding open her cabin door, the men carried Martha Brown inside, laying her on the neatly made bed. Quinn covered her with a quilt from the waist down while Dr. Weber opened his black leather medical bag. He used a device — a wooden tubular stethoscope — to listen to her heart and lungs, then moved it to her rounded belly.

"What do you hear, Doc?" Greely asked quietly.

Dr. Weber glanced at the pastor. "It all sounds fine."

After a stir, Martha called out, "Greely?"

Her husband knelt and took hold of her hand. "Right here, Martha. I'm right here."

"You fainted," Dr. Weber told her. "How long has it been since you've eaten or rested?"

Instead of answering, Martha looked to her husband. Greely lowered his head, unwilling to face the doctor. "Too long," he admitted. "All I could think about was getting her here before birthing time. I was afraid she'd have the child on the trail with just me to care for her." The pastor looked up, his eyes scanning the room. "We lost two in birth already."

Quinn's hand went to her heart. "Still-born?"

Greely nodded. "Twins. 'Bout a year ago." Squeezing his wife's hand, he said, "I blame myself for not keeping her near another woman or a doctor. And for me not knowin' how to birth a baby."

Quinn said, "Well, you're here now."

"You look to be pretty far along, Mrs. Brown," Dr. Weber cut in. "I'd like to examine you, if you don't mind."

When her husband nodded, they all filed outside, leaving Martha alone with the doctor.

After a time, Dr. Weber came out and announced that he expected the baby to be born any day. "Can she stay here until after the birthing? She needs tending to — food, water, and rest."

Mrs. Crawford spoke up. "I'd be glad to share my cabin, or give it up to them since it only has one room. I suppose I could stay with Bill and Blue for a few days, but I'm ashamed to say, without sight, I don't climb stairs very well. In fact, stairs scare the dickens out of me. Is there another place for them?"

"I'd offer a room at the boardinghouse," Marshall said, "but Nettie don't allow men upstairs — husband or not."

"Won't do for Mrs. Crawford either," Bill said. "All boardinghouse rooms are on the top floor, so she would still have a long flight of stairs to climb."

"Is there no hotel in Fortune?" Pastor Brown asked. "Not that I have the money to pay for a room, but maybe I could do some work around the place in exchange for a night or two."

"No hotel yet, but we'll have one soon. Work just started on it today," Marshall answered. "It's gonna be a real nice two-story hotel."

"I could share my tent," Quinn offered.

"That's an idea," Bill said. Then to Quinn, "Not *your* tent, but I got one tent left in the store. I plan to get more on my next supply run. They've been selling faster than gold pans. I'll be glad to lend it out as temporary housing, as long as the rest of you don't object to not getting one for yourselves."

Dr. Weber nodded to the pastor. "This man's wife needs it more than any of us." When the rest agreed, he said, "I can make do with a lean-to for a few days."

"Good," Bill said. "We'll have the boys start building for you tomorrow. In a few days, you'll all have a roof over your heads."

Bill and Greely set up the pastor's tent behind the store, just a few yards from Quinn's tent, and, just as he had done for her, he outfitted them with two wool blankets and a lantern.

Quinn stole time away from the restaurant to help Mrs. Crawford make mattresses, one big and one small for the babe on the way. Without enough dry cornhusks, Blue helped cut long-stemmed amber grasses from the surrounding hills, bundled them, and carried them back for mattress stuffing.

On Saturday, October 20, 1849, Baby Brown, hollering at the top of his strong lungs, let everyone know he had arrived.

Soon after the birth, Quinn brought Martha Brown a bowl of vegetable soup. "Today is our first day to serve lunch. I thought you might be hungry." She set the bowl with its red broth aside as Martha lightly pulled back the blanket so Quinn could see her suckling baby. "He's beautiful," she told the new mother. "Are you pleased about him being a boy?"

"It wouldn't have mattered one way or another as long as we got a healthy baby." Martha cuddled the newborn. "God finally saw fit to bless us."

"Praise the Lord," Greely murmured from where he knelt near the tent's opening, looking out.

Quinn turned to the pastor. "Have you decided if you'll go on to another town when the baby is stronger?"

Greely continued to stare out through the open tent flap. "The Lord leads us where He needs us." Then with a glance back at his wife, he said, "We still got a little time afore winter sets in."

His eyes were hollow with worry, causing Quinn to shift her focus to Martha, whose gaze had settled softly on her husband, sharing his burden.

To distract from their unease, Quinn reached out and lightly brushed the infant's fingers. "Have you named him yet?"

Martha glanced at Quinn, then back to her husband. When their eyes met again, Greely stood, his head nearly grazing the sloped canvas top, and came to his wife. "I been thinking 'bout that, Martha. When I first laid eyes on this child, I felt the Holy Spirit, and, soon after, I thought I heard Granddaddy callin' to me." He knelt at her feet as she lay on the mattress. "What do you think of naming him Arthur Winfield Brown?"

A pleased smile came from Martha. "I like that name." She looked down at her baby. "Do you like it, too, little one? Arthur Winfield was your great-granddaddy, and his is a fine name for a boy." With a kiss for the newborn, she said to him, "I hope you'll be tall and strong and live a good long life like your great-granddaddy did."

On her way back to the restaurant, Quinn found Catherine Muir, the thirteen-year-old wash girl from the boardinghouse, waiting outside the restaurant tent.

"Catherine, hello! Are you coming in to eat?"

"No, miss," she said quietly. "I been released from the boardinghouse 'cause I can't holds me temper, so I've no money for food."

"Oh dear," Quinn said. "What will you do without a job?"

Catherine dropped her gaze, letting her long brown hair hide her scarred face. "I talked to Miss Libby, and she thinks kindly of ye." Her head popped up in apology. "As do I, miss! I didn't mean . . . Oh, me muddled up words gets me into such trouble."

"That's all right, Catherine. You're not in trouble. Not with me, anyway."

"Thank ye, miss." Her shoulders relaxed. "It's just that Miss Libby thought ye might be able to gives me some work. I have nowhere to go and no way to get there, so I might as well stay in Fortune, but no one's agreein' to hire me. Thirteen is too young, they're sayin', and there's not a thing I can do about fixin' me age. Not even that galoot Mr. Parker wants a thing to do with me. He says me scarred face is too ugly, and he don't want me scarin' away his customers."

"He has a few scars himself, Catherine, but unlike you, he earned his."

Contemplating job possibilities, Quinn looked around, scrutinizing work that needed doing. Mrs. Crawford and Blue were in the garden weeding and watering. Libby was hurrying back and forth between the workroom and the cooking fire. She knew Bill was inside tending the store. "I suppose you could help me serve meals and clean dishes."

"Oh, I can clean anything, miss!" Catherine blurted. Then her eyes and her voice both dropped. "But I wouldn't want to serve meals because . . . *because* of me face makin' folks sick, but I can clean dishes good." With an upward glance, she pointed to Quinn's food-stained apron. "I can wash clothes, too. I can wash anything, miss. Just so long as ye keeps me away from the customers so me unruly temp don't insults nobody."

Quinn stifled a laugh. "Of course, Catherine. Consider yourself hired."

Catherine bolted forward and squeezed

Quinn in a hug. "Ye won't be sorry, miss. I swear it on me maw's grave."

CHAPTER TWENTY-EIGHT

Bill Beaudry had pried a feeling of womanhood from Quinn. It came fast, furious, and barely controllable, which made it hard for her to maintain a reputable businesswoman's stature when he was near, but focus she must, because her business was booming, just like the gold rush. The restaurant expanded its service to three meals a day. Even though breakfast only offered a plate-size flapjack with sorghum or molasses, the tent filled to the brim daily.

With a full bucket of water, Quinn hurried through the door, sloshing only a little before setting the pail on the work counter.

"Quinn?" Bill called. He entered the workroom carrying an armload of Mexican blankets. "Look what I bought!"

At the sight of a dozen colorful folds, her eyes widened. "They're exquisite, Bill." She fingered the woven fabric of one. "Where did you get these?"

"Some fellas had half a wagon full, so I bought a few for the store."

Quinn unfolded a light-red blanket, outlined in darker red. "This one is lovely."

"I'll make it a gift to you." He leaned in and kissed her cheek.

"No, I'm earning money. I'll buy it. How much is it?"

Instead of answering, Bill set down the blankets and pulled her to him.

Far too aware of his scent, his touch, his warmth, her eyes closed, avoiding the attraction lest her heart melt completely, but at the sound of three-year-old Blue outside urging Rufus to fetch, his embrace released.

Quinn's strength of mind returned, bringing with it a wave of guilt. The longer she kept Henry and her marriage secret, the harder it would be to tell Bill. She fastened her gaze on a sunspot that was working its way across the floor. With posture steeled, she readied herself for raw honesty, but when her eyes found the radiant blue of his, the only thing she knew for certain was that today was not the day to reveal her truth to him.

Supper brought in more than fifty miners for roast beef, potatoes, and carrots, and the bread pudding sold out to the first twenty customers. Frankly, the restaurant had outgrown its ten-man tent, and it was too short-staffed for all the incoming orders. Libby slaved to meet demands, but cooking over an open fire had its limitations, especially with so many men to feed.

Quinn collected money, delivered plates of food, and cleared the tables afterwards, but it was nearly impossible for Catherine to wash and dry dishes fast enough for re-use during the same supper seating. The restaurant needed more workers — especially a woman to pour coffee, help serve, and clean up.

The next afternoon, Quinn went looking for Nadine. She was perfect for the job, and it would get her out of the Dancehouse.

Serious-faced card players occupied every table in Medford's Saloon and Boarding-house, so Quinn went unnoticed when she entered. Behind the pine bar, stacking whiskey glasses, she found Monique.

"Do you know if Nadine is upstairs in her room?" Quinn asked.

"She went out a while ago. Probably visiting Johnny again. I swear she lives up there at that cemetery." Monique turned to Marshall. "Oh, I almost forgot, Nadine said to tell you she borrowed something of yours."

"What was it?" he asked.

"I don't know, she just said to tell you."

Quinn left as a loud card game went awry, only to hear Marshall shout, "Where's my Colt?" Blood ran cold in her veins.

She hurried up the cemetery path beneath the afternoon sun, which surrendered its golden light to the hilltop as if life itself was focused there. Though she wasn't high enough up the trail to see the cemetery, the faint sound of sorrow-filled words drifted down to her.

Quinn's lips parted as she prepared to call out, when a gunshot sounded at the crest. She bolted up the incline, but at the plateau, her knees buckled.

Nadine's blue floral dress was blood-spattered, and her mouse-brown hair, loosened from its pins, lay saturated in a crimson so deep and dark it blackened the ground. Nearby was a thirty-one caliber Colt, its walnut grip in her open hand.

Quinn turned away, vomiting into the autumn grass.

Gunfire, whether from hunting, fighting, or the joys of a strike, was common, so the echo of the fatal shot drew no one to the hill for some time. Eventually, Bill came looking for Quinn.

"Holy God," he said when he saw the body. "What happened?"

Quinn pointed to the Colt, its bluish barrel glinting in the sunlight from where it lay. "She took Marshall's gun . . ."

"How long have you been here?"

"A while. I was moments too late."

"I'm sorry."

"So am I, Bill. Nadine had no one." When Quinn reached for his hand, he helped her to her feet. "A fifteen-year-old all alone, trying to deal with the death of her beloved. It was a bad decision to assume others would care for her. I should have accepted the responsibility myself."

"Fifteen?" Bill asked. "She had to be older. No one younger than eighteen works in the saloon. Marshall and Nettie's rule."

"She lied about her age."

Bill nodded. "I'll get the boys and some canvas."

Before the gravediggers broke ground on the far side of Johnny, Quinn stopped them. She had promised the girl a final resting place between the two men. Awkwardly, she stared at the ground while the diggers awaited her instruction.

"I'm sorry," she told them finally. "Go on with your digging."

Nadine might have thought she deserved one foot in hell with Bob Riddle, but Quinn did not.

The next morning, Quinn spotted Catherine under a lean-to made of pine boughs. The girl was emptying pebbles out of her boot that had worked their way inside through a hole in her worn-out sole.

Had she been living in the woods since leaving the boardinghouse? Quinn put down her basket of carrots, went to the lean-to, and took Catherine by the hand, helping her onto her feet. "You're moving in with me."

The two of them gathered blankets, a hairbrush, two dresses, a tin plate and drinking cup, and a bucket of homemade soaps. They carried all of it to Quinn's tent.

"One of these days we'll live in a proper home again," she told the thirteen-year-old.

"I never lived in a proper home, miss. We was always in a shanty or worse."

"Well, I'm growing tired of primitive living, so we're not going to do it much longer."

It was almost midnight before Quinn finished her restaurant duties. Dog-tired, she found Bill inside the store at his cashbox tallying the day's earnings, then recording them in his journal. When he saw her, he stopped, his gaze lingering.

"Long day," he said.

"Yes, and I don't see the day getting any shorter tomorrow." Quinn went to the stove and poured herself the last of the coffee, then sat on a nearby stool. "Would you like to share?" She held up the cup.

"Had more than enough. You go on ahead and enjoy the last of it." Bill came and sat beside her. "The restaurant did good today."

Quinn nodded. "Libby and Catherine are wonderful, but we've got to hire more help. The three of us simply can't go on doing this alone with so many customers."

"I know," Bill agreed. "But I've done my best to bring more women to Fortune. I was lucky to get you." He smiled at her. "What if you wrote to the ladies in Stockton? Let them know how well you're doing here. Even if you only convince one or two to come, it would be a big help."

"No," Quinn said with a shake of her head.

"Why not? It's worth a try."

Now would be the time, she thought, to tell him the whole horrid story. Her marriage. Henry's death. The accusation of food poisoning.

"Maybe you could invite them to the wedding," he said softly.

The words caught Quinn by surprise. Her

back straightened, then arched as her eyes searched his for an explanation. "Whose wedding?"

Bill reached for her hand and said, "Ours." He leaned closer, then gently kissed her. When he pulled away, his gaze was soft and adoring. "I'm head over heels in love with you. I want you to be my wife."

Without conscious effort, she withdrew her hand and stood. "Oh, Bill, no . . ."

"No?" Brow furrowed, he also stood. "You're in love with me, too, aren't you?"

Of course she loved him! He was the man of her dreams, when she dared to dream at all. "It has nothing to do with love. I won't tie you down in marriage. I can't." She started to pace, her eyes focused on the floor. "I'm not even sure love is real."

Bill's tone turned hard. "You're mistaken if you believe that, Quinn. I loved Blue's mother with my whole heart, and I never thought I'd feel that way again. But because of you, I do. It never occurred to me that you weren't feeling the same about me."

Quinn lowered her eyes, not wanting to acknowledge the barricade building between them. "No," she whispered, not to Bill, but to herself. Her eyes rose, meeting his. "The goodness you deserve is gone from me. Every life I touch, I ruin."

His reply was almost as low as her own. "These past few weeks must have meant *something* to you."

Her mind spun. This thing called love made men weak, and women weaker. It possessed them. Consumed their very being. A ruthless monster who stole even self-survival, forcing those in its grasp to believe a life other than their own was most important. Love could not be God's will, or it would not have such controlling influence. It was the devil's poison.

"Love is different things to different people, I suppose," she said, trying to reconcile her thoughts.

Bill stood back and regarded her. "Love is love. Maybe some just have more of it than others."

Weak kneed and yearning for his embrace, Quinn tried to look into his beautiful blue eyes for a sign that he would still feel the same about her after she said what she had to say, but she could not. Instead, she focused on the floor. She had to free him. "Love is just a word to describe the indulgence of desire. If I've misled you, I am sorry."

Bill turned. Tense, he walked straight to the front door and lowered its locking bar before snuffing out the oil lamp. His hardened steps carried him back past her with just a passing glance. At the counter, he closed his open cashbox. Brusque, he said, "Would you care if I fell off a high boulder and cracked open my head? Died right there?"

"Of course, I would care!"

"What would you do? Would you mourn me? Miss me? Would you shed a tear for me?"

"Yes! Yes, of course I would!" The timbre of her voice rose with the absurdity of the question. Then, more quietly, she admitted, "I would cry for days." She glanced at him, and her heart softened under its deep ache. "Maybe weeks. Maybe I'd never stop crying."

Bill took her in his arms. "That's love, Quinn. Not desire. I don't know what you were expecting, but that's its name. *Love.*"

Quinn could have stopped his kiss, but she needed him with every fiber of her being. She lifted her arms, caressing his neck and shoulders, leaving her breasts purposely defenseless. His hand slid closer, cupping her firmness as his manly arousal strengthened, until a relentless banging on the door jolted them from their intimate entanglement.

"We're closed!" Bill shouted to the intruder, but the hammering continued until he unbolted and opened the door.

"We're in need of a doctor. Do ya have any in town?" beseeched the man who stood there. Behind him, a woman knelt in the bed of an open, low-sided wagon with a young girl, holding onto her like a bear cub. "It's our son. He's been snake bit."

Without a moment wasted, Bill pushed past him out the door and ran for Doc Weber's office.

Quinn lit a lantern, then hurried out to the wagon. She leaned over the side panel and peered in. A boy, no older than ten, lay flat on his back shivering. His pant leg was torn to the knee where his mother clutched a cloth tightly twisted into a tourniquet. The boy's ankle was swollen, dark, and discolored. He was mumbling incoherently.

"I'll get a blanket." Quinn hung the lantern on a hook bolted to the back of the driver's seat, then hurried back into the store, returning with a gray wool covering. She handed it to the woman, who instructed her daughter to take it.

Worry paled the mother's face as she held tight to the tourniquet. "Unfold the blanket," she instructed. "Lay it over your brother." With her free hand, she helped cover the boy, then she looked at Quinn.

"Much obliged."

The woman's husband gave a nod to the boy. "Seth was worried about coyotes gettin' his pup while out doin' his business, so he went with him. I never should have let him go out like that after dark. The rattler got the pup first, then Seth."

When Bill returned with Dr. Weber, they both climbed the endgate into the back of the wagon. Bill held the tourniquet, relieving the boy's mother, as Doc set his black leather bag down beside him, focusing his attention on Seth.

Feeling inadequate to help further, Quinn moved back to the porch steps and turned her eyes skyward. Midnight brought a chill to the evening, lending a shimmer to the faintest of stars in the near moonless night. She recognized a few of the constellations, which she had learned while attending the Oregon Institute, but many she could not name. When the distant howl of coyotes brought a frightened whimper from Seth's little sister, Quinn went to the wagon and raised her arms in an offering to take the girl.

"Would you like to look at the stars with me while Mommy and Daddy are busy with Seth?"

When the girl nodded, Quinn lifted her

from the wagon. "My name is Quinn. What's yours?"

"Alice," said the flaxen-haired girl, softly.

"And how old are you, Alice?"

"Three." The girl held out her hand with her pinky finger curled beneath her thumb.

Quinn carried Alice several steps from the wagon, then stopped and pointed to the sky. "Do you see those seven stars? They're in a constellation called Ursa Major." Still pointing, she drew an arch in the air, following the bright points of light. "That's the Big Dipper."

Still focused on the sky, the girl quietly asked, "Is Seth gonna die, too?"

Quinn leaned her head against Alice's just as a star streaked across the sky. "Look there! Do you know what that means?" When the girl shook her head, Quinn said, "It means whatever you wish for will come true. Close your eyes. Make a wish."

After a moment, holding the girl high on her hip, Quinn returned to the wagon. "May I take Alice inside for some raisins?"

"That's nice of you, thank you," the girl's mother said with a nod and a look at Alice. "I'll come get you soon as I can." She turned her attention back to the doctor as he worked on Seth.

Quinn was filling a clean sardine tin with

raisins when the girl found Blue's toy top on the floor. She tried to make it spin as if she understood its workings, but it simply slid across the floor on its angled side.

"Here you go." Quinn handed her the raisins, then pulled a stool nearer the stove as the girl's mother came inside the store. "How's your son?"

"Doc says Seth needs to stay with him tonight. He thinks he'll be better by mornin'. I guess that rattler didn't have enough venom left to kill Seth after it killed the dog. Praise be . . . glory to God!"

Quinn pulled another stool to the stove for the woman while Alice sat cross-legged on the floor between them. The girl picked one raisin at a time out of the tin and ate it.

"Sure grateful for your help tonight, and for takin' care of Alice."

"Yes, of course. I'm Quinn, by the way."

"Liza Ward," the woman offered. "Edward is my husband. Seth and Alice are our only two young'uns still alive."

Without taking her eyes off her raisins, Alice said, "Gracie died."

"Gracie?"

"She was our baby. Died two months back."

"I'm sorry."

"We come out west from Nebraska.

315

Started building us a cabin yesterday, just a mile or two from here. Edward said it's where the good Lord told him to stop. I think he was wrong about that."

Edward peered inside, his eyes searching the dimly lit store for his wife. "Liza, get Alice and come on. We're movin' the wagon with Seth in it to Doc's place."

Liza grabbed hold of Alice and lifted her up as she rose. They headed for the door. "Much appreciated," Liza called back.

Quinn gathered the empty tin coffee cups from around the stove and carried them to the back room where Catherine's wash buckets stood ready for a new day. She rinsed and dried the cups, then turned them upside down on the wood plank counter for the night. She was yawning when Bill returned.

"You must be exhausted," he said as he put his arm around her. "I barred the front door again and blew out the last lamp. Come on. I'll walk you to your tent."

Except for the croaking of frogs and the call of a night bird, all was quiet. It was nearly one in the morning, and even the saloon and the Dancehouse at the other end of town were silent. Their short walk came to an end when Quinn reached to open the tent flap.

Bill caught her hand and held onto it. "I'm not going to rush you," he said. "But I'm also not going to lose you to some senseless notion that love isn't real. For now, if companionship is all you're offering, I'll take it." He gently lifted her chin and kissed her. "I trust you. I need you. *I love you.*" He turned and walked away.

Quinn watched as he climbed the stairs to the room above the store. When he reached the top, he quietly opened the door and disappeared inside.

With a sigh, she cast her eyes skyward, settling on the brightest star. "At what point in life do you know whether you are right or wrong?" she asked the heavens. Then she closed her eyes and listened to the silence.

Chapter Twenty-Nine

By November, Fortune swelled up and over the foothills, spilling down into the rifts with nearly four hundred canvas-topped houses, cabins, shanties, and lean-tos, facing every which direction.

Not so long ago, the air was scented with pine resin, pristine rivers, and healthy soil, but now the pervading odors were of horse and oxen manure, human sweat and filth, and smoke.

People dotted the land like foraging blackbirds gleaning insects, and civilization was no longer civil. Men stole, fought, and bullied or killed one another. It seemed a man a day needed doctoring or burying. A square of land held more value than a life.

The town rules were no better than rumors, so, on a trip to Sacramento City, Bill bought a hand press for penny prints, which he delivered to the town attorneys. By the following Friday, every business had an official notice nailed to its outside wall, and more were hammered to the trunks of trees, all within walking distance of the lawyers' office:

LEGAL NOTICE
HALT ALL BUILDING
IMMEDIATELY!

All persons are hereby notified that the Town of Fortune, California, has been surveyed and laid out by Attorney at Law and Land Surveyor Kent Hawley as directed by town founders Marshall Medford, Bill Beaudry, and Doss Parker. Designated lots are now for sale. If you have not legally purchased your land, you must do so within ten days or risk forcible removal. The Fortune plat is available for viewing at the lawyers' office.

Bill attended almost nightly meetings focused on how wide to make the streets, which direction the buildings should face, and what each lot should cost, as well as plans for future streets. He insisted the buildings on the north side of Main Street face south, the same direction as his store, because he wanted to build a home soon and intended to use the movement of sunlight and shadows as a means of telling time.

"Quinn, what do you think about letting similar businesses set up shop? A newcomer is wanting to open a pharmacy, but Doc has been supplying the need."

Although she had not been involved in any of the decision-making, Bill never failed to ask her opinion about agenda items.

"I don't know why my opinion matters. I am just one business owner."

"You're not just a business owner. You're my partner in the restaurant. You have a good head on your shoulders for trade and commerce, and I'd like to hear what you have to say."

Quinn wiped her hands clean on her laundered apron. "All right then, perhaps all business owners should be allowed to attend the meetings and voice their opinions on the decisions being made."

Bill lowered his head and chuckled. "Not sure the council wants to listen to anybody else. Folks don't have the same vision we do."

Her hands flew to her hips. "Then why ask my opinion? I shouldn't be treated differently than any other business owner. There should be equality among us, and all should have a right to be heard. Every business owner cares about the success of this town."

"All right." Bill stood. "If you feel that strongly, then you should come to the meeting with me and present your ideas."

Quinn stepped back with a shake of her head. "No. I'll not intentionally subject myself to the company of Doss Parker."

Bill cleared his throat. "I suppose I should just tell you outright. We've decided to visit the business owners to ask them to support the new establishments by attending grand openings. It's the civic-minded thing to do." He glanced at her. "That includes you."

Quinn's mouth dropped open. She gave an incredulous stare. "Do you honestly expect me to attend Cora McCready Night at the Dancehouse?" When he didn't answer, she shouted, "You can't be serious! You said yourself it's no more than a brothel."

"I know." Then he levelled his gaze at her. "But it also happens to be what's bringing men with pockets of gold to Fortune. Doss isn't the only one who's making money off these folks, Quinn. You are, too. They're eating meals at The Stewpot, buying supplies from the store, and some have already decided to stay permanently. Marshall swears his business is doing better than ever."

"As is the cemetery! A dozen men have been shot and killed this week fighting over a woman, liquor, or gold."

Bill slapped his hand down on the counter. "The Dancehouse only opened its doors a few weeks ago, and it's already made a big difference to this town. Maybe not all good, but not all bad either." He stared at her. "Men are coming from every camp around, and they're spending their money here, *with us.* That's what we wanted, wasn't it? A booming town with commerce?"

Clanging from the blacksmith's across the street frazzled Quinn. She clamped her hands over her ears, and, with a shake of her head, she exclaimed, "I can't believe you're expecting me to support the Dancehouse . . . *me,* of all people!"

"Quinn, this is business. It isn't personal."

"It may not be personal to you, but it is to me. Nadine is dead because of it, and don't forget about Doss Parker attacking me at his cabin."

"In fairness, you can't blame Doss for Nadine's death. She took her own life."

Quinn's unrelenting glare made Bill fidget. At last, she untied her apron and pulled it from around her waist. With it folded over her arm, she walked past him without so much as a word or glance in his direction. She left through the back door and headed for her tent.

Marshall and Nettie lived about a hundred yards behind the saloon and boardinghouse. From their front porch, workers could be seen adding final touches to the new two-story hotel, aptly named The Medford. Painted white, the hotel had a high porch — six steps up — with eight square columns that supported a matching balcony above. It was the only painted building in town, and the wet paint smell still permeated the air as its first overnight guests arrived.

Marshall greeted Bill at the door and directed him into the study for their meeting.

"On the way over tonight, I saw more folks I didn't recognize, standing in front of your office building reading the notices you posted," Bill told Kent Hawley and Conny Steele, who had arrived before him. "I know fewer and fewer people around here every day."

Conny puffed on his pipe in front of the crackling fire. "Fifteen arrived late this afternoon from a ship in the San Francisco harbor. Some came from as far away as

Germany and Belgium, but they're no different from the rest. Gold is all anybody wants."

Kent polished his spectacles with a cloth. "I saw some Chinese today, too."

"Nobody cares about foreigners." Doss walked in without a knock. "Let's get on with this meeting." He poured himself a whiskey from the decanter, then tipped back the glass, swallowing the amber liquid in one gulp. "Since I have the only worthwhile entertainment between here and San Francisco, the Dancehouse needs constant supervision. You boys have no idea how hard it is to keep sixteen beautiful dancers working instead of socializing for free."

The room — illuminated by two clear glass oil lamps — danced in shadow flames from the hearth fire. Each man took a seat in one of the upholstered chairs.

Smiling, Conny asked, "Doss, how's your grand soirée coming along?"

"Stop calling it a damn *soirée*!" Doss snapped. "Makes it sound like an upper-class affair, and there sure as hell isn't anybody here like that. Keep it up and you'll scare off my customers."

"Sorry." Conny folded his bony hands in his lap. "I was just wondering if you need help with anything?"

Doss nodded. "Me and Virgil are gonna check out things on the coast, and at first light I've got some of the boys riding out to post prints about Cora McCready Night in every camp for a hundred miles. It's being advertised in the *Placer Times* and *Daily Alta,* too." He stretched out his long legs and crossed them at the ankles, his pipe still clenched between his teeth as he looked around the room. "Mark my words — miners with pockets full of gold will swarm Fortune after hearing about Cora Mc-Cready. I watched men throw gold at her feet in San Francisco. Half that take will be mine." He set eyes on Conny Steele. "You're in charge while I'm gone."

"Sure, Doss."

Bill declined another whiskey when Marshall offered, then said, "I've got a bit of good news. Word arrived that Dan Gallagher is on his way here from Independence. He was a deputy there, but he's got gold fever. Wants to accept our offer to be sheriff. His father was a marshal, so he's experienced. I expect claim jumping won't be too much of a hardship for him."

"That is good news!" Conny raised his glass in a toast, but when Doss gave a disgruntled grumble, he lowered it.

Quinn's suggestion rumbled inside Bill.

"Any objection to having an open meeting once a month, so other business owners can discuss their thoughts about the town, too?"

"I like the idea," Marshall said with raised hand.

When Kent raised his hand in agreement, Conny Steele did, too.

But Doss shook his head. "This is our town. Who cares what they think?"

"I do." Bill raised his hand, passing the suggestion by a vote of four to one.

CHAPTER THIRTY

Fifteen miles south of the southern shore of San Francisco's bay, storm clouds broke away over Pueblo Valley — a plain surrounded by graceful, rolling hills watered by arroyos. In the aftermath of a downpour, indigenous grasses, wild oats, clover, and mustard grew hock-high, sometimes so tall their feathery tips grazed the underbelly of Doss Parker's red sorrel.

Near dusk, Doss and his hired hand Virgil rode into the muddy, rain-flooded town of San Jose.

In front of a partially built two-story building, Doss called to an acquaintance he recognized. "Señor Gomez!" The hunch-backed man was bent forward, struggling to pull his two-wheeled cart through the mud. In the waning daylight, its wet canvas covering, pulled back, revealed a cart filled with steeple-crowned sombreros and fiery-colored serapes. When the old man stopped and looked up, Doss said, "I'm looking for Josiah."

"Buenas tardes, señores," Gomez answered, his eyes shifting from one man to the other. "Señor Belden has gone to Monterey."

"What about Reed? Is he here?"

Gomez shook his head. "He's with Josiah."

Doss hesitated. "I heard this is the new capital. What are they doing back in Monterey?"

"Ask Señor MacCann." The man pointed at the building, then lurched with a heave, towing his cart onward through the mud and sludge.

MacCann?

"Ain't that the same name as Bill's cook?" Virgil asked.

"Yeah, it is." Doss dismounted, handing over his leather lead. "Stay here 'til I get back."

He went inside the building. Three men stood there having a discussion, all of them well clothed and trimmed.

Doss interrupted them. "Which of you is MacCann?"

The red-haired, green-eyed man glanced at him. "Who's asking?"

"Name's Doss Parker. Owner of the best

dance house in California."

"Is that so?" His gaze traveled Doss from head to foot. "In San Francisco?"

"Who's asking?" Doss countered.

MacCann's sharp glare softened. "Hugh MacCann." He offered his hand.

Doss stepped closer and shook it. "I came looking for Josiah or Reed, but I'm told they're in Monterey. Any truth to this being the new capital?"

"Yes," MacCann said. He waved a hand, indicating the building's interior. "But we're likely to have the first legislative meeting in an adobe hut at the rate this building is going up."

Doss glanced upward, then around the half-finished room with a nod. "Fortune's a three-day ride from here, but the legislature is welcome to meet at my Dancehouse. There'll be no shortage of space or comfort."

"Monterey is a day and a half. Why would we do that?"

Doss grinned. "Monterey — or San Jose, Vallejo, or San Francisco, for that matter — can't offer what I can. I guarantee the state's most important men will get the attention they deserve in Fortune. It's more than a gold town."

MacCann's steady gaze never dropped.

"Why haven't I heard of this nugget of a town until now? I'm a well-informed man, Mr. Parker."

"Fortune is just a few months old, but growing fast. We've already got a supply store, saloon, boardinghouse, even the makings of a restaurant." With cocked head, Doss said, "Matter of fact, the owner has the same name as you. MacCann. A woman named Quinn. Know her?"

Hugh MacCann's face hardened. "Quinn, you say? Owner of a restaurant?"

"That's right."

MacCann glanced out through the unfinished frame of a future window and pointed. "See that little adobe with the wild roses? I'm told it has a bar. May I buy you a drink, Mr. Parker?"

At an unadorned, rough wooden table in the corner of the noisy gambling den, Doss took stock of MacCann — a man of obvious wealth who commanded the room without a word. With just a flick of his fingers, two whiskeys were delivered.

"Señora," Hugh MacCann said, uplifting his full glass. "The bottle."

The fine-mannered woman spoke no English but seemed to understand. She returned right away with a bottle of whiskey and set it center table.

"Tell me," MacCann said to Doss. "Does this person with the same name as mine make money cooking?"

Smug about spurring interest, Doss restrained a grin. "I suspect so, but it's not her who cooks. She has women for that, but she seems to manage the place good enough to fill it every day."

"And what of her husband?"

Doss shook his head. "She's not married."

MacCann hesitated. Took a swig. "Henry is his name. Matheny. From Stockton."

Again, Doss shook his head. "No Matheny that I know of." At MacCann's creased brow, Doss said, "But you do know Quinn MacCann, don't you?"

"She's my daughter."

Doss leaned back in his chair. *His daughter!*

"You've not seen her with a man?"

"Sure I have, but what woman with such beauty wouldn't have a man? Beaudry isn't her husband, though. He owns the store, and he's a town founder, like me." Doss sipped his whiskey as MacCann poured himself a second, downing it in one gulp before pouring another.

"She had a husband in August. What do you suppose happened to him, Mr. Parker?"

Doss shrugged. "If it's important to you, I

331

can ride through Stockton on my way back to Fortune and ask around."

"Yes." MacCann nodded. "Why don't you do that — I'll make it worth your while."

At the hour mark, the whiskey bottle was empty, but Doss's curiosity was satisfied. He stood when MacCann did, the two shaking hands.

"It's agreed, then," MacCann said, donning his broad-brimmed hat. "A profitable venture for us both."

CHAPTER THIRTY-ONE

The morning was dry, almost warm for November, and the Sierra Nevada foothills were teeming with newcomers.

Squatters with cabins or shanties, or tents pitched on surveyed lots, lined up to legally buy them, and, though mining claims were not purchasable, squares of land — staked with notices posted — popped up all along the river. It seemed every prospector within Fortune's reach had one hundred square feet of land along the banks of the American River that he could rightfully call his own, as long as he worked it regularly.

Quinn thought nothing of the loud rumble and accompanying racket that moved down the main road. Even as the noise neared, growing louder, she kept rolling out pie dough without any curiosity whatsoever about the commotion.

Bill called, "Quinn?" from the front porch of the store. "Come on out here!"

"Must I?" she called back to him from the workroom. She had never made pumpkin pie before today and she was trying hard to follow the recipe exactly as recited to her by a traveling woman.

"You're going to want to see this!" Bill urged.

Quinn covered her dough with a damp cloth and started through the store toward the front only to have Blue dart past, shouting, "Look at all the wagons!"

"Oh, heavens," she moaned. "That's all we need. More wagons when I don't have enough tables, benches, or room to feed the people already here." But when she stepped out onto the porch with Bill and Blue, the line of wagons she saw were not the type she expected. There were no prairie schooners or farm wagons with bonnets — instead, she watched a dozen freight and delivery wagons roll down Main Street toward her. The lead wagon stopped short of Beaudry's Supply Store.

"What in the world?" Her voice was almost a whisper. "Bill, what is all this?"

He turned to her. "It's planed lumber. A lot of it. I bought out the mill. The rest of the wagons are loaded with furnishings and supplies."

"For what?" Quinn asked.

"We're building a restaurant. A real one. It'll have tables, chairs, and linen cloths. Dishes, too."

Quinn made her way to a porch post and steadied herself against it.

"Where should we unload?" The lead driver had a chaw of tobacco bulging under his bottom lip, and his broad-brimmed felt hat set far back, not shading his forehead at all.

Bill hopped off the porch and walked away with the man as curious townsfolk came to investigate the line of supply wagons. Quinn was still propped against the post when another driver walked toward her, asking, "Where do you want the rest of us to unload?"

With a glance, she said, "I haven't the faintest . . ."

"Over here!" Bill called. Pointing, he said, "Stack those furnishings inside the ten-man tent, and what doesn't fit, just set out back. We'll cover what's left with tarps until the building is raised."

Quinn's head jerked in Bill's direction. She called, "Where will supper be served if all this is stacked inside the tent?"

"It'll all be taken care of," he answered before turning back to the tobacco-chewing man.

Libby and Catherine appeared beside Quinn to watch deliverymen unload the furnishings.

"How long will it take before the restaurant is built?" Libby asked.

Quinn shrugged, her gaze wandering. "I'm not sure, this is all a surprise to me, but the hotel and the Dancehouse took no time at all. A week, perhaps?"

The men continued to unload the wagons. Piece by piece, things were carried into the tent through flaps tied open with rope, then set haphazardly. Eighteen dark wood tables and matching chairs came first and then a dry sink, a tall cupboard painted black, a bluish-gray pie safe with punched tin doors, stacks of linens, one crate marked *Tin Ware* and two others stamped *White Ironstone.*

Quinn grabbed hold of Libby's hand. "Ironstone dishware?" She focused her disbelieving stare on her cook.

Without meeting Quinn's eyes or replying, Libby raised her free arm and pointed. "Look," she whispered. "Is that what I think it is?"

Both wide-eyed women shouted in unison, "We have a stove!"

Four men unloaded a large cast-iron galley stove, nearly dropping it to the ground. After wiping his brow, the main man, who wore a sea cap, motioned to two others who promptly set down their crates and came to help. The six men, muscles bulging, lugged the big stove into the tent. Behind them was a seventh man who carried the stovepipe as if it were light as a feather.

When the men dispersed to their wagons, Quinn approached Bill and waited as he shook hands with the lead driver. After a word of thanks, the man climbed aboard the freight wagon, then turned with a wave to the drivers lined up behind him. When he received a "ready" signal from each of the other wagons, he slapped the reins of his own team, and their journey back to San Francisco started.

Quinn tightened her grip on her folded hands. "Bill, how much did all of this cost?"

"We got a good deal on most of it," he said, unaware of her angst. "It's from a Panama ship that docked two months ago in the San Francisco harbor. The crew abandoned her for gold country. When the sailors didn't come back, the captain started selling off what he had onboard, and that's how I got the galley stove. He sold his unclaimed cargo, too. Most of what we got here today was a shipment from the East for a French eatery called Truffi's. The owners never picked up their order, and they're nowhere to be found. I bought the whole untaken order from him."

"I'm glad it was affordable for you, but half this restaurant belongs to me, and you never asked me a thing about purchasing these items." She motioned to the lumber. "Nor did you say a word about immediate plans to build a permanent restaurant."

"With a separate kitchen."

"What?"

"A restaurant with a separate kitchen," Bill said again. "It's going to look exactly like I always thought it would."

"How will I repay you for all of this? I've made good money since the restaurant opened, but not enough to afford what you've purchased. How am I expected to reimburse you half the cost?"

Bill smiled. Gently, he brushed her cheek with his hand. "Don't worry. I told you I always planned to build a restaurant, re-member?"

Quinn suspected Bill was anticipating grateful acceptance, but instead she was angry and terrified. She straightened. Both hands went to her hips. "Which you couldn't do without me, as I recall. I told you from the start, I'll not take charity. You had no right to lay such indebtedness upon me."

The pride on his face fell. "I never said

you owed half."

"If we are equal partners, then there is no difference between half the profits and half the debt. Are we equal or not?"

"Of course, we are."

"Good," Quinn said. "Then there's something I need to take care of before this goes any further." She hiked her dress skirt ankle high and started off down the main road.

CHAPTER THIRTY-TWO

The Fortune law office was located halfway between Beaudry's Supply Store and Medford's Saloon and Boardinghouse. It had one long plank porch with a step-up and no overhang, two front windows, and two separate entrances. One door was marked *Conny Steele, Attorney at Law* and the other, *Kent Hawley, Attorney at Law and Land Surveyor.* Attached to the outside, between the two doors, was a large, white-painted display box for posting legal notices. Two newcomers, a man and woman, stood near it mumbling, their heads together.

Lightly, Quinn knocked on Kent's door and then opened it, peeking inside. "Hello?"

The young attorney, seated at a table with an open book, jumped to his feet when he saw her. "Miss MacCann, please come in."

From the doorway, she explained, "I am in need of an agreement."

"Yes," Kent said. He motioned her inside.

"I can draw up documents for most any purpose." When she still didn't move, the attorney gestured to a spindle-backed chair. "Please come in. What type of agreement do you need?"

When a glance behind showed no one she knew, Quinn stepped in and closed the door. She came over to the chair and sat. "Is our conversation confidential?"

"Of course," Kent assured her, straightening his brown waistcoat. "No one would talk to a lawyer otherwise." He laughed and pushed his wire-rimmed spectacles back up the bridge of his nose, then reseated himself.

The office had few furnishings. Beneath the front window was a table, which displayed surveying equipment, and behind his worktable desk stood a crudely built bookcase holding no more than twenty pristine-backed books.

Quinn placed her hands in her lap. "I am in need of a partnership agreement."

"All right." With pen in hand, Kent said, "Tell me about the partnership. I'll take notes today, and by tomorrow I'll have the document ready for signatures."

Quinn nodded, and then resettled herself to fortify her nerve and will.

"Now," Kent said. "Tell me about the parties."

"The parties?"

"The people," Kent clarified. "Who are the people involved in the partnership?"

Up until now, it had been comforting to know that no one had been privy to the details of her and Bill's private agreement, so the realization that she was now disclosing all of it — and putting it in black and white, no less — felt prickly and distasteful. Quinn likened this business burden to her father's daily transactions, and it sickened her to see herself as an image of him. A sourness rose in her throat, but she fought the urge to excuse herself. As a businesswoman, she needed to adapt to such circumstances, or settle for being a common domestic leading a life of wifely servitude.

"Bill Beaudry and myself," she announced.

"Bill?" Kent asked. "Does he know you're here proclaiming yourself his partner?"

Quinn rose from her chair. "Proclaiming myself? The restaurant is half mine."

He started to laugh, but her glare stopped him. Kent cleared his throat. "All right." He motioned for her to sit down again. "But before we begin, I'd like to be clear — you'll still owe for the preparation of this document whether or not it is signed by both parties."

How had she thought this pompous young attorney preferable to the pretentious Conny Steele? Perhaps the only elevated distinction Kent Hawley deserved was that he was not on Doss Parker's payroll. If she wanted an agreement drawn, her only choice was to hold her tongue and stay true to the business at hand. "I understand. Now may we get to the facts? I have a restaurant to run, Mr. Hawley."

When Kent had all the information, Quinn set out on her way back to the restaurant. She was so engrossed in thought, she did not see Blackjack hastening to catch her.

"Afternoon, Miss Quinn. What's your hurry?"

She stopped and whirled around. "I was beginning to think you didn't like our cooking. I haven't seen you in a week."

"Oh, that's not it, ma'am." Blackjack chuckled. "But I got somethin' to tell you."

"Good news, I hope?"

"Well, yes, I think so."

"Out with it," she teased. "I need to hear good news."

"I'd like to bring by my wife, Mabree, to meet you and Bill tonight. For supper, if that's all right."

"Your wife?" Quinn's tone caused Blackjack to chuckle again. "You didn't have one of those last week."

"No, Miss Quinn, I surely didn't. I met her in San Francisco and . . ."

"And you fell instantly in love."

"That's right," he said with a broad smile.

Quinn reached out and put her hand on Blackjack's arm. "Congratulations. I'd be delighted to meet Mabree. I'll save a special table for you at supper."

"Thank you, but we'll do just fine outside under the trees, as usual."

"Oh my," Quinn said with a quick glance toward the tent restaurant. "We'll *all* be outside under the trees tonight. Bill has stacked the tent full with new furnishings." She looked up at the billowing clouds. "I hope it won't rain." Then she turned back to him. "Bring your wife for a six o'clock supper. I'll be sure to save two pieces of pumpkin pie for you, although I have no idea whether it will be edible."

When Quinn returned, Bill was busy co-ordinating the delivery. He focused on the men as they moved the old restaurant tables and chairs outside, arranging them on the grass between her personal tent and the ten-man tent. Nearby, Baby Brown wailed, his newborn ears assailed by the sounds of their reorganization.

344

By evening, the restaurant was an outdoor eatery.

Quinn made her way to Libby as the evening crowd found its way back to the seating area. Two kettles of ham hocks and beans simmered. "I don't know how you do it, Libby, but I'm awfully glad you do." She was tying on her long white apron when Bill emerged alone from the big tent.

When his eyes found hers, he stopped, but Clive followed, engaging him in conversation. Although she could not hear their discussion, she knew Bill was pleased, because he nodded and then patted Clive on the back, which brought a grin to the young man's face.

She made her way through the gathering supper crowd. "Bill, can we talk while I have a few minutes?"

With a nod, he walked to the big tent's canvas sidewall before stopping to ask, "Where did you run off to this afternoon?"

"I went to see Kent Hawley. I've asked him to draw up a partnership agreement for us, so there will be no more misunderstandings. It should be ready to sign tomorrow."

Bill lowered his gaze. Nodded slowly. "All right."

She waited, but he said nothing else. "Don't you want to know what terms I've given him?"

His eyes met hers. "I already told you. I trust you. Whatever information you gave him is fine."

Quinn watched him as he walked away. Had she been rude? Ungrateful? She hadn't wanted to be any of those things, but a businesswoman needed backbone. Even when it meant standing up to a man in love.

As supper service began, Dan Gallagher — the man who promised to be sheriff — rode in on a dun horse the color of stone. Sunlight glinting off his badge gave away his identity to anyone willing to raise their eyes from their plate of food.

Bill greeted the man and took him to a quiet outer table before going straight to Libby to get the two of them a meal. They were still seated, talking together, when Blackjack arrived with Mabree.

She was tall, slender, and wore a blue dress dotted with tiny white flowers, its material thin and faded. Her dark skin had a black-satin shine, and her curly, close-cropped hair framed a blemish-free face.

When Quinn saw them, she went to the couple with a smile for the Negro woman. "You must be Mabree. Welcome to Fortune."

Mabree smiled but kept a tight hold on Blackjack's arm. "Thank you."

Quinn led them to a table. "Congratulations on your marriage. You're a courageous woman to brave these California wilds with a new husband. Did he tell you about the hardships of living in a gold mining town?"

"Yes," Mabree said with a smile meant only for Blackjack. "But wherever he chooses to go is where I'll go, too."

"Well, that's good for us, anyway. It's nice to have another woman here."

With the tables full, and hungry grumblings from customers beginning, Quinn excused herself, but she returned quickly with dishes of ham and beans, and two slices of pumpkin pie. "I'm sorry I don't have more time to talk, but men become unruly when their supper is delayed."

As Quinn turned away, Mabree stood. "Miss Quinn?"

"Yes?" she said as she turned back.

Mabree's hand crimped Blackjack's shoulder as he stayed seated. "In San Francisco, I served meals to the fishermen at the wharf. I was hoping . . ." She stopped and looked down at her new husband. "I mean, Jack says you might be hiring."

"Hiring?" Quinn repeated. "Servers?"

"Yes, ma'am."

Quinn came back a step and laid her hand on Mabree's shoulder. "Those are the sweetest words I've heard in weeks."

"Does that mean you'll hire me?"

"Hire you? I'll beg you to take the job! How soon can you start?"

Mabree smiled. "Will tomorrow be all right?"

"Six o'clock, right here, tomorrow morning." Quinn gave a pat to her shoulder, and then she smiled at Blackjack. "Now enjoy your meals. They're complimentary tonight."

Dan Gallagher kept his eyes on Quinn throughout supper service, much to Bill's annoyance. It seemed no matter the topic, the newcomer rarely let her out of his sight. Finally, in the midst of Bill's description of the office the town had begun to build, the man pointed to Quinn.

"Tell me about that redheaded beauty over there. Is she taken?"

Bill adjusted himself so that he, too, faced Quinn, following her every move as she served the restaurant patrons. *Is she taken?* Without any intent of being overheard, he mumbled, "I wish I knew."

"Well, I plan to ask her," Dan said.

"Ask her what?"

"If she's taken. She's a true beauty. What's her name?"

"Quinn MacCann," Bill said with no enthusiasm. He turned in his seat, facing the new sheriff. "This is her restaurant."

"She's a businesswoman?" Dan leaned back and crossed his arms tight across his chest. He grinned. "I'll bet she can do a lot more for a man than just cook his meals."

"Oh, she can't cook," Bill said before realizing his slip. "She's learning, though. The most important thing is that she's a good businesswoman."

"That wouldn't be the most important thing to me. I'd like to meet her."

Bill fought back his unease. He had no hold on her. She had made that clear. "Yeah, sure . . ." He stood and waved to Quinn, catching her attention. As she started toward his table, Bill quietly waited. When she got close enough to hear him, he said, "Someone would like to meet you."

The new sheriff stood.

"Hello," Quinn greeted him. His face, with a sheen like a china doll's, had low, arched brows, flat cheekbones, and rounded brown eyes.

"Dan Gallagher." He nodded in greeting. "I'm the new sheriff. Miss MacCann, is it?"

"Yes," she said, giving him a friendly

smile. "You're just what this town needs."

He fixed his eyes on her. "I sure hope so."

Quinn took measure of him. He was a dapper gentleman with his dark frock coat, smartly tailored and bearing extra decorative buttons at the wrist. It hung long over his waistcoat and high-collared white shirt. His smoky-brown hair, combed forward with a flip at the hairline, was long all around and raggedly cut as if self-trimmed with a dull knife.

With a glance at the waiting line of unfed patrons, Quinn said, "I should be getting back to my customers, Mr. Gallagher, but it was a pleasure to meet you."

He reached out and took her hand. "It's Dan, and I hope to see you again soon."

"Yes, well, if you're accustomed to eating, I expect you'll see me daily. We are the only eatery in Fortune." With a smile, she slipped her hand out of his and hurried off to the cook's station.

At ten o'clock the next morning, Kent Hawley came through the door of Beaudry's Supply Store holding several black-inked pages.

"Good morning." Kent greeted Bill, who sat on a stool behind the cash counter with an open journal. "Did Miss MacCann inform you that she asked for my legal services yesterday?"

"You mean about the partnership agreement? Yeah," Bill said. "You want me to go get her so we can get this thing signed?" He stood without waiting for an answer and started for the back room where Quinn was working.

When he opened the door, Quinn had her back to him. Bent forward, she inspected the daily vegetable baskets delivered by Mrs. Crawford and Blue. One by one, she separated carrots and parsnips. Blue often stripped off the leaves trying to pull them from the ground, which made it difficult for Mrs. Crawford to know which was which. Both were of similar shape and size and covered in dirt.

"Kent Hawley is here," Bill said.

Quinn straightened, then glanced at her dirt-covered hands. "I'll need to clean up," she said without making eye contact.

"Go on ahead and wash, then come on out here so we can get this paper signed."

When Bill left, she went to the vegetable wash bucket and dipped her hands in it. Using a sliver of bar soap, she scrubbed, but a line of dark soil seemed permanently wedged under her short fingernails. She dried her hands, swiped red stragglers off her brow, and then re-pinned her hair before she stepped through the doorway into the store.

Quinn walked to the cash-taking counter and stood side by side with Bill while Kent went over the specifics of the agreement. When he finished, he looked at the two of them. "If these are acceptable terms, you'll need to sign on the line above where your names are printed." He turned the papers so that the print faced them.

Bill pointed to the other pages held by the attorney. "What are those?"

Kent laid the papers on the wood counter for Bill to see. "I've made three copies — one for you, one for Miss MacCann, and one for myself. You'll sign all three, then I'll sign as preparer and witness." He held out the last paper, which was different. "This is a promissory note spelling out Miss Mac-Cann's repayment agreement for half the furnishings and half the building materials purchased for the new restaurant."

Bill took the paper and silently read it.

Quinn watched for any expression, but when she saw none, she said, "Twenty dollars a week until paid in full is all I can afford. Are those terms agreeable to you?"

Without a word, Bill nodded, then signed the first page before sliding it along the top of the wood counter to Quinn for her signature. He continued signing until all the pages had signatures.

While Kent signed, he said, "I'll place a legal notice for you in the *Daily Alta* and the *Placer Times.*"

"Why?" Quinn snapped. "Must you do that?"

"Yes, a notice must be made to inform the public of your partnership."

"In the newspapers?" she asked.

Kent nodded. "Yes, is that a problem?"

Bill stared at Quinn as she fidgeted.

Fumbling for an answer, she said, "I don't see the necessity. Why must everyone be told? What purpose does it serve for unknown persons to know our personal business?"

"It isn't *personal* business," Bill answered. "Folks have a right to know who they're doing business with, who owes them money, and who they owe money to."

"It's the way it's done," Kent added.

Quinn grabbed the papers from Kent and turned away from the two men. She held tight to the pages. Her father, Hugh Mac-Cann, and Henry's mother, Myra, would both know she was in Fortune, part owner of a restaurant.

Bill placed his hand on her shoulder.

"What has you so unsettled?"

She couldn't tell him, not with Kent Hawley present. This was something that deserved privacy. Yet she was the one who had forced the partnership agreement. She had created this situation. The chance of someone finding her was *her* problem, not Bill's.

"Yes, I understand." Quinn handed the papers back. "I apologize for misunderstanding. File whatever is needed." She brushed her sweaty palms downward on the skirt of her green plaid dress. "How much do I owe you?"

"We," Bill corrected. "How much do *we* owe you?" He looked at Quinn. "Everything is fifty-fifty now, remember?"

"Yes, of course."

As they settled with Kent, Quinn focused on her future. She officially owned a restaurant. It was co-owned, but its control was in her hands. If it was a success, she was the reason, and if it failed, she was the reason.

Quinn glanced at Bill as he shook hands with Kent. Somewhere inside him was an angel. He had given her a chance, treated her fairly, and he had befriended her when she had no friends. He loved her in spite of how unlovable she felt, and, even now, in this prickly business dealing, she was drawn to him like a miner to gold. Surrendering what was left of her heart would be so easy, but she couldn't bring herself to allow it. It was a tiny, tainted piece, barely recognizable as a heart at all. This man had given her his trust, his respect, his loyalty, and his heart, never knowing that the value of her love was not worth the weight of its burden.

CHAPTER THIRTY-THREE

The newly erected restaurant, officially christened *The Stewpot* by its black and white painted sign above the entrance, opened its doors in mid-November. Its construction was of planed boards, with wood floors and windows all around. There were no wall decorations or curtains, but no one except Quinn seemed to notice. Still, she worried things had been forgotten.

She wandered the empty dining room in preparation for her first meal service. Eighteen tables covered with white linens, and forty chairs, were the only furnishings. The back third of the building housed the kitchen, which had the galley stove, pie safe, dry sink, tall cupboard, and one long rectangular worktable with six chairs. The kitchen also had an open hearth big enough for vats of stew and soups to cook all day. She told herself it was enough, to stop fretting.

Behind the restaurant, out back near the

garden, was their new water well. As soon as it started to pull clear water, Catherine set up four empty whiskey barrels — two for clothes washing and two for dishwashing — beneath an attached lean-to near a workbench. Her scrub board hung on a sturdy nail, and a clothesline, strung tree to tree, was nearby.

When the hired hands finished building the restaurant, they had moved up the hill, where they started building another structure.

"Bill, why are the men building another place up the hill?"

"Didn't I tell you about that?" When Quinn shook her head, Bill said, "They're building a house for me and Blue with lumber left over from the restaurant and church. Nothing fancy, but Blue will get a room of his own. A boy shouldn't have to share a bed with his father."

"What do you plan to do with the room above the store?"

"I was hoping you'd take it. Move your things in," he said. "You shouldn't be living in a tent. You're a respected businesswoman, and you need a place of your own."

Quinn's thoughts settled on wood walls, a stove, and a window. "How much will you rent it for?"

"I wasn't planning to charge you for it. We're business partners, and whichever of us lives in that room above the store would be tasked with watching over things."

Quinn nodded. She liked that she would be serving a purpose by occupying the room. "I'll pay five dollars a month. A pittance, I understand, but with the added caretaker responsibility I feel it would be fair."

"It isn't necessary, Quinn," Bill said.

"It is to me."

After waiting for land to be cleared and labor to commence, the church and Reverend Albright finally stood ready for the town's first worship service.

Quinn arrived early to offer felicitations, but found herself in a long line of congregants. She pulled her tan flannel shawl snug around her shoulders during the wait and gazed about at the growing town and its newfound population.

Fortune now boasted two streets, the second being Church Street, so named for the new Episcopal Church. Beyond it, at the far end of the road, was Cemetery Hill.

The Medford Hotel supplied its leftover white paint, and two town founders, Marshall and Bill, donated a brass bell bought off an abandoned ship in the San Francisco harbor. Doss refused to chip in for the bell, but when parishioners threatened to boycott the Dancehouse, fearing women would not be drawn to Fortune without one, he offered to build a freestanding tower for the bell, promising it would be ready in time for the first sermon. As churchgoers arrived, Doss's men hurried to finish.

Prideful, Reverend Albright stood between the tower and the church door, greeting his flock, which included Quinn, Bill, Mrs. Crawford and Blue, Clive and Libby, Marshall and Nettie, the doctor, both lawyers, and Pastor Brown and his family. They talked together while a few miners filed inside, hats in hand. Mostly, families from passing wagon caravans filled the church. The small building, built for thirty, was full to the brim by the time Quinn spotted Edward, Liza, and Seth and Alice. Ten-year-old Seth still appeared pale and weakened from the snakebite, but he walked without hindrance.

As the workmen pounded the last nails into the tower, Bill shook Edward's hand, then knelt to introduce Blue to three-year-old Alice. "Told you other kids would come," he told Blue.

Although autumn's dazzling sunlit rays

delivered no heat this chilly morning, their intensity glinted off the bronze bell as it rose, tug by tug on its pulley rope, until it reached the top of the twelve-foot-tall, open-frame bell tower. Its jolting stop at the top gave a clang, sending two men scrambling up opposite sides of the ladder-like structure. One man stood below, holding tight to the pulley rope, while the two above tied the heavy bell to its crossbar. Their chattering stopped when Doss called up, "Don't make me a liar, boys! I said that bell would ring before service today."

"It's all right," the reverend told Doss. "We can ring it next Sunday." He motioned to the over-crowded church. "I should be getting inside for my sermon."

Doss shook his head. "I'm a man of my word." Then he tilted his face upward and yelled, "Ring that damn bell!"

Quinn angled her eyes skyward with the few who remained outside awaiting its first toll. *A splintery crack. A piercing glint.*

The collapsing tower sent the heavy bell plummeting, clanking and banging, until its final *clang, clang, clang* landed it with a *thwack!* On the ground beneath the fifty-eight-pound bell lay Reverend Albright, his skull bashed in.

Quinn's gasp turned into a scream.

There was no Sunday sermon, but instead a funeral attended by the largest gathering of God-fearing folks Fortune had ever seen. Pastor Greely Brown, who ended the short service with a quiet "Amen," gave Reverend Albright's eulogy.

Afterwards, Pastor Brown raised his bowed head, a creased look of bewilderment on his face. "The Lord surely does work in mysterious ways."

With so few possessions, it didn't take long for Greely to move the reverend's belongings out of the one-room parsonage built onto the back of the church and move in his own family.

The brass instrument, christened the "Albright bell," was moved to the cemetery. "Before burials," the pastor declared, "the bell will be thrice rung, forever acknowledging the reverence of its final three clangs before its fatal blow felled Fortune's first reverend."

This time, however, skilled builders built its new tower.

The following Sunday, Pastor Brown married Libby and Clive.

The tent vacated by the pastor and his family became their first home. It was convenient, considering it stood between

The Stewpot and Beaudry's Meat Market, but with the damp, colder weather, Libby caught a chill.

"You're stayin' in bed," Clive told his pregnant wife. "I don't care how many folks are expectin' supper."

"He's right," Quinn said after Clive's summons reached her and the doctor. "You need your rest."

Doc Weber listened to Libby's heart and lungs, the baby's heart, and then he checked her temperature. Afterwards, he prescribed fluids and bed rest. "She has a nasty cold," he said. "She's working a lot of hours, isn't she?"

A fluster came over Quinn. This wasn't *her* fault, was it? "Well, yes," she admitted. "She works daily from sunup to well past nine at night."

"Is she given any days of rest?"

Quinn shook her head. "No. She works every day, just like I do."

The doctor nodded. He stopped fiddling with his black bag and set his sights on Quinn. "But you're not with child. Libby is, and she's exhausted."

"Of course. I should have realized."

The doctor reached out and patted her hand. "Don't be too hard on yourself about it. She's young, strong, and healthy." Then he turned back to Libby. "Bed rest, doctor's orders. I'll check in on you again tomorrow."

When the two men stepped outside together, Quinn went to Libby's bedside.

Oblivious to her tangled mess of brown hair, Libby rubbed her pregnant belly, which rounded beneath the wool blanket. Her eyes settled on Quinn. "Who'll cook today?"

"I will."

"You?" Libby coughed, then sneezed. Nasally, she said, "Maybe Mabree can do the cooking."

"Fiddle-faddle. It's my restaurant. I've learned quite a lot about cooking since meeting you. Don't worry." Quinn patted Libby's hand. "Get some rest."

Mabree scooted aside on her way into the restaurant when four miners pushed through on their way out, all shaking their heads and grumbling. She was tying her apron strings when two more shoved past her.

When Clive stood up from a table with a plate of food, she hurried to him. "What's all them men grumblin' about this morning?"

"You gotta do somethin'." He held the

plate out for Mabree to see. "Libby's sick in bed, so Quinn is cookin', but her flapjacks are stiff as a planed board." Brows scrunched, Clive said, "Tastes a bit like wood, too."

Mabree dismissed all of his words, except the ones she considered important. "Is Miss Libby doing all right with the baby? Do I need to go get the doctor for her?"

Clive shook his head. "She just caught a chill, but if she hears folks grumblin' about the food, she'll get up out of that bed and come try to cook for 'em."

"Yes," Mabree said. "I see." She took Clive's plate. "I'll do what I can."

When breakfast patrons filed into the store next door asking for refunds, Bill argued, "It can't be that bad!" But when a man tossed his flapjack onto the counter and it landed with a *thud,* Bill refunded his dollar.

Throughout the day, when she wasn't serving, Mabree stayed close to Quinn. "I can fix us some nice corn cake, pork, and greens from the garden if you'd like, Miss Quinn."

"What a splendid idea! Corn cake seems simple enough."

The restaurant was full by the time Quinn thought to check the doneness of her corn cake. When she pulled it from the stove, it was firm and hard to loosen from the iron skillet. No matter how carefully she lifted a serving from the pan, it ended up in crumbles on the plate. Without a substitution, she topped the yellow heap with a ball of butter and served it alongside slices of fried salt pork.

Mabree served the meals without a discouraging word, but when a diner stood and spit his mouthful of food onto the floor as Bill walked in, she hurried back to his table.

"How much salt is in this hoecake?" the diner shouted.

"Too much salt, Freddie?" Bill asked on his way to the table.

The rail-thin man wiped his mouth on his shirtsleeve. "What the hell's goin' on, Bill? You got this nice new restaurant that's been serving dandy food up 'til today."

"Now, Freddie," Bill said. "Everybody has a bad day now and then. You want a refund?"

"Hell yeah, I want a refund! It can't be et!"

At that, other patrons laid down their forks and came forward asking for a refund, too.

"Every one of them?" Quinn asked when Bill told her.

"Yep," he said. "Not one dime earned here today."

Inadequacy soured inside her. She owned a restaurant, yet her cooking wasn't worthy of sating a malnourished miner. Whether goaded by embarrassment, or nudged by the desire to be a respected businesswoman, she wasn't sure, but she turned to Bill, and said, "Well, that won't do, will it?" She slid her hands behind her back and untied the apron, then she draped it over her forearm. "I intend to fix the problem."

Cooking duties fell to Mabree, who filled the menu with à la mode beef, stewed brisket of beef, roast turkey, duck, and venison — succulent aromas that drew miners to the restaurant same as gold drew them to the river.

Quinn helped with kitchen duties, collected money, and served meals, but her thoughts were never farther away than she needed them to be. *A businesswoman can run a successful restaurant without knowing how to cook.* Her intellect knew it to be true, but her heart ached at her shortfall.

"Would you be willing to share your crumb cake recipe with me?" Quinn asked Mabree. Of the dishes she attempted, none but her pies and bread pudding were worthy of serving. She could do better — she was sure of it!

"Crumb cake must be taught, Miss Quinn. Experience is the teacher. If you'll allow it, I would be pleased to show you."

Quinn agreed.

Throughout the week, Mabree spent time teaching Quinn to make crumb cake, sponge cake, tapioca, and sweet potato pie. Already armed with the ability to make apple pies, pumpkin pies, and bread pudding, Quinn ended the week armed with a newfound proficiency.

Saturday breakfast had concluded by the time Libby arrived at the kitchen, still an hour before the noon lunch.

"Libby, you're here!" Quinn headed to her with a *welcome back* smile. "It's nice to see you up and about." She placed her hand on Libby's pregnant belly. "You'll be glad to know that when time comes for the baby, Mabree has agreed to take over the kitchen again." She hesitated, then said, "I hadn't thought to ask. Do you plan to return to work afterwards?"

Libby's eyes went wide. "Yes, I need this job." She cast a look down at her belly. "Since it's our first baby, I thought I might bring her to work with me. I promise bein' her mama won't get in the way of me bein' your cook."

"Her?" Quinn smiled.

Libby grinned. "Well, I dream about it being a girl, but a boy would be fine, too."

"Of course, you can bring her with you anytime. Do you feel up to peeling potatoes?" Quinn held out a paring knife but turned toward the dining room when a commotion broke out. "Stay here, Libby."

She pushed open the dining-room door to find an unknown man rebuking Mabree, whom he had backed against a wall. "Here now!" Quinn shouted, hastening her pace toward the fuss. "What's the complaint?"

The rotund man, clearly an unskilled prospector by the mud-to-his-knees wool suit he wore, pointed his dirt-encrusted finger at Mabree. "I ain't givin' no dollar to a Negro!"

"She works for me. She is simply doing her job by collecting money for your meal."

The man backed off, dug in his pocket for a Liberty gold dollar, and handed it to Quinn. "Take it," he said. "Then bring me a meal." Agitated, he jerked out a chair in the otherwise empty restaurant and sat.

"Lunch isn't ready," Quinn told him. "It won't be for at least another thirty minutes."

"I'll wait," he told her. "Bring me some coffee." Before Quinn could respond, he waved a pointed finger at her and said, "But *you* bring it to me." His glare turned to Mabree. "I ain't takin' nothin' from a runaway slave woman."

Quinn tensed. "Mabree is a free woman. Not a slave."

Anger brought the man to his feet, his bulbous belly tipping over the table and knocking Mabree to the ground. "Ain't no such thing as a free Negro!"

At the sight of Mabree on the floor beneath the toppled table, Quinn leapt at the man in fury, the tip of her paring knife dimpling his double chin. "Get out of my restaurant!"

The man's hands shot up in surrender as he stepped back again, and again. "I'm goin' . . . I'm goin'," he rattled in a higher pitch than before. After another backward step, he said, "What about my dollar?"

Quinn tossed the gold coin onto the floor at his feet. With his eyes steady on her, he bent to pick it up. As he straightened with coin in hand, she stepped toward him, the knife still clenched in her fist, but the feel of Mabree's hand on her forearm stopped her.

"Let it go, Miss Quinn," Mabree said. "Let it go."

The man straightened, then kept backing away until he was through the door and gone.

Mabree took hold of Quinn's hand. She was lightly unfurling Quinn's fingers from around the knife when Bill charged through the kitchen door with Libby in tow.

"I heard shouting," Bill said, huffing out a breath. "Libby said there's a man . . ." He scanned the empty room. "I came quick as I could. Is everything all right?" When his eyes settled on the knife Quinn held, he said, "Are you hurt?"

"She's not hurt, Mr. Bill," Mabree said when Quinn didn't answer. Then, "Miss Quinn, you got to let go the knife now."

Quinn's eyelids fluttered. She took a breath and then turned to Mabree. "He shouldn't have spoken to you that way . . ."

"It's all right, Miss Quinn," Mabree told her. "Now let go the knife."

"It's not all right." Slowly, Quinn unclenched her fingers.

Mabree took the knife and handed it to Bill, then she held Quinn's hands. When their eyes locked, she said, "Somebody is always goin' to be offended by the color of my skin. You can't go pullin' a knife on every one of them." Mabree gave Quinn's hands a loving squeeze. "But I want to thank you for comin' to my aid."

Mabree stepped back, giving space to Bill. He pulled Quinn to him. "I'm glad you're all right. Did you know the man?"

The moment his arms were around her, Quinn's inner shield crumbled. "No, I didn't know him." She leaned into Bill, her head resting against his chest, then a kiss pressed through the soft strands of her hair.

Behind his tenderness was safety — a shelter against brutality without isolation.

Between them was *love.*

CHAPTER THIRTY-FOUR

With a flannel shawl pulled tight around her shoulders, Quinn knocked on the pine-scented door of Bill's new house, but the hammering inside overshadowed her arrival. When no one greeted her, she pushed the door ajar and peeked in. On the other side of the room was Bill, dressed in dark trousers and a gray shirt — his back to the door, unaware. She watched as he put down his hammer, picked up his rifle, and then situated it on the new wall mount.

"May I come in?" she called. "I've brought fresh bread."

"Bread?" Bill craned his neck to see her, then smiled and motioned her inside.

After kissing her cheek, he raised the warm loaf to his nose, inhaling its scent. "*Mmmm . . .* You've gotten better at bread."

"The galley stove makes baking easier." Averting her eyes from him was the surest way to keep her thoughts ladylike, so she spun around and walked to the fireplace, pretending to inspect the stonework. "The men did a lovely job, didn't they?" Her hand grazed the well-set stones. Beneath her feet, covering the plank floor in front of the fireplace, was a circular braided rug that Mrs. Crawford had made using strips cut from empty flour sacks.

Bill walked to her and studied the hearth. "It looks nice, but we haven't tested it with a fire yet. We'll light the first one tonight and see if the smoke goes up and out." He smiled, then said, "Take a look at the rest of the house."

The fireplace was in the main room, which also had two windows covered with sackcloth curtains, a table and four chairs, a bench, and a rocking chair.

When Quinn turned around, she saw two open alcoves divided by a wall. The left nook was a kitchen equipped with a black cast-iron stove — much smaller than her galley stove — a dry sink, and an olive-green cupboard. The right side held a new log bed, as yet unmade, but it was the items stashed on the floor that made her gasp.

"Bill, what is this?" She pointed.

"It's a gift for you." He smiled. "I was going to save it for your birthday, but I realized I don't know when that is. The man I bought them from said it's everything you'd need to start painting again — a canvas and easel, paper, paints, brushes. Was he right?"

She threw her arms around Bill and kissed him deeply. Tears came without sadness — a thing she never knew was possible.

When she pulled away, he said, "If I'd known I'd get this reaction, I would have given them to you a week ago."

Quinn laughed and then went to the art supplies. She knelt and opened a japanned box holding sixteen watercolors, six tin tubes of oil paint, and brushes. "I can hardly believe this . . ." She looked back at him over her shoulder. "Though I can't imagine finding time to paint — I will."

"Good. It would sure spruce up the place if we had some nice pictures in here. Maybe you could do some for us?"

"Yes." She stood. "Yes, of course I can. Thank you, Bill."

The raised bed frame cradled a straw mattress, atop which were two folded quilts, a gray blanket, and pillows. Beneath the mattress, directly on the wood frame, was the familiar blue-lined cloth of a feather tick.

The scent of him and his bed started her heart pounding. She forced herself to focus on practicalities rather than her heated desire. She pointed to the cushions.

"Shouldn't the feather tick be atop the mattress? For comfort?"

Bill shook his head. "Makes sleeping too hot for me, even in winter, but it's a good cushion for the straw mattress." Then he pulled her close again and kissed her.

A slow sweet shiver sunk deep inside her.

"Daddy?" Blue called, a downward drift to his voice. "When do we have to go to work?" Up above the double alcoves was a loft with a railing where the boy sat building a tower of wood blocks. The dividing wall between the two nooks supported a ladder leading up.

Softly, Bill said to Quinn, "Work always calls."

"Yes," she forced herself to say. "I . . . I suppose the restaurant needs me, too." Then a jumble of words sounding like "pumpkin pie people" tumbled out, and she stepped back, away from Bill. She cast her gaze downward, then smoothed her skirt as if it needed pressing.

Bill looked up into the loft. "Come on down, Blue. You can earn your keep by pulling weeds in the garden today."

The boy climbed down the ladder and then jumped with a flat-footed *thud* onto the floor. "Daddy, why do I always have to pull weeds? Why can't I do something else to earn my keep?"

The desire to feel Bill's touch again led Quinn to take hold of his hand. "Perhaps Blue can work with me today. I could certainly use help getting seeds out of my pumpkins."

Blue's eyes widened. "I can do that!"

Bill laughed. "Pumpkin guts. That's what Blue calls it when he digs out the insides."

Quinn gave Blue a smile. "Pumpkin guts?" When the boy nodded, she extended her hand to him. "Well, come on with me then. There are lots of pumpkin guts to be had today."

Not far from Catherine's wash station, Quinn set down two topped-out pumpkins beside an empty bucket. With Blue cross-legged on the chilly ground, she said, "Mrs. Crawford will want to save every seed for planting next season." She grinned at the boy's nod and wide smile. "Be sure to call me when you've finished."

Spending time with any child was a rarity, but one she was beginning to enjoy with Blue. His excitement over every little thing turned the mundane into a thrill.

Blue dug inside the first pumpkin with his bare hands, pulling out a handful of stringy orange pulp with clingy seeds, and then dropped them into the bucket. While Blue gutted the pumpkins, Quinn headed to the wash station, where Catherine was cleaning potatoes.

"Hello again, miss," Catherine said with a glance before turning her attention back to the potato she was scrubbing. She started talking as if Quinn had never been away. "Me maw loved neeps and tatties, but me paw was one tattie-hatin' Irishman."

"Neeps and tatties?" Quinn bent closer as she picked up a potato and then dunked it into the barrel of water. She began scrubbing.

Catherine gave her a crooked grin, then reached out and tapped a dirty turnip awaiting its turn at the wash barrel. "Neeps," she explained, then pulled a clean potato out of the water and held it up. "Tatties," she said. "These is Scotch grays, crisp as an apple."

"Oh," Quinn said with a nod of understanding. "Turnips and potatoes."

"Aye, miss."

"I assumed you were Scottish, but you say your father is Irish?"

"The Muirs is Scots-Irish, miss. Me maw was Scottish, and, seeing as how Paw died just after he set foot in America, our maw raised me brathair and me alone."

"I'm sorry. I didn't realize . . ."

Catherine dipped her hands into the wash water and began scrubbing yet another potato. Somber and reflective, she said, "Whit's fur ye'll no go past ye." She glanced up at Quinn. "That's what Maw used to say."

"Yes, I suppose she's right. What's meant to be, will be," Quinn said with a nod. "Where's your brother now? Donnan, is it?"

"Aye, miss," Catherine said. "After our maw died, Donnan and me came West fer the gold, but our wagon slipped o'er the trail edge and dragged the horses and me brathair with it. He was crushed to death." She continued to wash potatoes without looking up.

"And you continued on alone?" When Catherine nodded, Quinn pulled the girl into a hug. "I'm sorry. I lost my brother in a wagon accident many years ago, too."

In that quiet moment, Libby came around the outside corner of the restaurant with a hefty load of garden vegetables cradled in her lifted apron. She stopped at seeing the embrace. "Sorry, I didn't mean no intrusion."

"You're never an intrusion." Quinn pulled back with an affectionate pinch to Catherine's chin. "We were just talking about the things we have in common. Here, let me

378

help you," she said as Libby stepped up to the long, double-plank work counter. She raised Libby's apron higher, and together they emptied the vegetables out onto the "waiting to be cleaned" counter. Tapping a potato, Quinn said, "You're boiling these for tonight's supper, aren't you?"

"Yes," Libby said. "If the milk arrives in time. I wanted to mash them like my mama used to do, but the delivery is late."

"I'll ask Bill about it," Quinn said as she glanced back to check on Blue, but her eyes went straight to Nettie, who was trudging toward them.

With her scrawny finger pointed at Catherine, Nettie called, "So this is where you been hidin'!" She stopped just short of stepping in a mud hole near the water barrels. "You still owe me for the window you broke." She held out her hand to Catherine. "Now pay up."

"I'm waitin' for me wages, then I'll pay ye back. I said I would."

"Wages?" Nettie asked. "From who? No one's gonna hire a girl like you knowin' your age and sass."

Catherine dipped her head in Quinn's direction. "Me washin' job is here now."

"She works for me."

Nettie shook her head. "You're crazy to

hire that girl, but it's no skin off my nose." Her tone was disapproving. "She owes me thirty dollars. We got a sheriff in town now, and I ain't afraid to have him haul her in on charges of property damage if I don't get my money."

Catherine gasped. She turned to run, but Quinn caught her by the arm. "Stay, Catherine. It's all right." Then Quinn turned back to Nettie. "She's earned more than enough to pay for the window. If you'll accompany me to the store, I'll get your thirty dollars."

Waggling her finger at Catherine, Nettie warned Quinn, "You'll regret it. She's stubbornly belligerent."

"She's fiercely independent. I like that about her." Quinn headed for the store with Nettie in tow.

Once inside, Quinn went to the counter, where Bill stood marking his inventory pad. "Bill, I barely have enough in today's coffer to pay Nettie the thirty she is owed. May I sign for it from your cashbox until after lunch is served?"

Bill looked from Quinn to Nettie but never asked the reason. "Yeah, sure." Outside, an approaching wagon caught his attention, but he counted out the thirty dollars and then handed it to Quinn, who handed it to Nettie.

"You're paid in full," Quinn said. "Now, I'll kindly ask that you not harass my workers in the future."

"Harass?" Nettie laughed. "*Your* workers?" She turned for the door. "Considerin' Bill paid the debt, I'd say anyone workin' here is in *his* employ, not yours." She cackled and pushed open the door, leaving Quinn speechless.

Without raising his head, Bill's eyes angled upward. "I'm not gonna ask what that was all about." He put down his inventory pad, then said, "Will you watch the store for me for a few minutes? Lively Coons just pulled up in his wagon with our dairy delivery. I need to get it unloaded and paid for."

Quinn eyed the wagon. "I meant to tell you. Libby is waiting for milk." Bill nodded, then left through the front door. He hopped down off the porch and then directed the bearded man and his wagon to the back before he disappeared around the side of the building.

It was as good a time as any for Quinn to put an order in for restaurant supplies. She picked up Bill's inventory pad, flipped to a new page, and was inspecting the shelves, looking for the ingredients Libby and Mabree said they needed, when the door banged open.

Quinn turned with a jump, glimpsing Doss Parker. Long ago, she'd learned a smiling man was not always friendly, so she offered no greeting even though he was Bill's customer.

"Well, well," Doss said, removing his hat. "Bill gone?"

"No." Uneasiness washed over her. "He's out back checking on the dairy delivery."

"So you're just the pretty face."

"Did you need something today, Mr. Parker? Or are you just here as a nuisance?"

Doss laughed and thumped his way forward in heavy boots. He held a folded paper out toward her as she stood behind the counter. "Next time Bill goes to Sacramento for supplies, I need four boxes of extra fine Austrian cigars in polished maple boxes of a hundred each." When she made no move to take his note, he leaned over the counter with a smile. "He'll know where to find them. Give him that message for me?"

Quinn held a steady posture and reached for the paper. "I'll give Bill your order."

She tugged at the paper, but Doss held onto it with a firm grip. "I'd go myself, but it's a lonely trip." He stared at her without blinking. "Now, if you wanted to go along with me and do some shopping for yourself,

I'd be glad to make the trip. I could show you what it's like to be with a real man."

"And why would I want to do that, Mr. Parker?"

With a *pffft,* Doss released the paper and straightened up tall. Then, with a quick grab, he had hold of her wrist. He pulled Quinn close — the counter being the only barrier — until his whispering breath caught her face. "I'm hard to satisfy, but I doubt you are."

"Let go of me! Or I'll —"

"You'll what?" Doss released her wrist, then flicked his hand in a shooing motion. "Go on back to Bill's bed then . . ." But instead of turning to leave, he gave her a hard stare. "Don't think I haven't been studying you. Independent businesswoman, huh? You haven't done a damn thing by yourself, except spread your legs for weak-minded men so they'll give you what you want." He straightened. "I don't mind that, though. Remember that."

He walked back across the store and shoved the door open. Once outside, he turned. Held it open with his foot. Gave her an unsettling glare.

"I know more about you than you think."

When he released the door, it banged shut like a slap.

CHAPTER THIRTY-FIVE

The room above the store, although it had no real furnishings other than a bedstead for Quinn's mattress, blankets, quilt, and pillow, felt cozy with its one window and wood-burning stove. Its warmth, however, wasn't just inside the bare wood room; it was inside her, too.

She'd almost forgotten what it was like to have walls of her own. Truth be told, she never actually *had* her own walls — they always belonged to someone else. They'd been lent to her for privacy and protection, but they were never hers. She stood near the window, her fingers tracing the wall's patterned wood grain. In a way, she supposed, even these nailed up boards belonged to Bill Beaudry, but somehow, she felt rights to them. Maybe this sense of entitlement came with the paying of rent. Whatever it was, she was grateful.

In lieu of a chest of drawers, Quinn hung

a clothesline wall to wall for her dresses, but without a mirror, it took fortitude to leave her room each day, having no idea as to her own appearance.

The biggest missing luxury was a chamber pot. She could not see herself asking Bill to purchase one for her on his next trip to the city, so, instead, she made jaunts down the outside stairs to the outhouse when the need arose.

She gave Catherine her canvas tent and never heard a complaint about things the girl didn't have, so whenever she felt a yearning for material goods, a feeling of guilt invariably followed. The Scots-Irish girl was young, but she had an admirable handle on life.

In her long-sleeved red dress, Quinn draped a shawl over her shoulders and then started down the outside stairs through a thick veil of fog, heading for the restaurant.

Overnight, the cold, damp air had turned autumn's leaves brown and putrid green, sending them to the ground. Even the tree bark had darkened to a lonely, morbid umber in the cloud-like mist. She stopped at the bottom stair step and looked about. The dense fog concealed anything farther away than The Stewpot.

The world had gone still and quiet, with

the exception of a worrisome cough coming from Mrs. Crawford's cabin. Quinn went over and knocked, then waited at the door.

"Yes?" Mrs. Crawford called from inside. "Who is it?"

"It's Quinn. Are you well?"

The door opened. Mrs. Crawford stood there, wrapped in a yellow and black plaid shawl. "Yes, dear," the blind woman said. "I'm fine, but Blue is feeling poorly. Bill went for the doctor."

Quinn entered and went straight to the boy, who lay shivering beneath a pile of quilts. She placed her hand against his forehead. "He's burning up."

The shuffle of Mrs. Crawford's thick-soled shoes neared the bed. "Tell me, dear," she asked. "Will you look and see if he has spots anywhere on his body?" Then, "Look under his arms and on his belly and his backside for me."

Quinn nodded, then pulled back the quilts to examine him. Blue slept through his shivers as she raised his nightshirt. She checked his front side first, then gently rolled him onto his left side and inspected his bare back. There was no redness, no spots or splotches. "No," she answered. "His skin is clear and dry, but feverish."

Mrs. Crawford gave a relieved sigh.

"Good. By now you'd see a rash if he had smallpox, or the measles." She went to the wood-burning stove and felt for the handle of the coffee pot, then poured herself a cup. "Would you like some while we wait for the doctor?"

"No," Quinn said. "Thank you." Her hand rested on Blue's soft, young skin. Time hadn't the chance to weather it, burn it, or wrinkle it, but still she felt a fragile life in this boy. Lightly, her hand rubbed circles on his back, willing his body to heal, though no one she had ever cared for fared well — not her one-year-old brother, not her mother, not Henry, or Nadine. They had all died. Quinn took her hand off Blue. *Bad-luck charm.* She couldn't risk the curse falling on him, too. Why had she allowed this little boy to capture her heart? She knew all too well, as long as she had just herself to look after, she'd do all right, but Bill and Blue had changed everything, and she was at odds as to how to handle it. She stood and re-tucked the covers. "How long ago did —" Her question was cut short by the opening of the door.

Bill entered the cabin with Dr. Weber, who went straight to Blue without a nod or hello to the waiting women. He set his black leather bag down beside the bed and pulled back the quilts, just as Quinn had done, but this time the boy whimpered.

"It's all right, Blue." Bill patted his son's blond head. "Doc needs to examine you."

"I'm cold, Daddy," Blue whined. "And my legs hurt." Then his coughing sat him straight up in bed.

Quinn stood and watched the doctor use his tube-like stethoscope to listen to the boy's lungs and heart. When he finished, he returned the instrument to his bag, then rubbed his hands together vigorously to warm his touch. He pulled up Blue's long cotton nightshirt and brushed his hands over the boy's chest, neck, underarms, and back. "No bumps, bruising, or rashes," he said to no one in particular. "Is he a sickly child?"

"Lord, no," Mrs. Crawford answered. "He's a good, strong boy."

Using the flat of his fingers, Dr. Weber pressed lightly on Blue's belly without causing a cry or a whimper. Afterwards, he pulled the quilts up to the boy's chin.

"Is it cholera?" Bill asked.

"I don't think so," Dr. Weber answered. "You said he's had no diarrhea, which is one of the first signs of cholera."

Quinn stiffened. "Is it typhus?" She fingered the cameo pinned to her high collar as the memory of her dying mother darkened her thoughts. Typhus had swept through Oregon Country when she was thirteen. The disease had taken hold of her mother, refusing to let go. Quinn had stayed at her bedside, dabbing her mother's feverish brow, giving her sips of water, and administering calomel. In the end, with her mother mumbling incoherent prayers and clutching the cameo like a crucifix, disease and death had won.

Now, looking down at Blue, so fragile, the anguish of the unforgiving pestilence — surely at the devil's hand — again felt unbearable.

The doctor's brow furrowed. He shook his head. "I haven't seen or heard of a case of typhus in almost a year."

Tense and worried, she pressured him for a diagnosis. "But he has fever, a cough, muscle pains . . . all signs of typhus!"

Dr. Weber fixed his eyes on Quinn. "Those are common symptoms of many diseases, not just typhus."

"What, then?" Quinn asked.

The doctor looked back to Bill. "Influenza."

"Stars above!" Mrs. Crawford cried. She moved to the bedside and felt for Blue. With a wet cloth already in her hand, she dabbed his forehead. "Bill, I'm keeping Blue here with me. I know how to care for him after having the influenza myself last year, and I'm not about to lose this sweet boy." She stroked the boy's blond hair. "I should have put warmer socks on his feet when he went out this week."

Quinn's memory flashed back to Blue sitting on the cold ground cleaning pumpkins. She had placed him there and left him for over an hour before checking on him. His hands had felt frozen and his trousers were damp from the moist earth. Glancing at Bill, she said, "This is my fault for allowing him to de-seed my pumpkins on so cold a day."

Bill did not look at Quinn. Doting, he used his fingers to comb the boy's blond straggles off his feverish brow. "There was a wagon that came through last week saying they'd just buried their two-year-old and his grandmother. They said influenza was a death sentence for the young and old."

"For the weak, that's true." Dr. Weber picked up his medical bag. "I'll mix a powder to add to your son's tea." He laid his hand on Mrs. Crawford's shoulder. "Give a few sips every hour until his fever breaks. Camphor for his cough, too." He walked to the door and opened it. "Send someone to my office to pick it up."

"I'll go."

But Bill shook his head. "No, I'll go." Then to Dr. Weber, he said, "Half hour?"

"Yes." The doctor looked back and forth between Bill and Quinn. "Half hour is fine."

Mrs. Crawford picked up a pail and walked behind the doctor to the door. To Bill, she said, "Watch Blue while I get water for his tea." She had barely left the one-room cabin, shutting the door behind her, when Quinn turned to Bill.

"What can I do to help?" she asked him. "I'm certainly capable of picking up medicine."

Without looking at Quinn, Bill turned back to Blue. He tucked in the quilts around the sleeping boy. "I should have kept a closer eye on him."

An ache stung Quinn. She went to Bill and laid her hand on his shoulder as he sat on the edge of the bed. "I can't bear it when your eyes avoid me."

Bill glanced up, then dipped the cloth into the washbasin and wrung it partially dry. With it refolded lengthwise, he laid it across his son's forehead. "He counts on me. I've got no right to depend on somebody else when it comes to his safety."

"I'm not just *somebody else,* Bill."

"Are you sure? Because I haven't seen a real commitment from you — not personally, anyway."

Bill stopped talking when Mrs. Crawford returned with her pail of water, which she set on the floor by the stove. "Has he stirred?"

"No," Bill told her. "Not a peep."

The woman turned her sightless eyes to the log wall behind the stove where a row of pots hung. She reached up, feeling for the smallest pot, then pulled it down and set it on the cast-iron stove.

Bill stood and picked up the full pail. "How much water do you need poured for the tea?"

"Fill it halfway," she said. Then, turning as if she could see them both, she asked, "Who's going for the medicine?"

"I am." Quinn stood. She suddenly felt utterly out of place in this family affair. Without further explanation, she whirled her shawl around her shoulders and left.

The sun's rays had started to burn away the morning fog, giving way to a blue, blemish-free sky.

With her mind full of thought, Quinn trudged past miners in ratty jackets wearing mud-caked boots on their daily trek to the river. She was oblivious to men who gave friendly greetings and unaware of those who mumbled vulgarities. Her concentration focused wholly on the day of the pumpkins. Had Blue worn a jacket? Yes, she was fairly sure he had. Should she have given him work space inside the storeroom instead of outside on the cold ground? Of course — such a fool mistake. If he'd worked in the garden for Mrs. Crawford instead, would he still be sick? Of that, she could not be sure.

When Quinn reached the doctor's door, she knocked, but her introspections overshadowed his beckoning. She was head down, deep in thought when Dr. Weber pulled open the door.

"Come in, come in." His mutter was rushed. "I'm mixing powders," he said, motioning her to take a seat. "I'll have the medicine ready in a moment."

Quinn sat on the wooden bench, hands enfolded, watching the doctor funnel white powder into a dark blue bottle. "How does one get the influenza?"

Dr. Weber glanced at her. "Before leaving New York for the West, I read an interesting study on catarrhal fever, commonly called influenza." While he talked, he held the bottle up to the window's light, measuring its fullness, then set it back down on his table and continued to funnel white powder into it. "There is great diversity of opinion, but it now seems sufficiently conclusive to say the disease is ruled and spread by the influence of the stars."

The strength of her higher education was failing her. "Doctor, plain English, please?"

He turned to her. "Weather. Temperatures. The wind." He corked the medicine bottle and handed it to her along with a smaller, barely green bottle, which carried a strong camphor scent. "Sudden changes especially."

Quinn accepted the medicine. Still puzzled, she asked, "Are you saying the weather is to blame for Blue's influenza?"

Dr. Weber gave her an assured nod. "That is the professional opinion of our most learned physicians, including those from King's College in London."

She lowered her head and murmured, "Perhaps I am to blame."

"For the weather?"

"No." Quinn shook her head. "For Blue's influenza. He was in my care when it turned colder, and I failed to take precautions. I should have kept him indoors or dressed him warmer."

The doctor seated himself beside Quinn. His clinical, educated tone softened. "Influenza attacks thousands of people — in epidemic proportions these last two years — and it has never been particular about folks who dressed warmly and those who didn't. I don't think it's fair for you to blame yourself."

"Thank you. True or not, I appreciate your words."

Quinn took her leave and returned to the cabin with Blue's medicine, only to find Bill gone.

"I told him to go on to the store," Mrs. Crawford explained. "It'll help keep his mind off Blue. I can worry enough for the two of us." She tapped a good pinch of the bottled powder out into her hand before adding it to the tea and stirring. "You go on, too." She slid her arm under Blue's back, then raised him up, giving him a long sip of tea before laying him back down. "Ask Libby to make some broth, will you?"

"Yes, of course. I'll bring it as soon as it is ready."

The fog, lifting at its own slow pace, dampened everything it touched, even the air. After entering The Stewpot through the back door, Quinn hung up her shawl and dabbed her bundled hair dry with a towel. She set to work peeling and slicing carrots for the chicken stew, bubbling on the stove for lunch. Although she willed her mind to drift elsewhere, it seemed to be stuck, drowning in a pool of sadness, guilt, and worry.

At noon, Quinn delivered bowls of broth to the cabin for Mrs. Crawford and Blue. Then she headed for the store. After his only customer left, she approached Bill. "I've delivered a fine chicken broth to the cabin. Mrs. Crawford said Blue's fever is going down."

With a nod and a relieved sigh, Bill said, "That's good news. Thank you for checking on him." He dropped a few gold nuggets into a sack, tied it, and then slid it under his counter. "I was upset about Blue this morning, and I took it out on you. I owe you an apology."

"You had every right to be upset. Death and disease seem to follow me, then pick off the ones closest to me as if doling out punishments."

Bill cocked his head. "Your mother's death wasn't your fault." But when her head dipped, he remembered the lovesick fifteen-year-old girl. "Nadine's suicide wasn't your fault either. Two deaths that had nothing to do with you."

"More than two."

Bill's posture stilled as if frozen — his eyes glued to hers. "Who else?"

Divulgence without repercussion had a precarious balance between truth and deceit. If she fully disclosed the story of Henry and his death, everything she had worked to gain was at risk. Yet in her hesitant moment, the words *the truth will set you free* settled on her.

"My younger brother was in my care when, on his first birthday, he toddled out an open doorway and was run down by a carriage. Clearly, my fault." Then she steeled herself to reveal the one truth that held the power to ruin it all. Her stance straightened, ready for the emotional blow. "Bill, I . . ." But her confession was cut short when the man who could send truth-stifling thunderbolts into her womanhood took her in his arms.

"That's why you blamed yourself for Blue's illness, isn't it?" He pulled her tight, holding her. "I'm such a fool."

CHAPTER THIRTY-SIX

On November 24, 1849, amid howling wind and pounding rain, the Dancehouse held its highly publicized Cora McCready Night.

Although Quinn had previously refused to attend the soirée, Bill convinced her it was the civic-minded thing to do. To uphold her position as a respected businesswoman, she needed to make an appearance. And, frankly, when it came right down to it, showing allegiance to Bill and her business was far more important than her need to oppose Doss.

Flyers plastered the town, and every mining settlement and gold camp within three days' ride was posted up, too. Advertisements ran in the Sacramento *Placer Times* and the San Francisco *Daily Alta* newspapers, and it had paid off. For tonight, at least, the population of Fortune had doubled.

With her red hair bundled atop her head

and her hands neatly folded over the lap of her sepia-colored dress, Quinn sat and waited for Bill as the two hundred-seat, two-story building filled with smelly miners in drenched overcoats and sweat-stained hats.

The heady scent of Doss Parker's pipe tobacco arrived before he did. Steeling herself, she looked up, glimpsing his face, which still bore the disfigurement she had inflicted. It seemed his lower lip would forever bear a half-circle scar with an imprint of her teeth.

"I'm surprised you came," Doss said as he pulled a polished spindle-backed chair up next to her and sat. "I thought you might like to know, I ran into an interesting man when I was out spreading the news about the Dancehouse." His grin was misshapen but smug.

"Why should I care about that, Mr. Parker?"

Doss cocked his head and glided in close. With an angry squint, he stared directly into Quinn's Irish-green eyes. "Because he had lots to say about you."

A flutter of nerves caused her heart to beat faster, but she averted her gaze as if she were more interested in the fiddle music and the fancy dancers lining up to take the stage.

"A cook, are you?" Doss said. "You'll never cook for me again. Restaurateur, be damned!"

He knew.

She felt her eyes go wide. Sensed her paling face. Her hands knotted into clenched fists.

Doss grinned. "Though I hate to admit it, you're the only half-intelligent businesswoman in this town, and, before our little squabble, you said being a businesswoman mattered to you." He adjusted his chair. Leaning in, he whispered, "So I have another proposition for you. I've got sixteen dancers, and not one of them has a lick of brains. You've got spirit. Hell, you've got the guts of a grizzly, and, as you know firsthand, men have a tendency to get rough with a woman sometimes." He studied her. "My girls need a strong, business-minded woman to manage them. They need someone like you. You'll earn good money. I have no intention of cheating you."

"I have a job. My restaurant is doing nicely."

"It won't be doing so well tomorrow after I tell Bill and the town about your husband, and how he died from some kind of poison in his food. They say you ran off with all his money, too. His mother claims the poisoning was murder. She's got the law looking for you."

"It wasn't poison!" Quinn snapped. "Food poisoning is not murder!"

Doss leaned back in his chair with a grin. Arms crossed, he said, "No one is ever gonna eat at your restaurant again." He rose from the chair. "Don't worry, I'm willing to keep you and your secret safe, as long as you're here noon tomorrow for your new job. If you don't show up, I'll start spreadin' the news, starting with Bill." After a cursory nod, he turned and headed for the stage of dancing girls.

Quinn's dream was over. She had been living a farce. All a façade.

Why hadn't she told Bill the truth? Hiding her marriage of convenience and her husband's subsequent death, especially him dying of food poisoning at her own ill-fated hands, was another devastatingly poor decision. *Bad-luck charm.* Bill would never forgive this deception. She had put his reputation on the line and then failed to uphold it.

As fiddles played and showgirls in fanciful costumes took the stage, Quinn stood. She calmly smoothed the wrinkles from her dress skirt, then looked around the big room. It was full of boisterous men, some she recognized, others she did not. They whooped, hollered, and waved their hats in the air, but their eyes never veered from the stage. With her voice and her heart both benumbed, she turned for the door and stepped out into the night.

Without her bonnet or shawl, Quinn walked mindlessly down the rain-drenched road to the stairs leading up to her room above the store. She took the steps slowly without regard to the blustering rain. It wasn't until she was safely inside that she realized she was soaked head to toe.

Without a chair, towels, or an extra blanket to throw around herself, Quinn dropped down on the edge of her bed only to spring up when the chill of her damp cotton drawers met the back of her legs. The cold, blowing rain had soaked clear through her dress and undergarments. When a shiver set in, she went to the stove, added two pieces of wood, and lit it. As the room warmed, she stripped off her wet clothes and slipped into her cotton nightgown.

At the window, she stood and stared out into the darkness of night. *Freedom.* It had seemed so simple. *Independence.* A given with her autonomy won. *To be a businesswoman.* For a while, she thought she'd done it. Oh, how daft a dream.

Time had run out, and a deadline now stared her in the face. What was left of her world would come tumbling down at noon tomorrow.

Life, it seemed, was ruled by choices, of which Quinn saw only three. She could fight the accusation, stand strong, and refuse to give up her restaurant, but it was easy to see that a public charge of food poisoning would ruin her. Doss was right. No one would eat at The Stewpot ever again. Whereas, if she were to give up her eatery, she could salvage a livelihood by managing the dancers at the Dancehouse, and she could save the restaurant for Bill. Keep his good reputation intact. Doss had agreed to keep her secret if she worked for him. No one would know the truth. Her past could stay in the past where it belonged.

Or she could leave Fortune.

Tears blurred her vision as she skimmed the room. She had so little, scarcely more than when she'd first arrived, except money. Of that, she had plenty.

Without her here in Fortune, Doss would have no one to ruin. In San Francisco, she could make a fresh start. And Bill would be better off.

Bill.

Pieces of her heart crumbled. He would understand in time. Before long, he would find a good and decent woman to love, which she knew he would never do while saddled with her. All she touched turned to dust, not gold. *She was a bad-luck charm.* A curse to everyone, including herself. The greatest apology she could bestow upon Bill and Blue was to disappear. If she were gone, good portents would return, and Blue would get well, she was sure of it, and no one would hold Bill responsible for things a runaway woman had done.

Quinn lifted her largest tapestry bag onto her bed. Then she went to her dresses and, one at a time, she pulled them down, bundled them, and put each into her bag before closing it. She stowed all but her hairbrush and pins.

Her fingers swept across the canvas on its easel. Like her future, it was painfully bare.

With the room neat and orderly, she crawled into bed. Pulled up the quilts.

First thing tomorrow, she would hire a ride to San Francisco.

CHAPTER THIRTY-SEVEN

Sunup brought the morning fog, which Quinn welcomed as a shroud for her departure. On her way down the outside stairs, she heard Blue's persistent cough. An ache in her heart turned her towards the little cabin, but rational thought stopped her. She needed to stay away. She needed to *get* away.

Quinn set her bags down on the bottom step, then dashed across the road to the blacksmith shop, where she found Riley Boles, who sat on an iron anvil with a cup of coffee in his hands.

"Good morning," she greeted him. When Riley turned, she said, "I am in need of a ride to San Francisco. I can pay one hundred dollars."

Riley pushed himself up onto his crooked legs. "A hundred dollars?"

"Yes." Quinn drew closer. "But only if we leave now, without commotion. And you mustn't tell *anyone.*"

Riley scratched his head. "I should let Jary know I'm leavin' but comin' back. I cain't lose this job, not even for a hundred." The blacksmith had hired him when no one else would due to his disability.

Quinn gave it thought, then said, "Yes, but you'll not mention me, my name, or our destination."

"Sure." Riley nodded. "Let me hitch the wagon." His eyes skimmed her. "You got bags?"

"Yes. I'll go and get them and come right back."

Quinn hurried across the street and picked up her two bags. She lugged the heavy weight of them back across the road to the hitched and ready wagon.

It took both her and Riley to hoist her biggest bag up the side, but once the bags were set, Quinn climbed up after them. Before snapping the reins, Riley turned to her and, louder than needed, he said, "You should rethink us goin' it alone. I heared the Injuns is all stirred up betwixt here and San Francisco. They can be mighty skeersome. Wouldn't hurt to have a gun ride along."

She pressed a quieting finger to her lips. "No. This is between you and me. I don't want anyone else knowing."

Riley shook his head in a wide side-to-side swing. "It just ain't smart startin' out cross-country unarmed with a crippled old man like me." He reached for the saddlebag he had slung over their seatback, opened its flap, and pulled out a Colt revolver. He handed it butt first to her. "Tuck this under yer skirts."

With a raised hand, Quinn said, "No."

Riley gave a doubtful cock of his head as if maybe she hadn't understood. "It weren't a question. These mules here ain't a-movin' less'n you're armed and willin' to shoot, if need be. You know how to shoot, don't you?"

"Of course I can shoot, though I haven't always hit my intended target. I just don't like guns."

Riley waggled the Colt at her. With a nod toward the bun pinned atop her head, he said, "You'll like it well enough if an Injun is fixin' to lift yer topknot."

Her hand flew to her bundled hair. "I suppose so," she said. She took the gun and tucked it under the spread of her blue skirt where it flared out on the wagon's bench seat.

Before slapping the reins, Riley reached down beneath the seat, feeling for his double-barrel shotgun. Upon laying his hand on it, he gave a satisfied nod.

The night's storm had left a slurry of sludge instead of a trail, but deep, permanent grooves from countless other wagons marked the route. Gradually, they ventured out across the low bluffs, following the wheel ruts.

By ten o'clock, the fog had lifted, breaking under the sun's strong but heatless rays. Off to the right, on a downslope, Quinn spotted an aged wooden cross, crooked but still standing. "Look," she said and pointed. "How sad to be buried on the forgotten side of a lonely hill." She glanced at Riley. "Stop. I want to pay respects."

Riley pulled the reins taut until his two-mule team slowed to a stop. "We ain't even gone six miles yet." He set the brake bar. "No disrespect intended, ma'am, but we cain't be stoppin' every time we see a grave, or we might as well dig our own." He pointed higher up the tree line. "I feared mentionin' it afore, but I seen a bit of movement up yonder."

But Quinn had already climbed down off the wagon and was trudging toward the wooden cross. Beside it lay an old headboard made from split wood and nibbled apart by termites and weather. Crudely engraved on its front was the lone word

Mama and the year *1848.* Quinn raised her eyes to the sky. "Dear Lord, please bear this woman's earthly burdens and relieve her of any curse that followed her in death."

"Stop right there!" Riley shouted. When Quinn turned, she saw his shotgun pulled, aimed in the other direction. She ran for the wagon, but by the time she got there and had a thumb on the Colt's hammer, she heard a voice in answer.

"It's me, Riley! It's Bill Beaudry. Don't shoot!"

Riley lowered his shotgun and called back, "Well, hello, Bill!"

Quinn's jaw tightened. A clean getaway was not to be. She climbed aboard the wagon and leaned forward, spying Bill's buckskin horse. Bill rode up to them and stopped just shy of a nostril puff away.

Riley reached out and gave the horse a gentle rub on the nose as Bill leaned forward in the saddle, his eyes set on the wagon's passenger.

"What's going on, Quinn? I looked for you at the Dancehouse last night and couldn't find you anywhere. I figured you'd changed your mind about goin', but then when I went looking for you this morning, I found your room cleaned out and you gone without a note or anything." His hardened eyes shifted to Riley. "Jary said he'd seen her leave with you."

"Now, Bill, it weren't my doin'. The lady asked for a ride to San Francisco and offered me a good bit to take her there."

Bill's gaze shifted back to Quinn. "San Francisco? What's in San Francisco?"

"Bill, I'm not the woman you think I am. There are truths about me you don't know."

"So, tell me now."

Riley swiveled his head between the two without an utterance.

She looked at Bill. "Before coming to Fortune, I rarely cooked for anyone other than my husband, and for obvious reasons he was never very complimentary."

"Your husband?"

Quinn shifted on the wagon seat without taking her gaze off Bill. "Yes, a thing I failed to mention." She watched an awkward uneasiness settle on him. "Dead," she blurted. "Buried the day I arrived in Fortune."

The buckskin flinched. Bill repositioned. "You're telling me you came to Fortune as a grieving widow?"

"A widow, yes, but not a grieving one. He was a tolerable man. Well, he was a cheat, a liar, and a gambler, but what's important is that you know we were never in love. We barely knew each other."

The brows of both bewildered men creased.

"Henry and I had known each other mere days when we married, and he died two months later."

Riley shifted his gaze from Quinn, to Bill, then back to her again. "What did he die of?"

Quinn looked straight ahead. "The determination is sketchy, at best."

"Well, was he shot, or was his throat cut? Was he hung?" Riley sounded as if the detail of Henry's dying was more important than the dying itself.

"No." Quinn shook her head. "It was an illness, but if you don't mind, I would rather not discuss the matter with anyone but Bill."

"Where do you expect Riley to go while you tell the story, Quinn?" He didn't wait for an answer. "You've dragged him out here in the middle of nowhere to tell a truth that should have been told a long time ago." Bill rode the buckskin around the front of Riley's mules, closing the gap between himself and Quinn. Facing her on horseback, he said, "What else don't I know?" When she hesitated, he yelled, "What else!"

"Food poisoning!" She cringed, bracing for the backlash.

In the silence that followed, a whirl of wind caught the scolding call of a hawk. With her eyes turned to the sky, Quinn spied the judgmental red-tail, circling. When her gaze dropped, she found Bill with clenched jaw and furrowed brow. "The doctor declared Henry's death to be caused by food poisoning." In measured tone, she declared, "I was his cook. His mother accused me of killing him for his money."

Bill took a deep breath. He leaned forward in his saddle, knuckles white. For a moment, he quieted, as if taking in the facts. "Thought you were broke when you came to Fortune."

"I was," she answered. "After paying my wagon fare, I had fourteen dollars to my name."

"So what happened to your husband's money?"

Heartsore, Quinn turned away, forcing her gaze to distance itself. "Henry had no money. We were living off my dowry, most of which was stolen in San Francisco. He gambled away the little we had left, leaving me near penniless."

Bill quieted again, his hands cupping the saddle horn as he set his eyes on the hills. After a moment, he turned back to Quinn. "Why now?" he questioned. "Why keep this secret only to run out on me now?"

She tensed. "Doss Parker."

"What about him?"

"Doss knows the truth. He found out while delivering his flyers to the camps and towns." A quivering snaked down her throat. "I was at the Dancehouse waiting for you last night when he threatened to reveal everything unless I agreed to manage his sixteen girls. He said he'd tell everyone about my marriage and the food poisoning." Every fiber of her being was unraveling. "My deadline is noon today." She blinked, wishing away her welling tears. "My deceit has lost me my restaurant and compromised your reputation."

"Being a bad cook isn't a crime." His tone, and his eyes, had softened. "But why would your mother-in-law think you killed her son for money when he had none?"

"Henry was a braggart who loved nothing more than carrying on about his wealth — a lie he told everyone but me. When we met, I was desperate to escape my father's abuse, but I had no money and no way to leave. And after too many gambling losses, Henry hadn't a penny to his name either. He was trying to get back home to Stockton. Together, we devised a plan to marry, convincing my father to bestow a dowry upon us. It was more than enough for us to leave the Willamette Valley, and for me to find my independence."

"So when you both showed up in Stockton, his mother thought the money belonged to her son."

"Yes."

Riley Boles gave a throat-clearing growl, then asked, "What about the poisoned food?"

With an annoyed glare, Quinn clarified, "*Food poisoning*. It wasn't *poisoned food*. There is a difference."

"The question still deserves an answer," Bill said, defending the inquiry. "What about the food poisoning?"

Quinn felt ill. Spitting out the truth left her sour. "I used his mother's recipe. Myra was a witch of a woman, but she was a brilliant cook. I followed her instructions for braised beef and biscuits exactly, but after one bite, Henry collapsed. He died soon after."

Bill scratched his head. "Never known food poisoning to kill a man that fast."

"Evidently, it did." She looked up, noticing the sun much higher in the sky than when the wagon had first stopped. Its rays, now bright and focused, had slipped over the top of the covered wagon and found her.

She glanced first at Riley, and then Bill. "It's almost noon. I'm sure Doss has realized I'm gone."

"I'm sure your whereabouts has a lot of folks wondering," Bill said. "Leaving without a word sent Libby and Catherine into a tizzy. Mrs. Crawford, too. They depend on you."

"They'll do fine. They're strong women."

"And you're not?" Bill leaned forward, his chest grazing the horse's mane.

"No, not in the same way. They know their place in the world." She inhaled a deep breath and then turned to Riley. "We should be going."

Before Riley could answer, Bill guffawed. "You're not going anywhere but right back to Fortune."

Quinn's glance shot to Bill. With a shake of her head, she said, "I'll not work for Doss, and I'll not stay and ruin your reputation or your business."

Bill reached into the pocket of his tawny-colored coat and pulled out a paper folded into a square. He held it up. "We have a contract, and I'll not think twice about enforcing it."

She combed her memory for lines from the document. *Unless terminated by mutual agreement, both partners are expected to maintain regular and consistent attendance.*

"Why would you propose enforcing an agreement that is clearly a detriment to us both?"

Surely, he didn't want a war between them, but if that was the only way she could protect him from the catastrophe bound to happen, she would oblige.

"We have a sheriff now, remember?" Bill settled back in the saddle. "You can either come back with the stature of a respected businesswoman intact, or I can have you arrested for fraud, or for failure to uphold a contract, or any number of things." When Quinn glared, he said, "And I'm sure the sheriff would be interested in hearing about your husband's death."

Lightheaded and nauseated, she asked, "Why would you do this to me?"

Bill steadied his gaze on her. "Because I'm in love with you, Quinn, and if I let you go, I may never see you again. I won't lose you over this. I'll do whatever I have to do to keep you here."

She pressed a hand to her hammering heart. "Bill, so many things have happened. I can't promise you tomorrow."

He leaned forward in his saddle and reached to touch her hand. "Today is all I'm asking for."

CHAPTER THIRTY-EIGHT

Quinn's future was on the line, but returning to Fortune for it meant a fight was afoot.

It was a quarter past two o'clock when the wagon with her and Riley aboard rolled into town. With the twelve noon deadline come and gone, she feared by now Doss had spread the word. Had she already lost her restaurant? After all, how hungry must a man be to eat food he fears has been poisoned?

Although talking to Dr. Weber seemed a futile attempt to prove her innocence, she would take Bill's advice. She was determined to squelch what would surely be an uprising of rumors. Was she a terrible cook? Yes. She'd proven it beyond doubt, but Bill said it best — being a bad cook was not a crime.

She needed to trust Dr. Weber with the truth. He was the smartest man she knew.

"Biscuits and fresh braised beef aren't

likely to cause food poisoning," the doctor said in answer to her question. "Was your husband acting strangely before supper? Had he been ill?"

"No, other than from drinking too much whiskey and gorging himself on brandied almonds." She shivered at the memory of Henry's dying day.

The doctor eyed her. "Were the almonds from your own tree?"

Quinn shook her head. "We hadn't a single tree of any kind," she told him. "Not even a shade tree. Though his mother had trees aplenty — so many it was hard to find a spot of sunshine anywhere — but the one almond tree she had was dead."

The doctor stood, straightening his tall frame. "So, you bought the almonds?"

"I would think almonds to be the least of my worries, Doctor, but no, Henry had spent or gambled all our money, so luxuries from the store were out of the question. He had no money nor credit left. The almonds were from his mother's peach trees."

"You mean almond tree," Bill corrected her.

"No, peach trees." She turned to the doctor. "Myra grew fig trees as well, although hers were very small. Not like a tree at all."

Dr. Weber cocked his head. "Are you saying your husband ate peach kernels?"

"I don't know anything about *kernels,* but Henry ate a bean pot of brandied almonds, and peach pies made with almond-flour crust. He was a glutton about those nuts. His mother made almost everything with almonds. She even had me saving more peach pits for her."

The doctor's eyes widened. "Holy God . . ." He took in a lungful of air, which seemed to clear his thoughts. "I feel it quite safe to say, your cooking did not kill your husband."

"How do you know?"

"Peach kernels — the thing that looks like an ordinary almond inside a peach pit — they're poisonous." The doctor arched a brow. "If chewed, or otherwise ingested, the kernel releases cyanide."

She grabbed hold of Bill's forearm — but her gaze was glued to the doctor. "How can that be? Cyanide is a gas, isn't it?"

"Commonly, yes, but it is also a poison. Before his death, did you notice any redness in his face? Did he complain of a headache? Was he drowsy?"

Quinn pictured Henry at his last supper. "All those things." She raised her hand to her forehead, willing the details to return. "He was so drowsy he could barely keep his eyes open, but after one bite of his supper, he collapsed. It had to be my food, didn't it?"

"From his symptoms, I doubt your beef and biscuits killed him," Dr. Weber said. "But eating so many peach kernels would have had enough cyanide to kill him in less than fifteen minutes."

CHAPTER THIRTY-NINE

The door banged shut as Doss Parker entered the store. He stared straight at Bill, who held up a forestalling hand.

"It's no use. I know about Quinn being a widow and the mistaken food poisoning."

"Who says it was a mistake?" Doss pointed to Quinn. "Her?"

"We just got back from talking to Doc Weber. Cause of death was plainly discoverable, even without an examination. The man died from his own ignorance and gluttony." Bill glanced at Quinn, who stood within an arm's length of him. Her posture staunch. "Look, Doss. You've got a good business. I've got a good business. Quinn's got a good business. No need to ruin it." His eyes narrowed. "You got nothing on her."

Doss laughed, then he lowered his gaze, and, with a nod, he focused on the floor. "Looks like you beat me, Miss MacCann. I guess you win this one."

Bill shifted, uneasy. "So it's settled? You'll drop the matter and not take it any further?"

But Doss didn't look settled to Quinn, which sent up a jittery wave of nerves.

"You might want to know," Doss said, "word got out about the poison."

Bill paled, which brought a gratified grin to Doss.

"Nervous about salvaging your restaurant, or just worried about losing your woman?" Without missing a verbal beat, Doss said, "You may not be used to dealing with women like her, but I am. She's just using you, but maybe you're too ignorant to know that."

"I am not using anyone!" Quinn shouted, her hand braced against her stomach.

"The Stewpot is her restaurant, not mine," Bill said as he stepped out from the counter. "And I love her, so I doubt I'll lose her."

"Love her! You're a damn fool. She's got you tit-whipped." With a dismissive hand, he turned for the door, which sent Bill into a rage after him.

"No!" Quinn grabbed Bill's arm. "Leave him be, Bill. He's not worth it."

Doss turned, fists primed, but on seeing Bill held back by Quinn, he lowered his hands and snickered. "Like I said . . ." With a push, he shoved open the door and held it. "Mark my words, that woman will be out looking for a new swindle soon."

The start of supper service was minutes away. Quinn needed to get to Libby and Mabree with the truth before gossip found them. She went through the back door of the restaurant into the kitchen where the two were working. At the sight of her, both women dropped their tasks and hurried to her.

"Mighty glad you're back," Mabree said, her hands on Quinn's shoulders. "We got lots of folks that need feedin' now, and we're countin' on your help." She nodded in the direction of the noisy dining room. "Half them people ain't even paid yet. They just piled in the door 'cause I can't be two places at once. You need to get on out there and manage things, all right?"

The last thing Quinn wanted was to rehash her circumstances, but both Mabree and Libby deserved to hear from her the rumors of food poisoning before it came beating down the door.

"We need to talk," Quinn said. "I want you both to hear this from me. I've been accused of food poisoning."

"Food poisoning?" Libby jumped on the words. "I've been doing the cooking." Her panic shot to Mabree, whose face was still as stone. "Most of it, anyway. Are you sayin' our food has made people sick?"

"No! Oh, no . . ." Quinn grabbed the hand of each woman. "It's *me,* not either of you." The rest of the words caught in her throat. Withholding the truth had been no better than a lie, and the weight of her deceit was heavy. Her eyes skipped from Libby to Mabree. "In my previous life." She gave a squeeze to their hands. "The important thing to know is that the rumors are untrue."

Obnoxious shouts from hungry men calling for their food came from the dining room.

Hesitant at first, Libby finally said, "Well, all right then." She hurried back to the galley stove. "We're gonna lose more customers by standing around not feedin' folks than we will by lies and rumors. We'd better get these plates of beef and biscuits served before that crowd in there tears the place down."

"Beef and biscuits?" Quinn swallowed hard.

"Braised beef. My mama's recipe," Libby said.

Though the lighted lamps cast a healthy glow all around, Quinn knew her paling face was evident when she saw the worried looks from Mabree and Libby.

"You all right, Miss Quinn?" Mabree asked.

"No." Quinn pulled out a chair at the worktable and sat. "Will this vile feeling *ever* go away?"

Mabree knelt at the chair. "What is it?"

"Beef and biscuits was the last meal I served to my husband . . ."

"Your husband!" The words stood Mabree straight up. "Does Bill know you got a husband?"

Quinn leapt to her feet. "Widowed! I thought I'd killed him with the meal I cooked, but now I know that isn't true."

Before she could say more, two gunshots silenced the restaurant crowd. Quinn rushed to the cook's door, unbarred it, and pushed it open. Not a diner remained inside. The front door stood ajar.

She and Mabree hurried through the dining room to the restaurant entrance with Libby trailing behind, holding her pregnant belly as if cradling a child.

The black slate publicizing "Braised Beef and Biscuits" swung from its only remaining nail. Two bullet holes pierced the sign.

"Evenin'," came a man's voice.

Out of the twilight walked Dan Gallagher,

425

the new sheriff. He approached slowly, almost in meandering steps. His frock coat hung open, revealing holstered guns on both hips.

"Thank heavens it's you," Quinn said. "Was there a strike? The men left without so much as a single shout of 'Eureka!' " She turned and pointed to her menu board. "But not before shooting holes in our sign."

His brown eyes, soulful like a puppy, yet wily and without innocence, settled on her. When he was a step away, he stopped and shook his head. "Gold didn't send the men running."

"What happened, then?" Libby asked.

The sheriff glanced at Libby and Mabree, but he didn't answer. His attention turned to Quinn. "I'd like to speak with you . . ."

"Please." Quinn raised her hand between them. "I'm not interested, Mr. Gallagher. I have someone." For the first time, the words meant something. *I have someone.* Her thoughts settled on Bill.

Without taking his eyes off her, the sheriff chuckled. "That's not what I came to say." He reached out and took her by the arm. "Charges have been filed against you. I need you to come with me."

"Ch-charges?" she stammered.

"Does the name Randall Waller mean

426

anything to you? He's waiting in my office. Myra Matheny is with him. She's already told half the town you killed her son by poisoning his beef and biscuits." The sheriff pointed to the menu board. "Never saw a place empty out so fast." He gave her arm a tug.

Quinn took a few languishing steps, then looked back over her shoulder at Libby and Mabree, who stood aghast, holding on to one another. "Find Bill," she told them.

The sheriff's office was a ten-by-ten building located closer to the Dancehouse than The Stewpot. Though the town had offered a salary and erected a building in hopes of luring a bona fide lawman, nowhere was there a jail. When Sheriff Gallagher ushered Quinn inside, she saw a black cast-iron stove, a six-foot-tall safe painted black with gold lettering, a desk, and three chairs — one of which held Henry's mother, Myra. Beside her sat a man — aged and lean — long-faced with hair the color of ash, but it was the presence of Doss Parker that unnerved her.

"That's her!" Myra jumped up, her gray-green dress pleated with wrinkles. "Murderer! Thief!" She pointed at Quinn. "Arrest her!"

"Now hold on!" Dan Gallagher out-shouted her. One hand held onto Quinn's arm while the other pushed the door shut. He led Quinn to a chair, then released his hold. "Take a seat."

Quinn looked straight into Myra's enraged eyes. She raised her chin. "I'd rather stand."

"All right then, stand." Gallagher motioned to Myra's companion. "Mr. Waller has a letter signed by fifty Stockton citizens that gives him the authority, if there is such a thing, to haul you back there for the murder of your husband and his missing money."

Quinn shouted, "There was no money!"

Louder, Myra yelled, "Henry always had money 'til you come along!" She raised a fist in the air. "You never had me fooled — not for a minute. You just married Henry for his fortune, and then you killed him for it!"

Myra turned to Randall Waller. "Get her and let's go!"

The lean man pointed to the only window in the small office. In a slow, haggard voice, he said, "It's after dark, Myra. You cain't be expectin' us to haul her all the way back to Stockton tonight. It took us all day just to get here."

Sheriff Gallagher cleared his throat, then motioned around the office. "Well, that could be a problem. Fortune doesn't have a jail to hold her overnight."

"You got a six-foot safe." Doss pointed to it. "Lock her in there for the night."

Quinn's jaw dropped open. "I'll smother locked in a safe all night!"

Feigning a sympathetic frown, Doss said, "That would be a shame, wouldn't it? Such a waste of talent and beauty."

"We're not locking anybody in a safe." Sheriff Gallagher tapped a finger against his chin, only stopping when Bill jerked open the door.

As soon as he saw Quinn, he started toward her, but he stopped when his gaze landed on Doss. "I should have known you had something to do with this."

"Thank heavens you're here." Quinn gave him a relieved hug, which set Myra on a rant, calling everyone's attention to her.

"My Henry hasn't been dead but a few months, and she already got herself another man! Not even a year of mourning. Shameful!" She pointed at Bill. "You'd better watch yourself or you'll end up dead, too."

Quinn took Bill by the shoulders. "We need Dr. Weber and Kent Hawley," she told him. "Will you go and get them, please?"

Bill shook his head. "I just came from the lawyers' office, and Kent isn't there."

"What about Dr. Weber?"

Again, Bill shook his head. "There's a note on his door saying he's gone out to one of the wagon caravans for a difficult birth." Bill looked at her apologetically. "No idea which caravan, or when he'll be back."

"Then I'll have no choice. They'll force me to return with Myra and the Stockton sheriff."

"Oh, I ain't no sheriff," Randall Waller admitted with a shake of his head. "I refused that job straight away after the last one got hisself shot. I'm just a deputy. I only agreed to come along with Myra 'cause she's my cousin, and I figured it weren't too hard to haul a woman back like the townsfolk wanted." He looked from man to man with a grin. "They're paying out a good reward for her, too."

"Stop your jawin', Randall!" Myra turned her angry squint on Bill. "The folks in Stockton are waitin' to hang her for killin' my son, Henry. She's a murderer, and the whole town knows it."

A flare of Irish ire struck Quinn. She glared at Myra. "The only thing the town knows is what you've told them, and nothing you've said is true." Her hands went to her hips. "Henry was penniless — he lied to you! The only money he had was my dowry,

430

and he gambled that away before he died."

Myra's quivering hand went to her heart. "Liar!"

The sheriff stepped between the two women. "I'm happy to let you each have your say, but I don't want this getting out of hand."

"Yes, of course." Quinn took a breath and forced a cultured tone. "The fact is, Henry died from eating peach kernels — those *almonds* you found inside the peach pits. They're not almonds at all, Myra. They're poisonous kernels. You made a crock full of brandied peach pit kernels for him, and then you milled more into flour for piecrust. He ate so much of it, he died from cyanide poisoning. My cooking didn't kill Henry. Yours did."

Myra froze, her eyes studying Quinn. Then she stepped back. Without turning around, she felt for the chair, then eased her hefty body down onto its wooden seat. Softer than before, she said, "You're lying."

Quinn went to her and knelt. "I'm sorry Henry died, Myra. I truly am, but his death was not my fault."

"Were you a witness to this almond eating?" the sheriff asked Myra. "And is she right? Did you make them for him?"

After a sniffle, Myra nodded, then pulled

431

out a white handkerchief and wiped her nose. She cleared her throat, straightened her posture, and turned a cold eye on Quinn. "There was a notice in the newspaper sayin' you owned a restaurant. I saw the place tonight, and it was full of customers, up until we told 'em about how you killed Henry. Was it my boy's money that bought it?" Her eyes stung, but the rage was gone. "Or do you got his money hid somewheres?"

"Myra," Quinn said, still kneeling. "Henry was poor as when we first met, which is why we decided to marry. We should have told you the truth, but he didn't want you to think less of him." Her tone softened. "My dowry was our escape from Oregon and his return to Stockton. Neither of us had a dollar other than my father's money."

Myra's fragility faded, and her dour disposition returned. She sprang up. "That's enough of your lies! There wasn't a day gone by that Henry didn't have money." When Quinn stood, Myra jabbed a finger at her, poking her mid-chest. "Give back Henry's fortune, or I'll make a claim on that restaurant you bought with his money." Vehement, she seethed, "Know this, you little gold digger, either way, we're takin' you back to Stockton tomorrow to face charges." She turned to the sheriff. "We'll be here at sunup for her."

She started for the door with Randall on her heels. Before pulling it open, she stopped and looked back at the sheriff. "I trust you got brains enough to know she'll be gone by morning less'n you find somewheres to lock her up."

CHAPTER FORTY

After deciding his office was the only appropriate lockup for the night, Sheriff Gallagher ushered Doss out the door after Myra and Randall, leaving him alone with Bill and Quinn.

"Dan, you've got no proof, right, or reason to hold her," Bill argued.

Quinn paced, fingering the cameo pinned to the high collar of her blue dress. How had it come to this? She stopped and turned to the sheriff. "When Dr. Weber returns, he'll tell you that I had nothing to do with the death of Myra's son."

"Was Doc there when it happened?" the sheriff asked.

"Well, no," she admitted, "but he has a plausible reason for Henry's death."

Gallagher knelt at the iron stove and added more wood to its low burn. He stoked the fire, then closed its heavy door. "That may be true," he said as he stood and dusted wood ash off his hands. With eyes on Bill, he said, "You advertised for a lawman, then hired me to ensure justice. 'A civilized town' is what you said you wanted, and the only thing that makes a town civilized is its justice. And not just for one man . . ." He looked at Quinn. "Or woman. Justice for all. The people have a voice."

"Not when they're wrong, Dan!" Bill's tone was heated. "You can't just let these folks take Quinn off to Stockton without evidence." He pointed outside. "Right now, they got no more proof of wrongdoing than we do of innocence. Give me one good reason why you would believe them over us."

"Because Deputy Waller hand carried a petition with fifty signatures from Stockton citizens that says she killed a man and stole his money." Gallagher grabbed a stack of papers marked *Confidential* off his desk and tidied them before shoving them inside his safe and locking it. "That's a hell of a lot more than you two are giving me. I can't just ignore them."

Bill paced, never taking his eyes off the sheriff. "The way I see it, there's two kinds of law — there's civilized law, and then there's vigilante law. You got both by the ears here." He stopped and pointed outside.

"You're letting them run roughshod over you with vigilante justice. They've already tried Quinn, convicted her, and are ready to let her hang for a crime she didn't commit." Defying the man that he himself had hired as sheriff seemed a bitter irony. "This right here is why the East sees California as a lost cause for civilized people. I was expecting you to enforce the line between right and wrong, otherwise Fortune isn't any better than a lawless town."

Gallagher grabbed his oversized coat off the chair back and put it on over his frock coat. "I'll give it some thought, but we're in lynch law territory. When there's no marshal or judge within a hundred miles, a lawman has got to enforce justice as he sees fit." He checked his pistols, making sure they were loaded, and then re-holstered them.

"Will you wait for Dr. Weber to return before releasing me to them?" Quinn asked.

"And a lawyer," Bill added. "Hear the two of them out before you let them haul Quinn back to Stockton."

The sheriff nodded, then fitted his wide-brimmed hat atop his head. "That's a fair request." He walked to the door and opened it. "I'll keep guard outside for the night." With tired eyes, he looked from Quinn to Bill. "I'll give you two a few minutes."

When the door closed, Quinn went to Bill and slid her arms around him. She pressed her lips to his lightly stubbled cheek, inhaling his scent. "I'm sorry about all of this."

Bill kissed her, deep and sensual, igniting a yearning. When their lips parted, his eyes skimmed her face. Then he scanned the interior of the sheriff's small office.

"I would say get some sleep, but unless you curl up on the floor without a blanket, there's not much chance of that." He brushed her cheek with the back of his hand, then leaned in, kissing her just under her ear. "I'm sorry I couldn't do better for you."

Quinn's head tilted, willing his breath to caress more of her, but when he pulled back, leaving a gentle kiss on her forehead, she gave a restrained nod. Quietly, she said, "I'll be fine." Her fingertips explored his unshaven face, lightly outlining his lips.

"I'll ride out and see if I can find Doc Weber." He gave her hands a comforting squeeze. "I promise to bring him back soon as I can."

When he left, she heard the door lock, which was calming in an odd way. There would not be any unauthorized access. Neither Doss, nor Myra, nor the deputy could niggle her again for hours.

Exhausted, Quinn pulled her shawl tight around her, then dragged a chair to the corner wall between the window and the woodstove. She sat back, using the angled walls to prop her head, and closed her eyes.

The flame in the oil lantern was low on the wick, lapping at the last bits of consumable air inside its clear glass chimney, when an opening door awoke Quinn. She lifted her head from the wall, cringing at the painful crick, and then stood with one hand cradling her neck.

"Yes?" she called, fully expecting Sheriff Gallagher, yet hoping to see Bill instead.

The door swung wide, shoved open by the arm of a masculine man who wore a tobacco-brown, almost black, thigh-length leather coat. His wide-brimmed hat was also dark, well shaped, and without a blemish. He closed the door in one fluid movement and turned around.

He pulled off his hat. For a moment, neither he nor Quinn spoke. Finally, "Well, look at you. A working woman now, I hear."

Quinn's nausea swam low at first. She pressed a hand to her stomach, hoping to steady its tide. "What is it you want, Father?"

Hugh MacCann approached the desk and

set down his hat, then went to the wood-stove and warmed his hands. "I am curious as to how you came to own an eatery. You never cooked a meal or washed a dish in your life."

He might have received an answer if he'd stopped there.

"I assumed your plan would be different." He turned and stared at her. "I thought by now you'd be buckled to a state officer, or married to a Boston banker."

Bantering with her father meant a black and blue ending, Quinn knew. She stepped back, closer to the sheriff's desk, silent.

"Even being the wife of an *alcalde* might have given you the luxury life you're used to living." A guffaw slipped through his lips without even the hint of a smile. He lifted his chin in an upward nod. "Was that your intent with the pissant you married? Did you think you'd turn him into an important man someday?"

He turned and warmed his hands at the stove again. "No coffee?"

Quinn crossed her arms to hold in her trembling. "Ask the sheriff. He let you in, he can serve you."

"On a break." He pointed a thumb at the door. "Parker let me in."

"The sheriff left Doss guarding the door?"

Without acknowledging the question, he said, "You should thank him."

"Me? Thank Doss Parker? For what?"

Hugh MacCann straightened and fixed admonishing eyes on her. "For sending a man to say you'd gotten yourself into trouble. Imagine a daughter of mine locked up by the law."

"He had no right!" Quinn nearly shrieked. She started for the door. "He's going to get a piece of my mind."

"Actually," her father said, calm but with forthright tenacity, "he's going to get a piece of your restaurant."

Quinn whirled around, her blue skirt swishing past her, green eyes ablaze. "What are you talking about?"

"The government transferred me to San Jose to prepare for statehood. My reputation is paramount, and I won't have you further disgrace me." Again he pointed at the door. "Parker and I have just finished meeting with that Matheny woman and her imbecile cousin. I've made them an offer, to which they've verbally agreed, that will make this whole embarrassing situation go away."

Mouth agape, Quinn stared at him. A barrage of words fell from her brain, landing just behind her lips, but a dam of disbelief blocked them. If she could turn nausea into rage, she might defend herself instead of standing here like a gutless, powerless child.

At the first sight of her hard-fought tears, his demeanor turned to ice. "A lawyer is drawing up papers for you to sign. You will transfer ownership of your restaurant to me as reimbursement for this redemption, and as repayment for the falsely obtained dowry. I know all about your sham marriage to swindle me."

He fitted his hat atop his fiery-haired head, then turned and strode toward the door.

"I will not!" Hatred rose in her throat, its taste more sickening than fury.

Hugh MacCann turned, her affront pulling him back across the room.

Piecing together a voice she feared would crack, she set her eyes on his and tensed. "I will not sign over my restaurant. Not to you. Not to anyone."

He stopped inches from her — so close, she felt his breath on her face.

"Women are not *fit* for business, not even one of my own flesh. Without a man's direction or control, you are out of your element. You have made yourself a social misfit by your atrocious actions, your lack of morals, and your abhorrent disrespect for the men

441

who offer you a proper place in society. My influence has saved your neck, but I'll not do it again." He pulled a pouch and several loose gold coins from his pocket, then tossed them onto the sheriff's desk. "Enough to send you on your way. I expect you to use it for passage East, or home to Ireland, I don't much care, but you'll not stay and make a mockery of me."

With one wide swipe of her hand, Quinn sent the coins flying off the desk.

His hand seized her throat.

Desperate, she clawed at his tightening fingers until he slammed her like a ragdoll against the wall. Her vision, an oxygen-starved speckled gray, was fading to black when she dropped to the floor, limp and gasping for air.

MacCann stepped back. Motionless, he stared at Quinn as she held her neck where her mother's cameo was pinned. She struggled to breathe. When her glance met his icy stare, he turned away and readjusted the fit of his hat. With her crumpled on the floor, he walked to the door, opened it, and left, closing it behind him.

For a long while, Quinn stayed on the floor shivering next to the stove's dwindling warmth. Firewood was stacked nearby, but the cold was good. It kept her awake, mind and body.

Her father's gold coins, strewn across the floor, were a pittance compared to her own earnings, but she reached for one. She held it in her hand and dreamed of a place far away, so far that no one would find her ever again. *Just start over,* she thought. *Start over. Start over.* Leave the trouble behind. Leave the memories, too. All of them. Her mother, her brother, the embarrassments and shame, the beatings and beratings. Leave Henry behind. Nadine, too.

But when she thought of Bill, a sob broke free. He wasn't the same kind of man as all the others. His soul fed hers in a way she'd never known.

Quinn fingered the coin for a moment, then threw it hard across the room. She got to her feet and walked to the door. *Locked.* If she beat on it, insisting it be opened, it would strip away her remaining dignity, and she was not willing to lose the little she had left. Instead, she went to the window and gazed out, but the night was so dark she saw nothing but blackness.

How many more hours would she be locked in this office?

CHAPTER FORTY-ONE

The morning fog dampened the bare wood walls, affixing its chill to Quinn. She had spent hours pacing the floor in the dark cold of night, but the break of morn brought an edgy restlessness.

She added wood to the glowing embers in the stove and walked to the window. Through dawn's haze, she spotted a lantern light. With it came two men, heads down, on their way toward the sheriff's office. When they drew close, she recognized Doss and his lawyer.

At the door, the voices of the men, including Sheriff Gallagher, were clear.

"She asked for a lawyer last night," the sheriff acknowledged. "Go on in."

"No!" Quinn pounded the door. "I wanted Kent Hawley!"

But the door opened anyway, forcing her aside. There stood Sheriff Gallagher with Doss Parker and Conny Steele, who was a shadow of a man compared to the others.

Perplexed, Conny stared at her. "I'm the only lawyer here. Kent went off to Sacramento and won't be back for a week." He held up a paper and waggled it in the air. "I just need your signature."

"I have no intention of signing that paper." Without any acknowledgement whatsoever to Doss, Quinn turned to the sheriff. "Have you heard from Bill?"

"Nope," Sheriff Gallagher said with a shake of his head. He looked from Quinn to Conny and back again. "But I promised you'd have a chance to talk to a lawyer this morning, so here he is."

When the sheriff turned for the door, Quinn shouted, "You can't leave me alone here with these men!"

Gallagher raised an eyebrow. "We went over this last night. You need to resolve the situation, or I'll be forced to." He pointed to Conny. "You two talk things over." He motioned Parker out, saying, "How 'bout a cup of coffee at The Stewpot?"

After the door closed, she stood there alone, facing Doss Parker's attorney.

"Now," Conny said while he walked to the desk, paper in hand. "You want me to give you an overview of the agreement, or you want to read it through for yourself before signing?" He laid the document on the desktop, then looked at her, awaiting an answer.

"I know what the document says, and I'll not sign it." Quinn turned away without further explanation. She walked to the window, hoping to spot Bill riding in through the fog with Dr. Weber, but all she saw were prospectors heading toward the river as they did every morning. By now, most of the miners had become daily customers at the restaurant. What must they think of her after hearing Myra's food poisoning accusations yesterday? Had anyone braved breakfast this morning, or were Libby and Mabree saddled with an empty restaurant? Her forehead sank down into the palm of her raised hand. She closed her eyes and rubbed, willing away her guilt.

"The way I understand it," Conny said, "if you'll sign this agreement — which, by the way, I stayed up all night writing — you won't have to go to Stockton, and you'll be absolved of all debts with Mr. MacCann." When she failed to acknowledge him, he walked to the window where she stood. "Did you hear me?"

She raised her chin, steadying her eyes on the view outside. "And if I don't?"

The attorney's head dropped a notch.

"Well, if you don't sign it, you'll be transported back to Stockton where they have a hanging planned . . . as I understand it."

Both stood silent. Finally, firm and steady, Quinn said, "And if I do sign it?"

Conny gave a nod to indicate she had hit upon the right decision. "Then you'll be free to go with no further consequences."

"No consequences?" Quinn turned and pointed to the unsigned paper. "That document forces me to relinquish ownership of The Stewpot. It leaves me nothing!"

"It leaves you with your *life*," Conny harshly reminded her. "A debt-free life."

"Get out." Quinn pointed to the door. "Take your paper and go."

Conny huffed back to the desk. Grabbed the document. "Maybe Doss was wrong about you. Maybe you aren't worth saving!"

Both Quinn and the attorney jumped with a jolt when the door opened and then slammed shut.

"It's rare that I'm wrong about anything, Conny," Doss said. He pulled off his hat as he walked to the lawyer and took the paper from him. "Go on, get out like the lady said. I'll handle this."

Conny Steele hurried out the door.

"Where's the sheriff?"

Doss gave a smug grin. "I bought him

447

breakfast. He's the only one in the place, too, so he's getting full service." He walked back to the desk and laid the document down, then offered Quinn his silver steel pen. "You know well as I do that this is best. Just sign it. I told your father that, once I had your signature, I'd make sure you left town, but soon as he's gone, he'll never know whether you left or not. If you want to stay, my offer still stands."

The sweetly scented oak burned hot inside the woodstove, its crackles and pops the only break in the silent standoff between the two. *The first one to speak loses.* Quinn stood quiet but firm and stared into his steely-green eyes.

Stalemated, Doss threw the pen on the desk and grabbed her by the shoulders, pulling her to him. She felt an all too familiar male rage in him, not lust.

"Listen to me, you log-headed woman! This isn't a child's game you're playing."

Quinn pushed against him, her hand landing waist-high on a sheath knife she hadn't seen.

With a quick grab, Doss had her by the wrist. He pulled her arm up behind her, twisting her into a front-facing restraint.

"Let go of me!" She struggled to free herself as Doss groped her breast.

Into her ear, he said, "I'm trying to save your life."

Quinn stomped. Her boot heel struck the arch of his foot. Doss bellowed. Shoved her. She stumbled, then turned. "Don't do me any favors! You're the reason I'm in this trouble."

"It wasn't me who caused you to marry a no-good gambler on a whim to bribe money out of your father, and it wasn't me who convinced you to run off after he died without first clearing your name. And it sure as hell wasn't me that told you to buy a restaurant when you had food poisoning charges against you." He shook his head. "No, it wasn't anyone but you who got yourself into this trouble."

The door bumped open. Sheriff Gallagher entered with an accomplished grin, a cup in one hand and a plate in the other.

"These flapjacks and sorghum are better than Mama used to make." He looked at Quinn with the grin still on his face, then set the plate and cup on his desk. "The ladies asked after you and wanted me to bring you breakfast and coffee."

Doss slapped his hand down over the document on the desk, his gaze glued to Quinn. "I'll leave this here for you. Think it over. You've got an hour. If it's not signed

449

by then, you'll be on your own hook. You'd be smart to re-consider my offer." With a nod to the sheriff, he left.

When the door closed, Sheriff Gallagher pointed to her meal. "Your coffee is gonna get cold." He picked up a stick of split wood and added it to the stove. "I can make you a hot pot, but mine is nothin' but brown gargle."

Though it was barely warm, Quinn took a sip of coffee, ignoring the plate-sized flapjack. After a swallow, she said, "I suppose you've not seen Bill or the doctor, have you?"

"No," he answered in a gentle tone without meeting her eyes.

Holding the cup with both hands, Quinn walked to the window again. The fog was lifting, but the day held to its wintry regard, casting a haze on the leafless buckeyes and cottonwoods.

With another sip, Quinn spotted a man. "He's here!" She hurried to the door, but the sheriff beat her to it.

With his arm outstretched, Gallagher held the door shut. "Oh, no, you don't."

"For heaven's sake, I'm not trying to escape! Open the door for Dr. Weber."

The sheriff gave an awkward, "Oh" and opened the door. "Glad to see you, Doc."

In his hand, Weber held a raggedly torn paper. He presented it to Quinn. "I found this note on my door."

She read it aloud. "Quinn's locked up at the sheriff's office. Urgently needs you." It was signed, *Bill Beaudry.* Her curious glance shot to Dr. Weber. "So Bill didn't find you himself?"

He shook his head. "Haven't seen him. Just got back from delivering a baby for a mother from Iowa. They're still ten miles out. The father sent a rider for me yesterday." He looked from Quinn to the sheriff. "Breech birth, but the infant is fine."

Sheriff Gallagher nodded without showing much interest in the birthing.

Quinn, nervous at not knowing Bill's whereabouts, said, "Doctor, please explain to the sheriff how my husband died, so that I can be released."

Weber turned his tired eyes to the lawman. "There's little doubt that an abundance of peach kernels, ingested in a short amount of time, killed the man."

"Just that easy?"

"It's not easy, at all. The kernels are hard and bitter. Sweetness is one of the few additives powerful enough to overtake their bitterness, leaving the cyanide toxin undetectable. A handful or two of brandied peach

451

kernels could have done it, but Miss Mac-Cann said her husband ate a full bean pot of them, and then in his drunken state, he ate an entire pie made with flour milled from the kernels."

Gallagher looked at Quinn. "So it looks like you're off the hook for poisoning the man's food. The Matheny woman admitted to making them for him herself."

Quinn could not pull her thoughts together. "Neither of you has seen Bill?" When both men shook their head, she said, "Something must be wrong. He wouldn't leave me this long knowing my predicament. He might be injured. Maybe attacked by Indians and can't get back to town."

"Bill's a big boy," the sheriff said. "He hasn't been gone but twelve hours or so. I'm sure he'll be back soon."

"I wish I were as sure as you." Quinn turned to Dr. Weber. "Thank you for gaining my release." She started for the door.

"Not so fast," the sheriff said. "There's still the matter of the missing money."

"You listened to my entire explanation last night. Sheriff, there was no money! And even if we'd had a fortune, which we didn't, the money would belong to me — not his mother. I was Henry's wife. Explain to me what right Myra would have to money belonging to our marriage?"

Gallagher gave a crooked grin. "I suppose you're right, assuming it was rightfully his money and not his mother's." He looked from the doctor to Quinn. "But considering you're a local business owner with a plausible defense, I guess I've got no real reason to hold you unless they can prove otherwise."

Quinn's legs nearly buckled at the liberating words.

CHAPTER FORTY-TWO

Quinn hurried to Beaudry's Supply Store in search of Bill, but as she feared, the store was locked up, and he was nowhere in sight. If he were still in town, the only other place he might be was with Blue.

"Mrs. Crawford? Are you there?" Quinn called after a knock. When the cabin door opened, she pulled the older woman into a hug. "I'm so glad to see you." Then she spotted Blue, sitting cross-legged on the bed drinking a cup of tea.

"Me and Blue have been worried sick about you!" Mrs. Crawford stepped back, giving her space to enter. "Come in. Tell us what has happened."

Quinn went to Blue straightaway. She pressed a hand to his forehead. "No more fever," she declared, then smiled when Blue's face broke into a rosy-cheeked grin. She gave his chin a playful pinch. "Seems you're winning the influenza battle."

In an excited voice, Blue said, "Mrs. Crawford says I can get out of bed today and play with Rufus. Have you seen him?"

"No." With splayed fingers, Quinn brushed back the boy's blond hair. "I've not seen that shaggy-haired dog of yours, but I promise to look for him."

Blue nodded. "Is Daddy coming?"

Before Quinn could answer, Mrs. Crawford sprang into an explanation. "Bill promised to tuck Blue into bed last night, but we fell asleep waiting for him, and he hasn't come this morning. That's not like him."

Quinn forced a smile at Blue. "I'll check on your father today, too." She stood and then reached out, touching Mrs. Crawford's forearm. "May we talk outside?"

The blind woman gently grasped Quinn's arm and walked to the porch with her. After the door closed, Mrs. Crawford whispered, "It's not like Bill to leave Blue alone for more than a few hours, especially with the boy being sick."

"Yes, I know," Quinn said, quietly. "I've checked the store. It's locked up tight."

"Where could he be?"

Guilt had a home in her heart, and it seemed to be taking over. "Bill went out last night to search the wagon caravans for Dr. Weber. He hasn't returned."

Head down, Mrs. Crawford said, "You've got to find someone to go look for him."

She gave the woman's hand a reassuring squeeze. "I'll find Clive. If I were a worthy rider with a horse of my own, I would go myself."

"Clive is good, dear. You go get Clive."

Quinn's first stop was The Stewpot. After a brief reunion with Libby and Mabree, Quinn asked, "Have either of you seen Bill today?" When both women said no, she asked Libby her husband's whereabouts.

Winter's mid-morning sun had burned off the fog with its bold rays, but it carried very little warmth as Quinn made her way to the butcher shop. She and Clive arrived there at nearly the same time, though from different directions. He carried four limp-necked geese, two in each hand.

"Mornin', Miss Quinn," he said, grinning proudly as he held up the trophy birds from his morning hunt.

"Good morning." Quinn followed him to the rear of the shop and watched as he laid the four birds down on a bloodstained butcher's block. "You haven't seen Bill this morning, have you?"

"No, ma'am. Can't say as I have."

"That's what I was afraid of," Quinn muttered. "It seems no one has."

"Is there trouble?"

"Possibly," she said. "Bill rode out looking for Dr. Weber last night. He was checking the caravans for him, but he hasn't returned yet. I need you to go look for him."

Clive lowered his head. "I'd like to, ma'am, but . . ." The normally talkative young man fell quiet except for a throat clearing. He did not lift his eyes.

"But?"

Sheepishly, Clive glanced at her. "But I owe a bundle to the livery for Sketch. See, I didn't have nowheres to keep him, so they been putting him up for me and feedin' him. They had to shoe him, too. They been dunnin' me to pay up, but I ain't been given any wages since arrivin' here, and I'm plumb broke."

Quinn patted her heart to calm its thumping. "Is that all? Clive, I'll be glad to advance you enough wages to pay the livery and get Sketch out of debt, so you can go look for Bill. How much do you owe?"

Clive's shoulders relaxed, and his head came up. He turned his face to the sky and started to mumble numbers until finally arriving at a figure. He looked at Quinn hesitantly and said, "Ought to be about fifty by now."

She gave him a smile. "I'll go get it and be

right back." Quinn hurried off to her room above the store for the money, which was still packed inside one of her traveling bags.

Bill had carried her belongings up the stairs yesterday, and then they had both left for Doctor Weber's office. She hadn't had a chance to return to her room to unpack a single thing.

Once inside, Quinn scooted her smallest bag to the edge of the bed, moving the borrowed Colt pistol to the floor beneath. The bag was so tightly packed, she couldn't push her hand far enough inside to reach a money pouch. Frustrated, she pulled out combs, hairpins, two books, her unmentionables, boots, and the daguerreotype of her mother, all strewn about in disarray. When she came to her leather pouches, she pulled just one from the bag. From it, she dumped all but a few coins into one of her white kid boots, then cinched the pouch before she stood and carried it toward the door. It was more than Clive needed, but she didn't want any surprises from the livery come time to pay the bill.

Quinn was halfway across the small room when Doss Parker kicked open the door. She dropped the coin pouch with a startled gasp. He stepped inside, his glare so piercing she almost felt its razor-sharp point.

Doss said, "I've tolerated you since the day you arrived, thinking you had something special wrapped up in all that beauty. But you've taken every opportunity I've given you and thrown it back in my face like bad whiskey." His eyes narrowed. "You've embarrassed me. You've scorned me. And now you've damn near broke me." Doss slammed the door so hard it popped opened again. "This time you're not getting away with it. You're going to give me what you owe me."

"Don't you dare touch me!"

"You swell-headed bitch! I came here for my money, not for what's under your skirts."

His words made no sense. Why would one of the richest men in town want her money? Tensing to hide her trembling, she pointed stiff-armed to the pouch on the floor. "Take it."

With a downward turn of his eyes, Doss spotted the hide pouch and scooped it up. He pulled open its strings and emptied the three coins into his hand. "This is sixty dollars." He looked at Quinn as he dropped the coins back inside. "Now all you owe is the other four thousand nine hundred and forty."

"That's five thousand dollars! Why would I owe five thousand dollars?"

"How do you think you got out of trouble?"

"Because I am innocent!"

"Innocent." He glanced down with a shake of his head. "Your brain is addled."

Quinn squinted a glare. "You must think me dead ripe for a swindle, Mr. Parker, but I assure you, I am not. If you think I'll hand over five thousand dollars for no apparent reason, perhaps it is you who is addle brained."

Doss let a raw, angry grin pull at the scar on his lip. "The fix you got yourself into damn near handed me what I wanted all along."

"Which is what?"

Doss stared, unblinking, at her. With a cock of his head, he answered, "You."

Speechless, Quinn eyed him.

"*You.* If you'd just done what was expected, I would have made you wealthy. You'd be the most powerful businesswoman in California. I would have made sure of it. And your gratitude would have paid off for me."

He said it with such warmth, it chilled her.

Wary, she eased into a step that edged her closer to the door. "Then why would you bring my father here?"

Quick as a lit match, his irritation flared.

With narrowed eyes, he said, "I needed someone with more influence than me to control you."

She took another step closer to the door. "My father would not have come here of his own accord." An icy feeling — a defiant strength unbecoming a woman — teemed.

His jaw tensed, and his steely-green eyes locked on hers. "You're right. He refused to come here until I threatened to use your murder and thievery charges against him, which would tarnish his name in the state's new political system." Despite his arrogance, Doss fidgeted. "I gave my word that you'd sign over your portion of the restaurant to him, which he would then sign over to me, but he bargains hard. I had to agree to repay the two-thousand-dollar dowry he gave to you and that gambler, and then another three thousand to satisfy the Matheny woman in return for her signature on a release of charges. I promised his name would stay good as gold if he kept his end of the deal."

"You did *what*?"

"He exchanged three thousand dollars of my money with the Matheny woman this morning when she signed the paper, which means I've paid out five thousand with nothing to show for it except your freedom."

"You blackmailed my father?"

"I'd say we made a deal that should have benefitted us both." He withdrew the folded document that Conny Steele had written and held it out. "Sign this bill of sale for the restaurant, or fork over the five thousand you've cost me."

"I will not!"

Doss stepped back, his eyes taking her in as if the line between business and personal was blurring. "If you don't sign it, he'll burn the release of charges, and Deputy Waller will come for you."

"Too late. The sheriff knows I didn't murder my husband, or steal anyone's money."

"You think he's going to fight the town of Stockton for you when Deputy Waller says he has rights to take you back? All Waller has to say is that it was Myra's money you stole."

Though she knew it was a risk, she took another step closer to the open door. "Bill will never partner with you."

"I don't expect him to. Without you, he'll gladly sell his half to me, making me the full owner of the only restaurant within fifty miles." A satisfied gleam settled in his eyes. "If you stay, I'll let you run it for me. That's what you want, isn't it?"

Knowing an amiable tone might clear the way for yet one more step closer to the open door and her escape, Quinn said, "Since I refuse to work at the Dancehouse, you'll let me stay on at the restaurant. Is that it?"

Doss smirked. "You've been too dim-witted to see it for yourself. You and me, we're the pair that should be — not you and Beaudry. I gave you time to figure it out, but you didn't. I've known it all along. You're manipulative and thieving, which suits me fine."

She bolted for the door.

In an instant, Doss had hold of her. She screamed as he wrapped his arm around her waist and lifted her off the floor, spinning her back into the room. His other hand clamped over her mouth.

"The problem with you is that you haven't been tamed. You'll be a changed woman when I'm done with you. Hell, you might even be grateful for it."

Thrashing and kicking, Quinn clawed at him as he muscled her toward the bed. With one hand locked around the back of her neck, Doss forced her down, face-first onto the mattress with her scattered belongings. He held tight, using his other hand to toss up her skirts, exposing her backside through the loosely draped opening of her cotton drawers.

With no awareness other than the weight of Doss Parker and his savage touch, Quinn struggled to breathe, drawing in just a wisp of air through one corner of her mouth.

When his heaviness abruptly lifted, she gasped, then boosted herself half up off the mattress. She turned in time to see Doss being yanked back through the air before he crashed to the floor.

The sun's glare from the open door fell on two grappling men. As they struggled, Quinn pushed herself up further, slipped, and landed squat on the floor. It took her a moment to realize the brown wool pants and gray shirt pinned beneath the raging Doss Parker belonged to Bill Beaudry. Doss had him in a stranglehold, thumping his skull on the floor and then slamming his head against the iron stove. Sunlight struck the silver blade of a double-edged Bowie knife as Doss raised it above Bill, who'd gone limp.

A scream, guttural and painful, came from inside her. Her hand found wood and cold metal, the shape of Riley's Colt. She rose, thumbed back the hammer, and pulled the trigger.

The blast knocked her off her feet. She hit the floor, shaken to the bone. Black powder and sulfur stung the air.

"Bill!" Quinn scrambled to him. He lay still and silent, blood oozing from beneath his head.

She heaved Doss Parker's body off Bill and onto the floor. Blood soaked Parker's shirt, high on his back and in front. Even as she watched, he expelled his last breath — a slow, steady lungful of death's air.

"Who's up there?" Mrs. Crawford yelled from outside. "Quinn, are you all right?" Then louder, *"Quinn!"*

Bill's shirt bore spatters of blood and a wet, red patch the size of a fist. Quinn wrenched her gaze from it, rose, and staggered to the open door. "I need a doctor! Hurry! I think I've shot Bill . . ."

Mrs. Crawford turned, yelling, "Help! We need a doctor!" Her blindness hindered quick steps, but she moved steadily toward the main road in front of the store crying, "Help! Somebody help!"

Returning to Bill, Quinn knelt. With a sob, she raised his head, kissing his still lips. "Please don't leave me."

CHAPTER FORTY-THREE

The outside stairs vibrated under the thundering steps of Dr. Weber and Sheriff Gallagher. Both men burst through the open door and stared in shock at Doss Parker's dead body. A second later, Doc Weber hurried to Bill.

As the doctor examined him, the sheriff knelt by Doss. After a moment, Gallagher stood. Quinn kept her focus on Bill. She watched as Dr. Weber held two fingers to his throat.

"Is he alive?" she asked.

"He has a pulse." He gently turned Bill's head to examine it, then pulled up his blood-spattered shirt and checked his torso.

"Is Bill all right?" called Mrs. Crawford from the outside stairs.

Quinn pushed to her feet, then went to the door and stepped out onto the landing. She saw Mrs. Crawford halfway up the stairs, holding tight to the railing and pulling herself along, one slow step after another. Quinn went to her and guided her up the rest of the staircase. "He's still alive."

The two women held onto each other as Dan Gallagher surveyed the room. He pointed to the bed, then said to Quinn, "Considering the gun is way over there and you're the one who's still standing, I've got to assume you fired it."

"Yes," Quinn said. Her eyes were set on Bill. "Doss attacked me. He had a knife and was going to kill Bill, so I shot him."

The sheriff reached down and picked up the Colt. "Is it yours?"

"It belongs to Riley Boles. He lent it to me for protection."

Gallagher nodded, keeping hold of the weapon as he turned to the doctor. "How's he doin', Doc?"

"Can't find a bullet wound. No skull fracture, either." Dr. Weber passed smelling salts under Bill's nose. When his eyes snapped open, Doc said, "How you feeling?"

Still prone on the floor, Bill winced as he turned his head, looking for Doss. "He's dead?"

The sheriff stood, looking down. "The bullet pierced his heart."

Bill gave a half nod, stopping with a

grimace when his head met the floor. "I'd be dead if you hadn't shot him." He stopped, drew in a breath, and went on. "I'm indebted to you."

"Oh, it wasn't me who shot him." Sheriff Gallagher pointed to Quinn, who came and knelt beside Bill. "She's your good-luck charm."

"I had to shoot him, Bill. He would have killed you." She held his hand close to her heart. "I was afraid the bullet struck you, too. Other than that nasty bump on your head, are you hurt anywhere else?"

"No," Bill told her, still dazed. "Don't think so."

A clarity settled in his eyes. He tried to sit up but could only rise halfway before he lay back again. He reached out and brushed the back of his hand downward along the line of her chin. "I came in and saw . . ." He stopped and then started again. "You all right?"

"Yes, thanks to you."

Bill reached back and felt the lump on his skull.

"Careful, now," Dr. Weber told him. "You've had quite a blow." He closed his black bag and stood. "You'll have a good headache for a few hours."

Louder than was needed in a small room,

Sheriff Gallagher announced, "Let me get some boys and get this body out of here." As he was leaving, he said, "Sure wish Fortune had an undertaker."

Quinn doused the spilled blood with a bucket of water, then scrubbed while Bill watched from the bed. She was still in her bloodstained dress when Libby, Clive, Mabree, and Blackjack came upstairs to inquire about events.

"I'm sure sorry about sendin' you back here for the money," Clive said.

"It wasn't your fault. I'm grateful Bill arrived when he did."

When Bill tried to sit up, she insisted he lie down. "By the way," she said. "Where were you? Clive was set to go out looking for you."

Bill pushed himself up onto an elbow, dismissing Quinn's caution. "Know how many wagons are out there? There must be hundreds scattered across the countryside, and they're all clamoring for news about the gold. I'll bet I talked to a dozen caravans before coming across the one where Dr. Weber helped birth the baby. And I didn't find them until after sunup. They said he'd already headed back to town. I turned around and got here fast as I could." Then his blue eyes, soft and warm, settled on her. "I was scared you'd be gone by the time I got back. Why haven't they hauled you back to Stockton already?"

"Oh, that," Quinn said. "It seems Doss blackmailed my father into coming here by threatening to use the charges against me to ruin his reputation. Father paid Myra for a release to save his own name, not mine." Then with a gasp, she stood. "The paper! I must find my father before he leaves town, but I don't want to leave Bill unattended."

"I'll stay, dear. You go," Mrs. Crawford told her. "Can anyone check on Blue for me? He was asleep when I left."

Libby took hold of Mabree's hand. "I'll find Catherine to stay with Blue if you'll check the cornbread. It's been in the oven too long."

Mabree started for the door, but Blackjack kept hold of her hand, preventing her from leaving. "Miss Quinn, before we go, do you need me to come along with you? I'd be glad to, if you need me."

"No, this is a personal matter." She looked at Bill. "My father has possession of the release Myra signed. It clears my name, now and forever. I intend to get it from him."

Bill threw back the blanket and stood, but his legs faltered. Dizzy, he sat down again.

"Just let me catch my balance. I'll go with you."

"I'll go," Clive said, stepping forward.

"No," Quinn told the men again with a shake of her head. "This is something I must do on my own." She leaned to gently squeeze Bill's hand. "I'll be back."

The town of Fortune had grown threefold since Quinn first arrived. The wooded green land she had so loved was now almost barren, strewn with hundreds of felled trees, the hills ravaged by gold-hungry men. The miners had become sophisticated in their techniques, with some learning to divert the river from its original channel, forcing it to dredge its own gold. The foothills felt strangely dismantled. The wild, untamed spirit of the land had been beaten down.

In her bloodstained dress, Quinn walked the main road, which was sloppy and scattered with drunks, horses, and pigs, all of whose stench was only slightly overpowered by the stink of poorly built outhouses, or alleyways that served the same purpose. It seemed one personality thrived on the east side of town where Doss had built the Dancehouse and Marshall had his saloon and boardinghouse, while the west side, where The Stewpot Restaurant and Bill's store were, had another — it was as if two towns boomed under the same name.

The hustle and bustle between newcomers and old-timers was a growth unforeseen, but the influx of women was a welcome sight. After months of overland travel, newly arriving wives sought fresh fruits and vegetables, flour and tallow, fabrics and bonnets, while men who fancied themselves gold miners came in search of planed boards, hammers, and nails to build wooden rockers for washing gold or for erecting cabins. Customer demands were no longer met by just selling mining camp supplies — now a wide range of everything was needed, which had turned Beaudry's Supply Store into a general store.

Fortune, California, had changed, both in its land and its people.

Busying about between the saloon and hotel was a flurry of folk Quinn didn't recognize. She searched for only one man — Hugh MacCann.

He stood on the high porch of the Medford Hotel with Conny Steele. His tall stature in the tobacco-brown leather coat and stout hat commanded a wide berth, deflecting those men who feared confrontation while drawing women who craved male companionship. His gaze sloughed off a scantily dressed, adoring girl and fell upon Quinn.

Though it was hard to be certain from her angle, she thought he wore a faint smile.

Her father reached into his coat pocket for a coin, then poked a passing lad with it. He pointed to the livery, which sent the boy scurrying down the white painted steps, bumping several people on his errand.

Quinn climbed the steps with a silent shudder and faced her father forthright.

With planted feet, Hugh MacCann gave a disinterested glance at her bloodstained dress as he slid his hand into a black leather riding glove. "I hear you're good with guns now." He donned the other glove. When she made no reply, he said, "What you did doesn't matter to me. Parker was a bastard of a man. You actually did me a favor by killing him. He was always going to be a problem."

Quinn stretched out a hand. "I'll need the release of charges Myra signed."

"I paid a good bit of money for that document."

"You paid *nothing* for that document. Doss Parker, however, paid three thousand dollars for it. Now that he's dead, you have no need of it."

Without lowering his eyes or changing his

expression, he said to Conny Steele, "Give me the paper."

"But Doss said —"

MacCann held up a hand. He kept steady eyes on Quinn while he spoke to Conny. "Parker's dead. There shouldn't be any doubt as to whose orders you'll obey."

"Yes, sir." Conny reached into his coat pocket and withdrew a folded paper, then handed it over.

Her father looked at it first, then at Quinn. "It's worthless to me now anyway." He held it out to her.

Quinn took it, closing her fingers tighter around it than intended. Hugh MacCann was not a man she'd dare turn her back to, so, with eyes on him, she stepped backward, inching away until the veranda railing and the stairs were within reach. She had taken a single side step down when the errand boy, whose face and brown hair were as dirty as his well-worn clothes, arrived with a saddled stallion.

"Here's your mount, sir," the boy called. "Will you still pay the extra dollar even though I'm late?"

Quinn stopped to see; she had to know. When a tossed coin landed in the boy's hand, he grinned and shouted, "Thank you, sir!" and then he was off on another run.

It was done. Hugh MacCann would ride out, never to be seen again. Doss Parker was dead and gone. Henry and his mother were at peace in different worlds. And through it all, Quinn had held tight to her business and felt stronger for it. The air of freedom was brisk as she turned and hurried down the final few steps, her thoughts focused on Bill.

"Did Parker tell you —" Her father shouted over the chatter of busy people.

Quinn froze.

"— about me holding title to the Dancehouse? In perpetuity, of course, until his return with a signed bill of sale, which would then authorize his idiot attorney to deliver the release of charges to me as agreed."

Quinn whirled around. *What?*

In his raised hand, he held another paper. "With Doss Parker dead, I suppose I'm the sole owner of the Dancehouse now." He refolded the paper, then tucked it into a pocket. "I do hope it's profitable."

Nauseous — so queasy, bile rose — Quinn pressed a finger to her lips, inhaling so deeply her nostrils flared. She expelled a lungful of sour air before starting back up the steps. She pushed past the weasel-faced attorney and stood face to face with her father. "How much do you want for it? I'll buy it."

A glimmer of pride sparkled in his eyes. "You've become a real businesswoman after all, haven't you?"

His gratification sickened Quinn. Her jaw clamped shut on gritted teeth. She focused hard to unclench it. "This is not a business decision. I despise you with such intensity I'll do whatever it takes to be rid of you."

Hugh MacCann laughed. "I can't say your mother would be proud of such grit, but I am not wholly disappointed by it."

"You have no right to bring up my mother. She was the only thing good about the three of us, and you did nothing to save her. You blamed her death on me when it was you who didn't come home."

His eyes dropped to the cameo pinned to Quinn's neckline. "You're nothing like her, you know? You can tell people whatever you will, but they'll see it's MacCann blood that lights that fire inside you." He started down the steps, leaving her speechless.

Mounted on his stallion, he turned to Conny Steele. "Keep the Dancehouse running, as agreed, until my return." Then he steadied his Irish-green eyes on Quinn. After a long, silent look, Hugh MacCann rode away.

■ ■ ■ ■

Quinn navigated through herds of people on her return to Beaudry's. She was only steps from the store when she heard the Albright bell clang three times from the top of Cemetery Hill. Its brass clangor was hard to ignore as it proclaimed the burial of Doss Parker.

She climbed the steps to her room, and, although it was still her home, she knocked.

"Who's there?" called Mrs. Crawford.

"It's Quinn." She opened the door and stepped inside. "I'm sorry," she said. "I don't know why I knocked. I'm a bit out of sorts, I suppose."

Bill slowly sat up, swinging his legs out of bed and planting his feet on the floor. "Did you have any trouble getting the release?"

Trouble. The word had greater meaning now than ever. "I have it," Quinn said as she held out the paper to him.

He silently read it. When he'd finished, he looked at Quinn with a nod. "This is all you need — it's proof you never stole any money from your husband or poisoned him." He stood but swayed.

Quinn slipped her arm around his waist, then found herself fully embracing him. She needed to hold him — needed him to hold her.

Bill wrapped his arms around her. "Hey, you all right?"

Mrs. Crawford reached out, feeling for Quinn. "Dear, if you'll just help this old woman down the stairs, I'll leave you two alone."

Quinn pulled herself away from Bill. "Of course." She took hold of Mrs. Crawford's hand, but her focus stayed on Bill. "I'll be back with a dish of food for you."

But Bill said, "I need to check on Blue and the store. It's been closed all day."

"You'll do no such thing," Quinn told him. "I'll check on Blue, and the store."

"All right," Bill said as he eased himself down onto the edge of the bed. "Take your time going down those stairs, and tell Blue I'll be by to see him as soon as I'm not so wobbly. Don't worry the boy with details, though."

CHAPTER FORTY-FOUR

At Quinn's knock, Catherine swung open the cabin door.

"Miss, where ye been? Ye had us worried sick!" She pointed to Blue, his eyes swollen red. "He's feelin' a bit limsy, but mostly it's from worry, methinks."

Quinn and Mrs. Crawford hurried inside. With a hand to the boy's forehead, Quinn said, "No fever. What is it, Blue? Are you sicker?"

The boy moved back against the wall, his wide eyes on Quinn's bloodstained dress. "I want my daddy!"

Mrs. Crawford sat on the edge of the bed. With her arm around Blue, she pulled him to her bosom. "Your daddy is fine, Blue. He's resting up in Quinn's room."

"Was he shot?" he bawled.

"Oh no, Blue," Mrs. Crawford said. "He just has a bump on the head, that's all."

Teary-eyed, Blue peeked at Quinn over

Mrs. Crawford's arm. "There was some men outside talking, and they said she shot Daddy."

"Oh, fiddle-faddle," Quinn said. "Mrs. Crawford is telling the truth. Your daddy has a nasty bump on the head, but he's perfectly fine otherwise. He'll be by to see you as soon as he can, but I don't expect it will be for another few hours."

Blue's head pulled up. "Really?"

"Yes, really."

"Well, then," Catherine said. "That's a bit of good news, isn't it?" She started for the door. "Me washin' is waitin', and it's likely piled high, so I should be gettin' to it." She nodded to Blue and then said, "I'll be takin' good care o' Rufus for ye 'til yer feelin' well again."

Blue grinned. "Thanks."

"So is that where your shaggy dog has been hiding?" Quinn asked.

"Uh-huh," Blue said. "He's been sleeping in Catherine's tent. She likes him a lot."

Quinn leaned over and gave Blue a kiss on the forehead, then ruffled his blond hair. "I'm going to check the store and look in on the restaurant before going back upstairs with your daddy. I'll have the ladies bring you two some lunch as soon as they can."

Inside The Stewpot's kitchen, Mabree

480

peeled parsnips as Libby stirred the kettle of stew that hung over the fire in the hearth. Curious, Quinn opened the dining-room door a crack and peeked in. The restaurant was half full with men she didn't know. "Is this the lunch crowd?"

"Afraid so," Mabree told her. She tilted her head. "Ever since them rumors of poisoned food got out, all we get is mostly newcomers."

"Food poisoning." Quinn's hands went to her hips. "It's not the same as *poisoned food.* And I'm innocent of those charges."

"Somebody needs to tell folks that," Mabree said.

"Yes, right. For now, perhaps I should greet these new customers and invite them back." She patted her bundled red hair.

"You won't make things any better for us by going out there in a dress with blood on it."

Quinn's gaze dropped to her dress front. "Oh! Yes, of course." She backed away from the door.

The store was barred from the inside, so Quinn entered through the workroom. Scattered about were stacks of delivered supplies that needed to be put away, but all else looked secure and untouched. When her movements inside the store caught the attention of several men waiting outside, they began to knock, calling out, "Are you openin' up today?"

The louder they called, the more men it attracted. Soon, a mob of customers waited in front of the store. Shouts of, "I just need a pickaxe!" or "a shovel" or "supplies for the river" came from the pleading faces that peered in through the grime-smeared windows. It wasn't until now that she understood. The commodity that drew folks to California was not gold: it was *hope.*

Quinn went into the storeroom and grabbed her long white apron. She tied its strings around her waist so that it covered the blood, and then she went to the front counter, pulled out Bill's ledger book with prices, and unbarred the door.

For the next four hours, men filed into the store one after another, buying a piece of hope: shovels, axes, hatchets, pans, and food that would barely sustain a malnourished man. Luck was in their eyes, and the thought of giving up was as far away as home.

As the sun sank lower on the horizon, the customers dwindled.

When Quinn sensed movement behind her, she turned. "Bill . . ." He leaned against the back wall with a smile. She went to him.

"I'm sorry about not returning, but there were so many customers. The men just needed a thing or two, and I didn't have the heart to keep them locked out."

"The businesswoman." He nodded toward the counter when a man approached with a bag of coffee beans and tobacco. "Don't let me interrupt."

Quinn weighed the man's gold nuggets, then thanked him for stopping in. Seeing the store empty, she followed him to the door and was ready to bar it behind him when she saw Edward Ward and his son approach. She held the door open for them. "Look at you," she said to ten-year-old Seth with a smile. "That snake didn't keep you down for too long."

Seth held up a ginger-haired pup. "Pa said I could come by and show off my new dog."

"Just look at him!" Quinn knelt and took the puppy in her arms. The dog licked her face while his behind wiggled. "Where did you find him?"

Edward pointed across the street. "There's a fella at the blacksmith shop needin' homes for four pups. Says he has enough trouble keepin' the dogs he's already got. Seth was beggin' when he saw them, and I figured the boy needed one after that snake got his."

"I won't let this one wander at night,"

Seth said as he took back the pup in a cuddle.

Quinn turned to Bill. "Blue needs a puppy."

Bill laughed. "You're as bad as the boys."

"Don't pretend you're not as puppy-struck as me. I see the gleam in your eyes."

"Yeah," Bill said with a grin. "All right, but you'll have to go pick it out. I'm not feeling up to dodging horses and wagons just to get across the road for a pup."

"You go on to Mrs. Crawford's cabin and see Blue. I'll be there soon."

Quinn followed Seth and his father out and waited to hear the locking bar drop across the store door before saying goodbye. Then she started across the street.

In the back of a wagon stopped in front of the blacksmith shop sat a teenaged boy dressed in gray wool pants and a long-sleeved shirt. He paid no mind to Quinn's approach. It wasn't until she asked, "Do these pups belong to you?" that he looked up at her.

"Yeah, I guess," he said mournfully, then he looked back down and petted the pups.

"They're mine," a man called to Quinn as he started around the wagon. "You wantin' one?"

"Yes," she told him. Then, glancing at the

boy, she said, "Unless this young man has decided to take them all."

"No," the man said with a shake of his head. "That's my son, Paul. He's soft-hearted and don't want to give a one of them up, but he ain't got no say in this." He pointed to the remaining three playful pups. "Which one you want?"

Quinn looked at the teen. "I promise the puppy will have a good home. You're welcome to visit." But the boy just shrugged. The little pups were doing their best to run on the bed of the wagon, but their legs were still small, and they tripped and tumbled over one another only to roll onto their feet and try again. One was black with white paws, another was golden-haired like Rufus, and the last one looked like Seth's pup. Quinn reached into the wagon and patted its rough boards. All the puppies stopped and turned toward the sound, but then the red one came running. He jumped on her hand and began wrestling it, which caused her to laugh. "This one."

Giving only a light knock at Mrs. Crawford's door, Quinn waited outside.

When Bill answered, he had a grin for the puppy. "Go on," he told Quinn quietly. "Take him his pup."

"No," she told Bill. "You should give the puppy to him."

"How 'bout we both do it?"

Quinn smiled and nodded.

As soon as they entered, Quinn put the puppy on the floor, where he began to spin like Blue's toy top — round and round he went chasing his tiny tail until he fell over.

"A puppy!" Blue jumped out of bed. He was on the floor with the dog in no time. "Is he mine?"

"Yep," Bill said. "If Rufus will let you have him, then it's all right with me."

"What are you going to name him?" Quinn asked.

The boy picked up the ginger-colored pup. He held him up, turned him this way, then that way, looking him all over, then said, "Red!"

"Blue!" Mrs. Crawford scolded. "You get back up here on this bed and keep your feet off this cold floor."

Blue scooped up the dog and jumped back onto the bed, hiding the wiggly pup under his quilts. He put a *shhh* finger to his lips, then giggled with a glance at Mrs. Crawford.

"Red and Blue," Bill said with a laugh. "I like it."

Chapter Forty-Five

At nightfall, after Blue was asleep, Bill led Quinn outside. He looked up. "Looks like a clear night."

Quinn raised her eyes to the sky. "Stars will be out soon, and winter stars seem to be the brightest." She crossed her arms for warmth and then glanced up at Bill. "Do you realize we've never had supper together?"

"That's pretty sad for two people who own a restaurant."

"It is, isn't it?" Quinn said. "And I understand there's no waiting line for a table tonight." They both laughed.

With a step back, Bill reached out and took hold of Quinn's hand. "Would you care to join me for dinner, Miss MacCann?"

"I'd be delighted, Mr. Beaudry." Quinn held out her dress skirt in a half flare. "But I'm afraid I'll need to change out of this dress and do a bit of clean-up first."

Bill looked down at himself. "I suppose I should, too."

From the top of her stairs, Quinn watched Bill walk to his cabin. Only after he was safely inside did she open her own door.

Inside, her scattered belongings were strewn everywhere. She had taken no care to pick them up when Bill needed the bed; she'd simply swept them off onto the floor. Her eyes settled on the easel, paints and brushes in the corner, then swung to the daguerreotype of her mother, its red case splayed open. She picked up the frame and stared into the silent eyes of the woman she had tried so desperately to emulate. Was her father right? Perhaps she was nothing at all like her mother. They had not been given enough time on this earth to know. Quinn set the photograph down, went to her largest bag, and opened it. Bundled into a fold on top of her other dresses was her best visiting gown — the earthy autumn-yellow dress with rows of red wisps and leafy green vines. She pulled off her blue dress stained with blood and silently vowed to burn it. Until such time, she tossed it onto the floor.

Quinn washed her face, put on her clean gown, brushed and pinned her hair up into a soft bundle, and then pulled a shawl over her shoulders before she headed to The

Stewpot. Instead of going through the back door into the restaurant's kitchen, she walked around to the front as if she were a full-fledged customer. The blackboard, re-hung but still bearing two bullet holes, listed the day's menu: *Roast Goose, Browned Parsnips, Federal Cake.* She opened the door.

Two tables had one man each sitting at them, but near a window in the far corner of the dining room sat Bill. His eyes were glued to the kitchen door. His blond hair was combed in the university style she liked, and he wore a tan waistcoat, brown jacket, and silk scarf tied into a flat half-bow. He never stirred as Quinn approached, which caused her to smile.

"Looking for someone?" she asked.

Bill turned, surprised. "I thought you'd come through the kitchen." Then, before she could answer, he stood. His eyes skimmed her head to toe. "You clean up real nice."

During dinner, Quinn divulged the facts, as she knew them, as to how her father came to own the Dancehouse. Afterwards, when silence fell between them, she said, "I can't pretend he is the sole cause of every difficulty. So many things I've done myself — *to* myself."

"Don't sell yourself short," Bill told her. "Look at all you've accomplished."

Quinn focused on his crystal-blue eyes. "In the beginning, had I told you the truth about my marriage, Henry's death, and the food poisoning accusation, would you still have offered me a partnership?"

Bill picked up his fork and inspected it as if it needed polish. "I don't know."

She had known the answer even before asking, but a place deep inside needed to hear it from Bill. Composed, she said, "Before coming here, I trusted no one. Independence alone was my only hope of winning a place in this world as a businesswoman, but it was never my intent to be dishonest with you."

"I know, but silence is just as dangerous."

"I realize now that withholding the truth is as damaging as a lie." She gave a faint smile and then reached across the table for his hand. "I suppose the underlying truth to independence is that it doesn't happen alone. I would not be a businesswoman without help from you, Mrs. Crawford and Blue, or Libby and Mabree."

"Probably true. And I wouldn't have a store if my father hadn't taught me how to run one, or without the help of Marshall and Nettie. Quinn, accomplishments rarely happen alone."

"Hmmm . . . *fathers,*" she said, focusing on the folds of her linen napkin. More to herself than to Bill, she said, "I wonder if it will always be so ravenous."

"Will what be so ravenous?"

She lifted her eyes. "Hatred. In my heart, I know God didn't intend for me to hate my father — no child should."

Bill squeezed her hand. "A father isn't supposed to give his child a *reason* to hate him."

Soon, the full moon — a high, lucent orb through the window — made the lateness known. They rose from the table.

Outside, boisterous shouts, laughter, and the sound of breaking glass emanated from the Dancehouse at the far end of the road. Business boomed, even without Doss Parker.

Bill took Quinn's hand and lightly closed his own around it. The two walked toward his cabin without much thought of their course. Wood smoke, barely perceptible on the breeze, tinged the air.

When they came to the door of his cabin, Quinn glanced across the clearing stubbled with dormant grass, to her room above the store.

"I should go." Her hand delicately brushed

his cheek as a shooting star — bright, bold, and beautiful — caught her attention. She closed her eyes and made a silent wish. When she opened them, Bill's gaze was there, taking her in.

"Stay with me," he said. "Marry me."

His words whispered through her thoughts.

"Yes." Softly, she said, "Life wouldn't be life at all without you."

ABOUT THE AUTHOR

Karen (K.S.) Jones grew up just a few hours south of Sutter's Mill in California, the site famously credited with the discovery of gold in 1848. Stories of the Mother Lode, and the ways courageous women coped in a land dominated by men, mud, and mayhem, captivated her. This is her first Gold Rush novel.

In 2014, *Southern Writers* magazine awarded K. S. Jones their grand prize for "Best Short Fiction" of the year. Soon after, Karen's first two novels, *Shadow of the Hawk,* a young adult historical, and *Black Lightning,* a middle-grade sci-fi/fantasy, saw publication. Her work has garnered numerous awards, including the coveted WILLA Literary Award. Today, Karen lives in the beautiful Texas Hill Country with her husband, Richard, and their three dogs.

CPSIA information can be obtained
at www.ICGtesting.com
Printed in the USA
BVHW050101191022
649770BV00002B/7

9 781432 888336